# TRUE NORTH

# GARY ELLER

# TRUE NORTH

A NOVEL

Livonia, Michigan

Editor: Jamie Rich
Proofreader: Tori Ladd

"Party Lines" and "Catch and Release" were originally published in the *Wapsipinocon Almanac*. Reprinted by permission. Copyright © Gary Eller.

"How Different This World" includes scenes originally published in *Wellspring* under the title "Uncle Foss." Reprinted by permission. Copyright © Gary Eller.

"What Was Wrong With Them" includes scenes originally published in *Flyway* under the title "Whole Wide World." Reprinted by permission. Copyright © Gary Eller.

"Ghost Shirts" is a much-revised story originally appearing in *Aegis Unicorn* under the title "The Scarlet Blanket of Florence Ida Little Shay." Reprinted by permission. Copyright © Gary Eller.

Quote from *Julius Caesar* by William Shakespeare. Public domain.

# TRUE NORTH

Copyright © 2021 Gary Eller

All rights reserved. No part of this publication may be reproduced, distributed, or transmitted in any form or by any means, including photocopying, recording, or other electronic or mechanical methods, without the prior written permission of the publisher, except in the case of brief quotations embodied in critical reviews and certain other noncommercial uses permitted by copyright law. For permission requests, please write to the publisher.

This book is a work of fiction. The characters, incidents, and dialogue are drawn from the author's imagination and are not to be construed as real. Any resemblance to actual events or persons, living or dead, is entirely coincidental.

Published by BHC Press

Library of Congress Control Number: 2020937799

ISBN: 978-1-64397-239-8 (Hardcover)
ISBN: 978-1-64397-240-4 (Softcover)
ISBN: 978-1-64397-241-1 (Ebook)

For information, write:
BHC Press
885 Penniman #5505
Plymouth, MI 48170

Visit the publisher:
www.bhcpress.com

# TABLE OF CONTENTS

13 | Ghost Shirts
36 | Black Marks
50 | The Road To Prophetstown
79 | How Different This World
96 | Firegoat Was Right
109 | To Have A Husband
121 | Something To Eat
137 | Catch And Release
151 | The Bull Halsey Chapter Of The Sons Of The New American Revolution
180 | What Was Wrong With Them?
203 | The Things You Learn
234 | In The Neighborhood
242 | A Newfound Grip
258 | Party Lines
263 | Everything Flows Away And Down
291 | Consequences
308 | Something To Look Forward To
325 | Laws Of The Hills
338 | No Good Reason
344 | Just A Little War
357 | In All The Days In This House
360 | A Kind Of Courage

*For my sister Karen Milne in whose eyes I could never do wrong.*

"But I am constant as the Northern Star, of whose
true fixed and resting quality there is no fellow in the firmament."

~ Shakespeare ~

# TRUE NORTH

# GHOST SHIRTS

## 1 | Berry Picking

In that time and place everyone was poor. Everyone was hungry. The common dream was to go away, to get out. While dreams could not fill bellies, they remained the last thing that the white man could not take away.

In the sad home of the Little Shays, rain fell all morning, painting dirty streaks on the broken kitchen window. Early in the afternoon when the emerging sun turned the air hot and sticky, Papa ordered Ida Florence out to the woods north of town, telling her not to return until she had filled a bucket with saskatoon berries. The berries, fat and juicy this time of year, were much prized by white people, who found a use for them in pies, jam, bread, or even wine. A bucketful was the price Papa must pay Tiny Turcotte for a ride to the sweat lodge at Border Butte. There, near the point where the Turtle Mountains reached their highest level, Papa would fulfill his obligation to share a vision quest with Ida Florence's brother Manny before presenting him with the Ghost Shirt in honor of the boy's twelfth birthday.

In her haste to fill the bucket, Ida Florence soaked her canvas shoes and anklets to the skin, ignoring even the puffball mushrooms and wild onions that she loved, for this was a day that Eddie Pakela might come to town. Those hours with him represented one of the rare occasions that she felt free. In a few short weeks, school would resume, where she must face the nuns at St. Ann's who hovered over her like great black raptors and thwacked her knuckles till they bled when she couldn't tell them the product of nine times nine. And as the days grew cooler and food even less plentiful, Papa would yell at her when she absentmindedly fried the salt pork, letting it turn hard as chunks of coal.

Eddie, a Finn from a farm in Towner County, was, in the opinion of Ida Florence's younger brothers, Manny and Roy, too dumb to know that white kids stayed away from Bucktown, the five-block area of Rolland west of Jackrabbit Road consisting of tar paper shacks. To Ida Florence, that didn't matter. Eddie represented a dream—unlike her, he was rangy and tall, handsome as a cowboy, with misty, sad eyes and money in his pocket. Best of all, he owned a car—a '27 Chevy that he'd cut down, bolted a box to, and painted egg yolk yellow. It was only the third vehicle Ida Florence had ever ridden in—not counting the St. Ann's school bus.

Ida Florence knew that her flawless skin and a cleft in her chin fascinated Eddie, especially after she let her dark hair grow down over her ample chest and put on lipstick red as cherry Life Savers that he bought her for a dime a tube at the Ben Franklin. But if she had an unattractive feature it was her hands, which were large and work-calloused, encouraging her to sit with her arms crossed and her hands out of view. Those strong hands, however, worked well to keep Eddie at bay when one of his own rough farmer's hands dropped gracelessly from her earlobe to her shoulder, around to the front of her breasts and down to the buttons on the side of her jeans where she seized and held it with a bear-trap grip until he sighed and pulled away.

*****

While Ida Florence labored in the woods, swatting water bugs and searching for the bushes with the richest clusters of berries, Eddie Pakela's cobbled yellow pickup rumbled into Rolland. Eddie was supposed to be working in the field pulling the binder, but the morning rain blew through the farm, drenching the hay.

He coasted past the Little Shay shack on the chance Ida Florence might be outside. From there, he drove toward Larry Laroque's filling station, where he spotted Manny across the street, sitting in the shade of the coal shed picking seed pods off the pigweeds to make a whip. He pulled over.

"Hey! Tonto! Where's your sister?"

Manny looked up at the pimply-faced whitey, not caring whether Ida Florence had hopscotched to Winnipeg, Manitoba or drowned at the bottom of Hooker Lake when he spotted the six cans of Grain Belt beer in an open bag resting in the truck bed. He had tried beer just once, a single warm can of Hamm's that somebody left back of the dance hall on a Saturday night—and though to him it tasted like skunk piss, he liked the way it made his muscles feel bigger and his tongue sharper.

He made his offer. For two of those cans he would help find his sister.

Eddie didn't bother to answer. Ramming his makeshift truck into gear, he floored the footfeed and sped away, spitting gravel into Manny's face.

Manny's brother, Roy, appeared from the opposite direction, hiking through the mustard field carrying the decrepit old rifle he'd found near the dump. Roy had been sent by their father to retrieve Manny in preparation for the vision quest that evening. The gun was a half-stocked, rusty Stevens .22 that fired so irregularly that every trigger pull was either a happy surprise or another disappointment.

Manny, a skinny kid with ears that stuck out like rhubarb leaves, seethed from the encounter with Eddie Pakela, and birthday or no birthday, he had no desire to waste time on a vision quest where the old man would be spouting his bullshit about how the family's Sioux blood was better than the Chippewas' that they lived among. Manny was so sick of hearing about the Little Bighorn that he wanted to poke needles into his own eardrums like the Sioux did to Custer. And as if that wasn't bad enough, he'd have to pretend he was proud to take ownership of a dirty old rag that smelled like a dead cow.

Made from a coarse, leathery fabric, tattered and darkened by time, the Ghost Shirt was kept wrapped in a deerskin and stored in a woven birch basket that itself was falling apart with age. Papa owned the garment by right of his existence as the sole fourth-generation Little Shay descendant of Lame Wolf, a Hunkpapa warrior who could talk to the buffalo and was a second cousin of the prophet Sitting Bull, the greatest of the Teton Sioux chiefs and conqueror of the preening magpie Custer. According to the belief that Papa held dear, Lame Wolf counted coup in a hundred battles while protected by the Ghost Shirt without once suffering harm.

Manny's thoughts were interrupted by the yellow car pulling into the filling station with its radiator steaming.

He watched as Eddie jumped out of the car and went for the water hose hanging from an outside wall. "Let me see that," he said to Roy, reaching for the gun.

Roy twisted away. "Hell no, I only got one bullet."

Manny grabbed his pigweed whip and lifted it menacingly toward his brother, but, catching sight of the cloud of steam engulfing Eddie's car, he had a sudden brainstorm. He explained his plan to Roy.

Dropping the .22 in the thistles, Manny approached the pickup where Eddie stood shielded by the open hood.

"Looks like you never found Ida Florence," he said, tapping a finger on the fender.

Eddie, his face red and dripping with sweat, didn't look up. "Get lost, papoose."

"Gimme four cigarettes and I'll tell you where she's at," said Manny.

Eddie lowered his gaze to his shirt pocket as if to check his cigarettes. "Like you know."

"I do. The old man made her go berry picking." As he spoke, Manny watched his brother tiptoe through the steam to the pickup bed.

"Where at?" asked Eddie. "I'll give you a cigarette."

"Two. One for Roy."

"All right. Tell."

"Gimme the smokes first."

Eddie shook out two Pall Malls from his pack. "Well?"

"You take the road up past the junkyard."

"Yeah, and then?"

"Go look around where that old barn collapsed."

Eddie slammed the hood and pulled out, leaving the brothers to watch impatiently as the truck pulled out of sight. They ran for the coal shed, where they used Roy's jackknife to poke holes in the tops of two cans of the pilfered Grain Belt.

\* \* \* \* \*

Ida Florence could always tell when Eddie had been drinking beer because his car smelled like fresh-baked bread. This time when they kissed his mouth tasted like Juicy Fruit gum. She wished she dared ask for a stick, but he didn't like it when she talked while they were kissing. He reached around her to brace the back of her head and thrust his tongue between her lips. His hand slid from her head down her neck and around to the front. She knew what was next. It was a well-trod path—outside her shirt, then under and beneath the dish towel that served as her brassiere. She allowed this. It felt good. Only when the hand tired of the breast and began the movement downward did she summon her resistance.

She worried how long this might go on. It became harder to avoid giving in. Eddie's Uncle Wes owned a trucking outfit in St. Paul and had offered Eddie a job once he got the right license. She dreaded the arrival of that day for surely it would put an end to the romance.

Ida Florence had never been to St. Paul, but she'd heard about it from Francis Belgarde's mother, who went there once for an operation. She said she saw grocery stores big enough to fit all of Rolland inside, coolers filled with gleaming packages of hamburger and chicken unlike the smelly gray meat covered with flies that sat for days in Ferris's Grocery. It had streets that didn't turn to mud when it rained, electricity that didn't go out four times a day, and water that you didn't have to pump from a well a block away.

Eddie's fingertips wormed inside the waistband of Ida Florence's panties, but as she reached to stop the advance, Eddie's glance fell on the bed of the truck. He broke off the kiss and sat up.

"Those little shits," he said. "I knew they were up to something." Leaping out of the car, he jerked the spare aside. "Sonofabitch!"

Ida Florence said later that for the first time ever Eddie never bothered to comb his hair before he had the car in gear and pointed toward town.

## 2 | Indian Girls

During the days preceding the passing of the sacred garment on to his son, Howahkan prepared by weaving his hair into braids that dangled from his head like peas from a vine. He donned a beaded smock and moccasins, making him stand out further from the Chippewa, who had taken to wearing hats and overalls like the white man. To him, living among the inferior, weak-willed, corn-growing Chippewa, who spoke the mongrel language *Michif*, meant disgrace for a descendant of such a noble people.

In the opinion of Howahkan's Chippewa neighbors, the blood of his superior ancestry was well watered-down by the time it reached him, while in his children they found no trace at all. The whole town knew that his daughter ran around with an ice monkey from out by Armourdale, while his boys revealed not much interest in anything but biding their time for the day they reached the age of eligibility for prison. Howahkan himself—"One-Horse Howie" they called him—though widely scorned, was however credited with knowing a bit of Lakota magic. How else could he stay so fat when none of them got enough to eat? But beyond that his family was stuck in the same poverty as everyone else on the reservation, selling gopher tails for the nickel-apiece bounty they paid at Staggs Hardware, getting by on fry bread during the waning days of winter, and going hat in hand to the fair-haired devils when they needed a favor.

* * * * *

At the moment that the enraged Eddie Pakela raced with Ida Florence toward the filling station, Howahkan Little Shay completed his rituals in anticipation of the vision quest. He'd donned his eagle feather headdress, readied his medicine bundle, and placed a handful of pemmican in a pouch to throw into the fire and feed the souls of the dead. Lastly, he slipped the Ghost Shirt over his head for the final time and set out to retrieve Manny, having decided Roy must have gotten sidetracked.

Before departing, he bowed in all four directions, four being one of the sacred numbers of the Sioux, corresponding not only to cardinal directions but to all growing things: roots, stem, leaves and fruit; the four stages of life: babyhood, childhood, adulthood and old age; and the divisions of time: day, night, moon and year.

As he reached the door to depart, he held it for a moment to let the bad spirits out and set off downtown.

Half a mile away, Manny and Roy sat on the ground, the .22 between them. The brown paper sack with one remaining still-cool Grain Belt rested beside the rifle. Manny calculated. Swallowing as fast as he could he'd managed to down nearly two of the four beers to his brother's one. Things swirled in his vision and the wooden flagpole in front of the post office kept doubling. Nevertheless, he gulped so hurriedly in an attempt to get the last can that the bubbly liquid backed up into his nose, making his eyes water.

The thumping of an engine sounded as Eddie's yellow Chevy turned and came to a stop, rocking on its springs. Eddie's bleached face hung out the window, scowling. Manny leaned forward, trying to bring the picture into focus. Beneath his piss-yellow hair and bulging eyes, Eddie's jaw worked, but through the clatter of the motor Manny couldn't make out what he was saying. Whatever it was, the skinny Finn looked angry and dangerous. When he shouldered his door open, Ida Florence opened hers and came around the front of the car, hoping to restrain him before he got too close to her brothers. When she grabbed Eddie's arm, he gave her a shove and she fell facedown in the gravel.

Manny grabbed the .22, braced himself on one hand and wobbled to his feet.

Howahkan Little Shay hiked up from the ditch and into this sorry state of affairs, bulky and huffing. There before his disbelieving eyes stood his son training a gun on a white man. On the ground sat his daughter, Ida Florence, weeping into her hands.

In an instant, Howahkan perceived what was happening. Wakan Tanka had arranged an opportunity for Manny to prove his readiness to accept the Ghost Shirt. The white man must have threatened the honor of Ida Florence, and Manny was about to make him pay for it. Pride tugged at Howahkan. In another time long past, he might have allowed such an act to proceed, but not on this sacred day. He raised his arms and cried out, but no one heard him. He thrust out his chest, displaying the Ghost Shirt, and stepped toward his son.

Weaving and wobbling, Manny managed to get his target in the sights, but the target moved continually.

Roy clambered to his feet when he saw his brother settling his aim on the Finn. He grabbed for the gun and got a hand on the barrel just as Manny squeezed the trigger.

The rifle fired, producing a soggy, muffled pop while the bullet, redirected, spun toward Howahkan. It arrived with just the required force to penetrate the Ghost Shirt and lodge in his chest. He went down silently, rose to his knees, and collapsed onto the gravel.

Ida Florence stumbled toward her father, screaming, bringing Larry Laroque from under the hood of a Studebaker where he'd been replacing the points and plugs. He pondered briefly what to do when Tiny Turcotte joined the scene, prepared to collect his saskatoon berries and deliver Howahkan Little Shay and his son to Border Butte.

Together, Larry and Tiny managed to drag Howahkan into the back of Tiny's pickup. Tiny did his best, honking his feeble horn to clear the way to the hospital. Eight minutes passed before he wheeled into the hospital grounds. Another two went by as he maneuvered the truck, which lacked a reverse gear, into the visitors' space. Another was wasted before he could summon help. By then, One Horse Howie had bled to death.

In the ensuing investigation, Eddie Pakela wasted no time in making himself scarce around Rolland. The BIA authorities eventually sent Manny and Roy to boarding school down in Flandreau while Ida Florence was placed in the girls' dormitory at Saint Ann's, where the nuns assigned her to help tend to the younger girls in payment for her room and board.

* * * * *

"How come you don't know no better than to have a Finlander for a boyfriend?" Etienne wanted to know.

"I told you before. None of your business," said Ida Florence. "And besides, he's not my boyfriend anymore."

At first Ida Florence appreciated the attentions of Etienne Morinville, a boy from the hills up north who took care of the livestock at St. Ann's and also worked as a part-time janitor. Furtive in movement and difficult to understand because of his habit of shielding his mouth when he spoke, he remained distant from most of the staff except Ida Florence. To her he spoke of his plans to one day have his own farm, not on the reservation because the land there was no good for farming, but up in the bush where the soil, though not much better, was cheaper.

But as the months passed his conversation moved away from talk of the future to his complaints about how the Indian students and help ate Crisco sandwiches while the white priest and his nuns enjoyed roast beef and potatoes. Now Etienne's often-indistinct words centered on the evils of white people as well as personal matters that made her feel like a bug in a pail of milk.

"Whites, they only want one thing from Indian girls," said Etienne one morning as Ida Florence stirred batter for the pancakes.

"Is that so?" She hated it when he came into the kitchen in his smelly barn clothes.

"You ought to know. I bet you and that Finn done it plenty."

"What? I can't hear you when you mumble."

He repeated himself.

"Oh, just shut up."

"You need to learn a lesson. You know what happens to babies that got Indians and whites for parents?"

Ida Florence left the spoon in the bowl and dropped her hands to her hips. "How come you hate whites so much?"

"Everybody hates them."

"You talk about getting your own farm up in the hills. Don't you know you'll have whites for neighbors up there?"

"I'll see they don't treat me the way they do the rest of the Chippewas—stealing the allotments and all."

Ida Florence felt her anger rising. "The rest of the Chippewas? Tell me your name."

"You know my name."

"Say it out loud."

Etienne began backing away. "Etienne."

"Both names."

"Morinville. Etienne Morinville."

"Is that a Chippewa name?"

"What do you mean?"

"Your name. Is that a Chippewa name?"

"It's an Indian name, yeah."

"I figured you didn't know this. You talk about weegies and finners, but your name is just as white as theirs, and you got more white blood than you ever dreamt of."

Etienne sneered in derision. "I know all about you. Your old man liked to brag that he was related to a Sioux chief. That didn't help him much when his own kid shot him."

"What?" Ida Florence glared at him. "That was an accident. You seen it yourself."

"Maybe. But what I'm telling you is you better keep clear of them whites."

"And I'm telling you that you don't know nothing about nothing. You don't even know that you got a white name, a French one."

"Bullshit."

"Just like everybody else on the reservation almost. LaFountain, Bercier, Peltier."

"Where do you get that?"

"It's true. Nobody talks about it. It would be maybe your great-grandfathers. They fought in Canada against England with another Frenchman named Louis

Riel. Long time ago. They lost the war and escaped across the border. They married Chippewa women."

Etienne stared at her. Ida Florence could see the stubbornness in his face.

"And you're nothing but a dumb girl that makes up stories," said Etienne. At that moment they heard Mother Superior shuffling down the hall, her beads clacking. Etienne turned and made for the back door.

Resenting Etienne's prying and cruel remarks, Ida Florence added an extra Our Father to her chapel prayers in hopes he would hurry up and own the farm he claimed to want. When he turned up at early mass to kneel beside her, she prayed that the thunderbird totem she carried everywhere would cause him to be struck by lightning—a sin that she immediately begged the Virgin Mary to forgive.

But his annoying attentions only increased. She felt his suspicious eyes on her as she met him on the stairs with her heavy loads of laundry, as she scrubbed the stains in the floor of the sacristy, as she gathered dandelions for the nuns to make into wine for Father L'Esperance. Her happiest moments came during the single hour she had to herself after the younger girls were settled in their narrow beds and the lights went out—a period of relaxation that ended when the girls began waking up after wetting their beds and crying out for their mothers who died or ran off to California.

The more Etienne talked about Eddie—a man he didn't even know—the more Ida Florence wanted to defend him. She wrote his name in the snow, then erased it with her foot before someone could see. She stayed hurt and angry that he disappeared when she got sent to St. Ann's. The nuns were right. She was a foolish girl. One day God would punish her.

* * * * *

On a Saturday morning in February, six months after that terrible day at the filling station, Sister Margaret Rose tapped Ida Florence sharply on the shoulder as she yanked the mop back and forth over the tiled floor of the sacristy.

"There's a young man here to see you," said Sister, and reminded her that as soon as she finished the floor she was wanted in the kitchen.

Waiting outside the monsignor's dim office, having planted himself in a puddle of meltwater on the freshly mopped floor, was a gangly, nervous man in his twenties. He blushed at Ida Florence's appearance and identified himself as Eddie Pakela's brother.

Eddie rarely spoke of his brother. Ida Florence took a minute to recall his name. "You're Mason then?"

The man nodded and forced a smile, revealing a black gap in his front teeth.

"Where's Eddie—is something wrong?" asked Ida Florence.

"He's at the farm," said Mason. "He told me to tell you he wants to see you and for you to wait by your old house tonight."

His duty fulfilled, Mason pulled his wool cap on, adjusted the earflaps and, with great relief, made for the door, leaving tracks all the way to the steps.

\* \* \* \* \*

Standing in the cold and staring at the house where she'd grown up, now boarded and gloomy, Ida Florence remembered the days long past before her mother had died. She recalled helping fix meals that were skimpy but tasty compared to the watery soup at the mission. Her brothers were innocent and curious while her bearlike father with his booming singing voice filled the tiny house with joy. Then her mother got sick, too weak even to walk to the outhouse. The BIA doctor came and the next day two men in the white ambulance took her mother away. She never again saw home.

After that her father never rattled the windows with his laughter nor did he swing Ida Florence in a circle holding her tight by the wrists. He spent time at the sweat lodge or fingering the thunderbird totem and gazing to the west. Every evening the children were made to sit in a circle on the floor as they had before, but instead of playing the stick-passing game, they listened to their father's endless lectures on the greatness of their forebears along with the wisdom he'd learned from his grandmother White Buffalo Calf Woman. And when he spoke of Windigo, the supernatural being who craved human flesh, especially that of children, his eyes took on a melancholy expression and his voice dropped to a whisper. So intent was he on his own words that he failed to notice that Manny and Roy fidgeted restlessly, making spitballs with wads of paper and pinching each other. Only Ida Florence continued to pay respect to their aging father whose talk and actions left him mired in the past.

\* \* \* \* \*

Eddie looked different. He wore a rust-colored cowboy shirt with sequins on the collar and cuffs. He also wore glasses that slid down his long nose when he bent to check his watch. He was deeper-voiced now, but in other ways he stayed the same old Eddie, restlessly glancing in the rearview mirror, fiddling with the choke while he pumped the footfeed. After driving directly to their old parking spot, he'd barely pulled the hand brake when he reached for Ida Florence, kissed her off-center and placed a hand on her breast. She brushed it away, noticing his fingernails were clean for once.

"What's the matter?" he said. "Aren't you glad I'm back?"

"Back?"

"Mason never told you? I been trucking for Wes in St. Paul."

"All this time? How come you never let me know?"

"'Cuz Wes sent word to come right away or he'd get somebody else."

"You ever heard of stamps and paper?" said Ida Florence peevishly.

"Well hell, I never wrote a letter in my life."

"You could have told Mason to tell me."

"After all that stuff with your pa? I had to wait for that to cool off. Damned if I want to get threw in the reservation jail and eat dogmeat the rest of my life. Now come here." Eddie leaned in to kiss her, but she shuffled to the side and folded her arms over her chest.

"Well that's a fine how-do-you-do," said Eddie, resting his hand lightly on Ida Florence's shoulder. "I come all the way back to see you."

"You never come back to see me."

Eddie flung his hands up. "Huh? I must be dreaming because it sure enough looks to me like I'm settin' here right now with Ida Florence Little Shay."

Eddie had turned the heat up high and the cab smelled of gas fumes. Now Ida Florence would have to wash her best outfit—a cream-colored blouse and brown slacks—before the nuns noticed. "Just take me back to the dorm," she said.

"It ain't even nine o'clock," protested Eddie.

"That's no matter," replied Ida Florence. "I had to sneak out as it was."

"Then you could sneak back in, couldn't you?" He took her hand.

"You don't know what it's like at St. Ann's. They punish you for anything and they get the little kids to spy on you."

Eddie sat back and lit a cigarette. "Why don't you run away?"

"Where would I go?"

"Lots of places. Minot or Bismarck."

"I don't know nobody there."

"You know somebody in St. Paul," said Eddie, making a circle on Ida Florence's shoulder with his thumb.

"Right now I don't," said Ida Florence, catching Eddie's playful tone.

"But you will when somebody gets back there."

"When's that?"

"When they start hauling cattle again, hard to say exactly, but it'll be a while."

"What are you going to do till then?"

"Oh, they always need help on the farm. Maybe by then I'll get cooperation out of you."

\* \* \* \* \*

Ida Florence harbored no doubt about Eddie's meaning. She felt a tickling like feathers in the pit of her stomach when she thought too much about it. Two weeks later they sat in the pickup watching the airport beacon rotating a mile to the east and picking up the glint of discarded beer bottles and candy wrappers. They weren't the only couple to use this lovers' lane.

Eddie took off his glasses and pulled his knee up on the seat, so he could face her. She intended to make a kind of announcement, but no arrangement of words came to her that fit so she loosened the top button on her jeans, arched her back so she could slide the jeans down, and reached for his hand.

She felt a sting and a squeezing. Eddie grunted and just like that it was over. Maybe he wasn't the experienced man that his talk made him out to be.

In his haste Eddie knocked over Ida Florence's handbag. "What the heck is this?" he said, holding an oblong, dark gray rock.

"Nothing. Give it back to me."

"It's got a hole in it," said Eddie.

"If you must know, it's a thunderbird. That's its eye."

"What's it for?"

"Just give it here."

"No, really. I never heard of no bird called a thunderbird."

"It's a charm."

"Where'd you get it?"

"My dad found it somewhere."

"Is it some kind of Indian good luck thing?"

"It's the Lakota guardian of truth."

"The what?"

"If you lie to whoever owns the rock you can get struck by lightning."

"Yeah? I ain't afraid of no lightning. Me and Mason ride horseback all the time when it storms."

"All that means is that you haven't told me a lie so far." She took the object from his hand.

Eddie blinked twice and his mouth dropped open. "What a bunch of hogwash," he said, stepping on the starter, for once in a hurry to go.

\* \* \* \* \*

Ida Florence discovered she could go out and return by way of the furnace room with little risk. No one had need to be in the area during evenings, and the door outside was never locked, but as the weather warmed and the days lengthened, she found it more difficult to get away. Everybody stayed up late to enjoy the outdoors. One Friday night close to Easter she skipped the Stations of the Cross and took the back staircase to the basement. She unbolted the cumbersome furnace room door. The ceiling light was on. Etienne Morinville was sprawled out on the floor, a toolbox at his side, a wrench in his hand.

"Oh!" said Ida Florence. "You scared me."

"Where you going?" said Etienne.

"Nowhere," she said, flustered.

Etienne twisted a dial on the wrench, producing a metallic click. "I see you got your purse. I guess you're going to see your white boy again. That Finlander."

"No, I'm not," said Ida Florence, hating both herself and Etienne for creating the awkward circumstances.

He stood with a snort and tugged his pant cuffs down so they covered his ankles. "You never been taught that doing something bad is one thing, but fibbing makes it twice as worse?"

Ida Florence held her bag behind her back. "What are you going to do?"

"I won't tell if that's what you're afraid of."

"I expect I should thank you," said Ida Florence, still rattled.

"Up to you. You better go or you'll be late," said Etienne, picking up his heavy tool case, grunting with the effort.

* * * * *

Spring became summer. The school term ended. The children who had homes were sent to them. As a newly accepted resident, Ida Florence was assigned arduous duties including weeding and hoeing the vegetable garden. Digging in the rock-laden dirt, her fingernails became chipped and torn. It had been a moist spring, resulting in a mosquito-infested summer. She filled out the required form for Sister Margaret Rose requesting citronella oil. At the bottom, she penciled: *And some gloves. OK if they are old.*

Such items were unnecessary, said the nun. God would provide.

Eddie was also no help. "What for?" he said. "You get whatever you want free from the government, don't you?"

Etienne, pitying her, located an old pair of greasy men's work gloves from the shop that fit well over her thick fingers. In addition, he told her that up in the hills they used catnip to keep bugs away. Plenty of that grew in the graveyard. She broke up several plants and rubbed them on her skin daily. It worked some, but Eddie complained that it stunk and made him sneeze, so she abandoned the practice.

In late July, harvest began and Eddie showed up at their meeting place by Ida Florence's old house less often, leaving her lingering in the twilight. When she asked if he'd heard from his uncle about returning to St. Paul, pointing out that farmers with cattle might soon be sending them to market, he responded with anger. "Stay out of it. He knows more about trucking than you do."

\* \* \* \* \*

One warm night Eddie drove up near the old house with someone else in the car. It was Mason, who Ida Florence hadn't seen since the time he came to the office to bring the message from Eddie. At Eddie's invitation, Ida Florence squeezed in between them, uncomfortable and uneasy.

Neither spoke as Eddie turned north on the Hospital road leading out of town. When they reached the abandoned farm known as the old Dunlop homestead, he pulled in and parked in the alder grove by the little lake.

"Let's go take a look at the lake," he said, opening his door. Ida Florence followed him out the driver's side, while Mason sat in the vehicle, staring into the woods.

"I need you to do me a favor," said Eddie when they were out of sight.

"A favor?"

Eddie glanced over his shoulder. "Mason, he's never been with a girl."

"What you mean?"

"You know."

"No, I don't."

"He never had a girlfriend."

Through the trees Ida Florence could see the brother. He'd gotten out of the truck and stood against the fender with one hand bracing himself, peeing on the tire.

Eddie lowered his voice. "It'll be the two of us, me and him, one on each side."

"God! Something's wrong with you."

"No. I thought I should tell you first instead of just starting in."

"How do you dare think of such a thing?"

"It's OK. I don't mind. He's my brother. I happen to know they do that all the time down in the Cities. And everyone says you go back and forth, Indian girls."

"What?"

"I promised Mason."

"That's your doing."

Eddie continued, his voice becoming a whimper. "I thought you loved me."

Ida Florence looked back at the pickup where Mason sat with the window cracked open, the red tip of a cigarette bobbing.

"Please?" said Eddie.

Ida Florence took a step backward and turned away.

"You come back here or else," ordered Eddie.

When she saw him striding toward her in his clunky engineer boots, eyes furious, she broke for the woods, confident she could outrun him. Willows slapped her face and rose thorns dug long scratches in her mosquito-bitten arms, but she ran until she reached the lake, where she stopped to listen, hearing only the sounds of insects and an owl beginning its nightly hunt. The lake smelled of rotting vegetation. No one fished or swam in it, and it was overrun with blood suckers.

Daylight came full by the time she got back to the dorm. The cook would be up by now boiling the meal for breakfast. Ida Florence continued to the garden, knelt in the soil, and started in pulling weeds, as if she were simply getting a jump on the day.

## 3 | Parsley and Cinnamon

In a single weekend, Ida Florence had gone from dreaming about Eddie saving her from the misery of life at the school to hoping that she would never see him again. When she neglected her duties, hiding dirty laundry, letting the girls run from room to room, Mother Superior scolded her. Yet she cared about nothing, not bothering to bathe or brush her teeth. She burst into tears for no reason. She wore a sullen look that mystified those around her. When some evildoer—one of her young charges probably—reported that she stole a cough drop from Father L'Esperance's desk, she was made to stand alone in the hot, dusty attic of the leather shop for four hours. Life could not possibly get worse.

But it could. Ida Florence thought nothing of it when moon time was late. It happened before when her father died. Two weeks passed and then two more. She knew what it most likely meant but told herself it couldn't be so. She believed that the other workers didn't like her—they considered her stuck-up and lazy. They would never help her even if they knew what to do. But then one of them did, though quite by accident. The weekend cook, a stout, jolly woman who had numerous children, was making a salad in the kitchen when she held up a sprig of a greenish plant. "I ought to of ate more of this and I'd never of had all them babies," she said, laughing.

But what was that green plant, and would it still work if you were already pregnant? She could never ask. She had already decided that she dared not even confess her sin to Father L'Esperance for fear of being discharged from the only home she had—such as it was—even at the risk of burning in Hell.

On Saturday morning she hung out the sheets early, and on the way back, passed the kitchen window. Ida Florence peered in over the counter and cutting board to make sure the cook was there.

She was. But so was Mother Superior, who sat across from the cook at the table, each with a cup of coffee. Mother was dressed not in her usual habit but in a plain work dress with buttons to her neck and a scarf tied around her hair. The two women—Ida Florence had to try hard to think of Mother as a woman—were all smiles and chattering like old friends, like teenagers in the drugstore in town. She made her way, head down, to the laundry room, where she waited for the next load.

\* \* \* \* \*

Although she'd never been to the stables, Etienne did not seem surprised to see Ida Florence appear, tiptoeing around the cow pies and looking scared. He finished the cow he was milking, not hurrying, biding his time, and set the pail outside the calf pen where it couldn't be kicked over.

Nor did he seem upset in any way when she explained what she wanted.

"If you can just find out, I can write to Minnie and she can find it herself," she said.

But Etienne wasn't fooled by her tale of her cousin Minerva at Standing Rock who was in trouble and whose father might kill her if he found out what she'd done. He brushed off his milking stool and placed it beside the next cow, then went for his pail.

"Did you tell the Finlander?" he asked.

Ida Florence burst into tears. "I don't dare. You must think I'm the dumbest," she sobbed.

"You don't have to bawl," said Etienne. "But I don't know about stuff like that. There's this guy, he's always at the pool hall. He used to live out west and he's one of those know-it-alls. I'll get him to tell me if you want."

"Please," said Ida Florence, wiping her eyes.

"Whatever's gonna come of you anyway?" said Etienne, returning to his milking.

\* \* \* \* \*

Two days afterward, Etienne motioned to Ida Florence as he dropped off the soiled bedding from the dorm.

"Parsley and cinnamon," he said.

"You mean like cinnamon Sister Rita puts on toast?"

Etienne shrugged his shoulders. "That's all he said."

Sneaking around in the deserted kitchen made Ida Florence dislike herself and St. Ann's even more. She opened the refrigerator to find the bulb burnt out. She wasn't positive what parsley looked like, but she felt around. A few carrots, a couple heads of cabbage, some onions. A large sack of crab apples with dried leaves and stems still stuck to them. That was all.

At least she knew where to look for cinnamon. She went to the spice cabinet. Right next to the cardboard container was a smaller, similarly colored one labeled parsley with its seal intact. She interpreted that as a good omen. She poured half of each into her coin purse with the dime and penny she carried so she wouldn't be broke.

The cinnamon went down easily with water, but the parsley tasted like dried grass and made her gag. She put a pinch at a time into her mouth and chewed until she produced enough saliva to swallow. Within an hour she developed a stomachache. Even after running to the lavatory and puking into the sink her stomach churned like an eggbeater.

She waited ten days. Her breasts felt weighty. She was often too sick to eat, and by midday could only think of going to bed.

* * * * *

Ida Florence knew Etienne kept a key for the office. Grateful that he asked no questions, she dialed the number and waited while Etienne stood watch in the hall.

Two rings, four, and then a pause. Her luck held. Eddie himself answered.

"Eddie?"

Silence.

"Eddie, this is Ida Florence."

"What do you want?"

"I need to talk to you."

"What about?"

She planned that if forced to, she would tell him right then. But the phone seemed so flimsy with its thin lines that broke like string when it stormed. "Please, can I see you?"

Eddie spoke something away from the phone, then came back. "I can't go nowhere except if it rains. We're swathing."

"That's OK," said Ida Florence, thankful for the small boost. "Just come when you can. When it rains. To the house, I mean." She held the receiver for a moment. The line went dead.

"Thank you," she said, though not sure why or for what.

\* \* \* \* \*

For the second evening in a row she waited in the scrawny lilac bushes across from her old home, shifting her weight from one foot to the other and pressing a piece of oilcloth over her head to keep off the drizzle. Both times she'd sauntered straight out the main door of the dorm, no longer dreading the consequences of breaking the rules.

A car with a single headlight rolled past, splashing through potholes. A "one-eyed Ike," her papa used to call such vehicles, provoking giggles from her brothers. How sad the house looked with no one to kindle a fire or turn on a light. For many months, right after Sunday mass, she wrote a letter to her brothers at the boarding school in Flandreau, but as she expected, never received a reply.

All she had now was Eddie. Not one person at St. Ann's would even notice if she jumped off the steeple. There was Etienne, yes, but he was more like a pesky stray dog than a friend, a dog that spat tobacco and smelled like a barn. And while Eddie had his own faults—his grumpiness, his zits, his cruel billy-goat laugh—he had the power to take her away from all this. And of course, she owned a true connection to him now through the life growing unbelievably in her belly.

He pulled up well after dark, craning his head about impatiently before she emerged, soaked and shivering. She climbed into the cab to the familiar smell of sweat and cigarette smoke. Eddie lit a cigarette and frowned at her.

"You cold?" He reached for the heater control. Precious warmth flowed from the floor.

By the time they got to their familiar spot to park—Ida Florence never doubted their destination once they began moving—she was warm and comfortable. Practiced lovers by now, she let Eddie's hands go where they would. She lifted her legs in readiness. He unhitched his belt and slid his pants down to his ankles.

"Lay back more," he said, pulling her toward him with a hand under each of her thighs. When he judged the angle to be to his liking, he plunged into her in a single painful thrust. While she stared through the windshield at an alder branch silhouetted against a hazy night sky, he drove forcefully in and back like a machine as the little yellow pickup rocked on its squeaky springs. At last he let out a high-pitched grunt and went still.

After he withdrew, she lay unmoving and limp. She waited while he got himself properly arranged with his shirt buttoned and his hair combed, turning the rearview at just the right angle.

"Eddie, are you still going back to St. Paul?"

He inspected his comb before slipping it into his back pocket. "Yeah. Soon as we get the crop all in. Why?"

"You know you said you would take me with you."

"I shoulda known that was what you wanted to talk about."

"Did you mean it?"

"I said it, didn't I?"

"Yes. I didn't know after you quit coming."

The gentle rainfall intensified. Eddie wiped the windshield with his open palm to clear the fog.

"Well, you started acting funny and I got busy. I hope you learned your lesson."

Ida Florence could tell he expected a comment. She had a poor idea what he meant and feared saying the wrong thing. She understood mostly that this was no time to be telling him about her condition.

But Eddie wasn't waiting. "Because if you didn't, I can send you back just like that." He snapped his fingers.

\* \* \* \* \*

The next two weeks felt like the longest of Ida Florence's life. Every time one of the nuns approached her in the hallway, she expected she was about to be summoned to the office and then locked up somewhere. Etienne's expression made her feel like he was saying *I know what you been doing.*

For his part, Eddie guarded his intentions, speaking during their two brief meetings only of how poor the wheat crop looked, how difficult it was to drive a cattle truck and how things cost so much in Minnesota.

Every word he said added to Ida Florence's gloom. At the same time, she hated herself for not telling him her secret. Each day brought more torment. She checked her shape in the laundry room mirror for a swelling in her stomach. She tried to conceal her nausea by smiling or looking the other way. When fatigue plagued her, she ignored it, plodding forward sluggishly, waiting for nightfall and the comfort of her narrow bed.

\* \* \* \* \*

Ida Florence's imaginings had run so wild that when Eddie at last advised her when to be ready to leave, she at first thought that he must be lying. Her hopes rose when he provided details. He figured to make St. Paul in three days, he said. They needed to pack plenty of food and of course they'd sleep in the car.

The night before departure, Ida Florence told Eddie she'd like to visit her old house one last time. Some bandit had made off with the windows and doors. She knew the place would burn or be torn down before she ever came back, and she wanted to see that nothing of value was left behind, not that much of value ever existed.

"Just don't go picking up a bunch of junk for me to haul all the way to St. Paul," growled Eddie.

Eddie played his flashlight around the kitchen. Black tarry droppings on the floor gave evidence of a family of raccoons dwelling nearby.

"Jesus, how could anybody live like this?" he said.

Humbled, Ida Florence fought the urge to explain. A person like Eddie would never understand.

## 4 | Finland

They left Rolland traveling east on Highway 5. The town had given her nothing but heartbreak and tears. Still, like the leaky shack she'd grown up in, she assumed she'd miss it. But as the distance away from those memories increased, fresh wonders and fears arose to take their place.

Eddie had mentioned that Wes owned a large house. Most likely she would have her own room—at least till she and Eddie were married, that is. After that they'd move into their own home. She pictured a tiny apartment over a store, like the Jacobsons had above the dress shop, maybe only a bedroom and a kitchen combined with a living room. Try as she might, she could not fit a baby into this image.

She reached over and rested a hand on Eddie's leg. His knee twitched and she shifted her hand away. He was in one of his quiet, grumpy moods. She didn't mind. Her father used to have those spells.

"Where's your glasses?" she asked, after watching him squint at his wristwatch. The last time she'd seen them a Band-Aid was wrapped around a corner of the bow.

"The wagon run over 'em," he said.

Then, with no design and emboldened by her ability to come up with something unrelated to the situation, Ida Florence came out with it. "Eddie, we're going to have a baby." It was like someone else mouthed the words.

Eddie, after flicking another one in his endless stream of cigarette butts out the window, stared ahead at the road, neither happy nor unhappy, just observing the horizon as if expecting someone or something to jar him into recollecting where he was and where he was going.

He twisted the wheel, corrected, eyes forward. He licked his lips. "How do you know that?" he asked, glancing at her.

"I'm not stupid."

The pickup swerved to the right. Ida Florence wondered if he intended to take her back to St. Ann's or push her out the door. But it was only to avoid a crumpled cardboard box in the middle of the road.

"When are you planning on having this baby?" he said.

"What difference does it make?"

Eddie made no move except to purse his lips.

That must be how he drives his cattle truck, thought Ida Florence. Staring straight ahead like there's nothing else except that ribbon of a road.

\* \* \* \* \*

By sundown they approached Jamestown and Eddie eased to a stop. A line of vehicles formed up ahead. A truck transporting cars had pulled over, nearly blocking the road. The ramp on the carrier was down, and the truck driver was carefully backing the cars off and parking them on the side of the road.

As they waited, Eddie played his foot on the gas pedal, coaxing the engine to idle just so. Others stepped out of their vehicles, as it looked like the delay would be long. He turned off the ignition and leaned back on the seat.

"There is a factor to think about," he said, gripping the steering wheel tightly.

"A factor?" said Ida Florence. That was a word Eddie never used.

"Uncle Wes, he don't go in too much for Indians."

"Is that right," she said, resisting the urge to add, "What else is new?"

"He says you all got lice and ringworms." Perhaps unconsciously, Eddie scratched the back of his neck.

"You can't say ringworms," said Ida Florence. "There's only one. And it's not a real worm."

"But you get what I'm saying."

"Yes, I do," said Ida Florence.

"Not that all that matters," said Eddie. "He's got nothing direct against Indians. They got rights like anybody else. His gripe is how they won't work and would rather live off the taxpayer. And then they keep having more kids." He turned to catch Ida Florence's eye.

"Yes, those babies are a problem, aren't they?" she said.

"Don't get the wrong notion," said Eddie. "I'm just telling you what my uncle says."

To the west, the sky formed shadows, and raindrops began pelting the roofs of the cars. Up ahead, doors slammed as drivers rushed to their cars.

"Is that what you think too?" asked Ida Florence.

"Heck no," said Eddie, raising a hand defensively. "I took you along with me, didn't I? But I been thinking if you're really gonna have a baby, maybe it's best to keep it quiet."

Engines revved. Some of the older vehicles refused to start and had to be cranked.

"And how will we do that—because I really am going to have a baby."

Eddie poked his head out the window, trying to see ahead. He pumped the footfeed and tried the starter. The engine came to life. "There's this reservation, you know—Indian reservation—that I go past when I truck up toward Eau Claire in Wisconsin. It's not that far. I forget what they call it, but I think Chippewas live there, you know, like you."

"I'm Sioux," said Ida Florence.

"Well, the thing is, you could still find your kind there."

In response to Ida Florence's silence, Eddie spoke faster. "Because during my overnight runs, you wouldn't have nothing to do in St. Paul. And I could visit you on the Wisconsin trips."

A crack of thunder sent stragglers scurrying to their vehicles.

The sky darkened. Eddie raised his window. The wind came up, splattering the raindrops against the glass.

"But I would have things to do on a reservation I never heard of and where I don't know nobody. Is that what you're saying?"

"No—well, just at first. The reservation, they must have a deal where babies can get adopted out, don't they? Lots of families might like having a little Chippewa papoose." Eddie grinned.

"I told you, I'm Sioux. Oglalla Sioux."

"Well, yeah, but…"

The highway cleared ahead. A truck, its headlights bright, approached slowly from the other direction, illuminating the cab. Ida Florence scrutinized Eddie's jaw laboring, spitting out words that had no more value than a mouthful of straw. The truck lights hit him in the face. Little hairs became visible in his nose as did a pimply rash on his neck. An odd question came to Ida Florence's mind. Finland. Was that a country?

The sky turned from black to a strange green. The wind took on the sound of a train, swaying the car sideways on its springs. Ida Florence pushed on her door. The wind blew it back against her shoulder.

"Where you going?" said Eddie.

"Out," said Ida Florence. The wind eased abruptly. She heaved herself against the door and it swung open.

Stretching her jacket over her head like a hood, she began walking. Like a dog that won't stay home, the pickup kept pace beside her, its yellow flashily prominent among all the colorless cars and trucks. As they neared a gentle rise the engine misfired, making progress erratic. Now the pickup scooted ahead, now it fell back as Eddie played with the choke and gearshift, his head cocked to the side as he listened to the struggling engine. Then, tiring of the game, he shot a look toward the side, face fiery-red, mouth wide and black as he shouted something Ida Florence had no chance of hearing. The pickup accelerated forward, swerved around numerous vehicles where there appeared no space to get by and carried on into the blackness.

Paper and other debris swirled around her. Lightning flashed continuously, each following thunderclap seeming to increase the intensity of the rain. Ida Florence stumbled to the ditch where she lay down, her meaty hands over her head, the rain nearly drowning her.

The storm weakened quickly, and the day brightened. Rivulets of water carved pathways in the ditch. Ida Florence stood and gazed around. A grain elevator and water tower emerged ahead, the storm having concealed their existence. She resumed walking. Along the road, cars were stopped every which way, doors open. Others rested in the ditch, hubcap deep in fresh mud. Tree limbs, hay, and rags lay about the ditch and fields. Knots of people, including families with children, gathered, chattering excitedly and pointing toward the east where the sky revealed a churning blackness. Ida Florence marched on.

She reached a Texaco filling station on the edge of the town. She entered as an ambulance and fire engine passed, racing toward the north from where she had come. Inside the station, a cluster of wide-eyed people gawked at her. No one said a word as she made her way behind the counter to a phone on the wall. She lifted the receiver and listened for a tone. Miraculously, the lines had remained intact. She requested an operator and gave the number.

She waited, clothes dripping and glued to her skin. Customers looked away. The distant sound of a second operator came on through static, then another. It would take some time.

But when at last he came on the line, it was like he was expecting her. "What you want?" he said.

"Etienne," she responded. "Come and get me."

# BLACK MARKS

## 1 | Père

The cold blew down from the north—so intense that the trees outside the hut protested with a hollow pop as if struck with a rock. The girl drew closer to the fire and pulled the deerskins tight around her shoulders. Père lay in his bed across the room, groaning and coughing in his sleep. In her hands the girl held the book she'd found, the first she'd seen in her few years, though she had no understanding of what to call the compact bundle of whitish barklike material. The cover, after it became separated from the pages, had disintegrated into fine threads that exposed the cross patterns of its construction. She studied the tiny markings on a page with pleasure, deliberating what they might be. She saw in their shape a resemblance to the black specks left by flies on the sides of the goat stalls. She knew the marks must stand for something, just as the texture and shape of the various clouds in the sky told stories, at least according to Père.

A thick length of oak snapped in the fire, throwing cinders of blazing wood into the air that settled on the dirt floor at the girl's feet. She looked intently at an ember as it cooled, its color changing to a darker red, then flaring brighter before giving up its life and turning a rich black.

When it cooled, she picked up the finger-sized remnant and touched it to the paper, making a distinct streak of black that resembled one of the marks on the page. Fascinated, she tried to make more marks. So intent was she on the book and her discovery that she did not hear Père rise and shuffle toward her on his walking stick. Before she could react, he reached with a gnarled arm and snatched the book away. He squinted at it briefly, sniffed it, touched it with his tongue, and tossed it into the fire.

\* \* \* \* \*

The hut occupied a shelf overlooking the creek with low hills in three directions. Constructed by Père of logs chinked with saw grass and pine tar atop a waist-high foundation of mossy field stones, the dwelling, with its backdrop of aspen and ancient oak, appeared to be sprung whole from nature. Highway 43, a route to the larger world, passed six rugged miles south. An unmaintained section line road a mile east ran straight to the Canadian border, but no routes connected to it. An inconspicuous, rutted game trail wound northwest near the terminus of the gravel section line road, but it lay hidden by the snows in the winter and by bog and tangled nettles the remainder of the year. A connection to any road required a half day's walk in the best of weather and amounted to no more than a winding footpath along a creek that stayed dry from late summer up to spring runoff.

* * * * *

Either through a minor dispute between Canada and the United States or because of an inept surveying crew, the precise border location was vague. Officials on each side knew of the hut in the woods, but all held the opinion that the crude dwelling lay within the domain of the opposite country, meaning that the two occupants existed permanently isolated and forgotten, as inaccessible as the northern lights.

Over time, legends arose. Deer hunters insisted that their game, after being field dressed, often disappeared if left unattended, an unexpected difficulty blamed on bears that were known to frequent the area as recently as the turn of the century. Still, murky fourthhand stories told of a creature seven or eight feet tall being spotted from a distance loping through the trees like a giraffe. Inevitably, tales of yeti or bigfoot arose. Etienne Morinville, who farmed to the southeast, claimed to have come upon footprints the size of tennis rackets, but since he was Indian, no one allowed the story much credence.

* * * * *

By age fourteen, the girl stood six feet three inches in her bare feet, nearly as tall as her father, although winters in the low-ceilinged, smoky hut caused them both to develop a permanent stoop. She had acquired the soft, toe-first gait of a wild animal, knowing little of shoes other than during midwinter or the first thaw of spring when she would strap her broad feet with their splayed big toes into footwear made of layers of birch bark before tending to the goats or gathering the sassafras that she loved to chew.

The man was much older, by forty or more years. He called her *Enfant* or "child," which she heard as "Fawn," a word that she believed to be her name. Their language was of Père's invention—a crude patois of simple English and French combined with words of convenience appropriate to their existence. Even with that, silence often prevailed for days, communication being rarely necessary as events seldom varied. The man's ever-dimming memory enhanced the isolation.

His one useless leg, the result of an untreated compound fracture sustained in a fall while gathering eggs from a falcon aerie, greatly limited his mobility. Only once had he ventured as far as town, where the first person he encountered was a woman with a goiter the size of a melon, which he took as an omen of an outlandish or menacing creature. That combined with the stares and taunts of a cluster of rowdy young men alarmed him, and he never went back.

\* \* \* \* \*

The larger world knew nothing of them, and whatever that domain consisted of was unavailable to Fawn. That realm lay uselessly in unfathomable distances or—in Père's designation—beyond *les arbres*. The forest itself was their security. Whereas outsiders thought of the deep woodland as a foreboding place with shadows and menacing surprises, for the man and the girl they were a great curtain, an impenetrable barrier guarding them not only from invaders, but from the greater threat of change.

The girl never thought of history or a past. To her, life was attached only to the present, which must be remade each day. What came before consisted of a foggy puzzle, uninteresting and valueless. She lacked goals other than the concrete notions to complete tasks essential to live another day.

\* \* \* \* \*

Occasionally, on a calm, late summer day with the air thick about her, Fawn would sit on the knoll behind the goat shed and gaze into the woods, studying the patterns of light and darker green, the patches of yellow and tan leaves, the areas of black where no light reached, and wonder what lay beyond. A single aspen or birch with its quivering leaves promised gentle comfort—shade from sun, shelter from rain. In their vast numbers they were as plentiful as the stars and their end as unreachable. Eventually, she concluded that where *les arbres* ended must be where the stars began, for at night the sky did indeed descend into the treetops.

Because she and the glum Père existed, Fawn knew that others like them must similarly have life. Through her animal intuition she knew that she must have originated from a mother. When her breasts began to develop, she inferred that she was the type of being that could be a mother. She hoped she was correct, for then she could at last have a companion like herself—someone she could talk to, who would laugh with her when butterflies arrived and share the anticipation of the sweet crunchiness of a honeycomb.

On a spring day, after she'd watched a goat give birth, she asked Père about the mystery of nature by which newly formed presences came into being. Could she herself make a replica of a human grow within her? Père's face darkened, and he covered the girl's mouth with one rough, dirty hand with its yellowed, broken fingernails. At the same time, he used his other hand to lift her loincloth. Leaning in, he gazed at the place where her legs met, the same place where blood showed occasionally. Frowning, Père let the cloth fall back and turned away, leaving her baffled.

Fawn recognized the diversity of life through the presence of birds, rabbits and other wildlife, but it was mostly from the herd of tame goats that she came to comprehend the dynamics of existence. She acknowledged the importance of the goats for the milk, cheese and meat they provided. She knew how to nurture the stubborn animals, to see that they were fed and protected from the rain and cold. She knew that a goat would never walk around an object, even for water or food, and she helped Père construct crude fences to accommodate their instinct to move only in straight lines. She knew when they were healthy and to grab them by the pones where the chest meets the front leg to determine if they were too fat. She knew how to treat their diseases—mastitis and footscald, though those were not the names she used.

*****

Still, as Fawn was to discover, she was not as alone as she had once believed. An occasional presence visited her, something that could not be seen, only heard. When she turned suddenly to see what it was, nothing was there. Yet she heard it speaking.

*The coals glow so pretty. Touch them,* said the voice.

She hesitated.

*It will not hurt,* said the voice.

Fawn did as ordered, blistering her fingers, wounds that took days to heal.

Since the voice resembled the bleat of a goat and because she could not forget her burns, she called it *Feu-chevre* or "Firegoat."

Sometimes Firegoat made a cloud to steal the sun for a short while. Then, at the reappearance of the sun, Fawn laughed uncontrollably. Other times, a crow cawed raucously from the roof of the hut, causing her to cry out in fear. If Père was nearby, he would scold or even strike out at her.

But regardless of Père, the plight continued. When Fawn said yes, Firegoat said no. When she wished to go, Firegoat ordered her to stop. Often, she clapped her hands over her ears to still the voice, but that only made Firegoat shriek all the louder. Luckily, when she thought she could bear no more, Firegoat might stay away for a long time. And though she hoped he would go away forever, he never failed to come back, as surely as the approach of winter's inscrutable darkness.

\* \* \* \* \*

Unknown to Père, the book that he had tossed into the fire was retrieved by Fawn when the ashes cooled, for she sensed that it was more important than the twigs, dried leaves and other debris commonly used for tinder. The book, itself salvaged from an abandoned hut, though charred around the edges, retained visible markings. And there was something she hadn't observed in detail—a drawing of a man and woman hand-in-hand beneath a tree. The man looked not at all like the bulky, hairy Père, for he was young and fair of face. The woman was younger yet, Fawn's age perhaps. Her curiosity grew.

One mark looked like a crawling garter snake, another resembled an eye, one more like an armless man on his feet, but the head separated from the body. But how was she to connect the casual scratches to the joyful expressions on the faces of the youthful couple? She took the pages to the goat shed where she hid them. Later in the winter, when Père became sick with pain in his stomach, she sat before the fire with the pages on her lap, peering at the picture and trying to make sense of the markings.

\* \* \* \* \*

Spring, the time of green, arrived. Goats dropped their young. Shoots emerged from the ground. The creek ran with fresh, clear water. As the weather warmed, Père took to his bed, his pain resistant even to the chamomile and peppermint that Fawn prepared him. One bright day, while searching for the best plants for the meal, she was startled by the bleating voice of Firegoat.

*Across the creek grows asparagus as tall as your arm is long.*

She hesitated. She was never to venture to the other side of the stream, but Père still lay in his bed. In two strides of her long legs, she reached the opposite side, avoiding the sharp rocks on the bank, and entered the woods where the moss-covered ground soothed her tender feet. Yet she saw no asparagus, only the dead, moist leaves of the forest floor with their sweet smell of decay.

She paused again. She'd come so far that she could barely make out the hut through breaks among the green, but as no harm had come to her, she went on. She reached the hill and paused to listen. Living in wilderness, she'd become attuned to the sounds of nature. She could distinguish the beat of the wings of a sparrow from that of a thrush and could follow the passage of a breeze as it weaved from aspen to birch. When the grating cry of a squirrel sounded from the dead limb of an ash tree, her anxiety diminished.

*Go past the hill and you will find the asparagus.*

She struggled toward the knoll, twisting this way and that to avoid thick brush or roots that would snare her feet. Near the bottom, the air filled with the odor of reeds and cattails, and after a few more steps, the pillowy ground dropped, and she sank to her knees in the black muck of a marsh.

*Go toward the light!*

She slogged her way out of the evil-smelling marsh toward higher ground when the light filtering through the trees became brighter and she knew she'd find a clearing ahead.

Something stirred nearby. An animal. When she heard the crackle of dry branches and the rasping of dead leaves, she concluded that it was a careless animal, unlike one with the dainty, cautious steps of a deer. She dropped to the ground and with a long arm reached and parted the grass. There, within ten feet of her, stood the largest animal she had ever seen. But there was more. Beside the animal was a person.

She lay breathless but fascinated. This was the closest she had ever come to anyone other than Père. The person was a man, straight-hipped and muscular, wearing clothing of an odd-colored bluish material, unlike the skin of any animal she knew. On his head rested a round covering that concealed the color of his hair and the features of his face. As she watched, he loosened his pants and delivered to the ground a long yellow stream of urine that seemed to go on for minutes. When finished, the man pulled himself up on the back of the animal. The animal moved slowly away with the man on his back, the two of them looking like a single creature.

As Fawn rose a blackbird took flight noisily from a tree limb. The animal halted. The man turned and called out, "Hello?"

She shut her eyes.

"Hello?" the man repeated. "Who's there?"

Hearing him speak and sensing the ground quiver as animal and rider drew closer terrified Fawn. She bolted away, her feet covering ground in six-foot strides, heedless of the uproar. Spiky branches swatted her face and etched red stitchlike marks on her bare arms, but she continued until out of breath, hoping the animal—which she would come to know as a "horse"—could not penetrate the thick brush. Approaching the safety of home, she leaped over the creek. The goats in the pasture raised their heads in unison, looked at her dumbly and resumed their grazing.

## 2 | Sidney

In the peak of summer, Fawn scoured the area for the purple flower that revealed prairie turnips that would be dried and crushed for food. When the hours of daylight shortened, she began filling skin bags with a mixture of turnip, dried venison and various berries. This, along with yucca, sunflowers and honey that she gathered without disturbing the bees, made up the important share of the food that would sustain the two through the barren months.

While she toiled, kneading the fragrant mixture that turned her hands purple and lured clouds of flies, she thought of the man and his strange horse—an animal so big it would never fit through the doorway of the hut. And how unlike from Père was the man. His skin smooth and clean, not red and wrinkled. His voice soft and pure, not harsh and guttural. She remembered the words he spoke. They were not upsetting or demanding like the angry calls of Père. The memory of the man saying "hello" sent mysterious sensations through her. The intensity of her feelings surprised her, and she paused to lean on the fence railing, light-headed and confused.

Provisioning for winter continued. In a week she must begin the gathering and soaking of acorns for human food as well as to supplement the goats' winter diet. Woodcutting followed soon afterward. Père had managed to rouse himself enough to select aging trees to fell that would with great effort be reduced to fireplace length to provide fuel for heat and cooking during the long winter. Fawn, with her lengthy arms, assisted with this task, using one of the few tools available, a hand scythe that Père had laboriously ground notches into to create a crude saw. She bent to her chore. Push the blade in, pull it back.

Later, after carrying the ashes outside to add to the pile from which to sort and make soap, she returned to the hut to find Père slouched on his bed, his chin resting on his chest, his shoulders slumped. In that instant, she knew that he had become old.

\* \* \* \* \*

When Fawn completed preparations for winter, she gazed with pleasure at her accomplishments: the food ready for storage in a hole near the door and covered with rocks, the wood split and piled, the winter clothing mended and hung out to air. On an early fall morning with a light frost on the tips of the grass growing on the shady side of the hut, she took time to sit outside and enjoy the sun before the first snow covered the landscape. The strains of summer had kept her away from the book pages that she kept wrapped in leather in the goat shed, and now she wanted to make one more attempt at finding order and sense in the marks on the paper.

The sun turned the air hot with no breeze, and soon mites and mosquitoes made their annoying presence known, unusual for so late in the year. Fawn brushed her arm gently as she eyed the page, noting again how groupings of certain marks were repeated more frequently than others—*t*, *h* and *e* emerged countless times. She rubbed her arm again. She knew by the sounds of the insects and stillness of the air that something changed. The goats were silent, the birds roosting.

At first, she feared to look up. As a child she discovered that unpleasantness in the night went away if she refused to open her eyes to it. But this was not night. Whatever disturbed her surroundings would not vanish like bad dreams.

She raised her head and there the man stood, just across the creek in the shade, studying her with a level gaze. He'd taken off his head covering, baring his face, which was reddish from the sun but pleasant with a square chin and upturned lips that formed a natural smile.

"Hello," he said. "Might I come over to your side?"

She recognized only one word, the pleasant-sounding one, the "hello." At its sound, she lost her fear, even when he waded through the creek and stood before her.

"I left Alouette at the clearing so as to not make noise," he said. "Alouette, that's the name of my horse."

She smiled, pleased. She knew the meaning of the word "name" but not of "horse," and took it that the man was named Alouette.

She pointed to herself. "Fawn," she said, and repeated the word.

"Fawn?" said the man, who carried a peculiar smell.

The dappled green of the forest stretched around them in all directions. The man squinted at the sun and knelt by the creek as if to drink from it.

At once, Fawn reached for his shoulder to stop him. *"Nee,"* she ordered, using the word that to her meant "no," for it was not safe to drink from this part of the creek so late in summer, fouled as it was by the goats. His arm felt rigid like an aged oak branch.

She made him understand that he was to wait while she went to fetch a cup of good water from the pail in the hut. But inside she found Père up and stumbling about, searching for the cranberries she had picked that morning. Fearful that he would see the man outside, she located the basket, grabbed a handful, mashed them with water and honey the way he liked and offered them in a bowl. But by the time she got back outside, the man had disappeared.

Later, when Père took to his bed, Fawn returned to the creek bank. The air smelled of the man's presence. She cocked her head, listening intently as if to hear his voice calling to her. She heard nothing. She looked around self-consciously and put her hands to her mouth. "Hello?" she shouted, sending the word on its hopeful way over the creek and into the woods.

But only a mocking magpie in a cottonwood acknowledged the greeting.

\* \* \* \* \*

When the man came again, he lingered out of view of the hut, but Fawn knew he was there by the stillness of the air.

"Hello, Fawn," he called.

Her eyes dropped to the ground. After a moment, she returned the greeting. "Hello, Al-oh-et," she said.

She had practiced saying the name, but when the man laughed she knew she must have made a mistake.

"I am Sidney," he said. "Alouette is my horse."

Her reaction told him she did not comprehend.

"Sidney," he repeated, jabbing himself with a finger.

*"Da,"* she said, catching on and trying one of the words she used to communicate with Père.

"I saw your father," he said, pointing to his eyes. "But not your mother. Is it that she died?"

Though the question was complex, Fawn thought she knew the answer, but could not find the way to reply. Following another painful period of silence during which she briefly desired that he go away, she shook her head.

"Your father is sick?"

"Père," she said.

"Who?" said Sidney.

Then, suddenly, she caught on. "Sick," she said, gesturing toward the hut, pleased with herself.

It was time to tend the goats, but the man's gentle patience in the face of her virtual dumbness had eased her anxiety, and now she wanted him to stay longer.

Sidney caught on. "I will come back," he said, and from his pocket extracted a hunk of yellowish taffy. "It is good to eat," he added and made a chewing motion. She accepted the gift. After the man crossed the creek and vanished, she bit off a corner of the sweet candy. When the taste reached her tongue, she spit out the fragment and threw the remainder in the creek.

On his next visit a week later, as a cold rain forced them to take shelter in the goat shed, the man asked question after question: How old was she? Why did she and her father live hidden away like woodchucks? How long had they been there? But Fawn did not know and couldn't grasp the concept of time. She recognized instinctively, however, that Père would react with threatening anger if he learned of Sidney's existence, and she went to great lengths, including use of an impromptu sign language, to make him recognize the danger. At last, as she literally pushed him into a cluster of willows on the far side of the stream, he comprehended the need to keep out of sight.

At the same time, Sidney's questions and the beautiful words he used generated her own laboriously formed questions about him. Where did he go when he disappeared into the woods? Would his horse be good to eat? What animal provided the skins for the strange-colored shirt he wore? Yet even with signs and pointing she could not make herself fully understood, and she covered her frustration with shrugs and bashful giggles.

*****

Autumn that year was slow to arrive, with the days characterized by blue skies and a bright but weakening sun. When he managed to rouse himself from bed, Père behaved differently. He complained about the water pail being missing though it remained in its usual place. No sooner had he completed his meal of goat cheese and honey than he demanded more, claiming he'd had nothing to eat all day. But mostly he lay in his bed day after day, calling out in his troubled sleep, getting neither worse nor better.

Fawn became accustomed to the freedom from Père's constant demands and found that she could tend to daily chores more efficiently by herself, allowing her an hour or more to do as she pleased. At the same time, she and Sidney became bolder as they fathomed each other's speech with more clarity. Although the difference was slight, she liked the sound of Fawn more than *Enfant*.

One day, Sidney came upon her as she sat with what was left of her book, which was now falling apart.

"Can I see what you are reading?" he inquired, pointing at it.

She hesitated, fearing that he intended to make a fire of the pages. As she handed over the tattered page, he saw that she had been holding them upside down. "You don't know how to read, do you?" he said.

She shrugged. *Read.* Another unfamiliar word.

He took from his pocket the stub of a pencil and drew a circle around the snake mark. He made another around the mark that looked like a small tree with no limbs, and another around the one that Fawn thought of as a chair. He circled three more, each unlike the others. Next, in the margin he sketched the letters side by side: *S-i-d-n-e-y.*

"Sidney," he said aloud, and repeated it. "Sidney." And she saw the connection. That was how his name looked when it was made of the marks.

"Sidney," she said, and saw the marks in her head. This delighted her, and she let him know she would like him to make marks representing her name.

He did so, and then, catching her pleased reaction, he used the margin of a second page to carefully write out all the letters of the alphabet in two precise columns.

"You see," he said. "With these you can make any word you wish." He went on to explain that in such a manner her book—he paused to write out *b-o-o-k*—could speak to her. "See?" he said.

"*Da*, yes," she said, and laughed at the thought.

And so it was. In her delight at seeing through the mystery of the marks on the paper, she forgot that Firegoat had not spoken into her ear in a long while.

\* \* \* \* \*

In the following weeks, the two experienced the joy of learning to know each other, unrestrained by the weight of adulthood which would soon descend upon them—particularly upon Sidney, four years older than Fawn. Throughout their brief lives they'd known mostly regimentation and drudgery, the lot of children born into rural poverty. Now, even though their time together was limited, it was carefree. Fawn, who stood three or four inches taller than Sidney, loved to swipe away his hat and hold it out of reach. He reacted by snatching her by the ankles and dragging her like a fallen birch through the creek bed, which was nearly dry this time of year. Only once did their exuberant cries cause them distress. The door of the hut came open and Père emerged. He stood blinking in the bright sun, looking directly at Sidney. His mouth gaped open, but he made no sound before turning back into the hut. Alarmed, Fawn signaled for Sidney to go away, then busied herself at the woodpile breaking dead branches for kindling, expecting Père to reappear. When she overcame her dread, she found he'd taken to his filthy bed and was now sound asleep. Upon awakening, he made no mention of the incident.

While they sat in their favorite spot in the goat-cropped grass by the shed overlooking the creek, Fawn encouraged Sidney to repeat words unknown to her. Even when puzzled by complex sentences, she grasped terms and phrases readily, realizing as every good student does that the more one learns, the more one is able to learn. Sidney spoke of various things in the other world. In a soft, pure voice that sounded like the call of a mourning dove, he described automobiles, airplanes, electricity and vast huts the size of the largest hill visible from where they stood. He spoke of great oceans far away and of a machine that could create a picture identical to what the eye saw. Once, he talked past sundown as Fawn's head almost burst before he hurried away, fearful that his brother would be angry that he had not returned in time to do his share of the chores. But before he departed, he impulsively took Fawn's face in his hands, reaching up to do so, and kissed her on the lips, surprising and embarrassing them both.

The storms of winter arrived, making it a struggle for Alouette to push through the deep snow. During their infrequent visits, Sidney and Fawn spent their time in the relative warmth of the goat shed. There they sat amid the bleating and baffled goats while Sidney told her of places known as "cities," which held more people than it was possible to count. Other people, though fewer, lived on farms or ranches where they could walk for a half day and not see another person. He explained families. His own father had died, but he lived with his mother and his brother, who sometimes went away.

Fawn lowered her chin. She pretended to grasp such things as the watch he constantly pulled from a pouch in his pants and even his description of an automobile. But it was the image of other people that terrified her. Would they strike her the way Père sometimes did when she allowed the fire to go out? Would they take her food the way larger animals take from the small?

Sidney smiled and touched her hair, telling her not to be afraid, for if the time came to see other people, he would be there to protect her. She accepted his words and then his actions as he put his face on hers and lowered her gently to the blanket that was used to wrap the baby goats when they came too early in the spring. She observed every detail with detachment as he pushed his man-thing into her. But her disregard turned to fright when his face reddened and contorted as if he were in pain. Soon, however, he smiled, and she knew she had done nothing wrong.

*****

"What will you do when Père is gone?" Sidney asked as he showed Fawn photographs that he had carried from home, including one of his father.

At first, the question confused her. Like so many expressions, this one could be taken more than one way. *"Nee,"* she replied, indicating that she didn't comprehend.

"He will die one day," clarified Sidney.

Fawn knew about death. Goats grew old or sick and died. So must humans. Père would die like all else, but that event stayed ever in the unknowable future—a future so distant it was not worth contemplating.

"You can't live here by yourself," said Sidney, forming a look of disapproval.

Fawn laughed at the incongruity of this. While she had dreams, the days to come, though indistinct, could not be much different from what she knew—even with Sidney's extravagant descriptions of the unimaginable world that he insisted lay close by.

"You must come to my house—to my hut—when Père dies," he said.

He may as well have suggested that she go to the moon.

"I will come for you," he said.

"*Nee*, no," she said, responding as much to his insistent tone as to his words. "But I am learning to love you."

She was not entirely sure of his meaning but liked the soft sound of the words and the secret, reassuring look in his eyes when he spoke them.

* * * * *

The ceaseless cold and snow had lasted for three weeks, making even a walk to the goat shed dangerous and difficult. Now a fresh storm had come up with wind so fierce flakes of snow blew in through the cracks by the door and settled on the hearth to melt. Père lay in his bed, scarcely moving—like the bear who sleeps all winter, thought Fawn. Suddenly the door blew open. Fawn looked up. Sidney stood in the doorway, his face so wrapped in scarves that only his blue eyes were visible.

As Père stirred at the commotion, Fawn, in a panic, leaped toward Sidney, shouting a useful word she'd recently taken on. "Go! Go!"

But Sidney closed the door behind him and leaned against it, exhaling frosty breaths that seemed to fill the room. "I couldn't wait," he said.

Before Fawn could gather her wits, he told her that he would not return for a very long time. A war had broken out, he explained, making slashing motions with his hands. And he'd been summoned to help fight the enemy, he added. He went on, gesturing futilely, speaking of mighty armies from across the ocean led by evil men who planned to come and kill people, burn houses, steal animals and poison food.

Fawn tried to follow. What was war? What was enemy?

Sidney spoke hastily, too fast for her to make out a word. They were interrupted when Père roused himself from his stupor and stumbled toward the fireplace, where the hatchet lay beside the woodpile. Fawn pushed Sidney toward the door, crying for him to go.

Once outside, she pointed toward the goat shed, frantically hoping that Sidney would figure out that she wanted him to go there. Back inside, Père had collapsed onto his bed. Fawn spooned a plate of mush from the kettle over the fire and left it in sight on the floor.

Surrounded by the huddling goats, Sidney again tried to explain. He must go, he said. Some day he would come back, but he did not know when. It might be several seasons. He then handed her a paper on which he'd written numerous words, most of which Fawn could not make out the meaning. He reminded her that Père was old and sick. If he died, Fawn must go to the house where Sidney lived and give his mother the paper. He pointed in the direction from which he had come and pantomimed a person eating and sleeping.

Fawn looked where he pointed, scowling.

Sidney had anticipated this and produced a second paper, a map with a drawing of a house, one with something on the roof that he called a weather vane. Only with Sidney's finger-pointing and pleading did Fawn absorb the nature of a map. The weather vane topping the house looked like a "rooster"—a bird, he said, flapping his arms like wings.

But he had put great effort into the map including features such as the creek, a tiny lake with little waves, and certain trees, and at last Fawn understood. She believed, however, that she would have no use for such papers, for even if Père did die, she would go on as before—seeing to the goats and gathering food and fuel to stay warm over the long, cold months.

But because Sidney seemed to place great store in the papers, folding them carefully into a larger paper, she said nothing of her beliefs.

When there was no more to say they held each other close. The cold did not stop them from a last frantic act of lovemaking that only left them craving more before Sidney vanished into the driving snow.

That dismal night Fawn sensed a familiar chill.

*You will never see him again,* said Firegoat.

# THE ROAD TO PROPHETSTOWN

## 1 | An Inch of Land

His name was Harold Peavey, and honesty compelled him to admit that he could claim no relation to the family that owned most of the grain elevators in the wheat country of the Dakotas and surrounding states. Once folks discovered that, they tended to look past him, just another baby brother squeezed off the family farm like one too many eggs in a duck's nest. Except for what happened during World War II and just after, few people outside Chippewa County, where he was born early in the century, would have been likely to recall a thing about him.

Not counting his time in prison, Harold had been driving the dairy co-op milk route for a dozen years by the end of the war, and the numb look that forms on a man who's been doing the same thing too long began to show on his handsome face. Of medium height with brownish hair that stood up in an untamable cowlick, he wore the same outfit winter and summer—a wool shirt washed of any color with sleeves rolled to the elbows and high-waisted dark trousers long past the time they were considered fancy.

During those years, the Great Depression and war that followed turned the world inside out for most of the hill farmers that Harold serviced. Horses gave way to tractors, candles to electricity, under-heated one-room schoolhouses to stately brick buildings. While most embraced the signs of a better life, the changes overwhelmed the widowed Omar Tuttle. He had farmed his eighty acres the same way all his life, plowing, seeding and harvesting with ancient machines pulled languidly by a team of Percherons. While others welcomed the startlingly efficient milking machines, Omar stubbornly persisted by hand—moving from one stall to the next with his pail and stool, hauling the milk in battered buckets to the milk house for his daughter, Leah, to pour into the separator that spewed out rich cream to be collected for pickup by Harold on his weekly stop.

* * * * *

Outside, thunderheads rumbled, bringing an early gloom to the deep green countryside as Harold pulled into the Tuttle farmyard. While Omar worked in the cool of the barn, Harold graded and loaded the cream, then gathered his razor and the clean shirt that he carried in an old pillowcase and made ready to stay the night. The dairy paid Omar four dollars each time he put Harold up, money added to the cream check, that Omar badly needed.

Harold helped himself to a cup of coffee from the pot on the cookstove before wandering back outside, stepping through the creeping charlie and buttonweed that hogged the nourishing dirt where a garden of daffodils and iris once thrived. Finding a familiar resting spot beneath the undependable shade of a dying cottonwood, he half dozed while Omar completed his chores and Leah fixed supper.

Though just out of grammar school, Leah had, for nearly two years since her mother died, been grinding through the endless, wearisome tasks of a woman on the farm. Harold both admired and pitied her, knowing that nurturing the vegetable patch, canning string beans and beets that the dirt reluctantly gave up, scrubbing floors, scouring dishes and caring for the chickens robbed her of her youth. Although strong as an iron rod, her lithe muscle had lost its youthful tone and her once girlish, spry gait had become manly and graceless. On top of that, the North Dakota winters with her father as her only company had turned her inward, and the burdens surfaced on the girl.

Omar emerged from the barn and greeted Harold with an uncharacteristically hearty wave. Harold brushed off his pants, watching Omar as he approached. The man had tilled the land so long he'd become part of it, like a stalk of wheat, all head with a thin reed of a body.

In the kitchen, they washed their hands at the pump and seated themselves on wooden chairs.

"Smell that?" said Omar. "Leah saves her best cooking for you."

"Oh, Daddy," said the girl, her tired voice refusing to play along.

Making no effort to conceal the broadness of her build, Leah trod heavily between the range and the table as she set out the meal—chicken rolled in flour and fried in lard, potatoes cut in chunks and boiled, gravy thick with cream, carrots, bread and butter, all fixed the way her mother taught her. While the men ate, eyes down, arms bared, elbows on the table, she cleaned the dishes, her forehead red and beaded with sweat as she muscled a Brillo pad over the crusty bottom of the good frying pan.

Omar spoke to his daughter over his shoulder. "Never mind all that. Me and Harold want to talk. Go on and get started on the milk before the flies get to it."

The girl twisted away from the sink. "I want to hear."

Omar raised his head stiffly. "Do what you're told."

With an airy sigh, Leah untied her apron and hung it on the wall inside the pantry.

Omar waited for the door to close, his big-knuckled hands with their rough, yellow fingernails drumming restlessly on the table. Before he sensed an unusual uneasiness in the older man, Harold supposed he'd be tapped for advice on ailing livestock. After years around dairy herds, he could diagnose mastitis, deliver calves and even do simple surgery. The nearest vet practiced a hundred miles away in Devils Lake, and the hill farmers wouldn't think of going to the expense of summoning him for anything short of a catastrophe. Now and then a dairyman offered to pay Harold for his help, but he always shook his head. He figured that his cow doctoring was not entirely illegal so long as it was done as a favor, with conflict with the law being the last thing he wanted.

Omar struck a match on the floor and held it to the gas lantern hanging over his kitchen table. Concentrating, he twisted the valve to the right, lit the mantle and blew out the match only when it had burned so low it seared his calloused fingers. The lantern hissed steadily, the cloying odor of kerosene filling the room. Omar placed his palms flat on the oil cloth and looked at his visitor.

"Harold, here's what you need to know. You're gonna be my son-in-law."

Harold, jolted out of his fatigue, looked up. "Come again?"

"You heard right. I got it all planned out. You and Leah are gonna be married."

Mortified, Harold tried a disarming laugh. "Omar," he said, scratching his scalp through his thick hair. "I'm a good twenty years older than Leah. She's got schooling ahead of her. We can't do any such thing."

Omar closed his eyes, displaying their veiny lids. "She's just about the same age her mother was when we got married."

Harold searched the other man's sunburned face. "But like I say, there's the girl's education ahead of her."

Omar scooted himself forward, the legs of his chair squeaking hideously on the linoleum. "I don't want her in school no more," he said, his cold eyes revealing his conviction.

"And why's that?" asked Harold.

"She won't need it. Me and the wife got by fine with grammar school." Omar scowled, as if challenging Harold to prove it wasn't so.

Harold stirred uneasily. "What else is going on here, Omar?"

Intricate patterns of wrinkles formed around Omar's eyes. "Well, for one thing her and one of them Morinville boys got their caps set for each other."

The picture gradually cleared. Difficulties with Etienne Morinville's family reached back to the time Omar emerged from the outhouse for the biggest surprise of his adult life. Failing to check where he was going while trying to find the buttonhole on the strap of his overalls, he looked up and found himself face-to-face with the Morinvilles' bull, which had wandered through a gap in the fence. Cussing and struggling to hold his pants up, Omar maneuvered the bull through the ineffective fence and back home while threatening to haul out his double-barrel the next time such a thing happened.

Eventually, the Morinvilles sold off their herd and plowed up their pasture for wheat, but not before a descendent of the bull broke through the same gap in the fence, upended the henhouse and trampled half of the plants in the tomato patch. Hearing the disturbance from the hayloft, Omar climbed down and with no hesitation shot the bull. In no time, Etienne showed up eager to raise hell, accompanied by his husky son Sam, who was armed with his own weapon, a thirty-aught-six. Omar stood his ground with his still-smoking twelve-gauge, the unfortunate bull dead at his feet. Only the intervention of Lucille Tuttle, who outweighed her hotheaded husband by forty pounds, prevented the incident from escalating. Nonetheless, the distrustful sentiments continued.

Harold shifted his gaze toward the Morinville place easily visible through the west kitchen window. "I don't see keeping her out of school would stop anything."

"It'll sure as hellfire stop it if she's your wife."

"You're not hearing me, Omar," said Harold. "Which Morinville boy is it anyhow?"

Omar pulled at his boney nose. "Freddy. The oldest one."

"Is that so? I always judged Sam to be the troublemaker."

"They're all troublemakers. I had my way, I'd run the whole Chippewa outfit back to the reservation where they belong."

"Well, here now, Omar. There's good and bad. They must be doing OK. I see Etienne built a brand-new machine shed with a concrete floor."

"Yeah, and I bet the government provided him the cement mix to make it with," said Omar. "But listen," he added, brightening. "Here's the rest of it. Once you and the girl are married, I'm bringing you in with me. Partners."

Harold took a revised measure of the old man. The light from the lantern cast ugly shadows across his stringy neck. "Omar, there's barely what you need here to farm for the two of you."

Omar hitched his hand around his kneecap and rocked back on the chair. "I got it all worked out. First thing is we'll get a John Deere if that's what you want and seed more alfalfa. The hail spares it and we can milk a good twenty more head. You like to talk about having your own herd."

Harold shook his head in despair. The man refused to listen.

Omar pulled a writing tablet from the sideboard, licked the tip of a pencil and with a firm stroke drew a vertical line on the first page. "I'll plan it out for you. Look."

Harold attempted to examine the figures as Omar's brow furrowed in concentration. This was a sticky fix. To get cornered into an argument over numbers, most of them imaginary, would be to declare that he was interested. He tugged on his trouser legs. "Maybe someday I could think about buying the place from the two of you. But it'd take a long time to get that kind of money."

Omar set the pencil aside and wiped his forehead. "That's just it. Leah, she don't have the time. Things of went haywire."

"How so?"

"The girl got herself in trouble."

Harold's face flushed. He lifted the dipper from the pail and took a long drink of the brackish water. "I'm sorry to hear that," he said. "But I'm not the way out of it. You got to talk to Etienne Morinville."

Omar snorted. "I'll talk to the Devil first."

"These things happen, Omar. Why, there's the Legassee girl. She married the Azure kid from the reservation and they took over the farm when the old man died. They're getting on just fine."

The old man's lips tightened. He jabbed himself in the chin with his pencil and spoke in a low inflectionless voice. "No Morinville or any other Indian's getting an inch of my land and I don't give a damn what I need to do to stop 'em."

\* \* \* \* \*

In the morning, Harold awoke to the sounds of a household fully engaged in the demands of the day. Omar was busy with the morning milking as Leah stirred a bowl of mix for hotcakes.

Harold poured his coffee and took a chair. "How old are you now, Leah?"

The girl went about her chores, not looking up. "You know as well as I do I'll be fifteen next month," she said.

Harold sipped his weak, only slightly warm coffee. "Got a boyfriend then?"

Leah wiped her hands on the apron that encircled her ample midsection. "You don't have to pretend like that. I know what you and Daddy talked about."

Harold squirmed uncomfortably, but the girl wasn't through.

"Now you're going to want to know about Freddy Morinville."

"Well?"

"It isn't what you think."

"Heck, I don't know what to think."

"You'll think what Daddy tells you to."

"That depends."

The girl turned back to the counter. Harold took a long swallow of his tasteless coffee. "You know what I had to tell your dad about the notion of me and you, don't you?"

Leah spoke as if into the pasty liquid in the bowl. "Yes."

"You understand why."

"It doesn't matter."

"Sure it does," said Harold. "I don't want you believing I don't care what happens to you."

Leah whirled around, her face weary. "It's more tangled up than that," she said, sounding as tired as she looked.

"Grown-up business is that way, young lady. It would get straightened out in a hurry if you and your dad set down with Freddy and his folks."

Leah narrowed her eyes. "You know Daddy would never do that, and besides, Freddy ran away."

Harold sat up. "What? He did? Where to?"

With an enormous wooden spoon, the girl dropped batter into the black frying pan, seeming not to notice the grease spattering her unprotected arms. The spoon hovered in the air like a weapon. "I don't know. He never said goodbye. How many cakes do you want? I got to go help turn the cows out."

* * * * *

In the thirties, the route that Harold Peavey followed weekly into the hills became locally known as the Prophetstown Road. Originating as an ancient buffalo trail, it gained elevation as it skirted the edges of hilly fields farmed by families including the Breens, Maases, Gosches, Morinvilles and Tuttles before ending at a clearing of moldering foundations and broken glass once known as Prophetstown, hard against the Canadian border.

At its peak, the settlement claimed two bars, a blacksmith shop, three churches and a bank, the latter's location still marked by the blue walls of its vault, now protecting nothing but rubble. The churches stood side by side, a Catholic and a Lutheran separated by a Dunkard as if to keep the peace. On Sundays, as many as forty horse and buggy rigs tied up on the muddy grounds. The proximity of the churches to one another enabled the congregations to hear the others singing and each preacher trying to outshout his competitors on the wages of sin. Unfortunately, one of the houses of worship caught fire on a Christmas Eve and all three burned to the ground. Each flock accused another, and by the time the squabbling ended, all the faithful had joined a congregation across the border in Manitoba or in Rolland a couple hours to the south. All that endured of the churches was the weedy graveyard shared by all three, a gesture of unity at last.

The graveyard sat on a rocky knoll above Leonard Creek. On sunny spring days before the broom grass grew too high, Harold liked to stop along the creek to eat his sandwich and apple. From there he made out the grade of a railbed that once ran all the way up to Brandon in Manitoba. Omar Tuttle swore to Harold that a locomotive and coal car lay at the bottom of the creek where a trestle bridge once crossed, a claim that Harold shrugged off as a tall tale.

During wet years, Harold was forced on occasion to hike from the muddy road to the closest farmer, who would hitch up his team and pull Harold's panel truck through a low spot after a rain. If delayed too long, he might stay the night at the farm. This arrangement, however, resulted in awkward situations for Harold, a man who preferred certainty and organization in his life. Once, he hiked coatless three miles in a drizzle rather than take a chance on asking for help at the backwoods home of the Able clan, a notorious collection of recluses so hostile to outsiders that even the law left them to their own affairs. At one time he spent an occasional night at the problem-besieged farm of the Breens, but one of the sons, Foss, had become a dissolute and half-crazy alcoholic who kept Harold up half the night with his drunken rants.

Other reasons existed for staying with the Tuttles. Various families, grateful for a visitor, emptied their overflowing wells of gossip and misbeliefs late into the evening, unbalancing Harold's sleep habits. When Mrs. George Gosch tried to crawl in his bed while George snored away, passed out drunk in the next room, Harold knew he'd have to work something else out. When the county graveled the road in 1941, a predictable schedule became possible, and at his suggestion the creamery contracted with Omar Tuttle to put him up where he bunked in the mudroom, not minding that in winter half-inch caps of ice formed on the nails of the wainscot.

The Tuttles welcomed him, giving him the run of the place. He took to bringing treats from town that he knew the family had no access to—lemons so that Lucille Tuttle could rub away the smell of chicken gizzards, orange Tootsie Pops for Leah, the *Police Gazette* for Omar. On a winter's night, a stranger might have wandered by the window facing the road, seen them carrying on, the toddler Leah at their feet while they played three-handed whist by the light of the lantern, and concluded it was a happy family passing an evening.

Those good times ended when Lucille Tuttle developed a growth on her bladder. By all accounts a saint of a woman, she regarded pain and discomfort as a private inconvenience. When Omar finally apprehended that something wasn't right, he loaded his wife into the sole motorized vehicle he owned—a prewar Dodge pickup—and drove her to Dr. Thwarp in Rolland, who declared he could do nothing for her. She died seven weeks later.

\* \* \* \* \*

Raindrops cratered the dust rimming the ditch as Harold slowed and shifted into second to climb the gentle rise leading into the Tuttle farmyard. In the space of a week, the square house with its sagging porch no longer felt welcome. The clanking of cream cans in the panel stirred the hens scratching in the scraggly yard. To Harold's unease, Omar sat on the porch step, staring fixedly at the truck as if to discern what sort of creature had wandered into his farmyard.

"Thought you'd never get here," said Omar, rising jerkily.

Harold took the greeting as a hopeful sign that things hadn't changed, for by Omar's measure he was always either uselessly early or disastrously late.

"Mose is off his feed. I think maybe he got the clover bloat. Suppose you could take a look at him before we eat?"

Outside the barn, the flowering pigweed provided an early indication of the fading of summer. Inside, the not unpleasant smell of manure, hay and warm-blooded animals filled the air. Harold ran his hand over the horse's withers. "Why, there's the bother," he said, pointing. "See the abscess?"

He studied the animal's fetlock. "He's got a shoe loose, too," he said, straightening up. "Fetch me some clean water and that jar of salve in the house while I get my vet kit from the truck. And grab me your big flashlight too."

Omar held the light while Harold lanced, drained and cleaned the sore before bathing it in peroxide.

"I'll hand it to you," said Omar. "You got the healing gift. Hell, I bet you could even doctor up a human person."

Harold smiled. "No, sir, I stick to livestock. They don't bellyache."

"What if there was a 'mergency like a busted appendix?"

"I wouldn't know where to start," said Harold.

"I recollect when you stepped in for Mrs. Lawston that time when her baby come early."

"A woman doesn't need all that much help to have a baby." Harold held the horseshoe to the light. "Get me your rat-tail file, would you?"

Omar limped over to the bench. "But just say it come up. How would you go about it?"

"What—an appendix?"

"Yeah, just say."

Harold recognized the idle flattery. Just the same, he welcomed it as a diversion from the cockamamie proposals the man spouted on the last visit.

"The main thing is you'd have to go easy to keep from cutting blood vessels. That's your big danger, bleeding, that and having infection set in. What I'd do if it was me was make the cuts real shallow, like if you were trying to cut through the cover of a magazine and not touch the first page. Course that's the easy part. Next you got to locate the thing and tie it off, then get it out of there and sew it all back up before your knockout remedy wears off."

Omar scratched his head under his hat. "You mean like ether?"

"I'd never fool with any ether. It can catch fire just like that. That very thing happened down in Carrington once before the war. Killed the patient and burned the doctor so bad he never could operate again." Harold wiped his hands on his pants. "Chloroform's what's easier according to what I hear. All you got to do is pour it on a cloth and hold it to the face, but you got to watch them close so you get the right amount."

"Chloroform, you say?" Omar smoothed the horse's mane. "Learn something every day. Let's wash up for supper. I had the girl butcher a chicken."

The welcome aroma of baked food filled the quiet kitchen. The meal had been left in the warming tray of the oven, covered with a red-and-white dish towel. "Where is Leah?" asked Harold.

"Oh, she don't feel good again. Let's me and you eat in the living room."

The room had assumed a permanent gloom under a patina of gathering dust since the passing of Lucille Tuttle. It was as if the inhabitants, shrunken by a third, had to occupy that much less of the home. A copy of *Wallaces Farmer* lay on the wooden floor, still in its brown mailing wrapper.

The men sat ill at ease with plates on their laps. They ate in silence, the sounds of hefty cutlery on stoneware the only noise. Omar, who wore his straw hat throughout the meal, removed it after finishing, revealing a band of skin pasty as a cutworm.

"Yes, sir, Harold," he said.

The empty comment perished from its own weight. A moment passed. The old house shuddered. A car roared by over the gravel. Harold broke the awkward peace.

"Omar," he began. "What you said last week about Leah, about her being in her…" He struggled for a word. "…*circumstances* and you wanting me to step in. I don't see that as a direction you ought to take."

"And why not?" said Omar, setting his plate on the floor by his feet.

"Why, I give you the answers and they haven't changed in a week."

Omar leaned forward in a great show of earnestness, his shoulders squared, his gaze steady. "That's too bad, Harold, because I didn't want to have to mention this in a hurtful way."

Harold sensed the ominous tone in Omar's words. "Mention what?"

"You been coming by on your route for a good while now. There's been lots of times I left you and Leah in the house alone while I did the afternoon milking. It wouldn't of—"

"Hold on there," interrupted Harold.

"The girl's underage. All's I got to do is make a statement to the sheriff."

"Omar, you know as well as me I never been near the girl in any way that's not proper."

The floorboards overhead creaked. Both men craned their necks to the ceiling.

"Maybe so, maybe not," said Omar. "But it seems to me I'm making you a pretty good offer to keep from having to get the law involved."

"That's no offer and you don't mean it anyway. There's a better way to handle this."

Omar stuck out his lower lip, considering. "By god, I do mean it. Come Monday I'll be visiting the sheriff."

Harold shook his head. "You really think anyone's going to believe you?"

At once, Omar offered a reply both measured and dispassionate. "Could be, but it ain't been that long since the war and folks haven't forgot what you did. Especially the ones whose boys never come back. And I don't need to remind you who the sheriff is now, do I?"

Harold heaved a deep sigh. It seemed like nothing in this life ever went away on its own.

## 2 | Go About a Life

Countless times, Harold Peavey wished he could have stopped the world in 1940. With the Depression over, the land again became fruitful, and a man willing to work hard could earn a decent living. On the radio, Fred Allen and Jack Benny got rich making folks laugh. Two passenger trains a day passed through Rolland in the event a resident had a need to go somewhere. Three automobile dealerships in town supplied nice choices if you preferred to do your own driving. The whole world knew that unrest smoldered in Europe, but the countries on the far side of the Atlantic were bound to come to their senses before having to get into another war.

Harold had plans. He'd socked over $1,800 into a savings account at the Chippewa County Bank run by Garrison Foley, not bad at a time when you could buy a new four-door Nash for seven hundred. During his drives north he'd studied the countryside, picking out good pasture for the day when he'd saved enough for his own acreage, which he figured would be in about five years.

He'd gotten so he could come within a quarter percent of a cream's butterfat by tasting it, and he knew quality cows when he saw them. Holsteins were his favorite breed. He loved them not just for the way they shucked off scours and other bovine maladies but for how they looked, with their graceful gait and kind eyes, and the tone of their lowing. When it came time to be milked, they bunched around the pasture gate, swinging their huge heads with their appealing, sweet faces toward the barn. When the gate swung open, they strolled through one behind the other, predictable as logs floating down a river. Easily pleased they were—an armload of hay, a long drink of greenish water, the shelter of a stall against the cold of winter.

After winning a small raise, he paid a visit to Guenther's jewelry store to put ten dollars down on a diamond ring for Marlys Fagerstad, who helped with the books at the creamery. They'd known each other since ninth grade when Harold followed his brothers into town to high school. But when Hitler invaded the Netherlands, Marlys's brother, Linus, joined the Royal Canadian Air Force, and her parents let it be known they'd like the younger folks to wait on the wedding till Linus came back.

To Harold, having to change plans left him out of sorts, like walking around in a new pair of shoes.

"But it's just for a year, maybe less," Marlys assured him. Harold accepted the reasoning even if he couldn't comprehend why anyone would go off like that risking his neck over another man's quarrel.

On the first day of spring the following year, Harold pulled in from his route to find Marlys waiting at the loading dock.

"Daddy and Mom got word from Ottawa," she said, squeezing her purse tight.

Linus had been shot down over the Orkney Islands. Of course, they'd have to postpone the wedding once more. Again, Harold accepted the circumstances while wondering why events so far-removed couldn't just let a man like him alone.

\* \* \* \* \*

A month after that, as FDR saw fit to beef up the U.S. Army, Harold received a telegram with his draft notice. He took the telegram to his room over Doc

Thwarp's office, where he glowered at the paper with the words pasted on like in a book of paper dolls. *Greetings,* it said.

That was some way to put it.

In high school, Harold earned strong Bs in both civics and history, but the ways of the world turned out peculiar compared to how they told it in books. One country all of a sudden trying to beat the stuffing out of everybody in the next one because some tsar or kaiser got his toes trodden on. Two important people can't get along and a million others die. When he tried explaining to Marlys that he wasn't all that keen on being a soldier, she threw a fit. Her own brother, she insisted, never got into nitpicking or dillydallying—he just went when he saw a need.

At Uncle Sam's expense, Harold rode the Great Northern to Fort Snelling with eight other men from Chippewa County, most of them ten years younger than him. All through the fourteen-hour ride in the rocking passenger car, he sat thinking as he stared out the window at the graceful telegraph wires strung from pole to pole over the country. As he rocked from side to side, dozing now and then, he dwelled on how green and peaceful the land looked. Cows flicked their tails lazily. The sun was high and casting warmth. He knew that Germany was located at about the same latitude as North Dakota. He wondered, did the people over there look up at the same sun from the same angle and stew over how come those in charge of the countries couldn't figure out how to get along?

At Fort Snelling, they looked at his teeth, had him turn his head and cough, questioned him about matters such as whether he'd ever been exposed to TB or wanted to shoot himself in the head and finally told him he'd passed his physical. He lined up with the others, but when ordered by a barking sergeant to take a step forward and stick his hand up to be sworn in, he failed to move.

The sergeant noted Harold standing alone, marring the perfect line, and repeated the request. Harold remained as immobile as a streetlamp. The sergeant stepped toward him with his hands on his hips. "What's the matter here? You got a sore arm?"

Harold swallowed and looked away, feeling like his shoes were nailed to the floor.

The sergeant softened his voice and came closer. "Or could it be that you're afraid you'll get too excited when it comes to taking a shower with all these good-lookin' fellas?" He winked. "Is that it, Mister? You one of them queers by any chance? Or maybe you're just tired of humping sheep and you got yourself set on something a little more re-al-is-tic?"

Harold had no idea how to respond. His scalp itched, and he dared not move. The sergeant smelled of garlic. If only the man would back off a few inches. Finally, the sergeant snickered and stepped around to face the other draftees, where he got on with the brief oath, dismissed them and then signaled to two soldiers, who steered Harold to the side where they ordered him to stand still and remain silent though as of yet he hadn't uttered a word. The sergeant left the room and after a long wait returned with an officer decked out in ribbons and braid who asked him questions that he read from a paper.

Did he comprehend where he was and why?

Was he claiming exemption for health or moral reasons?

Did he know he was in the process of breaking federal law?

"Do you have anything to say for yourself?" asked the officer.

Harold considered the question. He had some sketchy notions for a response but putting beliefs into words was never his strength. "Not just now," he said at last. "Sir," he added.

The officer folded his paper into the pocket of his uniform pants. "You're older than the average recruit," he said. "You must know what's going on. There's enemies of our country that need to be stopped. You've heard of krauts and Japs, haven't you?"

Harold admitted that yes, he had.

"And you're not willing to fight the likes of them who are out to destroy the freedom of ourselves and our forefathers?"

Harold's eyes fell on the officer's name tag: Lt. Walter Weiss.

Lieutenant Weiss scowled. "What's your game anyway? You got voices in your head nobody else hears? Too late for that, you were supposed to tell the doctor."

Harold swayed on his feet and said nothing.

"Mister, once more. Are you or are you not willing to take an oath to defend your country?"

Harold looked the young officer over. Why, he was nothing but a boy in a play uniform, a kid so young he wouldn't know a popgun from popcorn. He straightened up, assuming what he imagined was a good approximation of what coming to attention must look like. Still unable to formulate what felt like a reasonable response, he bit his lip and stayed silent.

The officer glanced sideways at the sergeant. "All right. Well then, I'm obligated to inquire if you're claiming status as a CO."

Harold waited for elaboration. "How's that?"

"Conscientious objector. Is that what you claim you are?"

"I'm not making any claim I know of."

"Well, friend, that isn't what your actions are telling me," said the lieutenant.

Harold took a long look into the flawless Teutonic face of Lieutenant Weiss and found his tongue at last.

"Son," he said. "Back in Rolland there was a fellow everybody knew named Gerhardt Albrecht, only we called him Fritz. He was part of a bunch of us that used to stand around by the drugstore watching the cars go past. Fritz, though, he kind of hung off to the back and never said a word. He was odd-looking, bent over like an old man and he wasn't more than forty-five. And he wore a kind of mask made out of cheesecloth with holes for his eyes, and if you caught him with the light behind him, you could see he didn't have a nose. One night they had a magician come to town. Me, I didn't have the twenty cents to go and so I was hanging around there with Fritz wishing I dared to sneak into the show. After a while Fritz pulled a quarter from his overalls and said to me didn't I want to see the magic man? Well I figured if he had the dough, he ought to see the show himself. He said nope, he didn't like stuff like that, didn't like big crowds on account of folks couldn't keep from staring at him. Then without me even asking, he told why he wore that cheesecloth deal. It turned out he got gassed over in France in the war. The gas turned one of his eyes all white like a boiled egg and burned the inside of his nose so bad all that was left was a scar and two holes. Then he said if there was ever another war and I saw it coming, I better run like hell. Well, it seems to me it's about time I start running."

Two days later, they escorted Harold to a spacious, varnish-smelling courtroom properly decorated with a flag and a photograph of the secretary of war, a man named Henry Stimson. Harold looked up at the picture, vaguely bothered. How come a man in a banker's suit was in charge of running a war?

A second set of officers presented him the same questions as the first, and he was careful to give them the same responses. When they were through an older officer motioned him aside and asked one final question Harold knew wasn't on any paper. Was he, by any chance, a member of that rich family of Peaveys, the ones that owned all the flour mills?

They then advised that in consideration of the fact that he was otherwise a commendable citizen, having no record of activities designed to undermine the U.S. government, they would give him one more opportunity to take the oath.

Harold didn't hesitate. He'd already made his decision, and of course he was not a man who changed his mind easily.

This time, they put his wrists in a set of iron handcuffs and escorted him down two flights of stairs to a room with a thick wire screen over the window. The following morning, he was on his way to a federal prison in Rochester.

Deep down, Harold comprehended. The government wanted him under lock and key and there was nothing more to it. He was beginning to learn what unlucky others before and after him did: timing counts for everything. The worst thing that can happen to a citizen is to get on the opposite side of a belief at the wrong time. Ten years earlier and he'd have been OK, but the romantic notion of war had captured the popular thinking.

In prison, he expected to be placed with people who were contrary or at least confused by the compulsion of society to kill others that it bore no hostility toward. In their place he found himself in the company of individuals unlike any he had ever known. Instead of giving a hoot one way or the other about war, most prisoners preferred to dwell on the faults of a society that unfairly placed them in their various hopeless plights—unfair judges, crooked lawyers, cruel bosses, cheating wives. When they paid notice to Harold, it was to make him an object of derision, a person to be ridiculed for allowing himself to wind up with them over such a petty affair.

Harold tried in unanswered letters to Marlys to explain what he'd done. In his opinion, folks could hang flags over their screen doors till the doors broke off their hinges and sing the national anthem till their lungs wore out and a war would be just as pointless as ever. A million would die and in the end things would be about the same as before. Some people would starve and others would get fat. Dogs would still bark for nothing and worms would keep on living in rotten apples. The world would continue spinning and nobody would fall off the edge.

\* \* \* \* \*

After nineteen months, Harold was released from prison a convicted felon and with no place to go but home. He waited a week and then paid a visit to Marlys at her parents' place by the fairgrounds. They sat in the living room drinking grape nectar, and Harold asked her how come she hadn't replied to his letters.

A flush rose from her neck. "Do you think folks left at home got nothing else to do during a war?" she said petulantly. "There's the scrap metal drive and knocking on doors for the war bonds. Then, too, I been a Red Cross volunteer, and don't forget my job at the creamery."

"I follow how you stayed busy," said Harold. "But in going on two years you couldn't find a minute to write even a postcard?"

Marlys plopped her hands on her lap. "OK," she said. "In case you been up on cloud nine somewhere, lots of people don't like what you done, and that includes Daddy and Mom. They didn't want their daughter marrying a man who would make himself to be so weak like that."

Much as he wanted to know what part of his behavior revealed him as *weak*, Harold let it go. People had the right to think their way just like he did. He made his choice, and he'd just as soon cut off his big toe as shift his mind.

Marlys, a petite, nervous girl, set her glass on the coffee table and wiggled closer on the sofa. "But I've been giving it thought," she said. "They say land prices are down. If you took your savings and we bought a section near town to start in farming, I think the folks would change their mind."

Now Harold had more explaining to do. He looked around, gathering his thoughts. His eyes rested on a huge piano next to the stairway, its lid open and propped up by a polished stick. It must be new.

"I got to tell you," he began. "You met my sister Sally? Her and her husband got their crop hailed out three years in a row. That's while I was serving my time and I never had use for but a dollar or two a week for postage stamps and soap."

Marlys drew back. "You let them have the savings?"

"They were going to lose their place."

The blood drained from Marlys's face, making her lipstick look purple. Distracted and trying to think, she cracked three knuckles on her left hand: one, two, three.

"You are a foolish man," she said. "You gave away your own future."

\* \* \* \* \*

Cut loose by Marlys, Harold took to spending evenings at Manson's above the bowling alley, where he'd drink Grain Belt and play eight-ball with the codgers and 4-Fs. Now and then he drank until the balls in the far corner of the table blurred. When that happened, he would return his cue to its place, concentrate on walking to his room, and go to sleep, speculating what might come next in this peculiar life.

The weekend following Armistice Day, 1943, after an early ice storm, Sergeant Dale Aingher, the same man elected county sheriff a few years later, home on leave to recover from a neck wound and wearing his dress uniform complete with battle ribbons, tapped Harold on the shoulder and asked if he could come out back and help give a push to a guy with a dead battery.

Harold leaned his cue stick against the wall and followed. A few pool hall regulars, including Useless Johnston, watched him leave. Outside, someone with muscular arms—Harold couldn't see who—grabbed him from the back.

"What's going on here?" he said.

Aingher's first blow came like an electric shock, landing above Harold's left eye and snapping his head backward.

"That's what's going on," said his attacker.

The second punch found Harold's stomach. "That one's for a coward," said Aingher, a powerful man with a thick body. Harold curled forward, suspended by the grip of the stranger behind him.

"And this is to remind you to keep your chickenshit ass away from Marlys," added Aingher as his knee smashed into Harold's face, breaking his cheekbone.

Across the alley, the back door of Hagen's Meat Market opened, and two people emerged. One was Ronnie Michaelson, Harold's former teammate on the Rolland High baseball team. They paused in the doorway, trying to see what was happening. At this, the attackers, after delivering a last kick to Harold's ribs, trotted away in the other direction, their breath forming wisps of white in the cold air. Ronnie Michaelson and his friend disappeared back into Hagen's.

Harold rolled to his stomach, raised himself to his knees and finally to his feet. He limped to his room a block and a half away, leaving his jacket hanging over a chair at the pool hall.

Near the end of the following month, in the area's most festive wedding since Pearl Harbor, Harold's former fiancée, Marlys Fagerstad, married Dale Aingher in a Thursday afternoon ceremony at Saint Joachim's Catholic Church. Despite sugar rationing, the reception in the basement featured a four-foot-high white cake with red, white and blue piping.

* * * * *

Not long after Marlys's wedding, Harold made up his mind to try life out west. The Boeing plant in Seattle, where they made the bombers that would set German cities on fire, was hiring. He took a job making sandwiches in the plant cafeteria within two days after stepping off the bus, but after six weeks realized the life wasn't for him. Harold liked working by himself and making decisions without discussing it with eleven different people and their underbosses. In the big city, you risked getting crushed like a beetle just going to work. The rooming house was expensive and noisy with tenants gone before you knew their name. The smoky beer parlors were filled with floozies offering to take you to their rooms if you'd buy them a tap and a pair of nylons. Most tiresome though were the questions. Soon as anyone got acquainted with him for more than a day, they wanted to know how come he wasn't in the service, and second, of course, if he was related to the other Peaveys, the rich ones.

Having his fill of the west, he got on a Greyhound. Three days and three bus changes later, he stood in the street by the Vendome Hotel in Rolland, his suitcase at his feet, happy to be home. Four days later, he got his old job back driving the Prophetstown run but at five dollars less a week to help support the war effort.

His dreams gone, Harold filled his days with work, hauling cream, passing pleasant evenings with the Tuttles and picking up his check from the office on Saturday mornings. As he followed the route, surveying the prairie as it wrinkled and rose into hills and grass before giving way to alder and oak, he discovered that the thoughts drifting through his head were changing. Rather than pictures of barns stuffed with hay, he tended to wonder what movie they might be running at the theater that weekend and when the Red Owl might be expecting a fresh shipment of muskmelon. As he took to spending more time alone, he decided he ought to have a hobby, so he bought the best fishing tackle he could find from the war-limited stock available at Staggs Hardware.

Comfortable with having tossed aside dreams of owning the finest herd in the county, he took to contemplating others and how they went about their lives. He once thought that important people like Herbert Hoover and Helen Keller spent all their time handling matters like feeding starving kids or finding a cure for blindness. But in truth they must be just like him. They brushed their teeth, combed their hair and checked in the medicine cabinet for aspirin when they got a headache. They spent time deciding what to have for supper and what color shirt to buy. That was how you went about a life: just tending to what was in front of you.

## 3 | The Only Noise in the World

The loading platform on the south side of the creamery provided a view of the sheriff's office and its parking lot fronting the courthouse. All day Monday, Harold couldn't keep himself from stepping out every twenty minutes like a sparrow at a birdbath to see if Omar Tuttle's dilapidated rig had pulled up. He checked all week, and by Wednesday, as he loaded the panel to head north again, he decided the threat was just the jabbering of a half-crazed old man.

He came out of Gamble's with a spool of twine for Ben Drewry when the sheriff's black Ford stopped on the street and Aingher rolled down his window to ask in a polite voice if Harold would mind stopping at the office for a minute.

In the office with its high, frosted window and stacks of papers occupying every level space, the sheriff stooped to pick up a pen from the floor, exposing a pink bald spot usually covered by his lawman's hat. Motioning to a chair, he folded his arms and rested his bottom against the corner of his desk, trying his best to look at ease.

"After all these years you know the folks up around old Prophetstown pretty well," he began.

Harold went silent, slipping easily into the habits he'd picked up in prison—don't admit a thing and try hard to look like you don't mind one way or the other whether the sun comes up or takes the day off for a change.

"I'm told," said Aingher, unperturbed, "that there's conflicts involving Omar Tuttle and the Morinvilles."

Harold tried to read the sheriff's face. "Maybe," he said, the one-word reply weak in the air of the spacious office. "The both of them got tempers, him and Etienne."

"Right. Do you suppose that has anything to do with Freddy Morinville disappearing?"

Harold pictured the boy, a heavyset kid, light-skinned for an Indian, with big front teeth, not much resembling his younger brothers, Sam and Casey. "I was told the boy run away."

"Supposedly, yeah. Only his mother says she don't believe that."

"Pardon me?" Harold's thoughts had wandered to his old girlfriend, Marlys Fagerstad, now Marlys Aingher. He pondered what it must be like for the sheriff, going home every day to talk things over and eat food cooked by a girl as spoiled as Marlys.

"I'm questioning if you got an opinion on whether the boy really did run off."

"I couldn't say. Since Etienne sold off his herd I don't stop there no more."

Aingher nodded patiently. He'd acquired tact since the war. "But that doesn't have to do with my question."

"I wouldn't really know," said Harold.

Aingher tugged at his collar, freeing space for his ample neck. "I ran up there Monday just to have a look-see. Etienne didn't have much to say about Freddy except they had a squabble, just a family thing."

Harold began to relax. This had nothing to do with him. "But you say his missus didn't agree?"

"When I talked to just her, yes. Then when the husband come in right away, she shut her mouth." The sheriff slid to his feet, and his big black boots hit the wooden floor with a hollow thump. "That happens," he said. "That's my second trip up to the hills this month. We got word that Foss Breen's been seen in the area."

"Foss is back again?" said Harold.

"Back and raising hell. He's like a bad penny."

Harold bobbed his head in agreement.

"You never know entirely what's going on up in the hills, do you?" said the sheriff. "And I'm not even counting the Able bunch. Did you ever hear the one about the locomotive that supposedly sunk in Leonard Creek?"

"That was before my time," said Harold, turning to the door.

"One thing before you go," said the sheriff. "You might know that Omar Tuttle made some accusations."

Harold waited, steeling himself. "Is that so—what kind?"

Aingher folded his arms, rocking back against the desk. He was getting soft in the middle. "Don't think I owe you any favors. I got a job to do, that's all. I'm just going to tell you for right now I don't believe a word the man said. But then again, that could change."

\* \* \* \* \*

By the time he walked out of the sheriff's office and got the panel gassed and loaded, Harold told himself that this would be his last trip north. The complications put too much strain on a man who wanted to be left to himself. As he passed the city limits, however, the view to the northwest promptly took his mind away from Omar Tuttle and his contagious turmoil. Great thunderheads rose into the distant sky, menacing and black, the kind that washed out roads, blew down trees and, worst of all, brought hail. Of all a farmer's calamities, he feared hail the most, especially when it hit just before harvest. The reward for all that toil was at last within reach, only to have the frozen destruction from the heavens snatch it away.

He reached Five Corners and made the first of his stops at the Gosches, where he smelled electricity in the air. Swaths of their wheat lay flattened in the fields from an earlier storm, but further north the skies cleared, giving hope that farmers in the higher hills might be spared. Hail had a strange way, as if God couldn't make up his mind who exactly deserved a portion of reckoning.

Running late, Harold chose to skip the Breen farm till morning, which meant he'd have to double back to the west a good distance. After hearing from the sheriff that Sidney Breen's brother might be around, he didn't want to risk being stranded there. He drove on to the Tuttle place, his heart fluttering like a leaf, and as he turned into the gentle rise of the farmyard, the sun again disappeared behind a towering bank of clouds.

Other than the pigeons ruffling the still air above the hayloft, the place seemed quiet for a farm, which typically carried demands for every spare second of daylight. Harold backed the panel up to the milk house to off-load empties and pick up the fulls. He tapped the heavy lids with his mallet to smell the cream, expecting the satisfying aroma of sweet clover. At once he replaced the lids. The cream was curdling. It had been left out too long.

With little notion what to expect but wishing to give the impression that all was normal, he continued inside, deliberately slow-paced, to have a cup of coffee. The sight before him made him think again. The kitchen that had once been the pride of Lucille Tuttle, polished and neat as the mess hall at Fort Snelling, presented a clutter of dirty dishes and spoiling food. The slop bucket smelled and flowed over. The coffeepot sat empty on the cold stove.

Footsteps creaked heavily upstairs, and Leah came into view at the top of the landing, her midsection revealing a marked bulge. "Oh, I thought it was Daddy," she said.

Harold beckoned to her. "Can you come down?"

The girl took each step cautiously as Harold stood back to give her room.

"What is it that's happening here?" he asked. "The cream's going bad, there's a storm on the way and you got wash hanging on the line that looks like it's been there a week. And the kitchen, my goodness, young woman."

Leah, her eyes puffy, her hair tangled, turned her eyes toward the messy sink, as if the disgusting collection of unwashed utensils and pots represented news to her.

Harold studied her face. "Before I talk to your dad, I got to tell you that the sheriff's been asking about Freddy Morinville. You sure you don't have any idea where he went?"

She wore one of her father's old wool shirts and bib overalls that concealed any suggestion of a feminine form. "No, I told you. He never said."

A rumble of thunder sent a shudder through the house. "Could it be that maybe he wanted you to go with him?"

The girl grabbed a handful of her shirt and tugged it downward around her stomach. She took a long time responding. "At first, I wanted to wait and have the baby, then go to high school in Rolland next year. But Daddy said I was staying on the farm and that was it, baby or no baby. So I told Freddy I'd go with him. But when I tried to sneak out in the night, Daddy found my suitcase in the milk house and waited out there till I came for it."

"What happened then?"

"Daddy pitched a fit, said if he got his hands on Freddy, he would teach him a lesson."

Harold's heart dropped. "He never actually tried to go after him, did he?"

"You know Daddy. He cools off in a hurry. When he woke up the day after, it was like nothing happened. Daddy said it would all be settled after he talked to you."

Leah lowered her chin to her chest, wiping her eyes with the back of her hand.

Harold extended a hand to pat the girl's head as if she were a cocker spaniel. "There, there," he said.

"Stop it!" Leah cried, her unexpected reaction giving Harold a start. "You don't know anything about it."

"Take it easy now," said Harold.

Leah raised her head, her red face a picture of anger. "Is that all you can say?"

Harold pulled back in confusion "You don't have to act like that. Freddy'll be back. They'll find him."

"You just don't see," said Leah, her voice rising again.

"See what? Tell me."

Leah turned aside, maybe looking for an out, but the habit of obedience lived strong in her. "It's Daddy."

"What do you mean *daddy*?"

"Quit blaming Freddy. We never even had a kiss. It was Daddy."

Harold took a step back, bumping into the newel post. "What?"

Leah directed her gaze into his eyes as if daring him to contradict her.

"What are you saying?"

"It started after Mama died."

Harold gripped the girl's shoulders. "Listen, you're coming into town with me in the morning."

Leah hugged her chest with her arms, quivering. "Daddy won't let me go."

"If he doesn't, I'll get somebody to come out and that'll be the end of it either way."

Leah shook her head. "No, please. They'll put him in jail and what do I do then? Anyway, it doesn't happen anymore."

"This will pass. You're young. You can start over."

Leah leaned back on her heels. Positioned on the step, her gaze was level with Harold's. "You're a fine one, Harold Peavey," she said, her voice strong. "Everybody knows you got your heart broken and you never went near a woman since. When are you going to start over?" She twisted around and lumbered up the stairs, the tails of the bulky shirt dangling.

Feeling suffocated, Harold was overcome with a need to get out of the stifling house with its withered flowers and dusty doilies. He made his way outside only to come upon Omar sitting on the porch steps, cleaning manure from his shoes with the blade of an old butcher knife.

"I heard all that," said the old man, concentrating on his task.

"Then we got nothing to talk about," said Harold.

"Unless you want to consider that the girl's making things up."

Harold looked at his old friend, but Omar avoided meeting his eyes. "I imagine there'll come a time to hash all that out. I got my load set to go. Maybe it's best if I head out right now."

"I was you, I wouldn't be going nowhere," said Omar, gesturing with his head to the west where flashes of lightning lit the immense, black sky, the clouds rolling and dipping toward the horizon in three directions. At the same time, a quietness settled on the countryside as nature gathered itself.

Serene as one of his Holsteins, Omar switched his scraper to the other shoe, the dry, ratchety sound of his blade on leather the only noise in the world.

*****

As the weather stalled in the west by the higher hills, Harold rummaged around in the untidy kitchen for something quick to eat. The breadbox held a few crusts of dark rye, but as he reached for them, he found he had no stomach for food after all. He strode through the parlor with its peculiar emptiness. From the rocker on the porch, he surveyed the crackling green sky, knowing by the band of white that it held hail.

The storm forced its way closer. The house sent out groans and sighs of restlessness. Blue-white lightning flashed behind the barn. Progressing rumbles like the sounds of men bowling followed the lightning, sending loose windowpanes quivering. Worried whether he'd rolled up the windows on his truck, Harold hurried out into the yard to check, one hand over his head. The lightning came in continuous bursts now, adding a midday detail to the tufts of grass and rocky soil. A cool breeze swept through the barnyard, rattling the door on the old privy.

Instead of dashing back to the porch, he sat for a couple minutes in the truck. He lowered a window. A blast of wind-driven rain hit his face, chilling him. Through the water-blurred windshield he sighted the orange glow of a nodding lantern showing through the upstairs window of the house. That would be Leah's room. The ghostly light glided down the stairs, back up and then down and out to the porch. The screen door opened, the exhausted spring making barely a noise as Omar peered into the slanting rain.

Harold opened his door but stayed in the truck, holding the door ajar with his left foot.

"There you are," called Omar through the tumult. Holding the lamp high above his drawn face, he hollered, "Come inside. I need you."

A thunderclap stifled Harold's attempt at any reply. He followed Omar inside.

The old man teetered on his gimpy ankles as he led Harold up to Leah's bedroom, where the girl lay on the bed faceup with her eyes shut. A framed print of a collie standing guard over a lamb lost in the snow adorned the clapboard wall above the bed. A big ugly hook that once saw service in the barn held a lantern that cast a harsh, oscillating light over the face of the girl. An odd aroma Harold couldn't place saturated the air.

He whispered to Omar, "What is it—is she sick?"

"No. She's just out."

A brown bottle with a cork resting loosely in the neck sat beside a white dishcloth on the wooden nightstand. Harold held the bottle to the light and read the label typed in red letters. *Chloroform USP.*

"What's this all about?" asked Harold, his alarm growing.

Omar took the bottle from Harold's hand and replaced it on the nightstand. "Look here," he said, lifting the towel to reveal a row of silvery instruments—scalpel, forceps, sturdy sutures, bandages ripped from an old sheet. "I cleaned them up good," he added, pride in his voice. "Boiled 'em for a half hour."

Harold recognized the instruments as part of the kit he carried under the seat of the panel truck. "These are horse doctor tools."

Omar spoke with his eyes aglow. "In your hands they'll work fine. I read in a book how it's done. It's not even a real operation."

Harold's eyes went unavoidably to Leah's stomach. "It's not time for her baby."

Omar's face flashed the first sign of impatience. "I know that, and you need to get what I'm saying. She's not gonna have no baby."

Harold reached for the girl's wrist, checking the slow, weak pulse. "How much of that bottle did you use?"

Omar crossed his puny arms over his chest. "Just what it took to get her out, like you said. There's plenty left."

"My god."

"I got it all planned out, Harold. I do. We'll bury it where nobody knows, the creek maybe. When she comes to, we'll tell her you did your best, but the baby was born dead. Things like this go on all the time, you know that."

Harold leaned over the defenseless girl. What Omar said was true. Such things did happen. He placed a rough palm on the girl's forehead. "Open that window, Omar."

The old man looked at it. "It's painted shut."

"Then bust a pane. She needs air."

"Hold on now."

"Just get the window."

Omar scratched his cheek in puzzlement. "Sweet Jesus, why you fighting me on this? Do I have to go after my twelve-gauge?"

Harold recalled the shotgun hanging from a spike in the barn, handy to bag a goose from the flock that watered in the slough each fall. Back in October, he'd fixed the firing pin.

Leah's head twitched and her eyelids fluttered.

Harold leaned over her, shaking her gently, but got no response. "Omar, either help me or get out of the way. We need to bring her to."

But the man had left the room, the sound of his boots on the stairs eclipsed by the rising wind.

The windowpane shattered on the jab from Harold's elbow. And then came the rain, plump drops producing the splat of a wet rag tossed in a sink followed by the sharp, focused sound of hail battering the roof.

Harold glanced at the sagging ceiling, aware that a decaying half inch of wood and tar was all that stood between the doubtful security of the room and the broad dangers flung from the sky. Already a yellow drip of water was forming. He shoved the bed closer to the wall. As the clatter reached an unbearable pitch, he lay on the bed beside the girl, his broad arm over her face, his chest protecting her middle. As the noise abated only to come back stronger, he felt for a wrist, dreading what it might tell. But no, the pulse, though weak, continued constant. He tucked the bare arm back underneath the covers and waited, listening for the sound of returning footsteps or the passing of the storm, unprepared for either.

Stillness, upsetting for its own suddenness, descended on the room. As the clouds dissipated toward the east, a faint light from the emerging moon filled the window.

After pulling the blankets higher over Leah, Harold made his way cautiously downstairs and outside, smelling the fresh ozone. The soft music of water trickling in a network of rills through the yard concealed the sounds of the night. Wading through a tangle of tree limbs, storm trash and boot-swallowing mud, he reached the truck. He turned the ignition key and tromped on the starter. The engine turned easily but did not catch. He tried again. He got out and lifted the hood, suspecting what was wrong. Sure enough, the coil wire was gone from the distributor.

He considered trying Omar's old Dodge but guessed it would be disabled too. As he debated about going to the Morinvilles for help, a final flash of lightning lit the yard, revealing a motionless form like so many rags tangled in the wire by an erratic wind. It was Omar Tuttle trapped by the barbs of iron in his fence, the relentless hail having pounded his face into jelly.

Tenderly, Harold pulled the body by the suspenders and eased it to the ground, surprised by its lightness. He found the missing wire in the bib pocket, next to a pair of pliers.

\* \* \* \* \*

That night, Harold pushed the panel so fiercely that his fingers ached from squeezing the wheel. On through the darkness he drove, splashing through washouts that should have sunk him axle-deep, swerving around broken limbs, bouncing over rocks and potholes. With Leah lying in the back, unresponsive but for an occasional whimper, he reached Rolland at dawn and drove directly through the empty streets to the side entrance of the hospital.

To his surprise, Dr. Thwarp himself, whiskery and irritable, came out to meet him. "What you got here?" he barked.

Harold, who hadn't spoken a word aloud in hours, couldn't find his voice. "It's an emergency," he said, knowing he sounded foolish. The doctor wedged his way into the back of the panel, where he shined a penlight into an eye and put a stethoscope to Leah's chest.

"Her respiration's barely there. Has this girl been drinking?"

Harold tried his best to explain as the doctor settled his stethoscope on Leah's abdomen. "How far along is she?" he asked but didn't wait for an answer. "Bring her in," he said. Two nurses arrived, maneuvering a sturdy gurney over the rough surface of the parking lot.

From where Harold stood, he could see down the street where Mr. Mott turned the key to open his newspaper office while, one block away, Ralph Brown threaded the air hose onto its reel next to the pumps at the Standard Station. The business of the town proceeded.

One of the nurses, Mrs. Crosby, a woman Harold knew only slightly though she was his mother's first cousin, adjusted the doorstop with her shoe while Thwarp and the other nurse wheeled the gurney through. Harold followed. As they waited at the elevator, Harold turned to Dr. Thwarp.

"Do you need blood or anything?" asked Harold, desperate to be helpful.

The doctor patted his shoulder. "We have plenty of blood. You've done your part."

\* \* \* \* \*

Harold hadn't set foot in the cream-colored hospital since Lucille Tuttle died. As he sat in the cramped waiting room watching the starchy people move briskly through the hallway, he was struck at how sober and precise they appeared. Everywhere else in town, residents went through the day with a casual, unhurried air, calling one another by nickname, behaving as if not much was worth getting excited about.

Measured steps clacked on the tiled floor. Harold looked up warily. Sheriff Dale Aingher stood before him, rumpled and sleepy-eyed.

"Call come in—somebody saw you heading into town driving like a wild man," said the sheriff, taking a seat.

"I had to," said Harold, annoyed at having to apologize for his offense. "It was the Tuttle girl."

"Yes, and what's her problem?"

"Better ask the doc."

"Where's the old man? Where's Omar?"

"He's dead," said Harold.

The sheriff's face registered no emotion. "What happened?"

"He got caught in the hail. He's pretty messed up."

"You're positive he's dead?"

"Yes."

"And tell me again why you brought the girl in."

Harold sighed, realizing how drained he was. "All right," he began. He spoke carefully, too tired to embellish what had occurred.

At the end, Aingher frowned and tilted his head to look at Harold's muddy shoes under the table. "That's quite a story," he said. "The instruments and stuff, they're still there?"

"Far as I know," said Harold.

Aingher looked at his watch. "We'll have to go up there, me and you."

"Right," said Harold. "But can you hold off till we see how she's doing in there?"

"Of course. Omar's not going nowhere."

From behind the nurses' station, a typewriter clacked monotonously. The hospital janitor, old Pete Hunt, came by, in no hurry, emptying ashtrays into a canvas bag slung around his neck.

"Lots of hail up there then?" said Aingher, his pointed boot twitching nervously.

Harold had to stop and think, though he knew the other man was only making conversation. "Quite a bit."

Aingher gazed down the hallway. "Maybe I'll go check if they got the coffeepot on."

Harold said nothing. The sheriff didn't move.

A *Saturday Evening Post* lay on the low table. Aingher flipped through the pages disinterestedly. "You ever think about that night?"

Harold appraised the magazine as if it might offer a clue to the question. "What's that?"

"You know, during the war."

"Can't say I do anymore much."

"We were all drinking some."

"Yeah, I could see that."

"Something I often deliberated about," said the sheriff. "You were locked up for what, two years, and then you come home to find nobody on your side. Think you'd do the same if you had another chance?"

Harold gazed at the man's face. "You never know, but I imagine so."

They sat in silence for a time, each reflecting on the incident, which seemed to both that it came to pass in such a far-off place and time that it shouldn't count for anything. "Now you tell me," said Harold. "If you and them fellas had been sober that night, would you of done what you did?"

The sheriff didn't hesitate. "I can say now that it shouldn't of come to that. The main thing is I made a bad move bringing those others along. I ought to have been man enough to settle it on my own."

Harold laced his fingers together and leaned forward on his elbows, doing his best to think of how to respond. The double doors swung open. It was Mrs. Crosby. "Harold, you can come back now."

Harold came to his feet and followed the nurse through an area smelling heavily of disinfectant to a door at the end of a hall.

Leah lay on the bed asleep, strands of her hair damp on her forehead. Self-consciously, Harold stepped closer. "How is she?" he asked Mrs. Crosby in a low voice.

"She'll be fine. She's a tough country girl," said the nurse.

"What all did you have to do?"

The nurse smiled. "Not much of anything. She delivered a baby—seven weeks before it was due."

Harold blinked. "And it's all right?"

"So far so good. You can take a peek if you like."

The nursery held only one baby, shielded in the artificial world of the warm, oxygenated incubator. Through the window, Harold's eyes fell on a bundle wrapped in white. He looked closer. From out of the bundle protruded a purplish head with a darkish patch of wet hair—a small, squirming, quite ugly, but very much alive, human baby.

\* \* \* \* \*

In the full light of day, the damage to the Tuttle farm looked less than Harold had imagined. A granary no longer used lay flattened. Shingles on the toolshed and over a northern section of the house were missing. Several west-facing windows on the house were broken, and the siding hung loose. But the barn looked undamaged, no doubt because of the sturdy four-by-fours used in construction. Inside, the cows bellered to be milked and fed. The horses were still spooked but relaxed at the appearance of a human. Most surprisingly, the chickens all survived, huddled restlessly beneath the porch, which was ample to shelter them all.

While Harold pitched hay down to the mangers for the hungry livestock, the sheriff took pictures of Omar's crumpled body all twisted up in the gumweed and washed clean by the rain and melting hail. By the time Harold finished in the barn, Aingher had managed to get Omar wrapped in a brown blanket and tied with baling twine, making a presentable package, for which Harold was grateful. They hoisted the bundle and eased it into the spacious trunk of the sheriff's car. To Harold, the wrapped figure felt as light as the suitcases in movies that even petite women could hoist with one hand.

While the sheriff poked around a while longer, overturning bits of wreckage with the toe of his boot, Harold milked the cows and let the calves drink their fill, then turned the herd out to pasture and fed the chickens. By then Aingher had wrapped up his duties in the house, where he found the unused instruments and the bottle of chloroform.

On the way back to town, Harold related to the sheriff what Leah had told him regarding her father's threat aimed at the missing Freddy Morinville. Two days later, the sheriff sent a crew with a rented backhoe to the Tuttle farm. They dug behind the barn, in the pasture and anywhere else the ground looked soft. They uncovered only a few animal bones. They next checked around the Prophetstown cemetery but found nothing. The sheriff finished the paperwork on the missing boy and put the file away. The young man would turn up somewhere—probably staying with a forgotten relative in Montana or pumping gas at a filling station in South Dakota. With the election coming up, Aingher itched to get campaigning.

* * * * *

Folks in the hill country along Prophetstown Road hashed and rehashed the Tuttle tragedy for some time. Eventually they tired of the story and took up their customary talk of weather and wheat prices and why the heck the county couldn't get around to blading the road going into town.

About the same time on a late summer day, a wedge of geese journeyed south in no particular hurry, their wings beating the warm air. They glided over farmers hastening to bring in the last of their wheat, a knot of older ladies in colorful dress picking chokecherries, and a lone fisherman in a straw hat on McGillis Lake sitting quietly in a rowboat. Beyond the grove where the ladies foraged, a herd of Holsteins grazed in the warm sun.

Beside the pasture and separated from it by goldenrod and timothy growing in a ditch, a green Ford pickup of recent vintage made its way along the potholes and dust of the section road. Though he knew the road well, the driver took great care to preserve the safety of himself and his passengers. At the Tuttle turnoff, the vehicle came to a stop, and for a moment no one got out, as if the driver and passengers had come all this way only to find themselves unsure of whether to proceed.

Just then the breeze switched, catching the tops of the goldenrod, bending them toward the farmyard and its old wooden house, pointing the way home for Leah and her baby.

# HOW DIFFERENT THIS WORLD

Fawn found little time to long for the company of Sidney after he went away to war. The remainder of the winter delivered snows that nearly covered the hut, forcing her to scrape out a tunnel to the goat shed to feed the animals. Part of a wall of the hut fractured from the constant wind. She stuffed hay and skins into the breach, only to see it open with the next storm. The cold placed more demands for wood, and that along with food supplies ran low. The goats took on a spectral appearance, and before the first edible grasses of spring emerged from the frozen ground, three of them had to be slaughtered before they starved to death.

At the same time, Père grew sicker, barely moving from his bed even to sip the thin broth that Fawn heated from old, yellowing bones and bits of leathery meat that she took from the floor. When a sour smell filled the air about him and he quit eating entirely, Fawn knew that he must die soon. Yet she too fought hunger. To save her strength and to keep from dreaming about the foods she desired, she spent most of the day in her own bed. So hungry did she become that she craved strange items that she imagined to be bitter or tasteless, such as unformed buds of aspen or even black soil from the pasture that she believed she would stuff into her mouth if only it weren't buried beneath the snow.

Days passed. Her limbs felt heavier. Her feet pained her, and her stomach felt about to burst though it held nothing. Perhaps she was taking on the sickness of Père. Was she to die? Firegoat, the faceless voice that often visited to whisper in her ear, had warned that she would never see Sidney again.

Early on a morning when the winds outside settled into a gentle breeze promising spring, she awoke with intense pains just like when once, in a fit of hunger, she had eaten great handfuls of green chokecherries. This time the discomfort did not go away but increased in tightening surges. She twisted about on her bed trying to find a comfortable position. At times, she could not keep from shrieking and feared that her cries would awaken Père, who lay on his back in his bed across the room, his hands crossed over his sunken belly. But he did not move.

Not long after first light, she experienced a twisting sensation followed by a gush of water that soaked her bedding. Soon, the pains increased in intensity, and a half hour later she felt the baby emerging, followed by a sinewy cord attached to bloody tissue that caused her to fear that her insides were being expelled. But the baby immediately captured her concentration. It was a boy, noisy and active. Astonished but exhausted, she placed him at her breast and slipped the cord and placenta underneath the covers beside her, knowing her child was healthy in the same way she knew that a baby goat would live—by his appetite.

\* \* \* \* \*

When she awoke to the cries of the baby, she became aware that Père had not stirred. She concluded that he had died. At once she covered his face, fearful that the sight meant an omen of misfortune for her baby.

Hungry and very thirsty, she filled a cup with water that she swallowed in a greedy gulp the way Père once drank. When she stirred the fire to heat the kettle, the baby wailed. Returning to bed, she let him have her breast again. The cord, with its dangling, wiry tissue, stayed attached to him at the belly, but she had feared removing it. It looked harmless. She eased into sleep.

She awoke hungrier than ever. She stumbled painfully to the food cache, where she retrieved a bag of pemmican stiff from the cold ground. Removing a roundish, cream-colored chunk the thickness of her wrist, she worked it with her palm and fingers to render it chewy and warm. Though dirty from her hands and salty, she ate it eagerly. Taking a handful of dried grass from the tinderbox, she dipped it in water and wiped down the baby from the featherlike hair on his head down to the placenta, finishing at the tips of his teeny toes that she uncurled, the better to clean between them.

While washing her baby, Fawn took care to keep her body turned from Père, wanting to protect the child from the air of death. Wiping away the dried bits of blood and matter from his soft skin, she felt as if she were correspondingly removing her own stains. When the baby opened his misty blue eyes to focus on her own, a warmth of gratitude and love came over her. All pain and misery went away, at least for a while.

\* \* \* \* \*

When she awoke from this rest, strengthened, she forced her attention to the long, uneven form of Père, who seemed to be sinking deeper into his deathbed.

Sidney had told her that when his father died, his mother wrapped him in a sheet. Next, Sidney and his brother placed the body in a long box to which a cover was attached. With help from others they lowered the box with their father in it into a hole in the ground that had been dug for that purpose. Just imagining the steps involved made Fawn dizzy. The last part, making a proper hole, would be impossible. Two winters previously when the supply of prairie turnips ran out, Père ordered her to look in the frozen ground for any that had been missed during the fall. After stabbing at the ground for an hour with the crude digging tool, she could penetrate no deeper than the length of her thumb. And while the worst of the cold had passed, she knew she lacked the strength to make a hole big enough to accept Père.

She shivered, remembering the time she came upon a baby goat dead in the woods with evidence of raccoons and ravens having fed on it. If she couldn't bury the man, she must do something. She imagined the once generous flesh gradually shrinking until only the naked bones were left. She would try to drag the body outside and cover it with snow. She waited until her baby slept. Closing her eyes, she slid her hands under Père's shoulders and pulled. He couldn't be moved. She tried again, managing to maneuver him closer to the edge of the bed. When she pulled on his arm, his weight caused him to fall to the floor, where his head struck the rough planks with his face pointed upward as if in accusation.

*You see, he wishes never to leave his home. If you wait, he will come back to life.*

Fawn knew that could not be. Firegoat lied. Dead deer did not rise to feed in the bushes and offer their meat again. Sidney never spoke of his father returning from the hole in the ground. Her eyes settled on Père, motionless on the floor, then to her baby, squealing and alive. But what if it were so?

The choice came easy.

* * * * *

From a deerskin softened by chewing, Fawn fashioned a sling to carry the baby, along with a backpack that would double as a blanket. To the pack, she added what food she could find in addition to acorns, very dry pemmican and a pouch of goats' milk. She hoped she might supplement this with early-season mushrooms and other edibles. During the brief days of preparation, the placenta and cord dried and dropped off, leaving only a shred of tissue that stuck to the baby's plump belly.

Lastly, she retrieved from a hiding place in the rocks beneath an alder tree the papers Sidney left with her. She studied his map until she believed she understood it; the other paper she secreted in her clothing. The night before departure, she released all the goats that had survived the winter, hoping that a full summer with abundant pasture might strengthen them, allowing them to return to the wild with the coming of the snow.

At sunrise the following morning, she covered Père with skins and cloth for which she had no need. He still lay in the awkward position on the floor, but there he must remain. With a last look around, she secured the door, knowing that before two summers went by, vines and other greenery would encompass the dwelling, making it nearly invisible, creating for Père a kind of tomb.

After adjusting and readjusting the sling over her lanky body, she crossed the creek and entered the woods, picking her way to the open area where she had first glimpsed Sidney and his horse. If only Sidney had made a gift of Alouette along with the baffling papers. He said that the animal, since it could move with less effort through the deep woods and around the hills, took less than half a day to carry him from his house to the hut, but to walk using the same route naturally took longer. What Sidney called "the road" was itself a good distance from the hut. But for anyone ill, aged, or burdened with a load, it was best to use the road, though in all it would require more than a day's travel. And though Fawn, with her youth and strong, long legs, could once walk easily through dense woods and tall grass, she had lost strength during the final weeks of her pregnancy.

By the time she reached the open area where the grass stood waist-high, she was already weak and tired. She could not make the sling ride comfortably, and a knot chafed the exposed skin of her neck with each step. She rested only briefly to feed the baby and swallow a bit of salty pemmican before continuing. She should have allowed more time before abandoning the hut, but she could not endure another day with the body of Père. She shut her eyes, forming an image of Sidney sitting before a cranberry bush reading a book. At once she knew she'd made a mistake, for the now-familiar voice whispered in her ear.

*Leave the baby. Drop it! Put it under the bushes!*

She forced herself on, ignoring the thorns of a wild rose grown tall as a tree. Soon she lost any semblance of a trail. She drew the map out of her robe. Where was the road? Sidney said it was in the direction the sun rose in the morning. But now the sun, when it managed to be seen among the treetops, hung directly overhead.

The baby fussed. Fawn worried; might his cries of distress be heard by a bear or a prowling wolf? Every sound—the flutter of a bird, the rattle of a broken limb falling—forced her to a halt to listen for danger. She stopped before a scraggly pine. Its rich scent reminded her of the pines that grew on the side of the goat pasture near the hut, where, in only a few weeks, cranberry and chokecherry bushes laced with blossoms promising an abundance of fat, sweet fruit would appear.

*Leave the baby!*

The day progressed toward late afternoon while she struggled with her precious burden beneath the umbrella of the spreading, endless woods. With trees in every direction, light disappeared early. Finding no hollow or cave, she settled for a mossy area beneath the exposed roots of a hackberry tree that formed an arch from which she strung the extra blanket. Exhausted, she nursed her baby before nibbling on a clutch of fresh ferns that she knew were safe to eat, but which she hated the taste of. Then she shut her eyes for a rest.

She came awake to a roaring, clattering sound like hail on the roof of the goat shed. As it increased in volume, she hugged the baby closer, covering him with her torso, expecting to be pounced on by some ravenous clawed creature. Then, gradually, the sound receded, and as it did, the air filled with dust and a strange odor she could not place. She waited, motionless, hesitant to breathe. A breeze came up, and the dust and smell disappeared.

At last, the dawn, hazy and speckled, filtered through the forest canopy that had never seen ax nor bucksaw. Stiff and tired, scratched and still bleeding from thorns, sharp rocks and bugbites, she gathered maple leaves, weaving their stems tightly to clean the baby and use as diapers. Then she allowed him to feed as she gazed into his unquestioning eyes. Renewed by his look of trust, she took him up in the sling and proceeded on.

Ten minutes later, the woods ended, and a straight path covered with small rocks and sandy dirt extending in both directions came into view. At last, the road.

Once again came the roaring noise that frightened her in the night. A large, shiny object approached from the hill to her left, moving faster than a deer. She watched, astonished, as it flew by in a cloud of noise and dust. This must be what Sidney had described as an automobile. What an awful thing, the way it raised a cloud of choking dust and spit blue smoke that smelled nothing like the comforting aroma of the fireplace.

She let the baby nurse while she chewed and swallowed half of the remaining pemmican. She checked the map, by now greasy from use and curling at the edges. As she came to understand the various lines, some curved, others long and straight, she saw that the farm was not so distant as she had estimated even while using the road. Going through the woods and over the hills like a bird was faster, but a road made a better way to travel from one place to another. How unfortunate that automobiles chose to use it.

As she progressed, she became accustomed to her surroundings. In addition to chokecherry and cranberry bushes, she came upon hawthorn and locust trees, foxtail and wild oats, pigweed—all the same as those she knew from growing up. She smiled at her own naivete in assuming that similar growth around the hut was there for her convenience.

Sidney had said that his house was the first one she would reach, and there it was, amid various outbuildings that all looked unrealistically large, especially the barn, which looked as if it could enclose all the other buildings beneath its spreading gray roof. The house, square and white and seemingly made mostly of windows, sat on a knoll and exhibited the strange profile of the rooster that Sidney had called a weather vane. As Fawn came closer, limping slightly from a blister on her right foot, the rich aroma of manure reached her, and she spotted an animal by the barn. She recognized it at once—Alouette. The welcome sight of the creature, the first familiar living thing she had seen since forsaking the hut, filled her heart with gratitude. She would forever associate this with her first impressions of the farm.

She approached the house timidly, acutely aware that in her entire life she had known but two other people, not counting the squirming bundle in her arms that was awake and letting her know that it was hungry. As she reached the yard, overgrown with dandelions and quack grass, a dog came bounding toward her, barking furiously. Although Sidney had enlightened her on dogs and cats kept as pets, she heaved her body to the side to protect the baby.

From inside the house came a man's harsh voice. "Patsy, shut up!"

A door opened. Fawn gaped, stricken cold. It was Sidney!

Wanting to go to him, she stepped closer, but halted at the landing. The man presented the same straw-colored hair swept to one side and falling over his ear and the same determined boxy face. But it was not Sidney. This man was shorter and stockier. His gaze lacked the quick smile and rainbow eyebrows of Sidney. He must be Foss, the brother Sidney talked about.

"What the hell?" the man said, frowning, stooping to see what she was carrying in her arms as she instinctively covered the child with the blanket.

A woman's softer voice drifted from deeper in the house. "Foss? What is it? Who's there?"

"Some squaw with a kid," said the man.

A heavy-faced older woman appeared, shambling painfully with each step. "For land's sake, let them in," she said, appraising Fawn, who matched her height though she stood two steps lower. She frowned as she looked about the farmyard. "Where did you come from—are you on foot?"

Fumbling and uncertain, Fawn handed over the perfectly folded paper from Sidney. The woman, who wore a red cloth in her white hair, took a long time reading it, looking up to examine her tall visitor repeatedly.

"What's it say?" asked Foss, trying to see.

"It's from Sid," said the old lady.

"What? How could that be?"

"It's his writing all right, but it doesn't say nothing about a baby."

Foss reached for the paper. "Somebody's trying to pull something. Just let me see."

"It's got my name on it and I'll be the one who decides," said the woman as Fawn listened, not comprehending it all because the people talked so fast, but at the same time expecting to be sent away. The baby made a noise.

The woman leaned in. "Is it a newborn?"

Fawn held the baby closer.

"How'd you get so far from the reservation?" said Foss.

"She didn't come from the reservation," said the woman before Fawn could answer.

"She smells like it," said Foss. "She probably wants money. I can take and drop her off in town."

"You'll do no such thing. Can't you see the girl's sick?"

\* \* \* \* \*

As Foss glared, Alberta Breen led Fawn and the baby inside to the kitchen table, where she set out cold chicken and bread slathered with butter. She warmed milk for the baby, but Fawn misunderstood and drank it herself before baring her breast to nurse the baby in full view of the unhelpful Foss, who leaned unshaven and sullen in the kitchen doorway. From there, the older woman guided her to a narrow room with a wash basin, a pitcher of water and a white chamber pot, and left her alone with the baby.

Fawn craved rest, but with the uncertainty and newness of her surroundings, she could not keep her eyes closed. As she washed herself, she heard footsteps and a rustling at the door. Outside on the floor she found a carefully folded pile of clothing, including a tan cloth like the woman wore that she knew would allow mosquitoes to bite her legs, and a shirt of a soft fabric but with buttons that she had great difficulty in fastening. She set aside the underpants and brassiere, which she regarded worse than useless.

Disregarding the chamber pot, she lifted the window and slipped outside to relieve herself. While she squatted, an automobile rattled into the yard, this one of an unusual shape and having few windows. As she finished her business, the automobile went quiet. A sad-faced man with brown hair emerged and offered a greeting to Sidney's mother, who stood on the step wiping her hands in her apron.

Fawn stood fitfully in the shadow of the house, certain that this man and his automobile could serve no good purpose. But in no time he loaded two large, shiny containers into his vehicle and drove away, bouncing over the rutty yard. It took days until Mother—as Sidney had referred to her—convinced Fawn that the automobile, with all its massive, clamoring intrusion, represented no danger. Furthermore, the man who drove it was from the creamery in town and stopped at the farm regularly. Since the square white house with the figure of a rooster perched high on the roof stood within view of the highway, vehicles often came by.

* * * * *

The house itself contained many rooms with wide windows, allowing a flood of bright light that Fawn found disturbing after her years in the mossy hut with its candlelit semidarkness. Each room in the house offered a particular odor. The parlor smelled of Foss's tobacco while Fawn's bedroom, when she failed to open the window, carried the stink of the baby's diapers. Mother's bedroom offered the alluring scent of cedar, cinnamon and juniper, detectable throughout the entire upstairs. The kitchen with its many aromas became Fawn's favorite. She loved the smell of bacon that sizzled and smoked as it fried, yeasty bread that at first made her stomach rumble painfully but which she grew to crave, and boiling coffee with its faint aroma of the endive the goats ate when they had lost their appetites for other plants.

How different this world from the only other she had known. How puzzling that it existed.

Mother, who barely reached the height of Fawn's elbow, made her feel welcome in many more ways—particularly by helping her acquire familiarity with the many words and phrases to which she was exposed every day. Words such as "scour," "whim" and "swear" baffled her, as did expressions like "beat around the bush" or "raining cats and dogs." Unaccustomed to the presence of an energetic person like Mother—so much in contrast to the silent and indolent Père—Fawn viewed with admiration how Mother spooned lard into the frying pan, then hurried to gather eggs before the grease melted. She looked like a hen herself, with arms tucked in like wings around her expansive bosom, her small feet pattering the dust and propelling her in a straight line toward her goal.

For his part, however, Foss displayed less good will than his mother, believing apparently that speaking louder would enable Fawn to comprehend the meaning of terms favored by him. When she failed to do so, he turned on his heels in exasperation, shaking his head and sputtering yet newer words that stood for nothing to her.

Sidney had said that his brother had "a liking for the bottle," but as with so much else, Fawn knew not what that meant. Foss was constantly angry with everyone, especially his mother. He grumbled when the baby cried. He sometimes had to be woken as late as noon to milk the cows and feed the calves. Often, he disappeared for days at a time, and during those times Mother sent word for what she said was a "hired man" to tend to the chores until he felt like coming back.

While trying to absorb the countless, puzzling aspects of this new life, such as using a fork and having to eat three or even four times a day, Fawn agonized constantly about Sidney, who, Mother explained, had been sent to the Pacific, thousands of miles away. Often, when working in the kitchen with Mother, Fawn enquired when he might return.

The old woman shook her head gravely and looked away.

"God only knows," she said, returning to her mixing bowl, the wooden spoon a blur in her hands.

* * * * *

Fawn thought little of it the first time Foss came up behind her in the barn and pushed her leggings down so he could put his man-thing in her. It hurt sometimes but ended quickly with Foss grunting and squirting into her the handful of thick liquid that smelled like bleach. On hot days, he pulled off his grimy shirt, allowing Fawn a glimpse of his skin—the sunburned arms and neck contrasting with his white-as-milk belly. While she found the experience distasteful, after time she came to see it as just another chore, like changing the nests in the henhouse. This was the way of the world—the new and confusing world which she sometimes wondered if she could ever truly become part of.

On the Fourth of July, Foss announced that he was going to town to celebrate the holiday. One of his drinking pals came by in his windowless Dodge pickup to fetch him, and three days later the pickup had not returned and neither had Foss, during which time it had been discovered that he had helped himself to the egg money that his mother stored in the cracked sugar bowl on the top shelf of the pantry. The cows needed milking and the livestock awaited their feed while Alouette had to be combed and let out to pasture. When Fawn observed Mother trying to manage it all by herself in the barn, she wrapped Baby—as she referred to him—and, to the older woman's objection, hurried through a sudden rain across the farmyard to help.

She and Baby were soaked, and by the time the calves were fed and watered and feed was scattered for the chickens, they were trembling despite the warm, humid air in the barn. Abruptly, Mother bundled them into bed and brought the hot water bottle along with tea and lemon for Fawn and paregoric for Baby, which was all she had by way of medicine.

Fawn slept lightly and felt better in the morning, but Baby awoke red-faced and gasping for breath. Mother filled and heated the steam kettle, but the vapors did nothing to ease his breathing, and a pallor replaced the flushed color of his features.

"We must take him to the doctor," said Mother, wiping her brow.

Fawn did not like the sound of that word. "What is a doctor?" she asked, and then listened to an explanation that she liked even less. She then wanted to know where the doctor was and how they were to get Baby there

"In town," said Mother. "We will take the Ford."

"What is Ford?" asked Fawn, frustrated at being presented with yet another new word.

"You know, a car, an automobile."

The voice she was coming to know captured her full attention. *You must not listen to that old woman. A doctor will hurt the baby,* said Firegoat.

"Please get him dressed," said Mother.

"No!" said Fawn, shaking her head.

"But he might have pneumonia. He could die."

"No," Fawn repeated, wanting nothing to do with anything that involved crawling into the yawning cave of the noisy and smelly creature known as a "car," and even less to do with what awareness she possessed of a doctor.

Counting on an upset and confused Mother to watch Baby, Fawn followed the fence line to the end of the pasture where wild onions flourished. She brought in a handful of the pungent plants and chopped them into pieces so fine they resembled applesauce. She stirred the mushy bits into warm honey.

Hovering nearby with beads of sweat on her forehead and scarcely able to keep from interfering, Mother watched Fawn use the tiniest spoon in the kitchen drawer to feed the boy a bit of the mixture. She then set the bowl aside and took a seat by the crib. After fifteen minutes or so, she fed another portion to the baby, who breathed easier before falling asleep.

Still distraught, Mother forced herself to take a seat. While Fawn sat self-possessed at last, Mother clasped her hands between her knees, rocking forward and back.

"Fawn," she said. "Don't you think it is time to give the baby a name?"

Fawn thought it over. Aside from the half dozen or so people that she knew, she could think of but a single name. "Alouette?" she said.

Mother fidgeted and looked over at Baby. "You mean like Sid's horse? I don't know if I like that."

"What is your name?"

"I was christened Alberta."

"I name him Alberta."

"Well, you see," began Mother, but changed her mind. "How about Albert?"

Though unsure whether she liked the modification, Fawn smiled.

Within hours, the newly named Albert breathed normally.

\* \* \* \* \*

As the summer progressed, Fawn concentrated on learning the ways of this undreamed-of existence. Mother taught her how to prepare all the dishes Fawn would come to favor, such as fried cabbage and fresh tomato pie. Mother also fetched books from the library in Rolland to help Fawn improve her reading, including—to Fawn's astonishment—a copy of the first book she ever saw: *Evangeline: A Tale of Acadie*. Fawn couldn't wait to resume reading the sad story of the poor girl separated from the one she loved only to find him again when they grew old. But when she took up the book, she burst into tears.

"There, there, my dear," said Mother, misunderstanding. "It is only a book. It's all pretend."

Still, when not otherwise occupied, Fawn spent hours imagining life when Sidney came home from the awful war. At night especially, she fantasized he lay safely beside her. She yearned for the touch of his hands. She awoke listening for his breathing, but the only sound reaching her ears in the stillness of the rural night was the steady ticktock of the grandfather clock in the parlor below her room.

\* \* \* \* \*

By his first birthday, the baby Albert began to walk, and Fawn, with Mother's unrelenting encouragement, could read not only books, but follow most articles in *The Saturday Evening Post* as well as in *Turtle Mountain Star*, the weekly newspaper that turned up every Thursday in the little barn-shaped mailbox by the road. Sometimes the newspaper printed stories about the war—a subject that continued to bewilder Fawn. Often the magazine stories displayed photographs of handsome houses surrounded by vast green lawns and patches of stunningly bright flowers or of women with bright red lips wearing flowing dresses that reached the ground. Other pictures exhibited markets with long shelves laden with cans bearing pictures of pork and beans or corn, which she liked, or boxes displaying pictures of cookies or other sweets, which she didn't like but pretended that she did.

When Fawn asked why the images in the magazines differed so much from what she saw around the farm, the older woman smiled and said it was because the Breens were poor. Their farm was not large and the soil not productive. Their machinery was old, and their barn and buildings were falling apart. And further, all those deficiencies were made more difficult by Sidney having gone into the army. But in the end, said Mother, that did not matter greatly because rich people, who were the opposite of them, were not happy.

Fawn couldn't help but notice how, in her pleasantness, Mother avoided speaking bad about Foss. In her own reasoning, she puzzled over how if poor people were happy why Foss went about with such a sour look. Like so much else, she dwelled on the concept while not fully understanding it, forgetting that the life she had left was likewise characterized by abysmal poverty.

*****

When Fawn was told by Mother that she and the baby were to be taken in the family's rusty car to a place called a "church"—a name hard to say—where there would be lots of people, she recognized at once that she best not refuse a second time to travel. Gently, Mother explained that a vital reason existed for this practice. It was time for Bertie—as the baby had come to be known—to be baptized. The importance of this eluded Fawn even though Mother took pains to explain God and heaven. So serious was she that Fawn shut her eyes tight, angled herself and Bertie into the back seat and waited for their doom.

They set out in a light rain with Mother herself driving, Foss refusing to have anything to do with the situation. Wearing a new striped green dress with white bows sewn by Mother on her treadle Singer, Fawn sat rigid as a crowbar while Bertie crawled back and forth across her lap to take in the extraordinary sights such as stacks of hay, water running in ditches and a tractor in a field pushing great black clouds of smoke into the sky. The automobile, its driver wearing her best poke bonnet and balanced on two pillows so as to see through the windshield, bounced along at fifteen miles per hour on its broken springs.

The church turned out to be as large as a barn while smelling not of manure and straw, but pleasantly of garden flowers. But as Mother warned, there were many people present—men dressed alike in pants and matching short coats and women wearing a variety of colorful dresses and hats—Fawn knew the word now—into which dusty flowers had been fitted. All the attendees chatted pleasantly with others along their rows of wooden benches. Then, as if on command, the building went silent at the appearance of the tall, stoop-shouldered young woman—the girl raised by wolves, as she was rumored to be—with her toddler, accompanying Alberta Breen as they made their way to a place in the first row.

Fawn sat rigid and wary as a nesting hen through the songs and prayers until Mother took her arm to lead her to the altar where the robed, smiling white-haired man with a thick book pressed against his chest waited.

She took the hand of her son, unsure. Seeking to help, Mother led Bertie to the man, who turned toward a wooden stand supporting a large basin of water.

At that point, Fawn heard a familiar bleating voice in her head.

*He wants to drown Bertie!*

While Firegoat had never spoken of anything that came true, to Fawn the situation carried ominous hints: the water, the singing, the strong voice of the robed man calling out words that rang like warnings about some future calamity. Mother insisted that this was all for the good of the baby, yet Fawn remembered her solemn words about the afterlife. She said that everyone was happy there, but Fawn wanted Bertie to be happy now, never mind the afterlife—a place she neither understood nor wished her son to dwell in.

Setting his book aside, the man grasped the squirming Bertie with one arm locking his legs together and the other clenching his neck—he was well-accomplished in the maneuver—and lowered his head toward the basin.

Fawn turned to the congregation, seeking help. The women smiled at her peacefully. Several men fanned themselves with their hats. Mother folded her hands and bowed her head. As Bertie's head touched the water, Fawn lunged past Mother and reached for her son. The minister leapt to the side, knocking over the wooden stand with the basin, soaking the Sunday shoes of several people seated in the first row. Clutching her child and trying to run in the constraining dress, Fawn made her way straight down the middle aisle to the doors.

Two grumbling men attempted to flush her and the squawking child from the grove of lilacs behind the cemetery. Bleeding from the thorns and with her dress hanging in tatters, she finally emerged after repeated reassurances from Mother. Following a quick consultation, two of the rescuers rode with Mother back to the farm while a second car followed.

Gently, Mother asked Fawn why she had behaved that way. After all, no one intended to do Bertie harm. But Fawn could not explain. She could never tell Mother about Firegoat and the many times he came to shriek into her ear. As she recalled the events, the picture of the black-robed man suspending Bertie above the basin of water refused to leave her head. Had it not been for Firegoat, the worst may have happened. Before that, Mother wanted to take Bertie to the doctor where more harm yet could have occurred. Could it be she must listen more closely to Firegoat?

Over the next few weeks, misfortune after misfortune was visited on the farm.

First, Firegoat instructed Fawn to pour the contents of the chamber pot into the well, which resulted in water having to be hauled from the creek for drinking and cooking. Fortunately for her, the incident was blamed on Foss. Similarly, when Mother peered from her bedroom window in the night to see a haystack aflame, she assumed that Foss had discarded a lit cigarette nearby. The butcher knife was found ground flat on the stone. Fawn insisted it was Bertie who knocked over a bowl of eggs she had left on a chair and Foss who backed the grain truck into the granary door, smashing it beyond repair.

Not once did Mother chastise Fawn even when she told lies for reasons that made no sense, such as when she insisted that the jar of marmalade that she had eaten in its entirety must have been thrown out by accident when orangish stains were evident on her fingers as well as her pillow.

After these events, Firegoat returned for a long while to the black cave where Fawn imagined him dwelling while he rested and observed from afar. When he reappeared, chanting into her ears with no warning seemingly from all directions, he made a point of describing for her pictures of happy days at the hut where juicy berries ripened in the sunshine while she waited for the return of Sidney.

\* \* \* \* \*

A year rolled by, then another. Bertie presented indications of growing tall like his mother. Little by little, Fawn came to appreciate the ways of life in this strange world, even overcoming her dislike of automobiles to ride to town with Mother, where, amid the jostling people, she stared uneasily into store windows.

The fighting in Europe and the Pacific raged on. The war demanded vast quantities of food to feed soldiers and sailors, which resulted in the government paying high prices for every bushel of wheat or pound of butter the country's farmers could provide. As even the Breen farm began to turn a profit, Mother spoke with hope of the day when they could afford coal for the furnace and forego the backbreaking labor involved in cutting and splitting wood. Soon they could complete the delayed repairs to the granary roof as well as the porch screens that allowed every kind of insect into the house. But most of all, she wanted a new radio. The repair shop in Rolland no longer carried tubes that fit the old hand-me-down set. With a functioning radio, they could not only listen to *Stella Dallas* and *Fibber McGee* but also follow news of the war instead of relying on word of mouth and the newspaper from town that was often a week late. Each month when the statement from the bank appeared in the mailbox, Mother sat at the kitchen table after sharpening her yellow pencil with the paring knife, and following much figuring, announced in a buoyant voice how many dollars away from a new Philco they were.

\* \* \* \* \*

On a cold February evening with fresh snow on the ground, Mother sat down with her cup of hot water and the Nestlé tea bag, which by now had endured two soakings that day, to go through the mail that included the latest bank statement. She opened the envelope, unfolded the enclosed paper, then reached for her spectacles and studied it more closely. After a minute, she set her glasses down and massaged the bridge of her nose with her thumb and finger. Carefully, she returned the statement to the envelope and placed it with the other mail in the drawer under the bread box where they filed all the important documents along with Sidney's letters.

Later, Fawn heard her weeping in her bedroom. Dread came over her. Sidney must have been killed like so many thousands of others, including at least three from Rolland. She rapped on the door.

"Please," she said. "Is it Sidney?"

Mother wiped her eyes and looked up. "Oh, thank God, no. It's nothing like that."

Soon Fawn found out what had caused Mother's grief. Nearly a hundred dollars was missing from the bank account, three times as much as the cost of a radio, and there was no doubt where it went. Fawn comprehended at that instant what would never be admitted. As long as Foss was alive and present, nothing around the home would be tranquil and predictable.

Not long afterward, Fawn, still relieved that Sidney had come to no harm, was on her way outside to take clothes down from the line when a screech of distress sounded from the kitchen, where Bertie sat waiting for Mother to prepare his favorite afternoon snack—a crust of dry bread smeared with honey. Dropping the wicker basket, Fawn ran to the kitchen to find Bertie thrashing about in the old high chair while Mother stood over him holding a spoon in one hand and the back of the boy's neck in the other.

Behind them, Fawn spotted the open amber bottle and its cap resting by the sink. She could make out the words on the label, *COD-LIVER OIL*, but had no idea what that was. One morning out of curiosity she had opened the container and dabbed a bit of the dark, heavy liquid on her little finger and touched it to her tongue. Immediately, she spat it out. It was the worst-smelling, most awful, rotten fish-tasting thing she had ever encountered.

And now Mother was trying to force her grandson to swallow not just a small smear of the foul liquid, but a whole tablespoonful.

Red-faced and hysterical, Bertie looked to Fawn as if for help. But Mother was determined. Vising the back of Bertie's head into the crook of her elbow, she managed to pry his mouth open and slide the spoon as far back over his tongue as she could reach, producing an agonized, gargling cry of protest and a spray of greasy cod-liver oil over his shirt front as well as the sleeve of her own clean housedress.

"You must not of noticed," said Mother by way of explanation as she went for the dishrag. "He's been punky lately. Cod-liver oil. Full of vitamins." She held the bottle up proudly. "I brought both my boys up on it. Don't worry. He'll get used to it."

Fawn picked up her son and held him close, his face twisted in pitiful, childish agony, smelling on his breath the wretched, viscous liquid that she could not imagine anyone touching let alone swallowing. She glared at Mother, speechless. Never in her days and long months here had she spoken harshly to the woman. But now she began to see her in a new, alarming way. So welcoming at first, she must have come to hate Bertie as well as her. If only Sidney had never gone away.

After finally seeing her son partly pacified with his delayed snack, Fawn continued outside to collect the dry clothes. As she loosened a pillowcase from the line, she heard the close voice of Firegoat.

*One day Mother will try to kill Bertie.*

She folded the pillowcase over her chest. Could that be so? If it was, how could she protect him? Now that Bertie was a bit older, he was allowed to wander freely about the farmyard. A hundred times a day he was out of sight. He knew to stay away from the road, and with the help of Harlan Maas, their neighbor to the west, a heavy cover was installed over the well. But other dangers lay about. With a push, the boy could fall from the hayloft or drown in the slough.

She glanced about. A red-winged blackbird flew low over the marsh. A truck growled by on the road, throwing up rocks and gravel.

"What shall I do?" she said aloud.

As if they were conversing casually in the parlor, Firegoat's voice took on a refined quality, both convincing and sensible as he explained a plan.

Fawn must go to a certain corner of the pasture where grew a patch of deadly nightshade plants and gather a cupful of their leaves.

*Allow the leaves to dry before passing them through the meat grinder. Mix them with a like quantity of brown sugar.*

When ready, Firegoat continued, Fawn must stir the concoction into coffee or tea, both of which Mother drank in large quantities. After only two cups of the lethal mixture, she would grow weak and tired, and within an hour would be no more.

Fawn weighed the idea. Not only did it make sense, but a modification came to her. She would see that Foss also drank of the poison. She knew the plant well. Gathering it would be easy. She could fix the brew at night and serve it to Mother before the older woman went to bed. It would be easier with Foss, who always stayed up late drinking coffee, or whiskey when he had it.

All told, it would be less difficult than beheading a rooster for the stewpot—a task she performed practically weekly without the slightest regret.

Encouraged at every step by Firegoat, she had already gathered the leaves the next day when the news came, delivered first by Harold Peavey when he came by to pick up the cream and confirmed a day later in the newspaper.

The war was over.

# FIREGOAT WAS RIGHT

## 1 | Foss

On a fall Saturday a month after Sidney came home, thinner in his years away, he, along with his small family save Foss, drove to Rolland, where he and Fawn were married by the county judge. Sidney, whose old, moth-smelling suit hung on him like drapes, was forced to wear his uniform although no longer a soldier, while Fawn was fitted into a blue cotton dress stitched by Mother.

Gradually, Sidney took up the joys and responsibilities of his enlarged family. Delighted to find that Fawn had learned from his mother how to prepare the dishes that he loved like pork roast with baked apples, he was further pleased that his wife now read as well as himself, and that she had learned to write in a tiny but legible hand. While thrilled by his son, he worried that Fawn had been afflicted by what his mother said were *spells*, though he believed they would go away in time.

\* \* \* \* \*

Finding his brother Foss as irresponsible as ever, Sidney at first labored mostly unaided, reminded again how difficult it was to coax a living from the sandy ground with the worn-out, broken equipment that by then dated from the 1920s. Often rising during the busy summer as early as three in the morning, he ran the tractor until he could no longer see and dropped into bed deprived of supper. During his first full season home, hail ruined half the wheat crop and the cattle contracted a mysterious bovine malady and produced only thin, weedy-tasting milk. The family made it through the winter eating vegetables put up in Mason jars by Fawn and Mother following a growing season in which they saved the garden by hauling one bucket of water at a time from the well.

Still, the strength of youth helped the couple to absorb such trials. Before he'd boarded the immense troopship that carried him away, Sidney's worldview barely overshadowed that of Fawn's, who knew virtually nothing at all of an existence beyond what her eye took in. Back in the confines of the farm, he happily reverted to the provincialism of the hills that he'd been born to. If seed was left over from last year, why pay good money for a hybrid variety? What need had he of contour plowing if his father had come through the Depression bringing in crops grown in whatever rows were convenient?

Sid more than Fawn was astonished at the unlikely circumstances of their shared life—that he had found her living with Père like hermits, that he escaped unscathed through years of war, that they produced a thriving child. At night when time allowed, the two loved to sit on the porch watching the northern lights in their shades of yellow and green rising and falling like waves on the sea. Occasionally, and after much coaxing, Mother pulled from her trunk her ancient fiddle, warped and out of tune, and played "Turkey in the Straw." Then they'd drink coffee and eat pumpkin bread and talk of how things would get better. The drought would end, they'd buy a new John Deere, the cows would stay healthy. Soon Bertie would be big enough to help with the chores. In only a year or two he would start school, and by now, with his father leading, he was able to stay atop Alouette.

* * * * *

But evidence that Fawn had not been entirely assimilated soon surfaced. When Sidney called her by her name one evening, Fawn realized that her husband had something serious he wished to tell her. Nevertheless, when he reached around her and slid the pan of frying eggs off the burner, she playfully returned it to the heat. He nudged it to the side again and stepped back, his posture stiff and upright.

"I seen something," he began. "And I should of known from the first what could happen."

He was choosing his words too carefully. "Yes?" she said. The egg whites changed color and needed to be turned.

"You and Foss. How long's that been going on?"

She put the spatula down and thought carefully. "Going on?"

He took a fleeting look at the eggs and licked his lips. "That what's supposed to happen only with a man and a wife."

Fawn blinked in confusion. Sidney must be talking about earlier that day when Foss mated her as she swept the granary floor to gather chicken feed. She'd forgotten about it. "I was your wife at the hut?" she asked, confused.

"No, not yet, but you see, we were in love," said Sidney. "We cared about each other. Remember? We shared food and I helped you read your book."

Still, Fawn failed to grasp the meaning. She made summer sausage sandwiches for Foss and offered him water when he was thirsty just as she did for Sidney.

"I am your husband," said Sidney. "You must only do that with a man who is your husband. Don't you see?"

"Yes," she said, though she was far from convinced.

\* \* \* \* \*

Only a day afterward, when Foss entered the shed as Fawn poured fresh milk into the cream separator, she froze and shut her eyes, hoping he would go away. She listened as he fastened the hook on the door. The peculiar smell of soiled clothes and tobacco attached to the man was as familiar to her as the odor of the manure pile on a hot day. She concentrated on her task, aligning the vessels for skim and cream.

Breathing through his mouth and averting his eyes, Foss put a hand on her shoulder.

Fawn turned the crank and a thin stream of skim ran from the spigot.

"He's out in the field," said Foss, sliding his dirty fingers behind the bib of her coveralls.

The remark puzzled Fawn. Did Foss think she didn't know that? He opened her shirt to expose her breasts as he always did before mounting her. She backed away.

*He is your husband now,* came the owllike voice of Firegoat.

"Hurry up. Get your pants down," said Foss, pushing her back against the separator. He grabbed her breast, his callous hand scratchy on her tender skin. He entered her quickly.

"You are my husband now?" she asked when it was over.

"What?"

"My husband," she said insistently.

"Stupid bitch," said Foss, fastening his trousers.

With her long arm, Fawn reached behind her and pulled the separator crank from its socket. With no hesitation, she swung the heavy cast-iron object viciously, catching Foss squarely on his left ear.

Bending at the waist, he covered his ear with a hand, fixing Fawn with a look of hatred.

She raised the crank a second time. Foss stepped back. "You go back where you came from and take your brat with you or else." With that he straightened up and left the shed, his hand cupped over his ear.

After adjusting her clothing, Fawn cleaned and rinsed the separator, then hurried to the house to sort the eggs, keeping those cracked or undersized for the family's own use, her daily chore since her early days on the farm. But when she arrived, she found the sorting had been completed, with the market eggs packed into a cardboard carrier for Harold Peavey to take to town on his next stop. Mother must have completed the task.

Foss failed to appear for supper that evening. The meal was a quiet one, the only sounds following Mother's brief grace being that of forks striking plates and of the plates being pushed away on the oilcloth table covering. Only Bertie reached for a second helping of potatoes.

\* \* \* \* \*

That night in bed, Sidney lay on his back for a long time with his hands clasped over his belly. "I don't know what's happened, but he's gone," he said.

Fawn, nearly asleep, made no reply.

Sidney turned to the side. Soon he snored while an uncertain Fawn lay awake. She had displeased Sidney. At supper, Mother had looked at her with doubt, barely touching the food on her plate. Maybe Fawn herself should have gone instead of Foss. For once, she yearned for the voice of Firegoat to tell her what she should do.

\* \* \* \* \*

Months later, Mother received a cheerful postcard from Foss at Glacier Park boasting that he was employed by the railroad. Less than a week afterward, a letter came requesting her to send money for a ticket back, as he'd been laid off. Not long after that, Sidney heard in town that his brother was back in the country and tending bar at a tavern in Devils Lake.

The remaining family struggled through another winter. Sidney asked Fawn to take over kitchen duties so that Mother could help care for the livestock, including the two hogs they acquired from their neighbor Harlan Maas at a bargain price and the cheeping, yellow baby chicks they ordered every spring that were delivered to the post office in Rolland.

Although slowed by her age, Mother crawled under the porch to dislodge a raccoon that had taken up residence, and Sidney had to repeatedly intervene before she climbed the unstable ladder to the hayloft to pitch hay.

Still, her body fell short of her will. Her walk took on a brittleness, and at night she could barely hoist herself from the supper table, so exhausted was she. Sidney tried bringing in one of the Morinville boys to assist during busy times like calving or haying, but they were not much more help than Bertie, who was learning simple duties such as gathering eggs.

\* \* \* \* \*

On an August afternoon so warm and humid that the botflies barely buzzed, Fawn went to the barn as she did every afternoon to help Mother carry the burdensome pails of milk to the shed and found the woman flat on her back in a dirty stall, having fallen dead off a milk stool. Fawn thought at first that she had been kicked by the cow Suzy, who was known to be bad-tempered. But seeing no marks on her, Dr. Thwarp in Rolland said it looked like a stroke or maybe she just wore out.

Foss came home for the funeral from his latest job in East Grand Forks where he drove a bread truck part-time. He presented himself at the door wearing an ill-fitting suit but reasonably clean and sober—so much so that Sidney, knowing that running the farm would be even more challenging without their mother, struggled with the idea of inviting his brother to stay on awhile. He would decide after the funeral.

But Foss wasn't willing to wait for that, and he brought up the subject the first night home while assuming his mother's chair at the head of the table. Foss had long known that Sidney, as the older brother, would by custom inherit the farm, a matter that had forever been a source of simmering resentment for him, and now he made a proposal. He would offer his services in return for a half interest in the place.

Sidney coolly pointed out that the farm was barely of a size to support the family as it was. To divide it would be foolish. The best he could do, said Sidney, would be to offer Foss a position as a well-paid hired man until after harvest. If the harvest was good, the two would come up with a fair cash bonus.

Foss, a man who appeared more fearsome sober and calculating than when subject to the carefree jubilation induced by alcohol, pulled at his lower lip. "How much cash?"

Sidney stirred a lump of sugar into his coffee. "That depends on the crop." He mentioned a sum.

Foss wasn't impressed. "In case you forgot, I ran the place all by myself for more than two years when you were in the army."

"I remember. But it wasn't my choice, and as I get the picture, you weren't too reliable. Besides, you did have Ma to help some."

At that point, Fawn took Bertie straight to his bed, for her husband and brother-in-law were eyeing each other with hostility.

As she expected, male voices, raised frighteningly in anger, reached the bedroom far into the night. She awoke briefly when her husband slipped into bed and turned away, mute and restless. In the morning, she found the kitchen smelling of tobacco with dirty cups stacked on the table. She boiled coffee, recalling with pleasure how Mother arose earliest to set about giving the kitchen a cheerful warmth for those that followed.

Sidney came down, hoarse-voiced and bedraggled. Fawn handed him a coffee as he sat heavily in a chair.

"He's staying for a while," he said. "Then we'll see what happens."

* * * * *

In the weeks to come, Fawn fathomed more than ever that her husband had made a mistake in taking Foss back on whatever terms they had agreed on—if indeed any agreement at all had been reached. It wasn't that Foss reverted at once to his old habits; in fact, he disappeared but a single time, and that for two days. More upsetting was his ongoing manner—sullen, suspicious, furtive. She knew that a wolf or a wild dog behaved that way, silently hostile, ever alert for an advantage.

Foss, maybe reminded of the pain Fawn inflicted on him in the milk house, avoided touching her as before, but he had a way of passing in the hallway—twisting against the wall and following her with his eyes—that suggested he was about to tear at the buttons on her dress with his ragged fingernails. In his time away, his face had taken on a haunted, angry appearance that forced Fawn's astonishment that she ever saw a resemblance to the gentle Sidney. At night, he shuffled about on the creaking floor in his room, grumbling to himself or jangling the coat hangers as he rooted for something in the closet. His actions weren't meddling or rude—they likely served as an eerie reminder that Sidney and Fawn weren't alone. Ever aware of his menacing presence, they refrained from even normal conversation.

Amid the ongoing strife and tension, it occurred to Fawn that Firegoat had seemingly vanished. She'd become accustomed to the wavering bleat during times of trouble. Since coming to the farm, she'd linked Firegoat and Foss as one, the only difference being that Firegoat prowled out of sight, making him more frightening.

At least Bertie, with the instincts of a child, gave his uncle a wide berth. When in the presence of the boy's parents, Foss spoke to him in a feigned, too-sugary voice that barely elicited a response from Bertie and that was plainly not the one his uncle used when his mother and father were out of hearing range.

* * * * *

By summer's end, Sidney had grown ever more on edge as the wheat kernels lay full on their stalks, their weight nearly pulling them to the ground. They barely had a quarter of the crop in because of rain showers that came in the night rather than during the day when the sun and wind would dry the grain so it could be cut. It further upset him that Foss's wages led to an overdue bill at the feed store while Bertie ought to have new clothes to start school.

Following yet another rainy night, Sidney mentioned to Fawn that he intended to talk things over with Foss that afternoon while they replaced a bearing on the swather. Maybe Foss would agree to take a reduced payment in return for some other concession—although Fawn, who disliked numbers, avoided the headache-inducing thinking that all that demanded.

In late afternoon with rain clouds again gathering in the west, she hurried outside to take in the wash and heard men's raised voices from across the barnyard. Since this went on most every day, she gathered the clean clothes and returned to the kitchen.

She checked the clock over the door, noticing the single strand of a cobweb captured in a ray of the sun. It was past time to start supper. She set a pan of water on the burner and selected half a dozen potatoes that weren't too soft and sprouty from the bin. She grabbed the paring knife before deciding to boil slices with the peel on. They'd be good eating with plenty of butter—the men stumbling in so tired at the end of the day that they barely knew what they put in their mouths.

Footsteps thumped on the porch and the door flew open. It was Foss, wide-eyed and sweating. "You better come quick," he said. "Something's wrong with Sid."

Fawn had just lifted the saucepan from the burner. With steam condensing on her face, she looked about for a place to set it. Flustered, she rested it on the drainboard. She wiped her hands on her apron as she turned to face him, bracing herself for unhappy news.

"What is it—is he sick?"

"I don't know. He got hurt or something." She followed Foss across the barnyard, noticing flecks of dirt clinging to his hair, his shirt torn in the back. Hens skittered out of the way before stopping to resume their pecking at the dirt.

"Is Bertie with him?" she asked. Foss didn't answer. Seemingly in no rush now that he'd summoned aid, he plodded on with his odd side-to-side gait, walking like his mother.

Sidney lay on the rim of the stock tank wet down to the waist, one hand dangling in the water, the other resting on the cross brace. Foss blathered about finding him with his head under water.

"It must of been a heart attack maybe," he said.

Fawn knelt beside her husband. His eyes were half-lidded. His face looked clean and scrubbed, remarkable for having worked all day in the heat.

"Don't you think we need to do something with him?" asked Foss. "Jesus, look at him."

"We can do nothing," said Fawn. "Where's Bertie?"

"He's around here somewhere," said Foss unhelpfully.

Fawn called for her son but got no answer. With dread, she ran a long arm through the stock tank, probing the warm water that always smelled of algae this time of year. She ran back to the house, calling louder. She checked the garden and hurried to the paddock, where Foss stood gaping at his lifeless brother.

"Check the haymow," she said.

Foss blinked and looked at her but didn't move.

"Go!" she ordered, motioning to the barn.

At last, she found the boy huddled in the cool dim of the icehouse, wide-eyed, speechless and trembling like a baby robin. Fawn pulled him to her. "It's all right. Come to the house and we'll make some nectar."

## 2 | Bertie

When the rain ceased, a crew of men, consisting of Harlan Maas and others who farmed in the rocky hills nearby, took care of cutting and threshing the wheat crop. Then, with their silent, sad faces, they climbed into their battered pickups to return to their own fields. To no one's surprise, Foss vanished even before his brother's funeral.

At the church services—presided over by the same white-haired man that Fawn fled from at Bertie's thwarted baptism—Fawn stood with her son's teeny hand in her own, trying to avert her eyes from Sidney's gray coffin. One by one, women much older approached her awkwardly to shake her hand or reach up to give her a clumsy embrace while their own still-living husbands waited, trying to be inconspicuous.

Granted that she knew the intentions and necessity of this, what went through Fawn's mind while it played out was, of all things, tomatoes. At least three bushels awaited canning on the vine or in the windowsill.

These thoughts stayed with her on the ride back to the farm and throughout the afternoon while mourners who hadn't attended the funeral stopped by with angel food cakes, sandwiches, potato salad, cider and beer. Fawn sat anxiously at the table as Bertie clung to her thigh like a fishhook and people she didn't know swung cupboard doors wide searching for plates and glasses. The mood lightened. She heard laughter from the parlor as she imagined tomatoes turning a murky red, softening and spoiling.

Though she hadn't heard him, she concluded that Firegoat guided her next actions. Shaking Bertie loose, she stacked dirty plates and forks on the table to allow full use of the sink. The empty jars sat boxed on the pantry floor. She pulled the box out after waiting for Ida Florence Morinville to move so she could open the door. She required two burners to heat the bath, but the women had piled the stovetop with empty cake pans. As she moved the pans to the floor, she heard the voice. *Those women, see them whisper as they watch you from the corners of their eyes.*

But Fawn cared nothing about anyone else. The tomatoes needed canning.

Most of the women in the area who might have befriended Fawn—wives, eldest daughters, old maid aunts—had long avoided the Breen place. They all knew that the scarecrow-tall woman from up in the bush that young Sid Breen married often displayed fits of odd behavior. Daft was the word they used. And now, here before their eyes, she labored, wiping sweat from her desperate eyes and pink, featureless face. Her Sunday dress, stained and matted with tomato seeds, proved that they'd been wise to tend to their own business.

Steadily, they departed. Ladies gathered their cake pans, checking the name on the adhesive tape stuck to the bottoms, and caught the eyes of their sunburned husbands in the parlor. One by one, the men arose and came to the doorway, holding their straw hats in two hands.

But Fawn, in her concentration on her tomatoes, was unaware that the mourners had departed. She lifted a rack of full jars from the bath and couldn't find a place to put it because she'd set a box of empties on the drainboard. Balancing carefully, she stood on one leg and used her knee to move the box of empties to make room for the rack. Bertie said something, distracting her from a concentration so intense she was surprised he was present. The rack containing the jars of scalding tomatoes slipped from her hands to the floor in a startling crash. Shreds of superheated jars, steam, bits of searing vegetable and metal lids hot as branding irons went flying, settling on her stockings and soaking through to the skin.

She cried out in surprise more than pain, for it didn't hurt. What mattered was that food for winter was going to waste. She dropped to the floor, gathering bits of tomato, picking them from pieces of glass, blood and even seared flakes of her own hide. Yet she felt nothing.

Now Firegoat reappeared, whispering in her ear a message she would soon grow weary of. *Run from this unhappiness. Return to the hut where you once knew joy!*

\* \* \* \* \*

In days to come, strangers wove their way in and out of the bedroom like people checking a new gadget at Staggs Hardware in Rolland. An older man with a wrinkly, sunken face appeared. He wrapped her hands and feet in thick bandages that made it difficult to get into her clothes. She parted a curtain, thinking for a confused moment that she dwelled once more in the hut.

The first day up exhausted Fawn. She dragged herself from her bed and pulled on Sidney's overalls with their pockets still filled with rusty nails and pieces of string. Stepping carefully down to the kitchen, she set a pan of water on the stove for oatmeal and with which to make a cup of weak tea.

As she stood by willing the water to hurry and boil, Bertie came downstairs, rubbing his eyes. They made their way to the barn, where the cows clustered and awaiting milking. While Bertie tended to Alouette and the other animals, Fawn milked, resting her throbbing forehead on the flank of each cow. Instead of the two hours usually required for chores, the necessary duties dragged on until lunchtime and still tasks were left undone.

This became the pattern of their days as winter set in.

Some mornings, Fawn could not summon the will to move from her bed, turning to the wall with her knees drawn up, watching the shadows on the wall migrate down and across the room and disappear.

*There is food at the hut,* said Firegoat. *There is wood to keep you warm in winter. All day you can read from your book.*

\* \* \* \* \*

If his mother failed to appear by the time the bellering of the cows reached his ears, Bertie began the day on his own. He'd tagged after his father often enough that he knew how to take corn from the crib to feed the hogs. Scattering grain for the chickens had been his job for two years. His little hands, however, could not do much more than milk the cows enough to relieve their swollen udders. To get to the haymow, he climbed the worn ladder with its greasy rungs spaced so far apart he had to pull himself up by the strength of his slim arms. Once there, he would forego the long pitchfork in favor of dropping small armfuls of hay to the mangers below. Still, the cows were looking thinner, while the volume of milk they produced dropped to half of what it was.

\* \* \* \* \*

When Bertie told of seeing unfamiliar tracks in the snow near the barn, Fawn worried that the herd in its weakened state may have attracted predators. Sidney once spoke of slim winters during his boyhood when a pack of wild dogs migrated down from the higher Canadian hills to menace the countryside, preying on sheep and sick cattle. Since no such incidents occurred in Fawn's time, she hoped that the stories of red-eyed, fierce, wolflike animals were not true. As a precaution, she had Bertie hold a board while she nailed it over a hole adjoining the back stall in the barn.

*The goat shed is a safe place. Not even a weasel can get in.*

\* \* \* \* \*

A week before Thanksgiving, Fawn stood over the stove frying potatoes in grease from the salt pork they had dined on the evening before. Bertie entered the smoky kitchen and made a face. She knew he was tired of the same meal, but so was she. As a treat, she twisted the lid from the last jar of pickled onions, of which he alone had become so fond.

The next morning, she took a food inventory. The pantry contained a dozen jars of string beans, three or four of corn, the same of peas. The spare room held a hundred-pound bag of flour. She found barely less than a half bushel of spuds in the root cellar and two dozen jars of chokecherry jelly, a too-tart treat that only Sidney favored.

Like the livestock, she and Bertie became slimmer, and even at reduced consumption she could not see how the food could last the winter.

*You will starve even while full bags of pemmican and fat goats wait at the hut.*

In January, the pump in the milk house froze, forcing Fawn to chop a hole in the slough to water the animals. When the ax slipped from her hands into the hole, she was forced to step into the opening and plunge her already-numb fingers beneath the surface to retrieve it. By the time she completed the demanding task both feet were also frozen. For weeks, she found ugly patches of dead skin in her socks.

Worse came. When she opened the bag of flour, she discovered that mice had gotten into it, their black rice-sized turds flecking the contents like bugs in a pail of milk. She and Bertie sat under the gooseneck lamp trying to handpick the contaminants out, but the disgusting mess had to be thrown away. She then made a pitiful attempt at milling flour from wheat stored in the silo. Using the hammer and cutting board, she pounded kernels until her arm hurt but produced little more than a cupful peppered with husks before the board splintered.

Firegoat was right. They would starve.

During a black night, she awoke chilled. When her bare feet touched the floor, she knew the stove had gone out. The woodbox lay empty, but the ax was down by the slough. Remembering the tracks Bertie had spotted in the snow, she tried splitting a log with the insignificant hatchet, but it kept wedging in the frozen section of wood. She used a hammer to free it. She struck the wood again, and the hatchet stuck once more.

On the porch was a broken chair that Sidney had intended to fix. Fawn pried the hatchet from the log and attacked the chair. Now she had wood for a fire but lacked kindling. She found a dry branch by the front steps and carried it to the kitchen, where she began breaking it up by hand. One of the thin pieces of wood snapped and flew like a bird toward the sink and landed in an empty coffee cup. Fawn giggled. She tried it again with another twig. It went nowhere, but it was funny just the same. She laughed out loud. She found more bits of wood and tried to make them arc through the air, but they only fell to the floor like snips of yarn.

She stooped to retrieve them. The floor felt cold. That was sad. She burst into tears that turned into howling.

"Mommy, stop, please."

Bertie stood there, wide-eyed, wrapped in a blanket. Fawn tried to explain how funny the wood looked flying through the air like grasshoppers. Talking made her tired. She ordered her son back to bed and followed him up the narrow stairway. She grabbed the quilt and slipped into bed with him. It was still too cold to sleep.

*Remember the hut?* said Firegoat.

It is too far.

*No, it is behind the barn now.*

Fawn did not believe that, but she struggled out of bed to see for herself. She went downstairs and out onto the porch. She strained to see into the cheerless night. Nothing looked different.

*Keep going. It is there.*

She took a tentative step off the porch into the snow, then another. When she reached the fence bordering the yard and was still unable to see the hut, she hesitated. She looked back toward the house, unsure.

*You did not go far enough. Cross the fence.*

She raised her leg to clear the top wire, but the barbs hooked on to her coat. She tried burrowing underneath the snow like a fox. The elongated hole reminded her of a bed. She lay on her back, beholding the sky.

*It was a happy time at the hut. There were mushrooms and asparagus that you ate till you could eat no more. The sweet Juneberries were delicious. It was so warm in the hut. Go back to it. It is not far.*

Fawn knew she must rest first. She felt warmer. She pulled off her mittens so that she could unbutton her coat. Having no more use for the mittens, she threw them aside. Next, she untied her scarf and pulled it from her neck.

*The goats need you. They will give you their warm milk. They offer you their sweet flesh that you put in water and boil until it is soft like mushrooms between your teeth.*

She dipped her hand in the snow. It felt good on her parched lips. Above her, the stars blinked steadily through the blackness. She kicked off one of her boots.

*Père wants you to return. He has a fat rabbit for you to cook. Rabbit is good in the winter.*

"Mommy, get up."

"Not now. The rabbit."

She turned on her side to avoid the incessant tug on her arm. The snow against her cheek felt warm. The sky vanished.

Another form appeared, a man, drawn no doubt by the aroma of the rabbit cooking. Saying nothing, he wrapped his arms around her and pulled her backward through the snow. Her feet left a wavering trail. She tried to twist around to see the man, but his arms held her too tight.

It could only be one person.

"Père?" she said weakly. "I came back."

# TO HAVE A HUSBAND

## 1 | A Handful of Bones

Leah Peavey inherited one important lesson from her father—the determination to see a matter, trivial or critical, to completion. She could wring the neck of a rooster, pull its rusty plumage, sear the pinfeathers with burning newspaper, cut off the head and clean the carcass with no more thought than sneezing, and never mind the stink of the gizzards. Small, well-defined, intense responsibilities helped banish worry and cool the heat of the regretful thoughts that overcame her.

So when she spotted the black sedan with Sheriff Dale Aingher at the wheel pull into the yard and stop by the barn, she began pumping water into a pail to heat for a load of laundry, though she'd done a wash just the day before. By the time she gathered Richie Lee's fouled diapers, Aingher pulled away with her husband in the passenger seat, neither one caring a whit about letting her know what sort of doings was going on now.

For an instant, she did wonder if her husband had been arrested, and if so what for, and then about all the bother of getting into town to learn what came next. It seemed like some days she just cleaned up one mess after another. But as she watched, the car, rather than veering south back to Rolland, continued to the east. She went back to her wash, wishing the water would hurry up and get hot.

\* \* \* \* \*

She couldn't help but think of Harold as her opposite. Her blue eyes and fair skin stood up poorly to the summer sun while he turned brown as a Mexican. With no effort, he stayed slim and broad in the shoulders while she, especially after the baby, broadened all over, particularly through the hips. She liked to get out, visit with others. Harold contented himself with the livestock, sometimes speaking to his family no more than ten words a day. Even their ages set them apart, a twenty-year difference. Twin swaths of bare scalp were beginning to extend back to the top of his head while she couldn't yet cast a legal vote. Usually firm with people,

Harold exposed his softhearted side easily, barely able to part with calves in the fall while she saw in their soft eyes and useless tails not animals but money that would buy warm coats, fuel to power a vehicle to town, Pine-Sol to clean with and maybe, eventually, a telephone.

Shoot, if need be, she would drive them up the chute and into the cattle truck herself.

With one arm, she lifted the pail of water from the sink and set it loudly on the stovetop, stirred coals with the poker and crammed in a half dozen pieces of stove wood. She'd always marveled what it would be like to love a man, to have a husband. Now she had one, and so far it produced not much in the way of surprises. *Husband.* The word had a funny, final ring to it. Then so did *wife.* Sometimes she forgot, and it was like she awoke to find that she had become a ballet dancer.

Once, on a day when the rains chased him from the fields, Harold wandered in from the barn and found Leah upstairs in her old room scrubbing the floor. He knelt beside her, awkward as a man getting down from stilts, and put a hand on her breast. Usually their lovemaking took place on a Saturday night following the shopping trip in town. This was the middle of a workday. She liked that he could be unprompted if he tried, but she stopped him. She couldn't tell him that she could never have sex in this room. And that was the last time he tried except for the occasional Saturday nights, which now were about as frequent as blue moons.

Harold and the sheriff took ample time for their business. Leah listened for a car but heard only the squawk of a jaybird and the patternless clanging of the workmen erecting a steel grain bin at their neighbors, the Morinvilles. She poured Hilex full-strength from the jug into the diaper pail to rid it of the urine smell.

As she capped the jug, Richie Lee's screams from the bedroom interrupted her thoughts. She lifted the boy from the crib and pressed him to her shoulder, but still he cried. She felt the diaper. Nope, clean and dry. She offered the bottle of sugar water from the nightstand. He twisted away and screamed louder. She tapped his back and listened for a burp, sensing him working into another tantrum. He caught his breath and howled louder, each breath creating a piercing demand for she knew not what. When he relaxed slightly, she lowered him to the crib and left the room, only to return after five minutes when the cries rose anew. She leaned over the crib, seeing the boy's mouth open in a howl when he saw her.

"Stop," she said. "Please, I can't stand it! Be quiet!"

\* \* \* \* \*

After hearing Sheriff Aingher's brief explanation, Harold agreed to come with him, aware that the interruption would set him back. The days lacked adequate hours as they were, especially with the weather warming. And to think he'd insisted to Leah that if they went ahead and bought a milking machine and hay baler, he'd find plenty of time for other chores.

He stood with Aingher two miles away at the top of the south bank of Leonard Creek, nearly dry after a downstream farmer took it upon himself to knock down a beaver dam. According to the sheriff, the previous afternoon, three boys searching for arrowheads along the wash noticed what looked like a large black cylinder thrust up out of the creek bed. The stream now contained but a trickle of water following the failure of the earthen dam downstream, a victim of spring floods. The boys crawled down the embankment and realized that the pipe was actually the stack of a steam locomotive that rested still upright on its wheels. Trains were a source of wonder for boys, and the realization that this huge machine lay unguarded before them heated their curiosity.

After the boys clambered to the bottom, however, their excitement turned to horror. As they drew closer, what looked like an assortment of rags dangling by a rope and partially shielded by the stack took the form of a corpse. They ran for their bicycles and pedaled home, where one of their mothers phoned the sheriff.

The sheriff, assuming the bones were from an animal, intended to send his deputy, Stan Stankowski, out to investigate. But something in his lawman's logic made him reconsider. The area of the creek described by the boys lay near the Peavey and Morinville farms where two years earlier a homicide may have taken place. With Leah Peavey's father, the likely murderer, dead and his supposed victim, Freddy Morinville, missing and possibly also dead, it seemed a good idea to look into it himself. With Harold Peavey related to or at least knowing everyone involved, it made sense to call on him for help.

Now Harold stared at the muddy creek water, trying to get past his foolish hope that the gloomy event lay forever in the past.

"It's a steam locomotive all right," said Harold quietly. "Omar Tuttle told me it was here. I never believed him."

The sheriff started down the bank, but his boot caught in the scree and he fell backward, catching himself with his elbows. He got up and made it to the bottom by planting the sides of his boots in the rocks and taking measured steps. Harold followed in the same tracks.

When they had made their way through the mud-filled depression to the other side of the rusting, derelict locomotive, they saw what the boys had seen.

And as they'd reported, it did appear as not much more than a collection of rags. The bundle had snagged on one of the drive wheels. A rope attached to it was blackened and losing its braid from submersion in the water. Harold leaned closer.

"Better not touch it," warned Aingher.

Harold waited while the sheriff messed around with his new camera, trying to photograph the scene.

"I'll radio in to get the hearse sent up," said the sheriff.

"Are you of a mind that it's him?" asked Harold.

The sheriff let the question go unanswered.

"It would be good for Leah to have the rumors settled," added Harold.

"It'll take more than a handful of bones to settle this," replied Aingher.

The sheriff was avoiding the heart of the matter. "Can you say straight what direction you're goin' on this? I got to tell Leah something."

Aingher cleared his throat. "It's understandable that she wants to believe that her dad had nothing to do with it, Harold, but everything we know about it points to him."

During the brief ride back to the farm, Harold mulled over what he would say to Leah. He knew it would be the truth but knew also that the truth can take varied forms.

\* \* \* \* \*

Leah waited on the steps with the boy at her feet, watching the sedan pull into the yard. She looked at Sheriff Aingher, and he nodded a greeting. He was not an attractive man. His head narrowed at the top and widened toward his chin like an upside-down flowerpot. His top teeth didn't quite meet. He was married to Harold's old girlfriend, Marlys. A wild notion came over Leah. What if Aingher were to drop over dead or get killed in the line of duty? Being a lawman was a dangerous occupation. The deputy over in Bottineau got hit by a car he tried to flag down. Would Marlys try to get Harold back if she lost her husband? She studied the tan collar encircling his bull neck. She wondered, did Marlys iron his shirts? No, undoubtedly, she dropped them off at Kaleva's dry cleaner and the county got the bill.

"What'd he want?" she asked, searching Harold's face.

He reached for the boy, who twisted away and locked his small arms around his mother's leg. "I shouldn't say too much," he said.

"To your own wife?" Leah scooted over and patted the step with her hand, ordering her husband to sit. He did so, no doubt troubling himself about why it was that with a porch swing six feet away, they always had to do their conversing on the splintery step.

"Well, it looks like they might have found Freddy Morinville," he said quietly.

"Freddy?" she said, trying to absorb the news. "They did? Where was he?"

"No, no. Don't mistake what I say. They *maybe* found him or his body."

"Oh," said Leah. "He *is* dead then."

Harold wrung his calloused hands. "Not for certain. The body'd been in the creek a long time."

"Drowned?"

"Possibly. No one can say for sure yet."

Her husband's deliberateness exasperated Leah. So eager was he to save her from hurtful things or matters that didn't concern her that his powers of reasoning were as distant to her as the Great Wall of China. "When they do, it better put an end to it," she said.

Harold was still trying to coax the baby to come to him. "I don't know. It didn't sound like it," he said.

"It didn't sound like it? Well, then what did it sound like?" Leah knew that, like her husband, she was being evasive, unusual for her. Yet she couldn't bring herself to address directly the issue of whether this would determine finally whether her father was responsible for whatever happened to Freddy.

"I don't know. I wish I could say. These things take time," said Harold.

He was trying to find an easy way to end the conversation. He had stalls to clean before supper.

But that wasn't the end of it for Leah. "What did Aingher want with you along? He knows this country."

"I got no answer to that either," said Harold, growing more uncomfortable.

"Then I'll tell you why. He already decided it was Freddy, and 'cuz from the first he thought Daddy was responsible, he didn't want to be the one to tell me."

"We don't know that," said Harold.

"Well, just say I'm right. What would you have said?"

Harold was picturing the arrangement of the cows' stalls. He needed to separate Jupiter and Pluto.

"Huh? Oh, I don't know. Maybe I could tell him that I don't see reason not to let sleeping dogs lay."

"Why would you say that? You know I been wanting him to look into it more."

"That's not what I meant," said Harold, struggling.

"Well, what did you mean?" asked Leah, the color rising in her cheeks. In this early period of their marriage, husband and wife hadn't mastered the easy, almost wordless communication that comes eventually to most couples.

"I never told him in those words. I just think it would be smart to get past all that."

"Smart?" Leah threw the word back at her husband. "Where's the smart in letting people think we accept some kind of guilt?"

Harold knew he was in it now. This is what happened when a person spoke too quick. "Oh, people forget. I know that after what happened to me during the war."

The boy crawled to a patch of grass, yanked a dandelion from the ground and bit down with his baby teeth. Upset by the unexpected taste, he burst into sobs. Leah knelt beside him, wiping the yellow particles from his wet mouth with the sleeve of her blouse.

"Harold," she said when the boy quit crying. "That's not the same at all. What you did by refusing to go in the army came from a long process of decision-making. Everybody around knows you did it and you paid the price. Here, everybody thinks Daddy did away with Freddy, but no one's proved it."

"One way or the other we ought to let Dale do his job," said Harold, in agony now that the confrontation flared out of control.

"Do his job?" Leah's face formed contempt. "The only way he'll ever find out is if somebody comes in and confesses. He never even bothered to investigate the Ables. He knows very well they hate Indians. Freddy was a Morinville."

"Now be fair," said Harold. "You know he talked to all of us. He spent most of a day just with you."

"All he wanted to know from me was the part about what Daddy was making me do," said Leah, her voice rising. "Know how many questions he asked me after he found that out? None! He just shook his head and said that a man that would do that to his daughter had the makings of a murderer."

The boy resumed his fussing. "I got to feed him," said Leah, turning away.

Harold stood and rubbed his sore leg where a calf had kicked him. He'd been sitting too long. He looked at his young wife with her stained apron and frazzled look, deliberating whether she would remain ever a stranger to him, as would the suitable yet ugly words that were as much a part of their family as barn cats. *Evidence. Reputation. Body. Abuse. Murder.* He limped out to his sanctuary in the barn, feeling his wife's obstinate eyes tracking him all the way across the barnyard.

* * * * *

The sheriff requested that Doc Thwarp do an autopsy—the first in the county since before the war. After extracting thirty pieces of lead shot from the chest cavity, the physician reported that the victim had been approximately twenty years of age and in good health at the time of death. Then the sheriff's men dredged up a shoe that Ida Florence Morinville said belonged to her son, Freddy.

After it was clear that no more evidence existed at the site, the authorities asked that the locomotive be taken away—as if its presence might lead to more such horrible incidents, though it had been there, forgotten, for at least forty years.

The railroad refused, claiming the rusting hulk didn't belong to them but to their insurer.

As for the lead shot, the sheriff declared that while it proved that a homicide had been committed, unlike bullets, lead pellets were untraceable. Therefore, the investigation was ongoing.

## 2 | The Advice of a Drunk

The cottonwoods leafed out. The child began saying a few words. Spring passed, and haying season arrived. The milk was down but that was normal in the heat. Around the Peavey household, the topic of Freddy Morinville didn't come up, tabled by a mutual wish to preserve peace.

In August, Leah's uncle Orville died suddenly and the family made the half-hour drive into Rolland to attend the funeral and to comfort his widow Dolores, an eccentric woman whom Leah had become close with during the troublesome times of her father's death.

As Richie Lee slept in the bedroom, Dolores served Leah and her husband gin and lemonade in a large glass with a wedge of lemon floating in each drink, remarking that yes, it was ten in the morning, but the occasion, not to mention the heat, demanded it. Harold glanced dubiously at his frosty glass and set it on the end table beside his chair. Leah sipped hers. She liked the taste and took a large swallow, feeling it burn all the way down.

Common knowledge—as well as condemnation—around Rolland held that Uncle Orville had left Dolores not long after they were married to take up with a former girlfriend, an incident that Dolores now recounted with glee.

"Orv must have kept his baloney pony pretty well-hid from her in their younger days," said Dolores, her cigarette-ravaged vocal cords giving her voice the timbre of a mountain lion. She grinned and held the thumb and finger of her right hand an inch and a half apart so that only Leah could see.

Dolores remained a striking woman with long gray hair that arched daringly over her ears and a figure that resisted any matronly tendency. In her presence, Leah felt diminished, seeing her glide around the room on her high heels, not spilling a drop from the drink in her slim hand.

Dolores turned her head toward Harold, noticing that he neglected his drink. "Bottoms up there," she commanded. "We need good cheer to send Orville off. God knows he displayed damned little of it when he was alive."

At first, maybe because she began to feel the effects of her drink, Leah considered the remarks about Orville amusing. She turned her attention to her husband, stern and unsmiling as he obediently lifted his glass, which was sweating and sure to make rings on Dolores's varnished end table. Leah knew he would think such comments less than funny—if he thought about them at all. Most likely what occupied his mind was all the work waiting for him while he wasted his time in the musty living room of a wacky woman trying to get him drunk at ten o'clock in the morning.

Leah jiggled the ice in her glass the way Dolores did and took another swallow, her eyes remaining on Harold. He looked like he was aging even as he sat there motionless as a hat rack. In not much time he really would get old. He'd turn forty before Richie Lee started school. How outlandish. During Leah's childhood, Harold, with his candy, fruit and town gossip, had represented to her all that was wonderful about the vast, unreachable world outside the hills and woods of the farm. She imagined that if she were attached to a someone like him—like a baby kangaroo riding around in her mother's pouch—she would gain an entry into that world. Why, she could find modern places, leave the hills forever.

And then it happened. She got in the pouch all right, but the kangaroo went nowhere.

If only she could be like Dolores. Here was a woman still turning men's heads at her age—if stories about her next-door neighbor, a retired navy captain or something, were true. Leah knew that gossip about Dolores often originated with the woman herself, but there was no denying that she knew how to embrace life.

Richie Lee awoke with a sharp cry, and Harold took the opportunity to leap from his chair to attend to him, stranding his fancy lemon concoction on the end table. Dolores watched him as he headed for the bedroom. "Just because you love 'em doesn't mean you want to spend your life with 'em," she said, a remark she failed to elaborate on. But the party must end anyway; it was time to get changed for the funeral.

Leah had brought her good dress, though it was never her favorite. Dark blue with a pleated skirt and Peter Pan collar, it had short sleeves that revealed the drooping flesh on her arms. It looked to her like an outfit whose designer must have had funerals in mind. In fact, she had worn it when they buried Daddy and then again for her wedding, which had taken place a few months later. Odd how the two events were mixed in her mind.

Not that her wedding had been sad, just small. Considering the situation, they thought it best to have the justice of the peace preside. They were still living in town then, Leah and the baby at Mrs. Mundy's boardinghouse and Harold at his old apartment over Dr. Thwarp's office. Four days before the wedding, Dolores came over smelling of booze and shrieked at Leah not to do it—keep the baby or give it to a nice family, but don't by any means get saddled with some broken-down bachelor who'd sit in the shade spitting tobacco and drinking dandelion wine while she fried potatoes and hogback. Leah listened closely, but Dolores's words were slurred, and she knew it was not wise to take seriously the advice of a drunk.

The modest ceremony nearly didn't take place for want of officials. Uncle Orville had insisted on giving away the bride, which left no one to serve as best man. Various clerks and secretaries searched through the courthouse until they found the only man available, Sheriff Aingher, who was about to take the afternoon off to go duck hunting. Aingher generously agreed to stand up but ambled over from his office absentmindedly carrying his shotgun at his side, giving everyone a good-natured chuckle. The occasion was delayed one last time while the justice excused himself to fetch his reading glasses from his office. Finally, with Harold afraid his new tie was about to strangle him and Leah hoping the pool of sweat between her shoulder blades wouldn't show, they exchanged vows.

After the ceremony, Orville treated the party to steaks at the North Forty Café. Leah and Harold then drove over the border to Killarney, Manitoba, for an overnight honeymoon. And that was that. Young Leah Tuttle existed no more. That life was gone, as dead as President Roosevelt.

* * * * *

As Leah fastened her collar, Dolores burst into the bathroom. "Sorry, gotta pee," she cried as she hiked up her dress and squatted over the toilet. Leah wanted to escape the cramped room, but if she opened the door, Dolores would be exposed to the whole world walking by. Dolores sat just a second before she grimaced, and with a series of grunts and satisfied sighs, released her bladder. She pulled a yard-long length of toilet paper from the roll, wiped herself and flushed. As she shimmied around to straighten her slip, she grinned at Leah.

"Why, sweetheart," she said. "Look at you. You're a striking young lady."

Leah studied herself in the mirror, sharply aware of the fact that Dolores had been present for all three wearings of the dress. "I got my mother's build," she said.

"But look at your eyes and your complexion," said Dolores, touching her cheek. "So delicate."

"I heard it said that what's inside is most important, but I'd trade it for more of the stuff that everybody sees," said Leah, warmed by the compliment.

"Oh, but you don't need it," said Dolores. "Stand still and hand me that hairbrush."

Leah wore her hair up in a tiered bun the way her mother had taught her when she was ten years old. She stared silently in the mirror as Dolores pulled the pins out one by one and held them in her teeth. She closed her eyes as Dolores drew the brush gently through the long, dark blonde hair, training it to rest comfortably on her shoulders. Her head and scalp felt lighter, freer. She couldn't keep herself from running her fingers over it.

"Stop messing with it," commanded Dolores, her voice distorted from the hairpins squeezed between her lips. "If I could have had your hair when I was your age," she muttered.

"Now for the skin." She reached under the sink for her makeup kit, turned it over and dumped the contents on the counter. "Let's start with a base," she said, reaching for a white jar.

Whatever it was felt good and cool, like cream whipped until it's on the verge of becoming butter. Dolores gently rubbed it in, her soft, practiced fingertips sparking a tingling sensation that drifted down Leah's shoulders toward her own hands. She stood in silent appreciation as her pale, dry complexion with its minute freckles was transformed into luminescent porcelain.

"Don't you use lipstick?"

"I never got the habit. Out on the farm there wasn't anybody to put it on for."

"Well, that's all the more reason," said Dolores. "It's part of how a woman thinks of herself. You look in the mirror and see good looks and you'll go all through the day playing on those good looks. This shade ought to go nice on you. Here, pooch your lips out like this." She made an improbable sour expression that stretched over her face. "There," she said. "Now rub them together. Yes, that's right. Now let's see. How about the cheeks."

"Sometimes I put some of Mother's old rouge on," said Leah.

"Rouge?" said Dolores in mock horror. "Good god, the war's over. We don't use rouge anymore."

Harold's voice from the hallway interrupted them. "Leah? It's just about eleven."

Dolores answered. "In a minute, hon, Orville's not in any hurry." She returned to her task, applying a lighter shade of base, giving the skin a faint shadow in the hollow below the cheekbones. Next, she penciled on eyeliner that brought out the too-faint eyebrows. Finally, the mascara. She stood back, rubbing her hands on a washcloth.

Leah studied the mirror. If she looked hard, she could see her own familiar round face and determined eyes trying to find their way through, but still, her face lacked Dolores's character. The makeup could not produce lines of maturity and confidence that to her represented loveliness. With a thumb and finger she bunched the skin to form an experimental wrinkle over an eyebrow.

Dolores nudged her to the doorway. "Don't go ruining it before your husband sees you."

They shared a ride to the tall, white-sided Lutheran church next to the Ford garage. When Dolores sauntered in, wearing not a stitch of black, Leah couldn't help but notice every eye of the mourners was fixed on her. Whispers among the attendees, if not the whole town, centered on exactly how the inexperienced widow would handle the humiliating situation wherein her late husband had taken up housekeeping with another. But rather than admitting to humiliation, Dolores reveled in the attention, nodding pleasantly to Orville's girlfriend Rosarita, who sat unaccompanied in the back row, a veil over her face.

Casting her eyes toward the altar where Orville's bronze casket rested, Leah was reminded of when her father died. Omar hadn't been a churchgoer, and the service was held at the funeral home. Before it began, the director told Leah that it would be prudent to keep the casket sealed as the deceased wasn't presentable. "He doesn't look like himself," he'd explained, shaking his head.

Leah said that she wanted to see him one more time no matter who he looked like. Mr. Murray smiled sympathetically and tried to talk her out of it. She insisted.

The viewing room had long drapes and deep organ music that sounded like it rolled down straight from the heavens—except for the hollow gaps caused by the record changing. Murray twisted some screws, raised the lid and backed away, his arms behind him.

The hands looked like Daddy's except for the fingernails, which had been clipped and cleaned of their grease. The brown wool suit, awful hot for summer wear, was one Leah had never laid eyes on. The breast pocket held a clean hankie folded in with a point up, and a patterned tie was knotted in a smart style that Daddy could never have managed on his own. All was well except that a piece of cheesecloth lay over the face so that she couldn't make out details, just a profile. She held her breath and pulled the cloth away, sensing Mr. Murray in a dither.

The face really wasn't that bad, not like when you see an animal run over on the road. It looked like one big green-and-blue bruise with just a trace of rustiness around the nose and lips. One eyelid was slightly open, revealing a blur of indistinct skin like a cat's third eyelid. Satisfied that it was her father, she leaned closer over the face. Staring into the slit of the partially open eye, she ran her tongue around her mouth and upper teeth, gathering saliva. She pursed her lips as if practicing a kiss, then, having accumulated a sufficient quantity, she drew a full breath. *Ptuh!* was the sound she made as she delivered the full load of spit directly to the middle of the face of the corpse.

Of the service itself she had no memory.

\* \* \* \* \*

On the way home after Orville's funeral, Richie Lee slept in the back seat while Harold drove. Usually in the car they sat like every other married couple, silence prevailing. The gap separating them seemed as uncrossable as the south pasture after a hard rain. Heading home with the afternoon sun hot on their faces, Leah slid six inches toward her husband and let her head fall back on the seat. And when they got home at last, they went directly to bed. Before the familiarity of the farm submerged them and as Richie Lee fussed his way into agitated sleep, they tried, without enthusiasm, to make love.

After a compulsory five minutes, Harold sat up and pulled on his pants. Milking time was past due. Leah lay there for a dreamy moment, hoping to take flight in her mind while enjoying the comfort of the bed, but all she could conjure up was the image of the lid of a gray coffin being lowered over her father while, in her imagination, she thrust an arm out to hold it open. Could it be too late for that?

She swung her feet to the floor and reached for her housedress. Time to start supper.

# SOMETHING TO EAT

## 1 | How to Fix Things

Young Albert Breen reached home near sunset, carrying his gun to scare off the wild dogs as usual. He'd been to Dark Lake to try to hook a Northern big enough to fry for his mother in hopes she might eat it instead of nibbling on Nabiscos. Even before last winter when she came close to freezing in the snow, she mostly stayed in bed. When she came downstairs, she spent her time in her dirty housedress staring through the kitchen window at the road, her long arms, skinny as fishing poles, resting on her lap, saying not a word.

As he approached the barn, Bertie noticed light shining from the kitchen window—a good sign. His mother must be awake. Maybe a visitor had stopped in, a rare occurrence. Better yet, perhaps someone came to help with the farm work even though his mother kept saying they had no money to pay a hired man. No matter. Bertie would be happy to see practically anyone—anyone except his Uncle Foss.

At only seven years of age, Bertie knew he faced a great responsibility. At his father's funeral, Harold Peavey, who had been his dad's friend, knelt and put his hands on Bertie's shoulders. *You are the man of the house now,* he told him. Bertie understood. Soon he took on the chores—milking, hauling water, feeding the animals, including Alouette, his dad's horse which was his now. If only he knew how to harvest the barley or fix things like the barn door or windmill pump.

He set the rifle against the wall and opened the door. There before the cookstove stood his mother stirring a pot. He looked around, scarcely able to believe what he saw—a floor swept clean, his mother wearing her Sunday dress. Even from a distance, he smelled the soap in her hair. In a peach crate next to the stove, something stirred. His mother turned to him and smiled.

"Bertie," she said. "You got a baby sister."

\* \* \* \* \*

At his age, Bertie never pondered matters such as the origin of babies. He accepted that one day they happened along, crying and hungry, just as he himself must have. With the passage of time and his deepening love for her, Bertie nearly forgot that this jug-eared, squirming baby girl was not his true sister. For now, at least, it mattered not a bit, for he couldn't miss the connection between little Vickie's arrival and the changes in his mother. No longer keeping to her bed till midmorning, she now woke up with the baby. She helped Bertie with the milking. She carried the heavy slop pail to feed the hogs. She gathered berries and roots from the woods, the baby slung across her chest in a blanket she tied around her neck.

Once a week, as regular as the calendar, the family of three awoke to find a flour sack strung high on the porch door out of reach of the raccoons. The contents of the bag varied—honey, coarse-ground meal, a few potatoes. Once it held a ham bone and a double handful of dried peas that Bertie's mother cooked into a delicious soup. Bertie had no idea where these items came from, nor perhaps did his mother. But food, any food, fell into welcome hands with winter bearing down.

## 2 | No Trespassing

Earlier on the day of the baby's arrival at the Breens, Harold Peavey had looked up from the fence he was repairing to see a team of horses sluggishly pulling a homemade wagon with rubber tires. The wagon held two people, one driving the horses, the other holding a small cloth bundle. Harold placed his wire cutters on a post and called to the house for Leah to come out. Though he didn't recognize the adolescent couple, he conjectured that they were Ables, one of the few remaining families still known to make do with a horse and wagon. He pulled his gloves off and walked out to meet the rig, smelling the mix of sweat and leather that attended all horses and their tack. He bobbed his head in greeting just as Leah emerged from the porch. "Hello there," she said politely.

The two gaped at her. The young man, long-necked and wearing muddy overalls at least two sizes too big, nudged the girl with his elbow.

"This here's a baby but she's asleep now," said the girl.

"I see," said Leah, trying to get a closer look. "She's a pretty baby. Would you like to come in the house? I can make some ginger tea."

The girl, expressionless as a tomcat, looked away. One of the horses nickered. Leah waited for her husband to speak, but he had more interest in the horses. "What might we do for you?" she asked.

The girl turned toward the boy, maybe waiting for instructions, but received none, and blurted out in one long, practiced breath, "You take this baby to keep.

It's a girl named Victoria, but you can call her different if you want. We got no room for a baby down to our place."

The baby came awake, its icy blue eyes trying to focus as the girl leaned down, offering it to Leah.

"You want us to keep your baby?" said Leah, drawing back.

"She don't cry much," said the girl. "She's a good baby."

"But we can't do such a thing," said Leah, disbelieving. "We have a little one of our own."

"You got just one baby?"

"Well, yes."

The girl gazed toward the house. "Then you got lots of room."

Leah tried to catch her husband's eye. As usual in a domestic concern, he offered no help. "Listen here. If that baby needs a home you got to find a way to get it down to Fargo. That's where the people are that look after these things. You're liable to get in trouble otherwise."

The girl ogled her, a witless expression on her immature face.

The baby squirmed and Leah resisted the instinct to reach for it. "Right now, you best go home and get her fed."

"We ain't supposed to bring it back," said the girl.

Leah ignored the excuse. "What you do is get hold of the county nurse in Rolland. She can put you in touch with people to help."

The girl offered the baby again, but Leah folded her arms and backed away.

"Do you get what I'm saying?" asked Leah. "You want to contact Luba Groman."

Harold, noting the roundish faces and prominent ears on the couple, said quietly, "You young folks, you're Able kids, aren't you?"

The boy eyed Harold suspiciously, but remained mute.

The girl gathered the blanket in around the baby's face, murmured something to the boy, then brushed her tangled hair from her eyes. The boy, called to action, flicked the reins in a practiced manner. The well-trained horses completed a wide turn in the yard and followed the road out past the switchgrass, the occupants of the wagon sitting as erect and unmoving as two ten-gallon cream cans.

Harold and Leah watched them in amazement until they reached the main road.

"I heard about that happening in the thirties," said Harold. "Folks who couldn't feed the kids they had getting someone else to raise them."

"Shouldn't we do something? Contact somebody?" asked Leah. "What will happen to the baby?"

"Somebody will take it," said Harold. "Anyway, if they are Ables, I don't believe we want to get mixed up." He wiggled his fingers into his gloves. He had a hundred feet of fence left to check before supper.

\* \* \* \* \*

The boy driving the buckboard soon tired of all this. He wanted to go home and hunt gophers. But the girl, thirteen years old and destined to live but another year before being fatally stricken with polio, demanded he keep on driving. Early that morning, she'd been taken aside by her one-armed grandfather, who pointed his hand toward the barn. "Jake's got the team hitched up," he said. "You go where you need to, but when you get back, don't have no baby with you."

The place the girl feared returning to was, as Harold deduced, the home of the Able clan. Even if few outsiders had ever set foot on the property, many in the area knew its location. Area newcomers, traveling salesmen and duck hunters soon ascertained the need to keep a distance. But in fact, even accidental intruders hesitated to go near, discouraged by the muddy lane, arched over by poplar and berry bushes and featuring at each turn a series of increasingly larger signs warning *No Trespassing!* composed in runny red paint. In the event anyone failed to take warnings seriously, he or she came shortly to a plank resting across the road with long spikes driven point up into the wood.

Those rare individuals acquainted with the Able property described it as a grassless junkyard of decaying vehicles, a broken windmill, a temperamental generator and an automobile hoist. Strangely, various items of questionable use to the clan had found their way there as well, such as an X-ray machine, a complete set of accounting textbooks still in their original packages and, locked away in the dusty heart of the North American continent, a pair of lobster pots.

The *gang* or family—consisted of a dozen or so related members plus a variety of hangers-on and drop-ins that occupied three flimsy trailer houses and outbuildings set up in the vicinity of the main house. On their forty partly wooded acres, the family raised barley and root vegetables, shot game in season and out, scavenged when the opportunity arose, borrowed what they could and stole the rest. Following every instance in northern Chippewa County of a hog reported missing, a tank of gas siphoned or a gate left open, guilt was automatically assigned to the Ables. Even after evidence suggested the correctness of the accusation, an arrest rarely resulted. Other residents in the vicinity, exasperated with this failure of justice, spread rumors that Sheriff Dale Aingher was somehow involved with the gang. Neighbors even speculated to one another in whispers over fences whether the Ables had something to do with the disappearance of young Freddy Morinville, who had vanished without a trace following a dispute with Leah Peavey's father.

According to legend, Magnus Able, the family patriarch and a man still robust in his seventies, had once, while running whiskey down from Manitoba during Prohibition, shot out the windshield of a car of armed revenue agents hot on his tail. His booze-smuggling career ended later in a spectacular accident when his own vehicle, its headlights off, collided with a hayrack just north of the border, severing his left arm and the thumb of his right hand. After that he became known, at least in myth, as "Four-Finger Maggie." For two or more generations, children growing up throughout the hills were warned to behave or Four-Finger Maggie would get them.

In the years immediately after World War II, the relative prosperity that descended on the countryside missed the Ables entirely. Like their neighbors the Tuttles, the acreage belonging to the Ables proved inadequate for modern farming techniques. At the same time, deer populations declined, cutworms invaded vegetable gardens and feed prices climbed sky-high. By 1949, when drought devastated the hay crop, the family faced the need to sell all its livestock except for the team of horses. Late that summer, hail destroyed what was left of the garden while rust ruined the barley. And when one of the overweight granddaughters of Four-Finger Maggie surprised everyone with a baby, delivered fittingly or not in a manger, it represented one mouth too many.

And so, the sad little wagon rolled on west, away from the Peaveys. From there, the twosome with the unwanted child tried the Gosches—after skipping the Morinvilles, who were Indian and no fit home for a white baby—then rode on to the Michaelsons and Lawstons, following the road west up into the hills. At each dusty farm, the girl offered the baby, and at each, she silently endured rejection by families who shook their heads in distress and stared at the departing wagon while the inexpert, too-young mother rubbed honey from a rag on the baby's lips to keep her from fussing.

## 3 | We Will Manage

Even with occasional handouts from friends as well as anonymous donors, the Breen family, having endured the loss of its husband and father, suffered mightily as the months passed. With the arrival of colder weather, Fawn feared not only the austerity of winter but the return of the recurring illness that stole her powers of reason and her sense of reality, sending her to bed with headaches and hideous visions centered on a familiar apparition.

Yet there existed a non-phantom that she dreaded as much as Firegoat—her former brother-in-law, Foss Breen, who had not been seen since the death of her husband. For the sake of her family, especially little Bertie, Fawn hoped she might never see the man again, but not long before the first snowstorm of winter, a bang on the door sounded. Fawn went to it.

"How are you, Fawn?"

She blinked. "What do you want?"

"Looks like you could use some help around here," said Foss, his eyes falling on the muddy yard spotted with manure left by cows seizing the advantage of an ineffective fence. He went on to explain that he'd heard they had a new baby, and with Sid gone and freeze-up on the way, times might get tough. As it turned out, he'd been after a place to live for a while. Between jobs, as he put it. How about if she took him on as hired man for the winter?

Fawn's despair and fear flared as always when Foss lurched into sight, leering and digging into his ear with a dirty finger. She rested her hands on her hips, rocking back on her heels. She had to think. The smell of baking bread beckoned her to the oven.

Foss stood there on the step, a weathered version of his brother but clean-shaven and apparently sober. Fawn had two children to keep fed, one still in diapers. Poor little Bertie worked with the vigor of a grown man when he should be enjoying his childhood. Plenty of cause for concern that since his father died, he barely spoke and smiled only in the presence of the baby. And worst of all, the recurring invasion of Firegoat—a presence that on her best days she knew must reside in her imagination—left her powerless. She needed help. They all needed help.

Then again, this person standing before her with his pleading eyes had more than once been thrown off the farm for good reason by his own brother.

A head taller than Foss, she lifted her chin to make herself look even more commanding.

"You sleep in the milk house," she said. "You stay out of the house. Bertie can bring you your supper."

"That's agreeable," said Foss, offering a rare smile. "I'll be back in a couple days."

"When spring comes you go away," added Fawn.

The smile disappeared. "But you'll need help putting the crop in," Foss argued.

Fawn made no reply. She crossed her long, boney arms over her chest for a thoughtful moment and marveled at what she'd done.

* * * * *

Bertie recognized more than his mother what she had done. For most of his short life, he'd feared his uncle. Once, with his dad out of sight in the pasture, Foss grabbed him by the ankles and dangled him over the well, telling him he would drop him into the black water if he didn't behave. Other times, he threatened to snatch him from his bed and feed him to the pack of wild dogs that sometimes wandered through the farmyard at night scavenging for food.

When his mother told him of his uncle's pending reappearance, that he'd arrive that afternoon, Bertie pulled his barn coat from the hook and hurried outside so his mother might not see his tears. But rather than the barn, he headed for one of his secret hiding places in the crawl space underneath the toolshed. There, in the dank air among the rotting timbers, he sat, listening to the sounds outside—the frantic beating of pigeon wings rising from the roof, the flapping of the loose door opening and closing with the passing of the wind, all the while thinking: *Why did Mother let Foss come back?*

He emerged from his hiding place reminding himself that he was the man of the house, just as Harold had told him. Tall for his age and strong like his father had been, he could carry two pails of milk at a time. But he knew from past experience that the more work he did, the more Foss found for him to do. He went to the woodpile and picked up the ax to begin the chore he hated most—splitting the sawed logs. He set a one-foot section on its end on the chopping block and raised the ax high. The head came down and two pieces flew to the side in perfect halves. He repeated the action with another piece of wood, then another, stopping only when his chest burned and the ax became too heavy to lift.

He returned to the house to find his mother in the same place he left her, by the window, gazing past the barn into the field. When she looked like that it made him think of the time she ended up in that snowy field. Bertie had followed her but couldn't make her get up. He climbed up to the road, looking about desperately, when Harold Peavey came along in his truck and spotted him.

Now he waited with his mother, trying to comprehend the dread engulfing him. If somebody had to come and live with the family, why not Harold Peavey instead of Uncle Foss? Harold would keep Mama from harm and see that they all had lots of potatoes to boil and flour for spice cake. If Foss had his way, he'd leave them all out in the snow and eat the spice cake by himself.

Not long afterward, a shiny speck of a vehicle came into sight in the distance, throwing up dust. It turned into the farmyard and skidded to a stop. Uncle Foss emerged from the passenger side. The car left at once, barely missing a squawking rooster forced to take flight to avoid being run down.

* * * * *

The blizzard came on suddenly. The morning began warm with temperatures touching fifty and a pleasant southerly breeze. All across the state, residents seized the occasion to hang storm windows, dig a last few potatoes, or drive to a neighbor for a social call. But by late afternoon, the wind swung around, two feet of snow carpeted the earth and every road became indistinguishable from the fields surrounding it. From the Turtle Mountains to down past Bismarck, people died, suffocated in drifts or frozen in their automobiles, some still in their shirtsleeves. Near the South Dakota border, a six-year-old girl, a relative of the soon-to-be-famous Lawrence Welk as it turned out, made a trip to the family outhouse with the snow falling thick as cotton. Ten minutes later, while trying to find her way back into the house, she became disoriented and trudged about in circles before falling and dying ten feet from the door.

Outside, the wind shrieked. Now and then, a more troubling sound reached the house—the howling of hungry animals. The wild dogs had come back. Two of them ventured into the yard, but Foss raised his arms high above his head and clapped his hands. The dogs spun around and disappeared into the trees. The week before the blizzard, they'd dragged a buck deer across the frozen pasture, staining the snow with blood. By spring, nothing would remain of the deer but shards of bone with pearly gristle for the crows to bother over.

During the second night of the storm, the house trembled as if made of cardboard. Bertie awoke from his makeshift bed on the kitchen floor to tend the stove. He'd just set the poker down after stirring the coals when a pounding sounded on the door.

"Open up," cried Foss.

Too frightened to talk, Bertie waited.

"Open up!" repeated Foss. "The stovepipe blew down. I had to put the fire out."

Bertie hesitated, listening to the wind howl. His mother, abed with her headaches since the storm began, had made it clear—Foss must never be allowed in the house, especially after dark.

The pounding grew louder. Foss must be kicking the door. "Come on. Damn it, I'm froze!"

Bertie watched as the door bulged inward with each kick. When that happened, the stout bar holding it shut usually jammed in the bracket and could only be freed using the poker as a lever. Though he knew the door would resist even the strongest efforts, he wished he had a place to hide just in case. The pantry might be OK, but no, Foss would find him easily. He thought of the storage space underneath the stairs where he played in the summer, now filled with his dad's old clothes. He could burrow under the army uniform and winter shirts like a woodchuck and keep very still.

But what if he hid too well? Mama and the baby would be sound asleep with no one to protect them.

A sharp breaking sounded from the door, then silence. Maybe Foss had gone to the barn to wait until morning.

But no. He spoke again, but in a softer voice.

"Bertie, come on. Let me in just to warm up. I'm cold."

"Mama said I can't," said Bertie.

"What? I can't hear you. Take the bar off."

"Mama said you have to stay in the milk house at night."

"Listen, Bertie."

Foss lowered his voice so that Bertie had to strain to hear. Foss was telling him that his dad—*bless his soul*—would want Bertie to do what he was told. And his mother didn't mean what she said.

"So please, take the bar down. I just want to stay till it gets light so I can fix the pipe. We don't need to tell your ma. She won't care."

Bertie waited, expecting his uncle to continue pleading. A gust of wind rattled the windows. Maybe Foss got too cold to talk. What should he do? If only Mama would wake up.

A plan came to him. He would lift the bar from the door and then run as fast as he could up the stairs to his mother's room where she slept with the baby and lock that door behind him. That way, Foss could be inside where it was warm, and the family would be safe.

First, he lit the candle on the table. Crossing the floor in his bare feet, he used the poker to pry the bar free.

At once he knew he'd done wrong as the door flew open, knocking him backward. He regained his footing and raced for the stairs, the poker in his hands. He barely reached halfway up before Foss grabbed his foot. The poker dropped to the step with a clang.

"Where do you think you're going?" Foss demanded, dragging him back down the stairs, where the cold air seeped in from the open door.

Foss positioned himself so he could block the path to the stairs and remain close to the stove. Shaking, he wrapped himself in the quilt from Bertie's bed. "Close the door," he said, motioning with his head.

While Bertie labored to lift the bar back in place, Foss warmed his hands over the stove, his forehead streaked with soot, his face red as a rooster comb, the tip of his nose a frosty white. The thick, rancid smell of clothing in need of a wash filled the air. Swaying on his feet, he looked toward the top of the stairs then back at Bertie as if trying to make up his mind.

Drawing a brown bottle from inside his coat, he took a drink, eying Bertie. "If I had a kid like you, I'd take and drown him in the creek," he said. "Maybe that's what I ought to do."

Bertie backed toward the wall, away from the dim light of the candle, picturing himself in the icy water.

Foss blew his nose into the quilt and sagged to a sitting position on the floor with his elbows resting on a chair and his feet pointing toward the stove. Steam rose from the damp soles of his boots. Bertie recognized the boots as once having belonged to his dad.

"Or I could put you out in the milk house and see how you get by. Would you like that?"

When Bertie failed to answer, Foss repeated the question.

"No," said Bertie, his voice barely audible even to himself.

"Then how come you think it's fair that I got to?"

"I don't know," said Bertie.

Foss lifted the bottle and held it to his lips. "Half this place is supposed to be mine, and I got to live out there with the rats. Do you think that's fair?" He drank from the bottle and held it out toward Bertie accusingly. "Well, do you?"

Bertie sensed he should offer some response. "Mama said we get to live here because my dad died," said Bertie.

Foss turned his head sharply and shrugged out of the quilt. "Is that so? Let me tell you something. My brother, your dad, he pulled a fast one on me."

Bertie didn't know the meaning of those words. Foss must have read the bewildered look on his face. "He cheated me," he explained, tipping his bottle up for another swallow. Air bubbles gurgled up, lit by the candlelight. "The old lady got the will made different on account of Sid having a family and all and that he went overseas."

The slurred speech became a maze of terms that made no sense to Bertie, but he could tell by the bulging eyes and clenching fist that his uncle was growing angrier.

"And your ma…" Foss used his pointer finger to make circles in the air beside his right ear. "You know what's gonna happen one of these days?"

Bertie waited for the answer.

"I'll tell you. They're gonna take her away."

Bertie appreciated what lying meant. At the same time, he wondered if this were true. In some of his scariest thoughts, he imagined his mother running away or even dying like his dad. But what could it mean that she would be taken away?

"That's when I get even," said Foss. "And as for you." Foss got to his feet, reeling toward Bertie. "When I have this place, there'll be no room for brats running around."

Looking up, Bertie saw the spittle running from his uncle's mouth and the rage in his eyes. He twisted away and ran for the stairs, but Foss got hold of his nightshirt and held him fast as the bottle clattered to the floor. He raked his fingers over Foss's face, feeling the soft parts of the mouth, the rough beard on the chin. His nostrils burned with the smell of man-sweat and woodsmoke from Foss's shirt. Now his throat was in the crook of Foss's arm, and he twisted his head to bite at Foss's wrist as his breath was choked off.

"And don't go thinking—"

A loud cracking sound like a branch breaking caused Foss's sentence to go unfinished. Bertie felt the muscles of his uncle's arms relax, allowing him to breathe.

From the shadowy stairway, Bertie's mother came into view, the poker in both hands, her eyes wild.

"Mama!" cried Bertie, wanting to protect her and at the same time explain. He crawled toward her, throwing his arms around her legs. "Mama, he made me open the door. I didn't want to let him in."

On the floor, Foss grunted and passed his hand over his head like a man smoothing his hair. Dark blood traced right angles along the seams of the floorboards.

Fawn seemed unaware of her son clinging to her. She studied the poker for a second as if she'd never seen it before, then set it carefully on the floor. Pulling loose from Bertie's arms, she turned and remounted the stairs, one slow step at a time.

Bertie followed his mother to her bedroom and locked the door, fearful of being left on his own with Foss. As his mother folded the blankets back and eased herself into bed with Vickie, he waited, not daring to move, alert for any sound from below. After a time, he joined the others, stretching the covers over the three of them. While his mother joined Vickie in sleep, Bertie lay reflecting. It was all his fault. He took the bar down and Foss got into the house. Now what would happen? He listened for the sound of booted footsteps on the stairs. The wind howled, the walls creaked and the air in the little room became colder.

\* \* \* \* \*

When his sister awoke crying, Bertie shook his mother, but she mumbled and swatted weakly at him before jerking the covers over her head. Vickie's fussing continued, forcing Bertie to get up. He tiptoed to the top of the stairs, his bare feet hurting from the cold of the floor. He took a step down, then another. The bright morning light flashed off the newel post. He blinked.

He surprised himself by shouting, "Uncle Foss, *go away!*" He repeated the words, listening for the echo in the hollow air. The effort made him feel braver, and Vickie ended her fussing, calmed by the sound of a familiar voice.

He descended the stairs, pausing at each step to call out. At the bottom, he listened harder. He peeked around the corner and sighted a booted foot. He drew back into the stairwell.

Breaking the unsettling silence, Vickie resumed her crying. Bertie took another step and peered into the kitchen.

His uncle lay on his back, unmoving as a fallen tree trunk, one hand covering the side of his jaw as if he had a toothache.

*Dead things cannot hurt you,* Bertie told himself. A dishrag hung over the pump handle. With shaking hands, he draped it over Foss's face.

Vickie cried louder. Surely Mama must hear her. Bertie opened the door to the firebox on the stove. Glowing cinders furnished a mild warmth. He shook down the ashes, gathered several small pieces from the woodbox, added them to the stove, and soon a decent fire arose. He pushed the door shut and put on a pan of water to boil for Vickie's mush.

As he waited, he could not keep from lowering his eyes toward his uncle, though he could see he no longer breathed. Blood from his head lay congealed on the icy floor. The more he looked, the sicker he felt. He would have to hide the body where no one could see it. He couldn't stand to get near the bloody head so he knelt on the floor and tugged on a foot, hoping he could drag the body to the porch. He pulled hard and the boot came loose, but the body didn't move. His uncle was not fat, but he seemed as heavy as a log. He would try again after checking on his sister.

When the mush began to boil over, he slid the pan to the side to cool. When it was ready, he took a spoon and a bowlful upstairs to feed Vickie.

When Vickie refused to eat anymore, Bertie changed her diaper. As he lay her back in her place on the bed, Mama came awake. She raised herself to her elbows, glanced at Bertie and just as quickly resumed her sleep. Hungry himself by then, Bertie finished the mush by tipping the bowl to his mouth and licking it clean. The food made him feel stronger. He gazed at the other two sleeping so quietly. One more task lay before him.

It took all the strength he had to move the body even an inch. The slight rise of the threshold to the porch just about made him give up, but by bracing his heels against the doorjamb he managed. When at last the body lay in the porch corner and out of sight—at least from the kitchen—he covered it with old flour sacks. Back in the kitchen, he filled the wash pail from the pump and set it on the stove, then mixed in a handful of lye. Kneeling on the floor, he worked the scrub brush until the black stain lightened.

When at last the floor was clean—cleaner than before, it looked to him—he put things away, then sat down by the stove, put his head in his hands and cried for fifteen minutes, not caring who alive or dead might hear him.

Later, he carried Vickie downstairs so she could crawl around while he fixed another meal. When she began fussing, he found her favorite toy—the old fiddle that once belonged to Grandmother Breen. Though nearly as big as the baby herself, the fiddle was lightweight enough for her to drag around, and though beyond producing music in its state, it functioned beautifully to distract her or end her fussing. It had but one remaining string that Mama had tried to remove for safety, but the baby took such delight in grasping it in her pudgy fist and releasing it to hear the hollow *thunk* it produced that she instead fastened it tighter and let it be. She expected Vickie would grow out of it in time.

In the period after Bertie's dad's death and before his mother took sick again, he'd figured out how to cook a few basic dishes using the simple ingredients available. He could boil oatmeal, fry up salt pork and even make a flavorful kind of pancake that he invented from flour, eggs and milk. In fact, he'd discovered that his pancakes were one of the few things he could get his mother to eat. Now though, with Mama still in bed, he made oatmeal, for that was faster. He stood by the stove spooning portions of the gritty, gray meal into his mouth, tasting little. Soon he would have to go to the barn to feed and milk the cows.

He tried to imagine what his dad would think. Would he be mad because Bertie disobeyed his mother?

His thoughts drifted back to the previous summer—the limit of his memory. Day after day produced cruel heat and endless sun. In the afternoon, Bertie liked to visit the one place that offered relief—the little icehouse on the opposite side of the barn. There, he could sit on a block of ice covered by sawdust and feel the cool air surround him. One afternoon, the loud voices of his father and Uncle Foss interrupted his comfort in a frightening way. They screamed at each other using words Bertie did not get. He heard his mother's name mentioned followed by a loud splash like the time a cow stumbled into the water trough. Then all went quiet.

Bertie listened at the door. When he heard voices again, one of them his mother's, he opened the door just enough to provide a view of the yard. There on the ground beside the trough knelt his mother with her hand on Daddy. Uncle Foss stood over her, wiping his hand across his whiskers.

Bertie's next memory was of grown-ups in the house for his dad's funeral. Cousin Leah came with her husband and their little son, Richie Lee, who fussed and cried so much his mother took him out to the car. With Foss gone, Bertie and his mother lived alone until the baby Vickie came. Sometimes neighbors came by, turning their eyes away as they offered jars of canned beets or a slab of bacon. Then one day, Foss came back. After that, except for Harold Peavey, neighbors no longer dropped in for a visit or to offer food.

\* \* \* \* \*

On the morning of the storm's fourth day and asleep in his own bed, Bertie awoke to the cry of the baby and was worried again why his mother was not tending to her. He gathered strength to go check. Vickie was by herself in the bedroom. Usually his mother took her downstairs with her as soon as she got up. Just then, a cry came from downstairs, followed by the dull thump of a door being closed. Bertie raced down the stairs to find his mother standing in the porch doorway with a hand over her mouth. For some reason, she'd removed the bar and stepped out into the porch where Foss lay stiff in the corner.

From the bottom of the stairs, Bertie called to her to come inside. She whirled about and brushed past him, disappearing up the stairs. Hesitantly, Bertie walked out into the cold porch. A gray rat scuttled across the floor, followed by another.

He shut and barred the door. The wind had eased, meaning the storm was ending. He knew someone would come to the house sooner or later. When they saw Foss, they would want to know what happened. Maybe they would come and take Mama away as Foss had said.

What could he do? He remembered that when Daddy died, men dug a hole in the ground to put him in. But that was summer. Now the ground was solid ice.

By afternoon milking time, snow had sealed the back door, and the only way to the barn led through the porch and past the long bundle of Foss shoved against the outside wall. Bertie moved quickly, afraid to look, afraid not to. Even though he lay in exactly the position Bertie had left him, he imagined his uncle snatching at his ankles in the quick, tight way he grabbed the legs of a hog for slaughter.

An hour later when Bertie emerged from the barn carrying the half-full bucket of milk the skinny cows had given up, the sound of bells reached his ears. He paused and listened. In a second, he realized what it was. A team of horses pulling a sleigh approached, gliding over the snow-filled road. As the rasping sleigh came closer, he recognized the huddled form of Harold Peavey on the seat. Forgetting the bucket, Bertie ran across firm drifts to the milk house and grabbed the tattered and smelly horse blanket that his uncle had used for a bed along with an armful of old barn wear that hung from a hook by the door. Moving as fast as his legs would take him, he dragged the clothes and blanket across the snow to the porch and draped them over Foss's frozen body to make it look like a pile of old rags.

The sleigh pulled into the yard as Bertie fed wood into the stove and filled the speckled blue coffeepot with water just as his mother used to do when she and his dad awaited visitors. Then he changed his mind and put the pot in the dishpan. Harold got down carefully from his sleigh, took a minute to adjust the harness on one of the team, then high-stepped through the snow toward the house carrying a gunnysack. The horses waited in the yard, their breath rising in white puffs behind their blinders.

Bertie headed outside to greet Harold, but as he hurried through the porch, he spotted one of Foss's feet spearing out from under the horse blanket. But by then, Harold had reached the steps.

"Leah sent me to check on you folks," said Harold, removing his fur cap and unwrapping the thick scarf from his neck. "You make out OK during the storm?"

"Mama's sick," said Bertie, paralyzed with anxiety.

"Is that so? Does she need the doctor? The roads should be plowed by tomorrow. If we have to, I can help get her into town."

"OK," said Bertie, trying his best to fill the space of the open door.

"Is it her nerves again?"

Bertie still had no inkling what nerves were, but he took a chance. "Yes. She has to stay in bed."

Harold stood there reasoning it out. "I see you got your fire going good. That's important," he said. "How about the baby?"

"She's sleeping too."

Harold turned his head toward the milk house. "I don't see smoke from the stovepipe. Things look froze up. Where's your uncle?"

"I don't know," said Bertie, wrapping his arms about himself. He looked down at the well-tracked snow, afraid to face Harold.

"You mean he up and took off again?" said Harold. He pulled at his chin through his mitten. "We got to figure out how to get you some help. Can you make it a couple days?" He handed over the sack he'd been carrying. "Here's a couple loaves of fresh-baked bread and some cold chicken that Leah sent."

"OK," said Bertie, realizing too late that he should have said thank you.

"Tell you what, when your mother wakes up, let her know I'll be back tomorrow."

"OK."

Harold buttoned his enormous coat. "You're a good boy, Bertie. Your mother's lucky. You know what to do when things need doing, don't you?"

"Yes," said Bertie. "Thank you."

* * * * *

Bertie waited until the horses and sleigh were out of sight just in case Harold had forgotten something. Back in the porch, he stomped on the floor repeatedly, hoping the commotion would frighten the rats back into their hole. He then attached his father's thick leather belt to Foss's foot and cinched it tight. Leaving the blanket over the body, he pulled on the belt. As before, it moved with difficulty. He reached the outer door and the landing, where he tugged harder, and Foss came bumping down each step like a hay bale.

Wading through the fluffy snow, he pulled the body like a toboggan up into the stand of aspen, where it couldn't be seen from either the house or the barn.

The following morning, the sun came out. Bertie stepped outside without his coat. Looking across the rise, he spotted the dogs, their forms distinct in the blindingly bright snow. There were seven of them, zigzagging, sniffing the sides of fence posts, foraging, their hairy lower jaws dragging the ground, searching for something to eat.

By the time Bertie returned to the warmth and safety of the house, they were already approaching the trees.

# CATCH AND RELEASE

The first time he opened his eyes to the misty reality of what he'd done, the boy rolled over and tried to return to a dream. But sleep failed him, and he lay there fully clothed until the arrival of daylight and the demands from downstairs.

"Casey! Chores."

Casey rolled over, dropped to his knees and snaked an arm beneath the bed, searching.

It lay there against the wall, strange amid the dust motes and dead flies. Cool to the touch, it had in the passing of a few hours been transformed from an elegant object of beauty and desire to a symbol of disgrace.

It was a Zebco 33 Rod and Reel Combo to which Sears and Roebuck devoted an entire page, featuring a smiling white man in a matching tan cap and vest pulling in a glistening walleye that seemed to be grinning at being hooked by such superb tackle. Casey had scrutinized the advertisement so intently and so often that the paper lost its starch, curled away and marked itself.

The ad went on to proclaim the revolutionary closed-face design of the reel, its resistance to tangling, its distance and accuracy. *Only $16.99 (plus shipping and handling)* it said, making it six dollars less than the price tag attached to the Zebco on display in the glass case at Staggs Hardware in town.

His father called again. "Casey?"

This time, the voice carried a tone of taut restraint. As the Morinville family had long understood, this momentary quiet always foreshadowed the unreasonable, for Etienne Morinville's temperament performed like the motor on the old Minneapolis-Moline, idling contentedly before suddenly erupting with a gunshot clapping and a cloud of black smoke.

Two summers previously, during a confrontation over how best to fix the drive chain on the manure spreader, Etienne grabbed the chain and swung it like a whip at Sam. A broken link struck him just above his elbow, tearing through his canvas shirt and into the muscle, forming a wound that bled for an hour. But now that Sam had grown taller and heavier, he behaved as he liked, which included staying in bed all morning, and the boys' father transferred his angry flare-ups to Casey.

The kitchen smelled of the burnt toast that Casey's sister, Rebecca, liked, though Rebecca herself had departed for the henhouse to gather eggs. Etienne sat upright in his chair, chin high with one hand squeezing a knife and the other a fork, each pointed toward the ceiling like a cartoon character waiting for his meat and potatoes.

"What was that you and your brother were up to last night?" he asked.

Casey glanced at his mother, Ida Florence, who stood buttering toast, her back turned. As always in matters like this, she avoided the eyes of her husband out of fear that even a peek might be seen as disapproval. The scratching of the knife filled the charged air as Etienne waited for an answer.

The response came softly. "Nothing."

"Like hell. I heard you talkin' in his room and I heard the door when you went out."

Ida Florence set the plate of stacked toast on the table, careful to place it slightly closer to her husband. From the cupboard, she took a jar of strawberry jam and opened it.

Etienne slid the toast closer and used his fork to spear two pieces. "Was Sam drunk again?"

Casey looked closely at the jam, noticing the crumbs of old toast and slivers of butter mixed in with the sugary fruit. "I don't know. Ask him."

"I seen you on your way over toward to the slough," said Etienne, his voice accusatory, his bull shoulders thrust forward. He crammed half a toast in his mouth, chewing on one side. "Where were you going?"

Casey hesitated.

"Well?" said Etienne.

"Casey, you want coffee?" It was his mother. She knew well that Casey hated coffee but sensed that the moment was right to ease the strain.

"I better start milking," he said, skidding his chair back over the tattered linoleum.

\* \* \* \* \*

The cows milled about the barn door twitching their ropey tails, waiting to be let into their stalls. Casey located his milking stool, its pine surface worn smooth and its legs loosely connected with baling wire, making it sway like a rocker. After securing each cow in her stanchion, he bathed the udder with warm soapy water while checking for redness or swelling that would indicate mastitis, then used his shirttail to pat the udder dry.

He pulled on the teats with his calloused hands, drawing the sweet buttery-smelling stream that produced the encouraging tinny sound as it struck the side of the pail.

The rumble of the sliding door startled him. The cow's huge head swung around leisurely. Through the cloud of dust particles illuminated by the incoming sunlight came Etienne.

Casey rocked forward, glancing down into the white liquid that barely covered the bottom of the pail. His father lumbered the length of the barn, kicking at clots of dung mixed with straw before halting behind Casey, his bulky shadow blocking the light from the door.

"How you expect them to drink when the stock tank's empty?"

"I know it's empty," said Casey.

Etienne brought his beefy arm back sharply. Casey braced for a blow, but his father only pulled an oily rag from his back pocket and blew his nose. The door rumbled on its track and the light went away.

The gray barn cat padded by, stopping to assess the possibilities. Casey directed a water pistol-like spritz of milk toward it. The cat dashed off, only to return a few minutes later. Casey let his forehead rest on the warm flank of the cow and tried to think.

*****

The night before, he'd passed Sam's open bedroom door—a rare thing in itself—to see his brother lying on his back with the catalog open on his belly.

"So, you still looking to buy that fancy rod and reel," said Sam, his eyes trained on the page.

As he and his family knew, Casey had been calculating how he could come up with the money for the Zebco ever since the catalog arrived back in March. Because his father required him to complete his usual chores unpaid, he'd spent Sundays all summer painting and fencing instead of going fishing for crappies at Dark Lake, the agreement being that he would be paid twenty-five dollars after harvest. But just this week, workmen pulled up in their truck to pour a cement pad for a new steel grain bin, and his father told him money no longer existed for some useless fishing rod.

"So how come's you never sent for it yet?" asked Sam.

Casey glanced over his shoulder toward their parents' room, kitty-corner across the hall. Although Sam must know what happened, Casey explained things in a low voice.

"What about your money from them empties you got all over the place?" asked Sam, referring to the bottles that Casey gathered in a gunnysack from the ditches along the highway, for which the SuperValu in Rolland paid two cents each.

"Most everything's in cans now," said Casey, picking up the aroma of liquor in the small room.

"Why don't you save up your lunch money?" suggested Sam, a snide tone creeping into his voice.

Every Monday morning during the school year, their mother produced two dollar bills from her coin purse to allow Casey and Rebecca to pay for their lunches for the week. Sam himself had no need for lunch money—he always managed to carry loose change jangling in his pocket, though no one knew where it came from, and on the few days he bothered to go to school, he vanished with his buddies during lunch.

"Rebecca tried that but she caught heck when Ma found out she was using her food money to buy cigarettes."

Sam grunted. "Me, I'll take a smoke any day instead of that slop they give you in the cafeteria."

Casey could see the picture of the Zebco in the catalog. He knew the image as well as he knew the trackless, yellowing ceiling above his bed. The reel was said to be tangle-free, the nearly invisible monofilament line enclosed in a metal cover so polished it gleamed like the classroom floors on the first day of school. The rod, as thin as a pencil, was made of fiberglass and so strong it could be bent like a willow branch.

Sam reached beneath his pillow and withdrew a pint bottle of his favorite whiskey, Ten High. It looked half-full with the tax stamp on the neck loose and sticking out like a red flag. He took a pull, his eyes on Casey as if daring him to object.

"I know where there's one of them Zebco outfits," he said, smoothing the page with the flat of his hand.

"You mean Staggs?"

"Nope."

"A Zebco 33? Really? How much?"

Sam sat up, planted his big feet on the floor, and raised the bottle to his lips again. Anticipating a reply, Casey studied his brother, unable to shake his sense of shame. Sam was old enough to be out on his own, but here he was sitting in his parents' home in his filthy shorts, smelling of sweat and tobacco smoke, his dirty black hair over his ears, his belly flabbing out like that of a man three times his age.

"I don't know if it's for sale," Sam said teasingly.

"Who's it belong to then?" asked Casey.

Sam extended the bottle toward Casey. "Here, have a little taste."

Casey knew that kids who drank were looked upon with scorn. It was said of them that they were bound for misfortune. Sam himself had been suspended from school after the shop teacher found a bottle in his locker—though he avoided a more serious penalty by claiming somebody else put it there. That misdeed, along with others, produced an effect on Casey. He became known as the *nice* Morinville boy, a good Indian. He'd earned As in every subject except for a B+ in geometry. Moreover, he'd been chosen president of FFA, the first boy who didn't live close to town to be given such an honor—never mind that becoming a farmer was the last thing he wanted to do.

Sam noted his hesitation. "Oh, come on," he said. "It's time you act like a man."

What a dilemma. The image of a magnificent Zebco lay before him. He could almost feel it in his grip. Would Sam really know where to get one? He accepted the bottle, held it to his mouth and drank. At once, he spat it out, remembering the time he'd found a similar bottle in the hayloft and tasted it, curious about the attraction Sam held for the brown liquid that looked like the piss that sick cows grunted out with so much effort.

Sam choked back a laugh as he reached for the bottle to keep it from being spilled. "I expected that. Young Mr. Candy-Ass here never got taught how to drink."

He explained that with good whiskey you swallow it quick before it has time to burn the inside of the mouth. He demonstrated. "And not such a big slug at first. Here, try it again."

Obligated at this point, Casey saw nothing to do but follow through. Lacking a chair and not wishing to sit on the bed where Sam sprawled, he eased himself to the floor and rested his back against the wall.

His second attempt succeeded. The liquid seared his throat but settled swiftly in his stomach. He took another sip. It went down easily. He put his head back and rested.

He watched as Sam wetted a finger and turned a page in search of items more attractive to him, his lips sounding out the descriptive words. A sense of pleasantness came over him—a warm summer night, the lowing of the cows in their pasture and the loneliness of the hills made him feel a closeness to his brother that he hadn't experienced since his younger years when Sam took him horseback riding and taught him how to bat left-handed.

"So anyways, you interested in that rig or not?"

Casey turned his head upward. The calendar with the picture of the woman in a bathing suit over Sam's bed doubled in his vision. He squeezed one eye shut to make it right. "Hmm?"

"Your Zebco," said Sam impatiently.

Casey took a moment to consider this. "Where is it?"

Sitting with his elbows on his knees and looking like a man satisfied with himself, Sam lowered his voice. "Right next door."

That made no sense. "Next door?"

"Peaveys."

Casey frowned in disbelief. After all, though located almost close enough to throw a rock through a window, the Peavey farmhouse may as well have been in Paris, France. The families' shared hostility stretched back to before Casey was born. He knew few of the details other than that Mrs. Peavey's father was accused of shooting Freddy, Sam and Casey's older brother. Nothing ever came of it because the old man died before they could prove he'd done it. Etienne Morinville never spoke of the misfortune but made it clear to his family that they were never to go near the Peavey place, a rule he enforced with stern warnings followed by beatings.

"How do you know?"

"I seen it myself. It's in the shop in plain sight."

"That's funny," said Casey. "I never once saw Mr. Peavey going fishing."

"That's why that Zebco looks so new."

"Or maybe he's saving it for Richie Lee when he gets bigger," said Casey.

Sam grunted. "That spoiled little shit don't deserve something nice as that. Shame for it to just hang there gettin' rusty."

"You sure it's a Zebco?"

Sam's cheerless face turned toward the window. "I told you it was. Go see for yourself if you don't believe me."

Casey at once regretted expressing doubt. "No thanks," he said. "I don't want to get my head shot off." Desperately wanting to lighten the mood, he was aware that the tone of his voice belied the intent of his words.

"You chickenshit," said Sam, pulling on the bottle again. "That wasn't even Harold Peavey done that. It was old Omar that shot Freddy."

"Same family," said Casey, wanting another sample of the whiskey, but not daring to request it.

"What would you say if I told you I been to their place lots of times and you don't see no bullet holes in me?"

"You mean close up and not just from way off?" said Casey. "When?"

"I go whenever I feel like it just to check around. You take a night like this when it's black, no moon. You go round back of the slough and come in from the north."

"It's all marshy up there," said Casey.

"Not when it's dry like it's been. Come on right now. I'll prove it to you." Sam stood and pulled up his pants.

Casey turned his head toward the window. The Peavey place. That forbidden cluster of buildings that looked so much like his home, yet remained so mysterious. The Peavey son, Richie Lee, who was just a couple years older than Casey, rode the school bus with the Morinville children, though no one ever spoke to him except for Sam, who took a cruel pleasure in teasing the boy. From their potato patch, the Morinvilles could almost hear conversations in the Peavey barn. All of it so near but so unreachable.

"Well, you want to see it or not?" said Sam.

Casey got to his feet, weaving slightly. In just one evening he'd come a long way toward winning the respect of his strange and distant brother. If he didn't show any guts now, more might be lost than a Zebco that he'd likely never own anyway.

The black sky was speckled with stars. An easy calm blanketed the Peavey property, and at this time of night, no cars passed on the gravel road.

As the brothers weaved their way through the high grass bordering the slough, the frogs ceased their rhythmic croaking. The rich smell of cattails and decaying vegetation faded as they neared the barbed wire fence separating the two properties.

"That's the shop on the right where he keeps it," said Sam, hunching low like a soldier behind enemy lines. "You can't see the rod through the window. You got to go in."

Casey's eyes adjusted to the dimness as he took in the square angles of the building, the door, the single window. His apprehension grew when he detected hesitation on the part of his brother. He imagined all the things that could go amiss. A barking watchdog might come bounding out of the house, or Mr. Peavey could be crouched behind that shop door with a rabbit gun.

"Well, go on, we ain't got all night," said Sam, resting his foot on the bottom strand of wire connecting two posts.

"You're not coming?" muttered Casey. "I don't know the best way."

"The best way is underneath the fence straight over there," Sam hissed, his eyes pale slits of white. Then, perhaps believing he'd been too harsh, he added, "It's OK. Somebody comes, I'll whistle." He lifted the wire.

As Casey's whiskey courage faded, he wavered. He wanted only to be safely wrapped in the covers of his bed. The wooden fence post creaked. He knelt slowly, planting his hands in the soft, cool ground, and snaked below the fence, touching, for the first time in his life, the forbidden soil of the Peaveys. From earning his merit badges in Boy Scouts, he possessed a deep understanding of nature and woodlore—how to track, how to move quietly, how to know where he was. But this was different. No one was going to pin a medal on his chest for trespassing on private property. A sickness rose in his stomach as if it came up through the earth. Catching his breath, he stumbled for a few yards to an alder tree where he shielded himself. He looked back. Sam stood leaning on a post, relaxed, far from harm's way.

An open area that would be visible from the Peavey house lay between Casey and the shop. He dropped again to all fours, beginning a slow crawl like a caterpillar across the uneven ground, rutted and cratered from the hooves of generations of cows. Then, wary of encountering some still-ripe manure, he rose and advanced carefully on his toes until he reached the shop door, where he stood listening. A single mosquito whined in his ear and he waved it away.

He barely touched the old-fashioned thumb latch and the door swung halfway open with a screech powerful enough to wake half the county. He gazed back toward his own house. It never seemed so far away.

He pushed past the door into the familiar odors of antifreeze, rotted hemp and spilled kerosene. But unlike the Morinvilles' shop, tools were neatly placed, wrenches arranged by size and hanging from regular hooks instead of nails driven into the studs. Skippy jars held screws of various sizes. Mr. Peavey had nailed the lids beneath a shelf so the jars could be held in place by securing them to their tops. Unlike most outbuildings in the area, the shop had been wired for electricity, and a bare light bulb hung from the rafters.

Just to the right of the bench, he saw the Zebco hanging vertically from a brass cup hook, enchanting as a magic wand. He had already made up his mind. He only wanted to lay eyes on it, maybe run a hand gently along the curved reel casing, then depart quietly. Still, the shiny, never-used rod and reel looked out of place in this shed amid heavy and greasy pipe wrenches, bare floorboards and rusting tools long past their usefulness. Like every outbuilding, this one no doubt harbored field mice. Cutting with their razor teeth, they could easily nibble through the cork overlay of the handle or gather bits of line for their nests.

As gently as if removing a robin's egg from a nest, Casey lifted the Zebco from its hook. It clung comfortably to his hand. In a flash, the realization came over him that his brother no longer guided his movements. His decisions and their outcomes were now his own.

Carrying the rod carefully at midpoint, he pulled the door closed behind him, checked the latch and took a mighty breath. The Peavey house remained unlit and buttoned-down. In the distance, just beyond the slough, his own home waited. With giddy determination, he trotted across the open area to the fence, this time vaulting over and ignoring a barb that snagged his pant leg. On he went, through the reeds, over the soft marsh that bordered the slough with its sickly smell, then onto higher ground, his feet barely skimming the earth's surface. Vaguely aware of Sam's disappearance, he slowed only when he reached the front step of the house.

Yet once inside, a fresh wave of anxiety overcame him. Maybe his father waited at the top of the stairs, rubbing his eyes, his hair mussed. But all was alarmingly normal. On tiptoe, he climbed the stairs to his room. He waited with his ears attuned, prepared for calamity. But only the settling and flexing of the old house and the fluttering of a breeze through the cottonwoods penetrated the calm. Leaving the light off, he slid the Zebco under his bed and crawled in, fully clothed.

Lying flat on his back, he stared at the ceiling, his mind struggling for something that made sense.

* * * * *

All day, Casey's emotions flapped about like a wounded bird. One second his nerves tingled as if electrified, the next his limbs felt puny and useless. He had to force himself to stop checking and rechecking if the Zebco was still in its hiding place. He pictured the consequences of its discovery, aware that the Kaleva brothers had been kicked off the football team for stealing two packs of cigarettes from the drugstore. And the brothers were white—sons of the man who owned the dry cleaner. What would they do to Casey? Forget being FFA president, forget going to college. What more might happen at the hands of his father?

Several times, he wandered outside trying to look casual while he shot sidelong peeks toward the neighbors to check for the silhouette of Mr. Peavey in the shop—or maybe to spot the sheriff's car throwing up a cloud of dust on the road, its disturbing lights flashing.

"You got ants in your pants?" said Etienne, peeking up over his reading glasses, the newspaper spread open on the kitchen table.

Twice, he did see Mr. Peavey start across his yard, walking as if guided from afar and lost in worrisome thought. Both times, Casey looked the other way, trying to wish himself into invisibility. But no, the man merely meant to check the mailbox.

In midafternoon, as the heat of the day peaked, Richie Lee Peavey emerged from the house. The instant the boy spotted Casey, he ran back inside. In a minute, Mr. Peavey appeared, waved heartily and waded through the foxtail and pigweed growing along the fence separating the properties.

"Do you suppose you could do me a favor?" he asked.

Casey couldn't speak. He saw that his neighbor was wearing his house shoes, a sign that he must have been in a hurry.

"I don't mean to bother anyone, but we're missing a piece of mail," he said, his voice pitched high and careful in the artificial way a man talked to a kid when he wanted to be understood. "I thought maybe Howard might've left it in your box."

He wore a pair of clean striped bib overalls, and up close, he looked younger than Casey had imagined. He seemed to be making an effort not to get too close to the fence.

"I don't know," said Casey, speaking with difficulty through dry lips and mouth.

"Well, would you mind checking with your folks if they've seen it?" said Mr. Peavey. "It's from the bank, so I got to get hold of them if it doesn't turn up."

"OK," said Casey, wheeling around in his eagerness, soaring over the steps in two great bounds and letting the screen door slam behind him. His father, in his chair, scowled at the disturbance.

"Mr. Harold Peavey needs his mail," Casey shouted, breathless.

"What?" said Etienne.

"We got a letter that belongs to him," said Casey. "From the bank," he added.

His mother came out of the kitchen and peered out the front door. "All we have is our own mail," she said. "I'm real careful about that."

Her husband rose with a grunt and took his turn at the door. "Make sure you tell him that. We don't have nothin' of theirs."

With his parents observing him through the window, Casey hurried across the yard and related what he'd been told to Mr. Peavey, who grimaced in disappointment, thought it over briefly and strode back to his house.

Casey watched him go, his heart fluttering like a bird's. This would have been the time to take action, to confess what he'd done. A free admission should count for something. Then again, maybe not. There must be plenty of reasons why he'd been taught to stay away from the Peaveys. Besides, who knew? Maybe nothing would come of it. Maybe Mr. Peavey had forgotten about the Zebco. By late afternoon, when it came time for second milking, Casey yearned for rest. His thoughts of the Zebco, waiting beneath his bed like a bogeyman, had not left his mind for two seconds since he awoke. At the same time, the people that formed his existence had lost all that made them tolerable and human—his father seemed more stupid and hate-filled, his mother cold and distant. And his ongoing thoughts of Sam, his once-beloved brother, who, typically for him, didn't bother to wait for Casey the night before in the event something went wrong, nearly drove him to tears of disillusionment.

Pushing and coaxing the cows into the correct stalls, he concluded that a single opportunity was left for him to reverse what he'd done. If he were lucky enough for Mr. Peavey not to notice that the Zebco was missing and for neither of his parents to find it in his room, he just might be able to make his way around the slough again after bedtime and put the thing back where it belonged.

By the time he'd finished milking and turned the cows out for water, a line of pillowy clouds highlighted in orange by the setting sun formed toward the west. A good sign. Rain might keep curious eyes indoors while providing an added layer of cover. When the rain never materialized, Sam thumbed a ride into town. Casey kept to his room, trying to read a book about Gene Autry that he'd won in a spelling contest in third grade. His father went to bed. Casey listened for the sounds of his mother on her way to the bedroom, but apparently she chose to stay up late solving her crossword puzzle and monitoring affairs in Canada over CKY in Winnipeg.

At last, the floor squeaked under the weight of her weary footsteps. Casey forced himself to delay another unbearable twenty minutes to make sure she joined her husband in sleep. Carefully, he pulled the despised rod out from its hiding place and crept downstairs through the silent house and out into the night.

Bellying under the fence, he recalled a mystery he'd read in which the criminal was identified by a fingernail-sized swatch of his clothing clinging to the barb of a fence like this one. Setting the Zebco down, he ran his hand along the strand to make sure no evidence lingered of his snag from the night before.

The night gave the impression of being darker than the previous—a blackness that triggered a terrifying memory of the time Sam locked him in the old humpback trunk up in the attic. In a hurry and trying to escape the recollection, he passed too close to the slough, plunging his left foot into the vegetation-saturated water.

As he strained to free himself, the sticky muck engulfed and captured his shoe like a dust mote into a vacuum cleaner. Clumsily, while grasping the rod in one hand he felt around with the other, but the shoe had vanished. He'd have to leave it. And those were his good shoes. For a moment, he deliberated tossing the rod into the deep part of the slough, locating his shoe and going home. But the slough tended to dry up in years of scarce rain and he would always know it lay there awaiting discovery. And another consideration loomed—only Sam knew exactly what took place, and Casey questioned whether he could guard the secret.

A jolt of panic hit him when the shop door latch jammed, but a second tug allowed him in. He moved cautiously to the workbench, hoping no mousetrap or sharp tack awaited his bare foot. Securing the Zebco at the proper angle, he backed away to assure himself that it would appear exactly the same as the night before. Seeing that it failed to hang true, he lifted it from the hook again. The rod felt foreign and evil, capable of staining the palm of his hand.

Light flooded the room. "What do you think you're doing?"

Casey turned to face the voice, blinking and speechless.

Mr. Peavey stood in the doorway, dressed in long underwear, a light jacket and a red hunting cap.

"It's you?" he said, lowering the flashlight in his right hand. "I figured it would be Sam. Is that my good fishing rod?"

Paralyzed with fright, Casey tried to think of what he should do with the rod.

Mr. Peavey had not moved from the doorway. He waited for Casey to speak.

"I was putting it back."

The look from Mr. Peavey told Casey that he wasn't believed.

"At one o'clock in the morning?" He held out his hand for the Zebco. Casey passed it over. In the light, smudges of mud became visible on the reel.

"You take anything else?"

Casey would always remember that this stung the most. Mr. Peavey considered him a common thief.

"No," said Casey.

"What were you going to do? Sell it somewhere?"

"I just wanted to look at it," said Casey, resisting the temptation to elaborate on his small lie. Still, the look of doubt compelled him to add something. "I wanted to see what it was like to go fishing with it."

"Fishing?" said Mr. Peavey, seeming surprised. With his free hand, he waggled the rod, testing its flexibility, or maybe trying to determine if it had been damaged. "Where do you go to fish?"

Casey looked at the man. "Just around here. Dark Lake."

Mr. Peavey nodded. "Does anyone else know about this?"

Casey considered the question. "Just my brother." Now he'd brought Sam into it. Another sting of regret. The hurts were piling up.

Mr. Peavey studied the floor where muddy unmatched footprints revealed a trail from the door to the bench. "Where's your shoe?"

"It came off," said Casey. "In the slough."

Mr. Peavey appeared to be reasoning things through. "So you lost a shoe and you got found with something that don't belong to you. How you gonna explain that to your pa?"

Casey had no answer. The requirement to explain it all, should it arise, felt like an unfair burden on top of the act itself.

"Your brother, he put you up to this, didn't he?" said Mr. Peavey.

"No," insisted Casey after a pause. "It was just me."

Mr. Peavey's eyes bored into him for a long while. Finally, Casey broke the gaze. "Maybe I could pick bales," he said, his chin on his chest.

"What? Talk a little louder."

"To pay for what I done."

Mr. Peavey looked slow to understand. "I'm about done haying," he said. "I got my rod and reel back, so we're square on that. As for your oxfords, that's a matter you'll need to take up with your folks."

Casey glared at the evil Zebco in Mr. Peavey's hand, wishing it would disappear.

"You know, something bothers me," said Mr. Peavey, frowning. "Do you even know how to use a rig like this?"

"I used a rod and reel before," said Casey.

"A spinning reel?"

"I don't know. No," answered Casey cautiously.

"You see, this is what they call a closed-face spinning reel," said Mr. Peavey, using his thumb to rub away a smear. "It's quite the design. Use it right and you'll never get a backlash." He raised his hand in a casting motion, but the rod's tip brushed the crossbeam of the small room.

"Wait, let me turn the yard light on." He found the switch. Hesitant, Casey followed him to the cone of light outside, where Mr. Peavey wiggled himself out of his jacket and let it fall to the ground.

"Now, there's a special motion you use with a spinning rod," he explained. He raised his arm above his shoulder in an easy motion and returned it forward. The lure with the line trailing flew into the darkness with a soft whirring and struck the gravel on the road with an impressive clank. He reeled it in with his left hand.

"Once more now, watch," he commanded, and the lure soared into the night air, traveled a farther distance and dropped softly to the grass just past the road.

"OK, your turn," he said, offering the rod and reel to Casey, who accepted it cautiously with two hands.

"Here, grip the rod with your casting hand around the reel seat," he said when he detected Casey's uneasiness. "Good, now your pointer and middle fingers go ahead of the reel and your other two behind. Right, like that. Now go ahead."

Casey imitated the motion, but when he brought his arm forward the lure and line went nowhere, wrapping themselves loosely around the forward section of the rod.

"Oops," said Mr. Peavey. "We forgot the release." He explained that when pressed, the button behind the reel would free the line at the beginning of the cast and lock it again at the desired distance.

Casey followed the instruction but squeezed the button too late, and the lure skidded along the ground like a discarded bottle cap. On his next attempt, the lure flew nearly straight up in the air.

"Don't worry," said Mr. Peavey, sensing Casey's discomfort. "You play ball, right? OK, what I want you to do is pretend you're throwing a baseball."

He demonstrated with his arm. "Try and imagine you're in center field getting set to throw home. At the place where you'd let go of the ball, that's when you hit your button."

This time, the lure sailed up and out, nearly as far as it had in the hands of Mr. Peavey.

"That's better. Try it again."

He stood by patiently as Casey attempted more casts, nodding in silent approval or offering little tips such as to lift the index finger as the line is released as a way of indicating the direction of the target.

"Well, now," he said after a few minutes. "I might as well get myself a little more shut-eye before the day gets going. Just leave the thing in the shop when you're done, but be sure you shut the lights off." With that, he picked up his jacket and walked casually into his house.

Casey watched as his neighbor moved about in the kitchen, cupboard to table, table to sink, easily visible in his underwear and red cap. Then, as the house dimmed, Casey resumed the task at hand. As if propelled by their own power, the lure and line traced an invisible path into the blackness of the northern night. Into the dark, back to the light. Out again, and back. Darkness, and light.

# THE BULL HALSEY CHAPTER OF THE SONS OF THE NEW AMERICAN REVOLUTION

## 1 | Points of Order

What she'd come to contemplate in this loose plan still forming, Dolores knew, was improper. But she was also convinced that the pain she felt lately, the one down low that had her groaning in the night, was cancer of the pancreas, for which there was no cure. Never mind that she'd never been sure exactly where the pancreas was or what it did precisely—although something she read made her think of it as a kind of sponge that soaked up stuff like DDT and swallowed shreds of pink Maybelline lipstick.

Dolores had long been obsessed with the infinite causes of human demise, but as her own end advanced, her thoughts turned to other matters momentarily more important. After all, dead was dead. It made no difference how you came to it—an eaten-up pancreas in result amounted to pretty much the same as hanging by a rope from a hackberry tree. To her, these days the greater point was to have everything complete to go, which she was not but intended to be once she evened the score with those who contributed to the misery imposed on her since she alighted in this town four years ago this fall.

Two citizens in particular required dealing with. The first was one witch-jawed Rosarita Wallingford, who had the gall to steal Dolores's husband, Orville. Never mind that Dolores regarded this like absconding with someone's case of kidney stones. The larger point was that prior to Orville, not one of her multitude of companions, boyfriends or husbands had found cause to voluntarily end the partnership, a fact that became a source of great pride.

Especially since she regularly provided an abundance of cause.

However, the other person requiring a comeuppance, Orville himself, presented a problem, since he happened to be currently deceased. Not long after writing Dolores out of his will, he surprised himself, Dolores, Rosarita and other interested parties by yawning wide and slumping dead (of allergic shock) in Doc Tanner's dental chair following the shot he was given just prior to having a molar pulled, thereby destroying Dolores's chances to exact revenge on him.

That she could no longer square the score with Orville after he left her like a worn-out broom was a sad fact that she had at first thought she would take to the grave. Fortunately for Dolores's vindictive need however, there existed a conveniently available man—one Mr. Max Plummer—who made an ideal stand-in for her departed spouse. Not only was Max a loathsome character in his own right, but he was also the former best drinking buddy of her unlamented husband. Dolores believed with all her mutilated heart that Max and Max alone had encouraged, if not persuaded, Orville to walk out of her life and into Rosarita's arms.

There was Max now, sucking on his cigarette like it was providing the pure air of life and all decked out in sunglasses and a fancy embroidered cap with *USS Blakeley* stitched in gold on the crown. With his angry scowl and tight gut, his tickler moustache and the big jeweled rings on his knobby fingers, he looked like the kind of person God put on Earth to remind us that paradise is a long way off.

He crouched on one knee, holding a silvery cosmetic mirror to the ground. Dolores knew what he was up to—checking the bottoms of the pickets in the fence separating their properties for signs of dry rot. She supposed he'd like to maneuver that little mirror close enough to see up her dress, which was good reason to go without panties while puttering around in her rose garden, just to see if the old bastard had any red corpuscles left in those dry bones.

*****

On occasion, Max enjoyed a couple of snorts with his cretin pals, fellow Sons of the New American Revolution, who came around to help him polish and preen the antique car that he kept stored in his spacious garage. They hung about like toilet paper on a tree, those toadies, listening to Max carry on from below the car about bikers and assholes, dickfaces and little pisspots, raghead A-rabs, jerk-off democrats and especially the shameful way citizens of this great country failed to appreciate its greatest military heroes of World War II. Max himself had served honorably in the navy and he made it clear that he still felt duty-bound to honor leaders such as Eisenhower, Nimitz and, above all, his own personal hero, Admiral William F. "Bull" Halsey. Over and over, Dolores listened to that gruff voice riding the night air above his chemically polluted grass with the message that the first sign of a nation's decline came when they forgot brave men like Bull Halsey.

Then, maybe to lighten the atmosphere and prove that behind his eloquence he was just one of the guys, he let out that he sure could use a little poontang one of these days. The laughter, men's laughter, raucous and brutal as thunder, threatened to collapse the walls of both houses, generating just the effect Max wanted. What they didn't know wouldn't hurt them.

\* \* \* \* \*

Max was aware that Dolores was watching him through her east window but didn't let on. What captured his critical eye were the offending curls of white paint and the leaning pickets on the fence separating her property from his. He'd been conducting surveillance on that fence for a year now as it degraded, making for a sorry sight on top of the dandelions and crabgrass on her failed lawn. Lately, he observed that she'd neglected the trimming of her rosebushes on the north side, which to his eye looked willowy. But that's what was predictable when you had no man around.

It was common knowledge that every woman—and this one he had good reason to believe—needed a good pump on a periodic basis or they were likely to go dead in the water. Over several weeks, the more he thought about it, the sweeter the remedy seemed. He'd be performing a great favor by jolting her out of those female heebie-jeebies. The fact was he'd already gotten a start by convincing her to attend a SOTNAR meeting, never mind that she didn't contribute much other than raise a fuss claiming it was an insult to women members just because they weren't mentioned in the name. But that would pass when she came to understand the nature of the group. And on top of that, there was that sweet, secret little memory of her that he guarded like the crown jewels, ready to roll out on just the right occasion.

As he did every night before going to bed, Max wandered into the garage to admire his REO—a 1913 model he'd bought for fifty dollars from a kid shipping out to Okinawa. Max spent three years restoring it with endless coats of lacquer and parts he sent for from every corner of the country. What a picture of splendor she offered, those wooden-spoked wheels, the leather upholstery, the original isinglass shades—and made right here in the USA. Once a week if it didn't rain—plus Independence Day—he took the REO for a stately drive around town to allow the general populace the pleasure of gazing upon true quality of the kind that had ceased to exist in this pussified and indolent society.

\* \* \* \* \*

Shortly after Orv's death, and hounded into it by her neighbor, Dolores reluctantly accepted an invitation to a meeting of the Sons of the New American Revolution (Bull Halsey chapter). According to Max, the still-fledgling society had been wrestled to life to pay homage to his commander in the Pacific theater. According to Dolores, the reason for its existence was to provide Max with someone to give orders to following the passing of his wife (emphysema). That the organization was the first and only of its kind, and that it was located as distant from salt water as it was possible to get in North America, never became a consideration.

The group, consisting of less than a dozen dues-paying members, convened every other week at Pam and Joyce and Deb's Café. Perhaps because the frequency of a fortnightly meeting soon exhausted issues pertaining to its hero—a man who first gained wartime notice by referring to his Japanese foes as "yellow-bellied sons of bitches," the actual business of the group tended toward other subjects. Most popular among these were discussions of matters legal and medical, boisterous claims of the bushels of tomatoes that would have been canned but for the blight, the dangers of gas-powered lawn mowers in use now that the war was over and, increasingly, how to deal with criminal elements closer to home.

These sinister forces were believed to consist of a combination of Indians from the nearby reservation along with the Able gang, the secretive family from up in the hills to the north. Elements of either or both purportedly conducted periodic forays into town to siphon gas, steal lawn ornaments and tear around the streets on thundering motorcycles or in derelict cars so that no hen could nest and no decent person could get a wink of sleep.

Having attended the meeting at the pleasure of Max, Dolores interpreted the lack of a second invitation as an insult, for her attendance firmed up her conviction that the gathering of what should represent the town's finest citizenry was no more than a collection of nattering nincompoops. Moreover, she enjoyed the repartee, the chance to practice her natural talents as a wet blanket and born debunker. Plus, she realized that the gatherings provided her with the means to keep an eye on both Max and Rosarita, the people she had vowed to inflict some as yet undesignated vengeance upon for the sorry state her life had reached in which pain was her only pleasure. Never one to worry about correctness, she began to simply walk in at subsequent meetings, rain or shine, invited or not.

*****

Once again, the despised Rosarita Wallingford dominated the preliminaries with an issue going on thirty years old. Somewhat prior to luring Dolores's husband Orville away, Rosarita's own husband, Glen, was shipped overseas to fight during the first war and, never bothering to rid himself of Rosarita back home, stayed behind to marry a Belgian girl named Yasmine with whom he produced twin boys. After all this time, Rosarita, at age sixty and following the demise of Orville, had, without due consideration, up and married old man Dawson, whose wife had died (perforated intestine) after a misdiagnosis of acid reflux. Now, Rosarita's situation became more complex yet, for word had come from Antwerp that Yasmine had passed away (run down by a streetcar according to what Glen told Rosarita), Glen's sons had gone off to embrace their own preferences of Belgian mischief and Glen himself, having made a fortune in the brewing business, desired now to return to Rolland and reconnect with Rosarita.

Rosarita tended to speak very fast, and after listening to numerous editions of the story, Dolores still had difficulty in determining what was what. As best she could follow, the flighty woman wanted either Glen or his money or both back but didn't really trust the man not to repeat what he did to her once before. Of course, she'd have to divorce Dawson, but to do so would risk seeing him write her out of his will. On the other hand, maybe she was still married to Glen, in which case she would be a bigamist! Then again, maybe the laws of Belgium came to play in there somewhere.

"Why don't you just divorce the whole shebang and start over?" said Jordy Bates, who believed in quick decisions and broad actions, and in fact had just come from sawing down the last of his crab apple trees so as to keep the Indians from stealing the fruit.

Rosarita's freewheeling hemming and hawing convinced Dolores that, in addition to her deceitful habits, she really was the stupidest person ever to open a can of Beanie Weenies. In a town where gossip reigned as important as a full coal bin in November, the woman refused to shut her mouth.

Jordy, a red-faced, undersized, quick-on-the-draw fussbudget, had the right idea. Get rid of everybody. Dolores knew, being well-versed on the topic, that there was nothing to getting a divorce—pay the fee, fill in the blanks while the clerk tapped her pencil and yawned, then wait a while with your fingers crossed to see that the ex didn't pull something funny.

At the same time, she suspected that the real reason Rosarita resisted unbuttoning herself from Glen was that, by some ancient bureaucratic entanglement, a government check had been showing up in her mailbox every month during all the decades since the army first declared him missing in action.

As the discussion stalled, Dolores calculated what it might take to get everyone dragged out and machine-gunned in the town square. The problem with these people was they believed life was something you must map out and then get through—like a long sermon or a drive across Nebraska. Dolores hadn't figured life out and never wanted to. Better to wait and see what comes. She might have her name drawn and be crowned the 1950 Bingo Queen. She might even eventually understand why the world thought zucchini bread and Ernest Hemingway were so wonderful or, dubious as it was with time so short, get lucky in love.

Dolores knew such endless babble exasperated Max, who'd spent twenty years in military service and preferred an orderly agenda. Seeing the blossoming red grooving the man's forehead pleased her immensely. While the exchange continued, he made his way through the tables to the kitchen in search of the gavel, writhing in frustration, horizontal lines of skin bunching on the back of his neck. As usual, his gleaming and oversize Bulova with the blue anchor on its face showed forty-five minutes past time and the formal meeting had not yet begun.

Then, as Max and the attendees might have predicted, in walked Useless Johnston, who ambled over to the counter, adjusted the toothpick in his mouth and turned on his stool to face Max. Useless was not a SOTNAR member. Far from it. He was someone who hung around, appearing at every ball game, every house fire, every fender bender and especially every parade. No one knew what he did for a living or where he lived. He was seen most often tromping along downtown in his buckle overshoes, wearing his striped work cap to shield his shiny bald head and frowning at the sidewalk, looking like he'd dropped something small.

At last, everybody took a seat only to have Max force another delay while he stormed back to the kitchen to borrow Pam's meat tenderizer to use as a gavel. With three short raps on the podium, he brought the meeting into session and ordered his charges to rise and place hand over heart for the reciting of the Pledge of Allegiance. At its conclusion, Dolores pulled out her crossword puzzle, aware she would have to act before the town dolts resumed clawing and snapping at one another like a mess of crayfish in a washtub.

The issue, as it had been for weeks, was how to raise $1,500 to purchase two acres of land from the Stagg family, which would be used to create a park with playground equipment and picnic tables that, while it would be named after Admiral Halsey, would be dedicated in honor of all military veterans. But before they could get to the discussion, Max made sure to observe proper procedure, beginning with a tedious reading of the minutes by the acting secretary, Lilly Saint Claire, who first spat out a golf ball-sized gob of Doublemint into a paper napkin.

"I wish to make an announcement," said Dolores the instant the motion to accept the minutes was passed (by a vote of four to two, with Andy Anderson, a believer in strict neutrality, abstaining as always).

"Somebody's making off with my tea roses," pronounced Dolores in a shaky voice.

All eyes turned to her. Her pancreas delivered a quick, hot twist. An anxious murmur swirled through the room, for while theft was a problem and well-tended gardens a source of community pride, no one wanted to officially acknowledge Dolores and her outrageous purple dresses, her disrespectful attitude and her citified ways.

"Point of order!" interjected Jordy Bates, his comment partially smothered by the sound of Joyce scraping yesterday's grease from the grill. "You're supposed to come to your feet when addressing the chair."

"My feet hurt too much," said Dolores, who couldn't take her eyes off the baling wire keeping Jordy's spectacles intact.

"Probably Ables or Indians," said Leo Larush.

"Coulda been either one," said Andy after some deliberation.

"Were they on motorcycles?" demanded Max, allowing himself a rare distraction.

Dolores folded her arms across her chest, crossed her legs at the ankles and lifted her eyes to the ceiling fan. The truth was she wasn't even sure she was missing roses. She simply wanted to preempt the forthcoming arguments concerning teeter-totters and treated-wood Adirondack chairs.

With that, Rosarita Wallingford, her attention diverted from her romantic woes, piped in. "What varieties were them tea roses you claim disappeared?"

"Saint Patricks and David Austins," said Dolores, pleased with herself for having a tailored answer. Various members shifted their gaze out the window, where Marcil Deveau's dray wagon rattled by. Kasimir Kavorcek, SuperValu's rotund butcher, further interrupted the discussion to shuffle out and enquire of Marcil when he intended to deliver his case of blood sausage, now overdue by three days. With that resolved, the discussion resumed.

"Well," said Rosarita, who also cultivated roses. "Maybe where you come from tea roses are different, but anybody that knows flowers could tell you that Austins and Paddies don't grow this far north. Even if they did, leafworms and mold would get them before they were six inches high." With that, she sat back, hands on her belly, cheered by her botanical astuteness.

Dolores couldn't hear as good as she used to, but her head bones worked adequate to tell her that the yokels were snickering. Max Plummer straightened his cap and squared himself up on his chair to look more in command. He took up the meat tenderizer and rapped sharply three times on the tabletop. As the tumult gave way to order, Dolores fixed her gaze on Rosarita Wallingford while the details of a plan took shape.

\* \* \* \* \*

She waited until after midnight when KFYR signed off with a rousing version of "The Star-Spangled Banner" and dragged her old wooden stepladder outside, through the alley and into Rosarita's backyard. Careful not to put weight on her bad side where her pancreas was hardening into peanut brittle, she propped the ladder against the porch, placing it so the legs straddled the anthill at the base of the wall. With her brace and bit, Dolores drilled a half-inch hole into the shingled roof above where she knew Rosarita's bedroom to be, having used this procedure previously to check on her and Orville. Poking her knitting needle into the hole to make sure it went all the way through, she wedged in a funnel into which she poured half a bottle of Karo dark syrup, then dribbled a trail over the eaves and down the wall to the center of the anthill.

That night, Dolores slept better than she had in weeks, and even the pain down in her pancreas backed off to a kind of half-remembered, hollowed-out place.

## 2 | Old Henry

Not that she wasted much energy in reflection, but Dolores marveled now and then how she could have been so foolish regarding Orville. He'd grown up near Rolland and convinced her to leave Minnetonka, Minnesota, where she dwelled alone in a comfortable condo, trying to avoid boredom while telling her neighbors that she'd taken early retirement.

They'd met when a descending elevator in the Foshay Tower stalled on the twenty-sixth floor. By the time the five-foot-tall Norwegian repairman rescued them, they'd arranged to dine at Peter's Grill on the ground floor. She admired the delicate way Orville dipped his fries in his ketchup, took note of the sizable tip he left for their surly waitress, and before they reached the street, discerned that he was interested and she would treat the situation as a romantic encounter rather than a business proposition.

Things progressed without delay. Orville displayed a boyish innocence that Dolores found refreshing after all those jaded and world-weary spouses whose outstanding attribute turned out to be their skill in concealing from her what fast became obvious: they were in decline. "They're after a nurse and purse," warned her old pal Tillie Tyler, who prided herself on remaining free of legal commitment.

But Orville was a glib and youthful fifty-four. He spoke of the "Emerald City of the Turtle Mountains" with its pristine lakes and fertile fields, its approachable and progressive citizens, its reputation as a bastion of tolerance and equality. He assured her Rolland would be the perfect place to spend the rest of her days, neglecting to mention that they wouldn't be spent with him. They were married less than six weeks after the brake failure in the Foshay Tower elevator.

In Rolland, they took up housekeeping in a run-down two-story purchased from the widow of the John Deere dealer who had recently died (brain tumor, malignant) with what was left of Dolores's once-substantial savings. No sooner had Dolores gotten her roses planted, complete with a chunk of gypsum and a 16 penny nail to provide iron and calcium to each, than the recently widowed Max Plummer bought the place next door and set in to fixing it up, working like a madman while sneaking curious looks across the fence at Dolores. Next thing she knew, Rosarita waltzed along, and quick as a magician, snatched Orville right out from under her nose. Then, before Dolores's first rose blossomed, Orville took up residence with Rosarita, developed a bad molar and just like that, left them both in beggary.

In bequeathing her the house, such as it was, Orville committed no great act of generosity, there being a vacant place to be had for taxes every block on Rolland's south side. So here she was, broke, too old to ply her trade and stuck in a one-horse town with no jockey.

* * * * *

Dolores had been married now six times, the same number as that king of England, Henry VIII, who she knew about from a movie starring Charles Laughton. Often, she dreamed that she could rid herself of spouses the way old Henry did, by chopping their heads off. Instead, half of them took their time and died on their own, leaving Dolores to learn afterward that she'd been fleeced again, funerals and headstones going for what they did these days.

Thirty years ago and in business down in the Cities, she had money to burn. Youthful, trim and in demand, customers requested her by name. Dolly was the name she used, turning forty or more tricks on long weekends if the Pillsbury and General Mills paydays hit just right or Fort Snelling let loose on leave. Not once did she contract a disease, not even chlamydia, which among the girls was like catching cold. She would wake up in the afternoon after a good sleep, red, swollen and sore, but with a feeling of achievement and more than a thousand in cash hid in an old silk stocking—money that grew into a considerable sum only to be eaten away by successive husbands in the manner a mouse will nibble its way through the cheese until the trap falls.

Still, the marriages did provide temporary breaks from professional demands. It was pleasant sleeping with the same man night after night. You got to know their expectations and their moves, and it was a comfort not having to be on the lookout for ones that would grab their shorts and run. Then, over time, her enjoyment level got to be like her late husbands' headstones: each a little less substantial than the last. When the third husband passed on (complications of diabetes), she considered consolidating the graves, maybe layering them like planks in a lumberyard, but dropped the scheme, having no inkling how many more might come along in the future.

Frequently since Orville died, she thought of those husbands, and how each one maltreated her one way or another, dying being quite a slap in the face if you thought about it. Those men, they were like cars she'd owned, some brand-new, some used, a couple real lemons, but with this in common: all had good paint, no dents and drove OK before breaking down after the first little strain. But God knows, if she had the time, she would do it again.

It made her want to weep to think of the girls she knew and how much better off they ended up. Unlike Dolores, most of them hung on to their money. Enjoying the life of leisure down in Florida they were, owning villas with orange trees and servants to squeeze the oranges. Her friend Tillie wound up living in finery the year round on the *Queen Mary*, playing shuffleboard by day and entertaining the occasional first-class socialite at night while floating back and forth across the Atlantic Ocean.

Before departing for the meeting of SOTNAR—Snotter, as Dolores called it—she checked her behind in the full-length. The sight called to memory the time when she along with every woman wanted to look like the movie queens of her youth, the energetic and beautiful blonde Carole Lombard or the spellbinding Mary Pickford. And God help it, now with Carole forever in her grave and Mary plump in her dotage, they all did.

\* \* \* \* \*

Max was having a bad day. The two-person committee he'd appointed to formulate a concrete plan for the park had presented its report, but the committee, supervised by Jordy Bates and assisted more or less in name by Kasimir Kavorcek, had clearly exceeded its authority. Lacking completely any mention of Admiral Halsey, the statement suggested a single item, which Kasimir wrote out in block letters: MAKE A STATUE OF SIKORSKI.

On top of all that, the *Rolland Ripple* had at last responded to Max's pleas for publicity for SOTNAR, but in a story printed in the latest edition, managed to get every fact wrong, including the organization's history and purpose, while somehow crediting Kasimir Kavorcek as the head and force behind its founding. Max's name appeared nowhere in the story, while his hero was referred to as "Admiral Hall." Moreover, responding to the *Ripple*'s misinformation, the Rolland citizenry now deluged the group with letters separated into two general categories: those opposed to the whole half-baked idea, and those liking it while advocating absurdities such as a staging area for reenactments of famous battles, a bell tower, a children's carousel and a petting zoo.

Max, still steaming over Kasimir Kavorcek being identified publicly as SOTNAR'S top man, snuck a glance at the stone-bald meatcutter plopped on a folding chair in his bloody apron, looking glum. Why, the ignorant bohunk had yet to contribute a word at a meeting, evidently content to sit there looking sinister. But what could you expect of a man coming from one of those Commie countries?

The street door opened, sending the dangling strips of flypaper swinging as in sulked Rosarita Wallingford with pinkish calamine lotion smeared over her shrunken face, covering what looked to be red welts. Before the members absorbed this strange sight, Dolores showed up wearing a smirk like she got goosed with a yardarm. When he got up to use the head last night, Max had seen a light on over at her place. Maybe she was entertaining the troops and that's why she looked so satisfied this morning. As he regarded this remote possibility, Max himself had to beat back a sting of annoyance and a touch of jealousy. That sort of thing would sure as hell monkey-wrench his strategy.

The arrival of the two women marked another instance that made Max wish he still belonged to Uncle Sam's navy. He no sooner got the troops off the subject of chimes than Rosarita started in mouthing twaddle about red ants, only to be interrupted by Toivo Bergstrom holding up like an auctioneer's assistant a picture of what looked like a horse. Civilian life was for queers and nincompoops. All this debating and checking six ways over China to see if something was legit. He lit another Pall Mall. He may have been a noncom, but he made top rate and knew how to give orders to peewees and shitbirds. Straighten up there, swabbie. Either stick to the agenda or shut your trap. You want the brig, is that what you want, the brig?

At Rosarita's insistence, the detestable citizens put aside a pending empty-headed discussion about the effect horse droppings might have on the park to take up the matter of her fresher catastrophe involving predatory ants. The victim herself introduced a motion seconded by Jordy that SOTNAR petition the county to spray for noxious insects. The ensuing discussion about whether weeds might be sprayed simultaneously was interrupted by Lilly, who wanted to know how to spell "noxious."

In the time it took Leo Larush to dig out his portable dictionary, Toivo retrieved his horse picture and began waving it about. Kasimir Kavorcek stood up, grunting with the effort. "N-o-x-i-o-u-s," he said, and sat down hard on his chair and folded his arms.

Useless Johnston caused a minor disturbance when, responding to some attraction known to him only, he slid from his stool and made his way to the kitchen, past the walk-in freezer and out the back door.

But Max ignored all this nonsense. He'd been scanning the unsolicited letters of suggested features for the park when he came upon one for a "captain's rostrum constructed in the manner of a ship's bridge with a steering wheel to be painted blue like the sea," and it lent him an idea.

"Hold the reading and come to order," he cried, and waited for the squeaking chairs and murmurs to settle. "I'm now entertaining a motion that SOTNAR hold a community celebration along with the formal groundbreaking for our park and that it invite Admiral William F. Halsey to speak at the event."

The room went silent save for the clatter of dishes and clank of steam pipes in the kitchen.

"What was that?" asked Leo Larush, who was hard of hearing.

Max repeated himself.

Jordy leaped to his feet. "By god," he said. "I'll make that motion."

At least three members rose to second it, but Dolores outshouted them. "Why don't you invite Harry Truman while you're at it," she said.

The suddenness of her contrary remark sent the others into a brief silence before Jordy, still standing, wiped his mouth and pointed a bony finger at Dolores.

"I don't think we need to listen to people comin' here from the east to tell us what's off beam when they don't know bullshit from goose grease let alone one flower from another."

Dolores let the laughter play out while scrutinizing the evil smirk on Jordy's face and guessed she might need to live forever before retiring this particular debt. She returned the expression with glee, sustaining it while waiting for Jordy to look away. When he looked back she upped the intensity of her smile. He lowered himself to his chair and wiggled around uncertainly as he tried to conceal what everyone had observed: he'd sat on his cap. At once, he focused his sight on Pam, who stood chalking the lunch special on the board next to the door: *HUNGRY GOULASH 1.10 plus coffee.*

Dolores got up early the next day in time to see Max outside sweeping the nightly accumulation of cobwebs from his yellow porch light before proceeding to the center of his yard to hoist the American flag.

She waited until he disappeared into his garage to check on his REO to avoid having to reciprocate his eardrum-grating top-of-the-morning greeting. She settled in to weeding around the roses, liking the chore for its repetitive nature and the way it helped establish order for the unfolding day. Dig out a thistle, get postage stamps; pull a cocklebur, throw out the old milk; uproot a dandelion, call the drugstore for more water pills.

The sound of hammering from Max's garage broke her concentration, leading her to wonder what kind of husband he'd been. She figured she knew—pretty much the style of Harold Peavey, Orville's niece Leah's husband. Loyal, predictable, hardworking and fully in charge. In short, boring as Cream of Wheat. In fact, as Dolores herself had seen proof of too many times, women prefer bad boys. Women want men to be exciting—to bring flowers, to spend too much money, to shave in the shower.

Her thoughts went from husbands to boyfriends, of which she'd had more than Carter's Little Liver Pills, and to the thousands of tricks she'd entertained. Good men and bad men, they all fit particular patterns—wheezing and coming, groaning and coming, grunting like bloodhounds and coming, screeching like baboons and coming, about every tenth one claiming he loved her as he squirted like a punctured hose, never mind he hadn't known her at suppertime, and, at least once a month, a smiling repeater striding in with a diamond ring.

Then there were the drunks with their tedious, disgusting ways—hiccups, booze breath, piss spots on their underwear. She would give refunds now and then though never to the drunks. Occasionally someone grabbed his hat in the middle of arrangements like maybe he all at once gathered where he was and now chose to be above it all, like how could he think of baring his hairy ass to a stranger? Dolores could only shake her head in puzzlement. If you don't like banana splits, what are you doing in the Dairy Queen?

She excelled at bringing the timid ones around. It was a specialty of hers—she even accepted referrals from other girls. She developed techniques she would never divulge. It was all in the art—pretending an interest, going beyond minimum professional standards. The right words were as effective as the right touch.

She shook her head, recalling the shy customers, mostly but not all young, and more virgins than you'd think. Wary they might be, but open them up and they jabbered like monkeys, wanting to discuss most anything other than themselves. In conversation, they eventually got around to wanting to know why and how she got into the business. Playing psychology they were and wanting to help, like all you were waiting for was to be shown the way out. She let them think what they wanted. In fact, she had no hang-ups about daddies or abusive big brothers. She liked sex, sure, but that wasn't the whole story. She never even had a brother, and her dad, well, he never stuck around long enough for her to find much fault in him, having died when she was seven years old.

Clients would never understand that, like in any industry, graded levels of quality existed within the organization. Streetwalkers, they were the unfortunates. That's where you found the ones who'd been taken advantage of as fledgling girls or maybe got in deep with toot or big H. But the higher class, of which Dolores was a proud member, they kept their pride up and their heads on straight. They worked in a house or with an agent. Pimp—that was an ugly sounding word. The agents Dolores caught on with were responsible businessmen. They found you places to live, ran your errands, paid for your doctors, sent you on vacation and made sure no client mistreated you. One of her agents, Ray, oversaw her for nine years and they never had a squabble. She still believed she wouldn't be in a pickle now if Ray hadn't had a flat tire that time in South St. Paul and gotten his throat cut while walking for help.

As for those that look down on a girl, well, they just never thought things through. As a youngster, you're told to find something you like, then work hard at it and you'll do well. The fact was that she took up the trade for money—to pay the bills, to keep a roof over her head, and if she got rich, that was OK, too.

\* \* \* \* \*

Dolores had never seen anything like this for weeds. Buttonweed with its little star-shaped flowers, burdock, which she heard was edible but not for her, cordgrass so sharp it sliced the skin like paper cuts, coneflower with its many-colored blossoms and lemon scent, crabgrass which might even grow on the moon, dandelion that Dolores rather liked for the purity of its yellow but eradicated anyway knowing it to be particularly despised by generalissimo next door, pigweed that clung to the soil so tenaciously you broke your hand trowel trying to dig it out, the ghastly leafy spurge, bottle gentian too beautiful to be a weed and wild carrot which never did anybody no good. There were maple seedlings, mustard, jimsonweed, rape weed and volunteer corn plants from God knows where. And maybe Jordy was right, her roses weren't exactly thriving. If she didn't prune and fertilize them soon, they wouldn't be worth stealing.

She peeked through the gap in the pickets, smelling the tomatoes in Max's garden, where his vegetables were arranged in perfect formation just like on a parade ground—columns of carrots, rows of radishes. Dolores herself abandoned vegetables long ago, what with the rabbits, and now she hungered for them. She wished she dared pilfer a few, but being acquainted with Max, she imagined he counted every last cob of corn. They never bothered him, those rabbits. He owned a gun, but his scowl alone was likely to frighten Peter Rabbit along with the majority of North America's fur-bearing creatures. Her mind snapped back to her roses, and she pictured them replaced by rutabagas.

She'd had it up to here. What's more, her pancreatic pain had come back with bells on and felt even lower. It must be growing faster than rhubarb, having reached her hip now. Her world was spinning to a close. She was going to have to speed things up if she wanted her books cleared on this side of the light.

\* \* \* \* \*

At the next meeting of SOTNAR, the overriding question involved the formal vote to extend the offer to Admiral Halsey, the issue having been tabled when

Max perceived a swirl of dissension among the members. Now, however, he had reason to believe the plan would slide through quicker than a duck quack. After enduring Rosarita's concern over what type of fence should be erected to protect the grass—split rail or barbed wire—followed by Andy's impassioned diatribe about the responsibility of all organizations to respect the equality of all mankind since after all, fair is fair, and the best way around this situation was half split and half barbed, Max could wait no longer.

"If I may interrupt," said Max, raising a hand confidently. "I just received notice that the Stagg brothers have donated a parcel of land to our organization pending our agreement to develop it as we've discussed." He paused to let the news sink in, withholding, naturally, the information that the property offered was not the parcel bordering Main Street, but an oil-and-cinder-soaked dumping ground located up by Bucktown with no road leading into it. He hooked his thumbs behind his suspenders and continued. "That will naturally negate any concern over our ability to fund travel for the admiral."

"Wait. Did you say donated?" said Dolores.

"Most generously, yes," beamed Max.

"Then you must not be crowing the same Stagg brothers who own the hardware that charges a quarter each for tulip bulbs that you can drive up to Canada and get for two dozen a dollar."

The group became reserved and doubtful as Dolores fanned herself cheerfully with a breakfast menu. The hush yielded to ratchety throat-clearings as heads gawked around like gophers emerging from holes and everyone waited for someone else to speak.

*Damn*, thought Max, doing a quick tally in his head. The results were troubling. Leo Larush, a dependable yes vote, chose this week to go walleye fishing in Canada, and Lilly Saint Claire was laid up in the hospital with shingles. Andy Anderson, who wouldn't get off the fence to call off the Crucifixion, would recuse himself. Kasimir Kavorcek hadn't gotten over his snit at the quiet rejection of the Sikorski statue request when it became obvious that no one other than himself had any idea who Sikorski was. Toivo Bergstrom, though present physically, tended to get matters mixed up when drinking, which lately was pretty much all the time. Max briefly pondered enlisting Joyce from the kitchen, but the cook/co-owner was cranky as an old crow lately because half the attendees ordered water instead of coffee and nobody had bought a pastry in a month. He counted again. It could go either way. A tie would do, as Max himself, as chairman, would be allowed to render the verdict. But that was assuming either Toivo or Dolores cast an aye. Toivo looked a bit wobbly, so the sooner the polling came the better. Max straightened up on his stool, hacked into a paper napkin and advised that, barring objections, they would proceed with the vote.

And sure as the sun shines on Dixie, Dolores tugged at her dress as if it were too tight around her waist, came to life and demanded a discussion.

"What's to discuss?" asked Jordy. "Even the mayor endorsed the general idea."

Dolores cleared her throat. "I don't care if John the Baptist endorsed the general idea. What makes this admiral so high-horsed, and if he's that important, what makes you think he'd care to spend expensive time in this two-dog town?"

Max had driven himself apoplectic by the time Dolores completed her spiel, but then Ralph Brown spoke up and allowed how Dolores might have a point. If the group got turned down flat or worse, received no rejoinder at all from the admiral, it would likely make them all look more foolish than they already were.

Max signaled to Jordy, who leaped from his chair as if bee-stung. "I call for the question, Mr. Chair," he said.

In the absence of Lilly, Max, after gathering himself, called the names one by one. The vote was tied when he reached the name of Toivo Bergstrom.

"Toivo?" he called.

Toivo sat up and smiled but offered no response.

Max called again, louder and adding the last name.

"What say you, Toivo?" said Max as Jordy reached over and shook the man's shoulder. At this, Toivo's eyes rolled back and he dropped his head to the table.

Jordy shook him again. "He's passed out, Mr. Chair."

Max looked around helplessly. There with his spine against the counter sat Useless Johnston with a look on his face as blank and meaningless as a plate of leftover coleslaw. Max sighed. That left only Dolores. Barely able to get the three syllables out, Max called her name.

Sensing all eyes were on her, she paused as if agonizing over her choice. Max waited, a pleading look in his eyes.

"I believe I'll vote no," she said, smiling politely. "Or *nay* to be proper."

Max placed a finger in his collar and worked it around his neck, considering whether he had authority to impose martial law when Jordy Bates once again stood.

"Mr. Chair," Jordy said in his wheezy voice, "I make a motion to kick somebody out of our organization."

Max reached for the paper napkin dispenser to find it stuffed so full he had to dig the napkin out in shreds. "You are saying you wish to expel a member from our organization?"

"Yep," said Jordy.

"I go along with that," said Rosarita.

Max pursed his lips in feigned contemplation. "I see," he said sympathetically. "Which member in particular do you have in mind?"

"Huh? Why, that highfalutin Dolores, who else?"

"I see." Max cleared his throat. "And what should be the grounds?"

"At least twice now she never even stood up for the pledge," said Jordy.

"And accusing other members of this and that," added Rosarita.

"I won't even mention about her reading a book during a meeting," said Jordy. "I'm calling for a vote."

Max whacked the tenderizer a bit too sharply, causing Toivo to lurch to a short-lived posture of attention. "It being the wish of the members, we will proceed with a vote."

But Dolores wasn't quite through. "I demand a ruling under the bylaws," she said.

Everybody, along with the drowsing Toivo, knew that SOTNAR had no bylaws. Max so stated, calming the protest. Dolores was invited to exit the room for the balloting.

Dolores gathered herself and hobbled toward the kitchen, where she peered through the order window out at Max and his bylaw-less flock. There they were with their tired old expressions and willingness to look stupid, the condition with which anyone who had lived in Rolland for more than a year was afflicted.

She waited as the votes were tabulated, recounted and recorded. Except for Andy Anderson, who dumbfounded his fellow members by voting against the measure only to have it later discovered that he placed a second ballot in favor of it, each member cast an unambiguous vote to expel her. Dolores knew she would be busy in the days to come.

\* \* \* \* \*

Jordy lived on the south side of town, requiring Dolores to develop her plans with precision. She no longer drove after running into the loading dock at the dairy co-op. Harold Peavey, who still drove for the dairy then, was saved from grave injury only by the six cases of whole milk in half gallons separating him from the daggerlike silver ornament on the hood of Dolores's Olds 98.

In place of the heavy set of sockets, she dropped into her handbag a Crescent along with a medium Phillips, two sizes of flatheads and her spool of number 12 wire. At the last minute, she threw in pliers, and, once again following the KFYR sign-off, set out. Favoring her pancreas side, she limped past the Pentecostal church, the vacant lot where a livery once stood and the school where Orville didn't learn much.

Jordy was an old man, with fine white hair growing in his ears, which Dolores supposed he thought made himself look wise like Moses. He owned the only bulldozer in town, a machine as big as a school bus with which he contracted with Marshon Lumber to raze buildings, and in fact was about to demolish a rotting henhouse with in Bucktown just outside the city limits the very next day. Proud of his powerful machine, declared army surplus and purchased for a song down at Fort Abercrombie, he kept it tuned like a fiddle, making it all the easier for Dolores. She wired the throttle, clutch and brakes, and the next time Jordy hit the starter, the machine took off like a dragster and scraped all the topsoil from his backyard along with his crab apple tree stumps and his hedge of mulberries. From there it roared full-speed across the baseball diamond where it took out the backstop and the right field fence, and, with Jordy barely hanging on, came to rest half-submerged in the creek beyond the field. Trying to get a line on it, Jordy slipped on a rock, landed on his fanny in the gooey bottom and came up spitting with mud in his hairy ears. Later that day, he was forced to pay eight dollars to Ralph's Standard Station for use of the wrecker to pull the dozer out.

Once again, Dolores slept unbothered and pain-free.

*****

Curious about how high the noses of the town's overly energized, Pecksniffian hypocrites could go in their attitudes toward a leper, Dolores redoubled her nocturnal activities. Over two weeks, the following happened: When Mrs. Kasimir Kavorcek grabbed her clothesline to hang a freshly washed, expensive bedsheet, she received an electric shock that caused her to fling the sheet high in the air where the breeze captured it before it settled like a parachute over the compost heap. The wires powering the Standard Station's gas pumps shorted out, causing Ralph Brown to lose a half day's gasoline income. Toivo Bergstrom discovered that his driver and five iron had been hacksawed nearly clear through so that when he took a mighty swing on the first tee the head of the club flew to the side, striking a glancing blow to the skull of a client to whom he was hoping to sell five acres of swamp. Jordy Bates, deserving of a second dose of retribution, backed his Hudson out of his driveway only to have one of the wheels fall off, causing the vehicle to veer to the left and roll over his granddaughter's tricycle. Only Dolores's ambivalence regarding the Seventh Commandment protected young Reverend Paulson and his married church secretary from awaking in their separate residences to find the letter *A* painted in red on their front doors. Instead, Dolores contented herself with jamming the locks on the church doors, sending most congregation members home on a Sabbath morning while the remainder took turns crawling through a basement window in their Sunday attire.

Hearing the results of her toils, Dolores allowed herself a twinkling of regret that she was about to expire. At the same time, she anticipated the joy forthcoming when she completed her master project: the comeuppance of Max Plummer.

* * * * *

On Friday evening, she watched Max as he carefully backed the REO out of the garage to park it on the street. There, as usual, he left it in full display so that weekend passersby might build their anticipation before seeing the machine alive and cruising about town the following morning.

In the night, historically her greatest ally, Dolores sneaked out with a glowing ash can in her gloved hand and approached the REO, noting the moist spots on the street beneath it. This would be simple. She opened the passenger door on the street side, freeing the aroma of varnish and gas fumes, substances whose sole purpose in existing was to mate with a spark. She dumped the lighted coals on the seat just above where she knew the fuel line passed, closed the door gently and retreated to the safety of her rose garden.

Crouching amid the bushes and wary of being pricked by thorns, she examined her roses as she waited. The remaining Gingerbread Men looked well, the blossoms large, their shape accented by the night dew glistening in the moonlight. The Albas offered a less robust appearance, maybe even suggesting they were on the way out, leading Dolores to notice how bad her pains were tonight. She changed position, moaning with the effort.

It took a while. A bit of smoke curled above the door of the REO. Then, rather than the anticipated explosion, an earsplitting, steady roar came from down the street, and one of those big motorcycles grumbled into view.

She listened as the machine downshifted. Just as it reached Max's house, the noise lessened. Dolores lifted her head. The rider wore a kerchief over his head. The muscles of his enormous arms glistened as he glowered at the thick cloud of black smoke emitting from the REO.

The man dismounted and ran toward Max's door.

Max had wired his doorbell to play "Anchors Aweigh," and he leaped from his desk where he was reloading ammo for his .357. He moved stealthily to the door, peered through the peephole and saw bared brown arms, a hand tugging on the latch, a mouth forming nonsense. His foresight in installing a steel security door paid off. He backpedaled instantly to the hall closet where he stocked his weapons. Properly armed with his Colt 45ACP, he made for the door, head down, unlocked all three dead bolts, yanked the door open and leveled his sidearm at the chest of the deranged, would-be intruder, who yelped and threw his hands skyward. At that moment, the REO erupted in an orange flash that lifted it off the ground and three feet into the street where it burned pleasantly, sending off balls of smoke that rose straight up into the night sky.

As occasionally occurred, the fire truck refused to start. Volunteer Chief Tommy Keegan summoned Ralph to tow it to the scene of the fire, but by the time it got there, the blaze had faded into a series of soft explosions resembling those produced by large, damp firecrackers. Max had reeled out his garden hose, which didn't quite reach the fire but dropped its flume of water ten feet short, drenching two bystanders guilty of inattention. The motorcyclist gunned his bike, vowing that this would be the last good goddamn time he ever came to the aid of a citizen in this forlorn, fascist town.

Dolores's searing pain eased off into a gentle warmth.

## 3 | Eggs

To the concern of everyone save Dolores, the dates for the groundbreaking drew near and the admiral had yet to respond to the luxuriously worded invitation formulated by Max in consultation with the high school English teacher, Miss Rhoads, who assured him that all the commas lay in their proper place. Just the same, the loyal SOTNAR members put in long hours attending to every auxiliary detail. The whole thing would begin with a parade, and though Max could no longer lead it with his REO, numerous organizations agreed to provide floats and bands, among them the Shriners from Devils Lake, who would bring their tricycles. Following the parade, families could visit the fairgrounds, where they could ride the Ferris wheel, win prizes for knocking over wooden milk bottles, and participate in pie-eating contests, three-legged races and square dance competitions.

"Let them dance all they want," insisted the banished Dolores to her ex-niece Leah Peavey. "All the planning in the world won't keep their monkey business from folly on top of catastrophe. Who would want to spend a quarter throwing a ball at a milk bottle to win a five-cent peashooter? And if anyone wants music, they can stay home and listen to the CBC. And as for Admiral What's-his-face, a man like him ought to find more important things to do than waste his time with country hicks who wouldn't know a battleship from a carbuncle."

\* \* \* \* \*

As matters passed the planning stage, Max Plummer fathomed why Dolores forecast difficulties. When word got out that tents were to be erected, some pissant inspector in a hard hat descended on Rolland to make sure that riggers schooled in the art of canvas and rope were available and credentialed with the proper permits. On the heels of that official came a health department fussbudget advising guidelines for food providers. The carnival demanded an ungodly sum as a deposit before committing, and in an apparent fit of dogma-induced greed, three protestant operators of food stands jockeyed for the optimal position following the Catholics' announcement that they would not be serving hamburgers on Friday. But worst of all, nothing had been heard from the admiral. A second invite went out just in case.

Yet Max retained his resiliency, the quality that brought him through all those years in the navy while being cheated out of any duty more dangerous than escorting a liberty ship full of vodka, vermouth and olives to Bermuda, allowing the officers on that front to face the hazards of war. A path always existed—as demonstrated by the parliamentary maneuverings that rid the organization of that pain-in-the-neck Dolores.

Which, by the way, as he feared, was causing him regret. In the heat of battle, he'd allowed the underling Jordy to overstep authority. Why couldn't the banished member be Kasimir or even Jordy himself, either of which he would gladly order the keelhauling of. He couldn't keep from noticing that Dolores had been keeping to herself the last few days, no doubt depressed over being drummed out of SOTNAR.

He inspected her as she marched into her house with her purse tucked firmly against her ribs. Still a handsome woman with her long gray hair, she knew how to dress sophisticatedly with no frippery. Even for gardening, she wore a well-designed sundress with a bib that rode comfortably on her more than satisfactory chest. Max liked an ample woman. His late wife Marge tended to let herself go toward the end, acquiring a slouchy and saggy appearance, much to Max's disappointment, as he preferred a girl who would snap to.

Regarding himself as a man of reason, he saw now that not only had an issue been forced, but for the sake of his duty as a gentleman, he must, on behalf of SOTNAR, express his formal regret. And thus compelled, he saw no time better than the present. As he stepped over the picket fence toward her doorstep, he realized that never before had he come so close to Dolores's house. Once, long ago, he crossed into her yard with a glass of lemonade, but the woman surprised him by requesting that a shot of gin be added and then tossed it down so hastily she couldn't have tasted it, clearly spoiling good citrus.

But perched there on her crumbling step, a sense of bleakness descended on him. This house was decaying, the town was on its last legs and he was getting old. Out of such contemplations, he emerged, half a minute later, to alter a plan for once in his life without intense deliberation.

Dolores leaned over the cast-iron pan, frying eggs in butter, maintaining a firm hold on the spatula so as not to break the yokes, when she heard the door. Mormon missionaries again, no doubt, wanting to talk. She carried no objection to discussions about God—in fact, she herself chitchatted with a god, not to a special person with a beard and laundered saffron nightgown, but to a kind of spread-out element that made itself available and hung out everywhere like dust bunnies. She considered not answering the too-vigorous knock as the eggs looked just right but decided that at this point she best keep her options open.

She drew back in surprise at the sight of Max Plummer, who gave her the impression of being very much off his feed. "Well," she said. "It's Mr. Chairman himself, it is."

Max bowed slightly from the waist, his palms flat against his navy-issue tan slacks. "Pardon the intrusion, but I'm here to address a matter very urgent."

Dolores froze. "Well, come in then and get it over with," she said.

"Actually, two matters," Max added.

Uninformed about the different levels on the first floor and their artful concealment under a richly patterned oriental rug, Max stumbled and bashed his knee against the walnut coffee table.

Seizing the temporary advantage, Dolores went on the offensive. "I'm in a bit of a hurry here," she said. "Can you make it quick?"

Max used the back of the recliner to pull himself to his feet. "First, I come as a representative of the Sons of the New American Revolution," he began, and waited fruitlessly for a response. "Admiral Halsey chapter," he added, smiling. "As executive officer, I'm empowered to advise that you are restored to active membership with full benefits."

A brief period of discomfort ensued.

"And there will be no permanent record."

The eggs popped in the cast-iron pan. "What else you got?"

Red-faced and sweating, Max straightened to his full five feet nine inches, engendering a brief stab of pity in Dolores.

"I'm requesting that you accept my hand in marriage," Max said, his eyes glazing.

Dolores knew she shouldn't have worn this old duster. Every time she touched it, something outlandish came to pass.

With the difficult part out of the way, Max revved up his blubbering, spittle flying from his mouth. "First thing is we'll rip out the fence. You can keep the rose garden, but we'll want to resod the back lawn."

He went on, detailing his pension, their likely income, his life insurance and his intention to attend annual reunions of his shipmates. He pointed out the advantages of their reduced living expenses, the ability to shop in quantity—his PX privileges, after all, must not be sneezed at.

Dolores reviewed the speech in her mind, trying to bring up whether he listed love in there somewhere. She listened patiently until he paused to wipe his mouth. "I don't imagine you know you'd be getting damaged goods," she said.

Max looked her up and down, searching for the flaw. "At our age, we're all, well, knowledgeable in that," he said. A flush blossomed around his ears.

"In what?" said Dolores.

"Familiarity."

"Beg pardon?"

"Intimacy. You know." Max twisted his big hands together. A sorry expression of pain crossed his face. "You and me, we had, you know. Dealings. This was before I met Marge, of course."

Dolores comprehended, but let him proceed, hanging himself out. Though not the first time she'd met a former client in the broad glare of God's sunlight, this was certainly the most entertaining. "You don't say."

"I served outside Saint Paul for eighteen months back then. You used to call yourself Dolly. I always specified you only. Both times, I mean." He swelled up at the memory, thrusting his chest out enthusiastically.

Dolores was not exactly sure how to respond. Clearly, he wanted her to dredge up a memory of him. A swirl of faces and bodies passed. Trying to take decades off the raspy collection of aging bones standing before her was like trying to identify the mosquito that bit you summer before last. Why did men crave distinction when basically they behaved the same, like little taped-up garden hoses—a few squirts and they go limp on top of you, all sweating and stupid.

"You were younger then," she said.

Now he really blushed. "Yes, but I've not had certain of my powers diminish. May I assume your apprehension has nothing to do with that department?"

Dolores studied the man's face. "No," she said, not quite daring to brag about never having contracted a venereal disease. "It's cancer."

Max's ruddy face turned white at the sound of the dreadful word. "Cancer?"

Dolores admitted at once that, despite the absence of confirmation, she believed it was indeed cancer and that it resided in her pancreas. She offered no more information, though Max waited.

She then half listened as he explained in detail about how, as a dependent, she would be eligible for medical treatment at the VA hospital down in Bismarck.

They had the best medics in the country, by god, on account of all the vets coming down with cancer after duty in Japan where they dropped the A-bombs. Max apparently knew a lot about cancer, and he continued, listing the equipment they had at the VA. But Dolores heard only the last sentence, which was, "So the sooner we get going the better."

That jolted her back to the matter before her. "I got to clean my frying pan before it cools off," she said, deliberating if anything could be saved of the eggs. "Can I get back to you on that?"

"Of course, my dear," said Max Plummer, reaching for her hand and kissing it. She appreciated the gentlemanly gesture but continued to be pleased that she'd burned his REO.

\* \* \* \* \*

As Dolores observed with satisfaction, SOTNAR swelled with disagreement when new setbacks arose in readiness for Admiral Halsey Day, as the affair was being billed. With barely a month to go, posters awaited distribution, the water tower still needed repainting and roadsides lay cluttered with trash. Furthermore, Jordy and Rosarita grumbled openly over being assigned more duties than Andy or Toivo, and Kasimir Kavorcek, who volunteered to oversee security, left town with no notice.

Max enjoyed a short-lived joy over the appearance of a feature publicizing the event in *The Minot Daily News*, only to fall into despair when an alert reader detected that the photo accompanying the story was not of the guest of honor, but of Admiral Karl Dönitz, the Nazi commander in chief of the German Navy. The incident served to worsen Max's concern that he had yet to hear from Admiral Halsey. A third invitation went out, this one penned entirely by Max and therefore lacking the diplomatic touch of the earlier two.

To worsen matters, Max had failed to advise the association of his action in restoring Dolores's membership, hoping the woman possessed the good sense to stay away for a while. He'd just called the latest meeting to order when a stir passed through the attendees.

"Mr. Chair," wheezed Jordy as he got up from his stool, jerking his head toward Dolores as she stood in the doorway, looking smug in a purple dress.

Chairs scraped. Feet shuffled. Max chewed on his lip and pretended to scan his notes.

"Now see here," said Rosarita. "There's a certain someone here illegally."

"Mr. Chair," Jordy repeated.

Dolores barely took note of the commotion, realizing she'd erred in leaving the comfort of home and gin lemonades, for the pain had intensified cruelly since

Max popped the question, rendering her senseless. She flopped into a booth to catch her breath as Jordy held forth, citing the Constitution of the United States and the rights of majorities. When he turned to Dolores, hostility in his eyes, she reached for the sugar dispenser, telling herself that if the hairy-eared old numbskull took a step toward her, she would brain him. As she rose in preparation, she sensed a hot, prickly ball grating in the vicinity of her pelvis, and in a great swoon, collapsed to the floor.

Helpless to do anything but lie there, she tried rolling over to alter the position of fanny to heaven only to find that the lower half of her body would not respond.

Jordy leaned over her, tugging on an earlobe. Rosarita Wallingford, skeletal-looking in a pair of tight brown slacks, elbowed her way past Jordy to ask Dolores if she wanted artificial respiration. Powerless to speak to let Rosarita know that if she came any closer she'd slap her into the middle of next week, Dolores managed to generate a small globule of sputum that she propelled with an effort that left her gasping. Max banged his meat tenderizer.

The ambulance, currently in use for its true purpose—as a hearse at Murray's Furniture and Funeral Home—required fifteen minutes to be disencumbered of the coffined remains of Wilfred Mathison (coronary occlusion) and his numerous floral bouquets. While they waited at the café, someone placed a wad of paper napkins under Dolores's head and several layers of dish towels over her stomach and legs. Ninety degrees outside and now they wanted to suffocate her. Max eased himself arthritically to a knee, a look of profound concern on his red face, apparently fearing for the well-being of the woman he planned to marry while at the same time peeved at having his meeting interrupted.

Against her wishes, the volunteer firemen loaded her into the hearse and drove her to the clinic where Doc Thwarp waited. Doc, smelling as usual of bay rum and iodine, asked her what her problem was and how come she looked all bent over like a toad? He listened to her heart, looked inside her mouth and prodded a fat finger into her abdomen, after which, reckoning that even someone as bungling as Doc could spot the grave nature of her situation, she prepared herself for the news. By the time she got her dress buttoned in the back, she'd decided for sure she wasn't going through any radiation, her hair being her joy. Take the pancreas, but by Jesus, let me keep my hair.

But no, before she could spell out her demands, Doc and his nurse loaded her into a proper ambulance. In response to her complaints, Doc advised that she needed the kind of specializing that only Minot could provide. As they reached the Rolland city limits, she felt herself tumbling into welcome unconsciousness, but not before she noted that a gray-faced Max sat beside her in the ambulance, causing her to wonder who ran the meeting, SOTNAR never being in need of a vice-chairman before.

\* \* \* \* \*

At the Minot hospital, they undressed, gowned and wheeled her into X-ray. Following that inconvenience, Max sat stroking her hand with the rhythm and force of a man massaging a leg cramp. When, for the fortieth time in the last ten minutes, he wanted to know if it still hurt, she suggested he go somewhere and smoke a cigarette. His rare compliance with her wishes almost convinced her to change her mind and allow him to stick around long enough to see her into the grave.

The doctor came in, flipped on a lighted screen and, with a brisk motion, slid her X-ray onto the screen where it stuck like a swatted horsefly. The casualness of this upset her—after all, this was a picture of her insides, not a View-Master of Old Faithful.

"Here's the source of distress," said the doctor, who looked about seventeen years old. He pointed to a lined area surrounded by what looked like a blackboard improperly erased.

Dolores bent forward. "That's what a pancreas looks like?"

"No, ma'am, that's a pelvis."

"Then where's my pancreas?"

The impudent young twerp would do well to polish his bedside manner, for he grinned like a pumpkin. "See the hip here and the top of the femur?"

"No, but I'll take your word for it," said Dolores.

The doctor returned to the comfort of the X-ray, pointing with a finger so white and perfect that it looked bleached and dry-cleaned. "The pins go right here."

"Pins?"

"To give Mother Nature a little assistance."

Dubious, Dolores pictured safety pins attached every which way to shore up the non-appearing pancreas.

"Look right here," said the doctor, speaking too fast. "This lighter line. That's a fracture scar where the bone has begun to knit. You've been walking around with a broken pelvis!" He folded his hands and grinned as if he'd just told a joke.

Dolores could only grunt.

"You had what we call 'referred pain.' The pelvic area became so inflamed it felt to you like it originated somewhere else. And this here," he said, moving his manicured finger, "is a fresh break in the hip. You did that today. Once we get the pins in, you must slow down for a few months, but by winter…" He snapped his fingers. "You should be as good as new."

"Pins," she said, and smiled.

* * * * *

The morning after surgery, Dolores came awake to find a vase of roses on her nightstand. Frau Dagmar Hartopps from her own bushes, she bet. Beside them stood Max, hovering over the buds like a hummingbird. "Ah," he said.

Dolores growled. "Did they fix it?"

Max smiled broadly. "Shipshape. You're as fit as I am."

Dolores pondered this for about ten seconds and went back to sleep.

She awoke hours later to visitors. Orville's niece, Leah, with her husband, Harold, and Leah's cousin, Fawn Breen. The sight of Harold standing beside Max, deferring to all and securing his out-of-fashion fedora gracelessly on his stomach, reminded Dolores that she once thought him unfit for Leah, being so unassertive, mild-mannered and predictably dull. How the tables turn.

* * * * *

Upon release, she made the ride home lying flat in the hearse with Leah Peavey by her side to attend to her.

Two miles out of Rolland, they came to a brief stop beside the road before resuming only to halt again. Dolores elevated herself to her elbows. Through the slats on the windows, she observed a series of evenly spaced, shiny cars roll past. "What's going on out there?" she asked.

"Oh, it must be the motorcade for Halsey," said Leah.

"You mean he's actually coming?"

"Max didn't tell you? That's all anybody's talking about," said Leah,

Dolores gripped the built-in rail that helped caskets stay in place.

"Careful," said Leah. "You're not supposed to jump around too much."

Dolores ignored her and pulled the venetian blinds back. The last of the cars rolled by, windows shaded, flags waving from the fenders. Ahead, policemen directing traffic waved the funeral coach through.

As they reached the parade assembly area, Dolores counted twelve separate sets of uniforms—golds, blues, green on white, white on green. Real cowboys on horses waited near a contingent of Mounted Police down from Brandon. Bagpipers tuned their instruments, and a unit of muscular soldiers in camouflage outfits massed around a grinding tank.

Half a mile from the reviewing stand, the crowd stood ten-deep. Boys dangled from elm trees on Main Street. Vendors sold cardboard periscopes for a dollar each. Useless Johnston occupied his usual spot, leaning against the lamppost fronting SuperValu.

Yet another traffic controller, Sheriff Aingher, waved the hearse off the parade route, and shortly the party reached Dolores's house. However, when the driver of the hearse, Mr. Murray's son-in-law, Calvin, came around to assist Leah in transferring the patient inside, he met resistance. Martial music filled the air, announcing the beginning of the parade, and Dolores insisted on seeing it. Waving Calvin away, and with the help of a walker and Leah, she set out.

On the old football field, now repaired following Jordy's caterpillar disaster, appeared the biggest tent Dolores had ever seen. A sign identified it as the Bingo Barn. Smaller tents sheltered the dog show, the beauty contest and the poetry reading. From blocks away came the smell of frying onions, the grinding of machinery and the cacophonous roar produced by happy voices. The women found a vantage point across from the high school gymnasium just as the parade began to pass. Colorful military-themed floats representing virtually every organization within fifty miles made an appearance, including several from north of the border. At least four floats depicted battleships, one even outfitted with cannons that produced window-shattering booms while belching black smoke.

After the parade came time for the remarks of Admiral Halsey, who would be introduced by none other than Max Plummer, listed in the program as "Rolland's Favorite Sailor." No matter how they tried, Leah and Dolores found it impossible to get close enough to hear, especially with the cumbersome walker. In fact, Dolores hadn't seen so many people in one place since Orville took her to see Frankie Yankovic for their honeymoon. Later, she heard that the booths ran out of cotton candy and caramel corn and that so many tickets for the quilt raffle were sold that more had to be printed.

\* \* \* \* \*

Leah escorted Dolores home before departing to find her husband and son. On her own at last, Dolores prepared a drink of lemonade and gin to celebrate her return to life. Seeking a break from the noise and chaos of the midway, she turned the radio to KFYR only to find that the station was broadcasting live from the festival. She twisted the dial to the station in Brandon that broadcast classical music.

Dolores knew nothing about fine music but always found the sounds led her into reflection. Today they played an opera. She knew not which one, only that buried in those beautiful arias lay all the tragedy of her youth. Her mind went to the days when she was fresh and beautiful. She pictured the faces of lovers, customers and husbands. And of Max Plummer.

She brought her attention to the present. She wanted to check her garden, fearful that Max had allowed it to go to ruin. With a great effort, she unfolded the walker. She hobbled around the corner and a blizzard of red presented itself. The Cardinal de Richelieus stood as tall as she, with blooms six inches in diameter. The blossoms of the Frau Hamptons were as purple as beets. The Karen Blixens erupted with aroma, the five sepals and petals in perfect symmetry. She'd never seen such healthy flowers. Hobbling back toward the step, she paused to check the picket fence that Max wanted taken out. She rapped a knuckle on a picket and it reverberated with a solid, reassuring crack.

It too would last a few more years.

# WHAT WAS WRONG WITH THEM?

## 1 | A Real Dad

Around midnight, the Alberta Clipper whipped across the border, freezing pipes, nipping noses and reminding North Dakotans of the real source of their frigid winters. Hours later, snow swirled through the circle of yellow cast by the yard light as Harold Peavey used the heel of his hand to rub frost from the kitchen window. In the dimness, he pumped cold water into the percolator, filled the aluminum basket with drip grind from the red Folgers tin, plugged in the pot and waited. Nothing happened. That same fuse had blown again. Unable to find the flashlight, he went without coffee. He'd mess with the fuse later. He wanted to do chores before the bus came to pick up Richie Lee.

It still worried him that Richie Lee, who could not sit still for five minutes, had to ride a bus for an hour each way to get to school. When the brains in Bismarck shut down the country schools, kids even younger than Richie Lee made the long ride into Rolland. Never mind that Harold, his wife and everybody in the hills learned to read and write quite well in country schools.

He reached the barn to find the snow drifted against the door and the shovel inside. Getting a good hold, he struggled to get the door open wide enough to squeeze through. But when he pulled too hard, the top hinge came loose, the weight of the door pulled the other hinge off and the door dropped into the snow at his feet like a falling tree. He looked at it in disgust. Straining, he lifted the door and leaned it against the frame to provide at least a partial windbreak while he tended to the herd.

\* \* \* \* \*

Richie Lee kicked at the frozen ground. The top of the bus appeared beyond the hill.

"Here she comes," said his dad, like Richie Lee couldn't see. He took a step back from the road.

At the turn into the farm, the bus skated sideways on the ice, but Mr. Legassee twisted the steering wheel and the bus slipped back into two ruts. This lit up Richie

Lee's imagination, and he smiled. What if the bus slid all the way over to Hooker Lake and broke through the ice? He saw himself swimming out to save everyone.

Well, not everyone. Not Sam Morinville for sure because he hated him. And he didn't care if crabby Mr. Legassee drowned either. Vickie and Bertie Breen would get to be rescued since he liked them, especially Vickie because when his family visited the Breens, Vickie let him play her fiddle, and the noise it made caused them to laugh.

When Bertie Breen rode the bus, Sam never dared tease Richie Lee, but Bertie missed school a lot from having to help on the farm. Once Casey Morinville tried to make his brother, Sam, stop, but couldn't because his muscles weren't as big as his brother's.

The door swung open. Richie Lee climbed on past Mr. Legassee, not bothering to stomp the snow off his boots, knowing Mr. Legassee wouldn't yell at him with Daddy standing there. He took his seat, fourth row on the left next to the window, noticing that once again Bertie Breen was missing. A couple minutes further on, the bus pulled up at the Morinvilles, where Rebecca stood alone. Her brothers must be sick. Just then, here came Sam, walking slow with his head down, the oldest student on the bus, the oldest in the whole school probably. Rebecca sat with the rowdy girls in back while Richie Lee knew by the barn smell that Sam took the seat right behind him. When the bus started, the Morinvilles' dog chased it down the road as usual. While others watched the dog, Sam leaned forward and with both hands gave Richie Lee a Chinese burn on his arm.

"Stop it!" yelled Richie Lee.

"Shut up back there," said Mr. Legassee.

Sam laughed and twisted Richie Lee's plump arm some more. It hurt more than anything. He tried to pull away but couldn't. Tears came to his eyes, and that made Sam laugh harder. All the kids looked at Richie Lee. He knew what they were thinking. That he deserved to get picked on because he was fat. Some of the older boys smiled.

*****

Harold let the bus roll out of sight before addressing the broken barn door. He removed his gloves and examined the task in the growing light. The wood was too soft to take a screw. He needed the brace to drill new holes. Everything in the cold took more time.

If only he had help. Lots of jobs on the farm required two people—someone to guide you in centering the tractor over the plow hitch, someone to hold the gate for the cows, someone to fetch tools. At eight years of age going on nine, Richie Lee bared a sluggish streak when it came to work, and the place wasn't yet of a size to rate a full-time hired man. Harold sometimes wished that his family got on better with their neighbors the Morinvilles so he could get their son Sam to help with heavy labor, but then again, in Harold's opinion, Sam, though twice the age of the boy, would make even poorer help than Richie Lee.

After Harold and Leah took over the old Tuttle farm, Harold hoped to make something of the land that Leah's dad Omar never managed to. They were better off, sure, but nothing like Harold pictured. Cows tended to get sick more than ever despite better medicines, and Harold swore that barley grown with chemical fertilizers produced a thinner and softer grain.

Like every day since he married her, Harold dwelled on the age difference separating him and his wife: twenty years. He ought to give her a diary with a miniature key for her birthday. At first, during trips to town, it bothered him to be seen walking with her, and not because people judged him a cradle robber.

What transpired not long before they were married stayed on the minds of lots of folks. First, Leah took on a mournful and frustrating guilt over the consensus of opinion in the area that her father, Omar Tuttle, was responsible for the death of Freddy Morinville. Only when Freddy's body was found years later full of buckshot did Leah begin to accept that it might be the truth. At the same time, rumors persisted over who may have fathered Leah's baby.

Leah and Harold made an unlikely pair. Harold saw things in a way he wanted them to be instead of how they were. Leah was practical and smart—so much so that Harold felt like he held her back. Once, he spotted her staring moodily into the distance like she was gazing at something no one else saw. Harold asked her what she was thinking.

"I was thinking how come you won't take down that cottonwood when I keep telling you it needs to go," she said.

Different they might be, but now the two were chained to each other as sure as the cows were chained in their stalls.

\* \* \* \* \*

That night, Richie Lee pecked listlessly at his potatoes. When Leah ordered him to clean his plate, he hopped off his chair and disappeared. Following the meal, she called him to help with the dishes, but got no response. She glanced at Harold.

"Richie Lee?" he called.

A muted response came from the living room. "What?"

"You heard your mother."

The boy entered with head low, feet dragging. Shielding the sink from view he nudged a plate off the counter. It smashed on the floor.

"Look at that," said Leah. "You did that on purpose."

"No, I never."

"Get the broom and clean it up, and then go to your room," said Leah.

Later, she tapped on his door and called for the boy to come to the kitchen where his parents were drinking coffee.

"What's eatin' you, Son?" asked Harold. "Is something wrong at school?"

Richie Lee mumbled into the table.

"Sit up. We can't understand you like that," said Leah.

"I hate Sam," he said, wiping his eyes.

Harold and Leah exchanged glances. "Sam Morinville? Why is that?" asked Harold.

The boy looked first at his mother, as if the question came from her. "He teases me all the time."

"Well, heck," said Harold. "I've seen you tease others plenty."

"And he says mean stuff."

Leah leaned in closer. "What stuff?"

"I don't know," said the boy, barely audible.

"You can tell us," said Harold.

The boy looked away. "He said you're not my dad."

"Richie Lee," said Leah unhurriedly. "This is your dad, the only one you have."

"I know," said Richie Lee.

"He is your father. Do you understand that?"

"Yes," said the boy. "You don't have to keep saying it."

"Well then," said Harold, "I guess it makes no difference what the other youngsters claim, does it?"

Richie Lee lapsed into reticence.

"Are you listening?" asked Leah.

*"Yes!"* whined the boy and lowered his head.

"Then what's the matter?"

"Nothing. I wish Sam would drown to death."

Harold sat up stiff on his chair. Before he could say a word, Richie Lee was halfway up the stairs on his way to his room.

\* \* \* \* \*

In bed that night, Harold turned to his wife. "Do you suppose we ought to have a talk with the Morinvilles?"

Leah turned away. "What good would that do?"

Harold, long burdened by the ongoing strife with the Morinville family, often tried to patch matters. He plowed the neighbors' road after heavy snows, returned a stray calf and even lent fishing equipment to young Casey Morinville. But Mr. Morinville, a hard and unforgiving man, resisted all overtures, and tensions persisted among the two families who lived year after harsh prairie year a few hundred feet apart.

* * * * *

The previous spring when Leah and Harold drove to the cinnamon brick school building in town for Richie Lee's second grade parent-teacher conference, they were told that their son faced the probability of being failed, held back a year. His teacher, Miss Bateson, explained that the boy tended to be inattentive and encountered obstacles interacting with other children. Miss Bateson, who'd taught generations of youngsters in the area, attributed these difficulties to the isolation of a farm with no friends or siblings his age. Although likely to grow out of it after a couple years, the boy required better reading skills to move on. If she passed him, he'd most likely fall further behind in third grade.

But Leah wanted nothing of this. She saw such a move as tainting her son's attitude toward achievement.

"Please," she said. "If I promise to school him over the summer, could you pass him?" She went on to point out her familiarity with home study programs, having earned her high school diploma in that manner.

Miss Bateson, a diminutive woman with graying hair that seemed lastingly forced into a tight bun, added that another problem existed. While stressing she had no proof of Richie Lee's involvement, a classmate claimed he saw him shaking coins from the piggy bank the children used to store funds to send to the Minot Zoo to help purchase a giraffe. Again, the teacher couldn't be sure, so she said nothing to Richie Lee, but in any event, the money never turned up. It might have been—Miss Bateson chose her words tactfully—that the other child was upset with Richie Lee. Several ruckuses occurred on the playground in which Richie Lee was involved, and one girl received a bad bruise on her leg after being pushed from the teeter-totter.

Miss Bateson, of course, knew something of the family history. She ended the conference by advising the parents that she'd consider the request. Finally, after conferring with the principal, she consented, and Richard Peavey was passed into third grade.

Leah, however, despite her tenacious efforts, found progress difficult. To the surprise of both parents, Richie Lee expressed a desire to spend part of the summer helping in the fields. Harold, silent during the discussion with Miss Bateson in the confines of the classroom, allowed him a fair try, but as he supposed, the boy proved less than cooperative, ignoring instructions, agitating the cows by prodding them with a broom and damaging machinery with his negligence.

During the limited time that Leah worked with him, the boy demonstrated no more interest in improving his reading skills than in acquiring experience in the grueling labor of agriculture. He tended to stare uncomprehendingly at a page telling of Dick and Jane's happy lives as if the letters on the white paper made no more sense than cinders in a snowbank. When his mother sought to stimulate his imagination by reading aloud from *Treasure Island*, he displayed little interest, fiddling with the blade on the oversize jackknife Harold gave him for his birthday against Leah's wishes. At last, when the allotted two-hour lesson period—later shortened to an hour and a half—mercifully passed, the boy dashed away, open books in his wake, to wander along the nearly dry Leonard Creek or climb to the hayloft where he could spy on the Morinvilles.

Seldom had Leah so fervently welcomed school and cooler weather.

\* \* \* \* \*

As always, Thursday—baking day—brought a hunger-inducing fragrance of fresh bread to the kitchen while the oven warmed the air pleasantly. Leah had one hand in the flour bin when she glanced out the window and saw a black sedan racing over the hill, going way too fast for the icy road. As it turned into the yard, she recognized the car as the sheriff's. The porch door opened, followed by jackhammer footsteps, a loud knock and a window-shaking voice.

"Anybody home?"

To Leah, Sheriff Aingher looked permanently on the campaign, eyes protruding with expectation and false good will. People compared him to a bear, but to Leah he looked more like a walrus with his Groucho Marx moustache and pear-shaped head. She still held a dislike for him from the way he asked her all those questions after Daddy died. And then there were those rumors going way back about him and Harold, who never talked much about it. That was his way. The gossips in town even said that Harold was once engaged to the sheriff's wife. Anyway, Leah knew it meant nothing—to a man like Dale Aingher there was no such thing as a past. She untied her apron, but then he spotted Harold coming from the barn and hurried to intercept him.

She called to them from the porch. "What is it?"

The sheriff half turned toward her, trying to speak to both at once. "You better come to town."

"Is something wrong?" demanded Leah. "Is it Richie Lee?"

Aingher waited for Harold to get closer. "Your boy's OK, but they had some sort of fracas on the bus, and Sam Morinville ended up with a bad cut. I just come from his folks' place."

"Oh, lord," cried Leah, sensing the sheriff held a lot back. "Is it bad?"

The sheriff rubbed his arms briskly against the cold. "We don't know, but the kids all say it was Richie Lee that did it."

"What do you mean by *cut*?" asked Leah.

"It's a knife wound from what I gather," said the sheriff.

"Oh! Lord," Leah repeated.

"But Sam Morinville's twice the boy's size," said Harold.

Aingher cut him off. "The laceration is in the upper back. We can talk on the way in."

"Is he in danger?" asked Leah.

The sheriff blew on his hands, shivering. "I just said I don't know. They took him to the hospital."

Leah, apparently oblivious to the cold though similarly coatless, pressed on. "Where's Richie Lee?"

"He's down to the hospital too."

"The hospital?" said Leah.

"No, no, he's not hurt at all," said the sheriff. "We just want him where we can keep an eye on him."

Harold looked at his wife. "I'll start the pickup."

"No, just ride with me," insisted the sheriff in a voice leaving no room for argument.

\* \* \* \* \*

After lowering the furnace, extinguishing lights and Leah checking three times if the oven was off, they folded themselves into the sheriff's four-door Ford with its big V-8, Harold up front beside Aingher, Leah in back.

Hearing what was going on, Leah took comfort in the company of the sheriff. She shifted her eyes toward the Morinville farm directly to the west. She recalled long ago seeing Mr. Morinville confront her dad with a gun following a minor argument over a bull. What might happen now, she wondered, considering the history of hostility.

She leaned forward. "Sheriff, you know we have a phone now. Why is it you never called?"

Aingher fixed his gaze rigidly on the road. "I was in the car already, and you know how it is when it snows, half the time the lines are down."

Staring at the back of Aingher's thick neck, Leah knew, knew beyond doubt, that he already saw Richie Lee as guilty of a wrongdoing. He was only settling on how to proceed.

The boy and deputy Stan Stankowski waited in a vacant single room on the second floor of the hospital, Richie Lee seated on the bed, the deputy on the chair.

"Richie Lee, my god, honey," Leah said, reaching for the boy, who leaned back and lifted his feet to the bed. The deputy, a slight man with a narrow, reddish face, retreated to the hallway.

Leah had imagined her son in blood-soaked clothes, maybe hysterical. But it was normal, chubby Richie Lee, slightly pale, unruly hair the same color as her own and ever-shifting, suspicious, unsmiling eyes. "What happened, Richie?" she said. "What happened on the bus?"

"Sam kept on teasing me so I took my knife and stabbed him," said the boy, his small hands worrying over a comic book.

"How was he teasing you?" asked Harold.

Richie Lee dropped the comic to the covers and folded his arms indignantly. "I told you. Just teasing."

Leah spotted a dark stain on the boy's right shoe. Was that blood? "And that's why you, you know, hurt him with the knife?"

Richie Lee reached behind his chest. "Uh-huh," he said. "I stabbed him there because that's where your heart is."

"Oh my," said Leah. "That's not right. He might have died, and it would be your fault. How would you feel if you killed someone?"

"I don't know. My grandpa killed someone."

"What? Who told you that? Did Sam Morinville say that?"

"No. I don't know."

Leah glanced at her husband, who pulled the vacated chair closer to the bed and sat.

"Son, let's just talk about what all went on today," said Harold. "Did Sam make like he meant to hurt you first?"

The boy looked down. "He knuckle-rubbed my head and then called me a name."

"What name?" demanded Harold.

The boy looked up, doubtful.

"It's all right to say it," said Harold, leaning in closer.

"Bustard."

Harold sat up as a soft knock sounded on the door, and Sheriff Aingher beckoned him and Leah to the hallway.

"Sam's out of surgery. A punctured lung is what it was, and they got it fixed."

"Are his folks with him?" asked Leah, looking down the hallway toward the visitors' room.

The sheriff nodded. "This wouldn't be a good time."

Leah swallowed. "What about Richie Lee? Can we take him home now?"

"I'm afraid not," said the sheriff. "He's officially in custody."

Harold leaned forward so as to hear better. "He's arrested?"

"No, not like you think," said Aingher.

"He's eight years old."

"Well, of course he won't face charges that an adult would, but if the law sees him as a danger, it's my duty to protect him and the public."

Leah, her face reddening in anger, gazed into the room where her son sat. "And what if the public was the one that started the affair instead of the other way around?"

The sheriff sighed. "Mrs. Peavey, you're wanting me to be the judge. You know that's not how it works. Now why don't you two go back in with the boy. I'll call Joyce at the café to send over some hamburgers, and then in a little while you can get on home and get on with the chores."

Leah stared intently at the sheriff. Nothing he could say worried her as much as being addressed so formally and by her married name when he'd known her all her life. She wanted to correct him, but he'd turned away.

## 2 | The Empty Space

With no Chippewa County juvenile detention facilities available, Richie Lee Peavey was sheltered at the hospital under supervision with no visitors other than his parents allowed. Twenty steps down the hall lay the recovering Sam Morinville.

To foster the boy's educational progress, the school secretary dropped off lessons selected by his teacher, materials the boy mostly disregarded.

After two weeks, Leah Peavey drove from the hospital to Dale Aingher's office, where she begged for information about her son. Why couldn't he come home while authorities sorted out the matter?

The sheriff shook his head. Nothing could be done pending the preliminary hearing, and right now the circuit judge was tied up with a backlog of cases over in Bottineau. Perhaps, Aingher told her, not without sympathy, if she wanted advice, she ought to think about talking to a lawyer.

From the sheriff's office, she drove toward Aunt Dolores's house, hoping the worldly ex-wife of her late uncle could provide guidance. As she turned on the street however, she spotted Dolores's new husband, Max, exercising in the driveway, a puff of frosty breath marking each jumping jack. She sighed in frustration. The least mention of laws or government turned the man into a bulgy-eyed lunatic. She veered north without slowing so as to get home in time to fix a hot supper for her husband.

While she peeled potatoes, she deliberated. To her, bringing in a lawyer made it seem like you must be guilty. But still, the boy had inflicted a wound. She brought it up over supper.

"Prob'ly need to at some point," said her husband after a pause. He'd gotten up early with a bad stomach and looked half-asleep. "This kid from my class, Jerry Langerud, he took up lawyering. That's his office in town over there across from the Red Owl."

"Is he any good?" asked Leah.

Harold gave her a perplexed look, like it never occurred to him that gradations of skill could apply to such a profession. "He won the prize for speechmaking that the American Legion used to give out. I recollect that. But there's another side to it."

"What's that?"

"Getting involved with a lawyer is sort of like saying Richie Lee didn't do wrong but at the same time admitting in a way that he did."

"I had the same thought," said Leah.

Harold reached for the shot glass containing the toothpicks. "Then too it would be liable to give him a black mark."

Leah put her fork down. "Well, the black mark is already there. How much blacker could it get?"

And back and forth they went as hamburger fat congealed on the plates and leftover potatoes turned gray and cold in their bowl. With nothing fixed, Harold sat in the living room reading the paper from start to finish beginning with the want ads. From time to time he yawned, his mouth forming a huge cavern. Leah joined him and paged through her *Better Homes and Gardens*. When through, she set it on the coffee table and folded her arms, alerting her husband that she had something to say.

"Why don't you go ahead Monday and get hold of that guy Langerud?" she said.

"If that's what you want," Harold replied.

\* \* \* \* \*

At the hospital the following day, Mrs. Crosby, the nurse, took them aside to explain that Richie Lee had "thrown a fit" that morning and struck another nurse, and they'd been forced to temporarily restrain his arms with towels.

After a quick conference, Harold folded the shopping list into his billfold and headed downtown. Leah entered the room to find their son propped up by a pillow with a pad of paper and pencil on his lap. The restraints had been taken off. "What are you up to?" she asked.

"Nothing," replied the boy, his eyes down.

"Are you working on your lessons?"

No answer.

"Richie Lee, they said you were upset. How come?"

"They made it so I can't move my arms."

Leah pushed the image from her mind. "But they did that afterward. What made you so mad in the first place?"

The boy looked up from his paper. "Sam did." He squeezed his eyes shut tight. An odd smile of triumph passed across his round face.

As she leaned in closer, Leah caught the strong odor of urine. Richie Lee had wet the bed and was sitting in the middle of saturated sheets. A deliberate act, no doubt. She chose to overlook it and sat, gathering herself.

"Can I see what you're drawing?" she asked.

With a sigh of impatience, the boy threw the pencil to the side and held up the paper. Leah peered at it, horrified. Drawn crudely, the sketch featured a stick outline of a woman lying prostrate with a knife plunged through her chest and blood running into a pool.

"Oh my," said Leah. "Richie Lee?"

"What?"

"Why don't we change your bedding?"

"I don't care."

"But Daddy's going to be here soon."

"I don't care," he repeated.

"He misses you, you know."

"I don't care!"

Leah reached for him, but the boy threw himself backward, slamming his skull against the headboard and bringing a nurse in at a run.

"Maybe it's better if you left for a while," said the nurse.

Leah waited in the lobby. When her husband returned, they walked the three blocks to Pam and Joyce and Deb's Café for the Saturday special—meat loaf—a rare treat. When they got back to Richie Lee's room, they found his window covered with a sheet of plywood except for an opening the size of a baseball for the boy to peek through. They were told that he became riled at being served green Jell-O with pineapple chunks for dessert and hurled the dish at the window, cracking the pane. To the distress of the parents, the boy not only accepted the increased isolation but looked rather proud of it.

On Sunday, a late winter ice storm blocked the roads and snapped the phone lines. After chores and not able to go anywhere, Leah and Harold sat down for a game of gin rummy. Inspecting his discards, Leah couldn't help but see that her husband, ever the peacemaker, allowed her to win.

With the phones back in order on Tuesday, Leah called the hospital and learned that Richie Lee had endured a trying morning but was cheered when Aunt Dolores visited briefly, dropping off a cowboy hat as a gift. Harold then phoned Attorney Langerud, and an appointment was set for the following Monday. Over the weekend, the temperature rose to the mid-forties. Trickles of water ran off the south roof of the barn only to form icicles when the frost returned after sunset. After milking on Sunday morning, Harold surprised Leah by suggesting they go to church, a proposal that she rejected with little consideration.

\* \* \* \* \*

Reluctantly, they climbed the half flight of stairs to the office located in the ancient redbrick building that once housed a bank. Though they'd passed it hundreds of times, neither Harold nor his wife had set foot inside.

The appearance of the overheated room dismayed Leah. The huge desk, topped with a sheet of thick glass overlaying a blanket of green felt, was spotlessly clear. She had foreseen a clutter of papers and files, at least a telephone. Last year's calendar was thumbtacked to a wall, and a rotting banana lay on a small table next to a typewriter under a dustcover.

"Mister and Missus Peavey." Jerry Langerud looked at the floor as they exchanged handshakes, making Harold wonder how well "Gerald," as the stenciled name on the door advised, remembered him. With a fluttering of his hands, he motioned them to chairs.

"We're sorry to bother you," said Harold, instantly regretting his words. He'd be paying for this bother.

Langerud had grown into a roundish man and wore thick glasses that added to his spherical appearance. Twin circles of sweat showed on the armpits of his white shirt. "Now, where should we start?"

"Well, the thing is—" Harold began.

"You must have heard about it," said Leah, interrupting, and went on to recount the entire episode, beginning with Richie Lee's complaints about Sam Morinville harassing him.

Langerud waited for her to finish. "And what is your primary concern?"

"Well. If he'll have to go to reform school or something."

Langerud cleared his throat. "It might surprise you to learn that there's less we can do about that than if he were older." The lawyer paused. "Richard has reached a kind of age of reason, but not the age where he's deemed capable of plotting and carrying out a crime. If he were, we could go about questioning evidence, motive, calling character witnesses and so on."

Harold followed this less clearly than his wife and looked at her. She looked at the lawyer. "What does all that mean?" she asked.

"What happens is that the court surveys opinions of those who know the boy well. This would be teachers, maybe your pastor, individuals from the institutions with which he's involved. Does he participate in sports or belong to clubs?"

The sour smell of perspiration filled the small room. "Oh no," said Harold. "We're too far out in the country."

Langerud's face formed a concerned frown, causing Harold to wonder if he saw the boy as deprived. "And these opinions, what will happen if they're not good?"

A fly buzzed around Langerud's face. He waved at it. "The awareness of juvenile delinquency as a significant societal problem is finally reaching the rural areas of the state, and my friends in the prosecutor's office say they're feeling pressure to demonstrate that efforts to ameliorate the phenomenon are in effect. That would be worrisome."

"I see," said Harold. Suffocated by the lawyer's gobbledygook, he turned to his wife.

"Maybe you don't know about it, Mr. Langerud, but years ago, before Richie Lee was born, my dad and Etienne Morinville got into a disagreement, and there's been a sort of feud going on ever since."

"I recall something about that," said the lawyer. "Your concern is if that would impact the case?"

"Well, yes," she said, troubled. They'd only been here a short while and it was already being called a case.

"No, it shouldn't at all."

"Who actually makes these decisions?" asked Leah.

"The courts, naturally."

"The courts."

"The courts in the person of the judge, if that's what you mean," said Langerud, leaning forward.

"And when would we know what they decide?"

Though Leah led the questioning, the lawyer directed his responses toward Harold. "All I can tell you is these matters take time." He opened his desk drawer, checked something and slid it shut immediately. Harold felt worse than ever. Weren't lawyers supposed to help you?

Leah picked up the hints and snapped her handbag shut. "You'll let us know as soon as you hear anything?"

"Of course."

The couple left, thanking the lawyer though neither was sure why.

\* \* \* \* \*

Five weeks passed, and no discernible change occurred. Richie Lee lingered in the hospital. His parents pleaded with him to catch up on his schoolwork. Sam Morinville had long since returned to his family. Lawyer Langerud advised patience. At home, as the first signs of spring showed, the milk production went up. Early buds formed on the cottonwoods. Leah started tomatoes inside under a grow light. Harold began preparing machinery for the planting. The warm weather and longer days lightened both of their spirits.

Yet each parent harbored thoughts concealed from the other. Would this contentment continue if they brought their son home? What was not right about them that they allowed themselves such unearned joy?

## 3 | He's a Good Boy

Above the small pale-green residence of the Sisters of the Holy Resurrection, across from Rolland Memorial Hospital, a crow flapped its wings, settling through the shimmering spring air as it landed, dislodging a chunk of masonry that rattled down the canted wooden shingles. Richie Lee Peavey, watching idly through the peephole in his window, willed the object to plunge to the ground and maybe strike a passerby. But it lodged in the basin of the eaves.

A box of crayons on the bedside table drew his attention. He withdrew a red one, scraped the paper coat off with his fingernail, bit off a piece and swallowed it. He waited a minute, felt no different and ate the rest of it. The week before, he'd eaten a bottle of aspirin that the nurse forgot. They tasted icky, so he mixed them with chocolate milk and swallowed all but six of the white pills. When the nurse saw what he'd done, a whole bunch of people came to his room. They made him drink a jar of stuff that looked like syrup but tasted awful, and it made him throw up.

Throwing up hurt his stomach, but he wanted to do it again because it looked funny to see all the grown-ups running in and out of the room.

So he ate another crayon, this one orange.

When Richie Lee stabbed Sam that day, he hoped Sam would die. But Sam didn't die. He went home, and Richie Lee stayed in the hospital. Everybody picked on him. That's why he took that fifty cents from the money jar at school. He deserved it.

If only he had somebody to play with at home. Twice, he and Casey Morinville met in the dark so Casey could show him constellations, and another time they secretly played stretch with Richie Lee's knife. They kept those meetings a secret until Casey's dad found out and Casey got a licking. He wished he could visit Bertie and ride Alouette, his horse. He ate a green crayon, this one with the paper on.

* * * * *

Harold Peavey eased his pickup into the lot behind the hospital.

"Hello, Son," he said, walking in.

The boy looked up. "Hi."

This was encouraging. Usually, Richie Lee offered no response to greetings when Harold came alone.

"What did you do today?"

"Nothing."

Harold looked closer. "What's that on your mouth?"

"Crayons," said the boy, his chubby hand going to his lips.

"Color crayons? How'd you get 'em on your face?"

"I ate some."

"What? You ate crayons? How many?"

"Fourteen."

Harold grabbed the crayon box, noting that only two or three were missing. Were crayons poisonous? They couldn't be. The boy looked the same as usual. Harold pocketed the box. He and his son's mother had been advised to stay composed in incidents like this to teach the boy that bad behavior was no way to get attention. Besides, Richie Lee hadn't yet mastered numbers and tended to use whatever figure came to his mind.

"Guess what," he said. "The judge is coming to town next week."

"He's gonna make it so I go to reform school." The boy's words came quick as a reflex, as if he couldn't wait to offer the declaration.

"Oh, we don't know about that. We'll have to be patient and see."

Harold heard stories about the reform school in Mandan. Little difference existed, it was said, between the school and the penitentiary in Bismarck. Boys received beatings for minor misdeeds or found themselves in solitary confinement where they were fed only bread and water. Harold didn't believe it, but wondered—was Richie Lee aware of its reputation?

The decision, Lawyer Langerud had explained, would be based on precedent, as well as information on the child's ability to discern right from wrong. But of course, you never knew. In one case, a nine year old was ordered to reform school until the age of sixteen after wounding his fourth-grade teacher with a makeshift bow and arrow. In another, a boy Richie Lee's age, after using a wrench to fracture the skull of a gas station attendant who discovered him trying to steal a 3 Musketeers candy bar, was returned to the custody of his grandparents, who agreed to pay the medical expenses of the victim.

Harold's attention resettled on this person before him. With his hair matted and flattened on his scalp and flakes of colored wax desecrating his skin, he'd taken on the look of a captive. This was his son.

\* \* \* \* \*

The courthouse stood ageless, gray with authority. A sad shrine to the need for its own existence, its minimally ornamented facade barely concealed the starkness of the county jail and sheriff's office resting behind it.

The occasion lacked the dignity both parents believed it was due. Aside from the judge, a court reporter, a bailiff, the lawyer and the state prosecutor, no one else was present. Then, just as the bailiff called for the citizens to rise, Ida Florence Morinville entered from the rear, struggling for a moment with the clumsy swinging door. Wearing her Sunday best—a print dress that hung nearly to her ankles and a hat with a veil that she'd pushed out of the way—she quietly took a seat in the last row.

The attorney Langerud had stressed that the proceedings were not a trial as such, but a hearing. Leah failed to see a whole lot of difference except that at a trial, the person accused could be present. And now the appearance of her neighbor seemed to add a greater importance to the affair.

The prosecutor, Howard Ness, a weary middle-aged man who held his office because neither of the other two attorneys in town wanted it, spoke first. "Your Honor, this is a case involving a minor who attacked a young and unarmed man with a knife in an entirely unprovoked incident. We wish to enter into the records reports on the child's behavior prior to the incident along with the sheriff's statement and transcriptions of interviews with those in charge of caring for the boy since the event."

"Yes, we see," said the judge. He turned to the Peaveys' lawyer. "Mr. Langerud, do you wish to present documentary evidence on behalf of your client?"

Langerud, wearing a blue suit that imparted a pasty hue to his complexion, stood. "We offer a statement from social services along with accompanying handwritten notations."

"And have you been given opportunity to examine the reports submitted by the state?"

"I have, Your Honor, and I find them in order, although I wish to note the lack of any record concerning a visit to the boy's home or interviews with his parents."

"Is this so, Mr. Prosecutor?"

"Sir, we determined that such a visit would be gratuitous in this case. The state concedes that the parents are respected people within their community and that they've striven to be responsible parents."

"Nevertheless," said the judge, "the court will take a recess while we confer in my chambers." He stood and whirled around, his black robes ballooning.

Barely ten minutes into the procedure, both Harold and Leah were bewildered. Langerud said nothing as he followed the prosecutor and judge out the side door.

"What's that about?" asked Leah.

Harold didn't know. His mind was filled with memories of sitting in a similar courthouse following his refusal to enlist in the army.

The bailiff walked casually to the rear of the courtroom and lit a cigarette. After twenty minutes, the three reentered the courtroom. Leah tried to interpret the expression on Langerud's face but couldn't, adding to her impression that the joyless events swirled about with no regard to her or her husband.

The judge coughed into his hand. He turned to the prosecutor. "Is the state prepared to make a recommendation at this time?"

"We are, Your Honor," he said as he stood and threw his shoulders back importantly. "It is the wish of the state that the minor Richard Peavey, son of Harold and Leah Peavey, be placed under the protection of the North Dakota State Reformatory up to his sixteenth birthday or until the authorities in that institution are of the opinion that the boy is no longer a threat to himself or the community."

Leah struggled to get up as her chair slipped on the varnished boards of the floor. At the insistence of Aunt Dolores, she'd ordered a new skirt and sweater from the catalog, and the skirt clung to her hips when she tried to stand. "Wait," she cried. Her face reddened as she turned to Langerud. "You need to explain how Sam was getting after Richie Lee."

Langerud pulled her gently to her seat. "It's all right," he said in a loud whisper. "That's only Howard's recommendation. The judge will make the decision."

Leah looked at her husband, pleading with her eyes for him to say something.

During another brief recess, Langerud asked the Peaveys if they had questions.

"Yes, why don't you speak up for Richie Lee?" said Leah. "All the judge has heard from is Mr. Ness. What about the statements you wanted from people who say he's a good boy? Do they know about the paper from Dolores…" Leah struggled to come up with her aunt's new last name. "Dolores Plummer."

Langerud looked at his watch. "Don't worry. We will. Anyway, the court knows where you stand."

But Leah did worry, a concern that went unrelieved when, on the way out, Langerud passed the prosecutor and the two exchanged smiles.

\* \* \* \* \*

The judge stared through the thick glass of the courtroom window. The boy's attorney, Langerud, was speaking, and the judge was having difficulty concentrating. Four cases today and this one far from over. He'd heard of the Peaveys, the couple from the hills up north, and knew the contexts of the wife's father's death several years previously.

"In light of the investigative oversight, I move for a continuance," said Langerud. "This would allow time for a visit to the boy's home."

"But, Your Honor," protested the state's attorney. "There's no requirement in the code for such a thing. It is the opinion of the state that abundant information is available to the court and such a delay would serve no such purpose."

The judge looked past the prosecutor at the Peaveys and tried to picture their son. His mind again returned to the case he most regretted during his career. A girl with a history of violence who happened to be a distant relative of his wife had stood before him. He had ordered her set free and placed in the care of her grandparents. Six months later, she got her hands on a shotgun and killed them both.

"Your Honor?" Langerud broke the silence. "May we have a ruling on the motion?"

"Motion denied," said the judge.

"But, Your Honor, if I may."

The judge cut him off. "You may not."

This Langerud was a pompous little turd whom the judge had never liked. It pleased him that light reflected from his greasy scalp.

"The court sees no reason for further delay. Adequate information is available. You will all return at ten a.m. Monday at which time a ruling will be announced." He rapped his gavel.

* * * * *

For what they anticipated to be the day of pronouncement Leah wore freshly pressed slacks, her husband a dress shirt and shoestring tie. Jerry Langerud wore the same blue suit as before. The state's attorney arrived late and out of breath.

The judge began. "This is a problematic case. There are certain aspects that suggest that the boy understands what he did and that it was wrong. There are other reasons equally strong that tell me that he is not prepared to reenter society and that he could benefit from some level of rehabilitation." Out of long habit, he paused, allowing his words to penetrate.

"Nevertheless, in the absence of any testimony suggesting that the boy in any tangible way represents a menace to the community, and after careful consideration, the court rules that Richard Peavey be returned to the custody of his natural parents with the recommendation that he be examined every three months by a qualified psychologist."

The judge's gavel hung in the air when a disruption arose from the back of the courtroom.

"Hold it," commanded a man's rough voice.

Something dropped loudly to the floor. Chairs squeaked as everyone wheeled around to see who it was. Only Harold and Leah recognized the couple—Ida Florence Morinville, joined this time by her husband Etienne.

"Bailiff," commanded the judge. "Please see if those people have business with the court."

The bailiff, a man nearing seventy and crippled with arthritis, limped to the back of the seating area, using the top of each bench as a handhold. After conferring briefly with the Morinvilles, he made his way to the prosecutor's table and said something in the ear of Ness, who sprang to his feet and approached the judge.

Leah Peavey reflexively squeezed the arm of her husband.

"Sir," called the judge in a voice that seemed to Leah louder than necessary. "Please come forward and state your name."

Shoving his cap into his back pocket, Etienne did as directed, giving wide berth to the table where Harold and Leah sat with Langerud. When he reached the front of the courtroom, he paused, seeming to think he should go to the chair beside the judge reserved for witnesses.

"That's all right, you can speak from where you are if you're comfortable," said the judge.

Etienne gave his name, his hands hooked into the straps of his coveralls.

"We take it you are informed of the proceedings and have something to add?" said the judge.

Etienne dipped his head.

"Please speak up."

"I want to add."

"Go ahead."

Etienne glanced timidly at the Peaveys, shielding his mouth with his cap. "Sam's our son," he said, bobbing his head toward Ida Florence, who sat as rigidly as a piece of furniture.

"Yes?" said the judge.

"Well, he, Sam, could have died from that. He was in the hospital for three weeks. Somebody should pay because I—"

The judge interrupted. "Mr. Morinville, if that's why you are here, I need to advise you that such a concern would require being addressed at a separate proceeding."

"Oh, I know, I know," said Etienne. "But that's not all."

Again the judge stopped him. "What we need to know is how you might enlighten us on the matter of Richard Peavey and in your opinion what, if anything, should happen to him as a result of the attack on your son. Please limit your remarks to that exactly."

Then, from apparently encountering trouble organizing his thoughts, Etienne let loose a gush of words so lengthy that even his wife must have found it remarkable.

"Like I said," he began. "He could have killed Sam. My boy was just trying to get to school so he could maybe learn something and get the chance I or his ma never got, and along comes this kid with a knife he never shoulda had to start with and runs it into my son like he was a hog or something. It even came out that the other boy said he was going for Sam's heart, and like you know, Sam was lucky to live he was in the hospital for so long." Etienne paused briefly, growing more comfortable.

"You can talk to his folks." He gestured toward the Peaveys. "They can tell you something's been wrong with their boy. I knew him since he was born. We're next-door neighbors. Our farms join each other."

At this, Langerud came to his feet. "Your Honor, please," he said.

But the judge ignored him. "Go on," he said to Etienne.

"We got another boy, Casey—he's around Richie Lee's age. We don't let them play with each other. And then you go back a ways and there's the time her old man tried to shoot me."

At that, Leah Peavey and Harold simultaneously rose to their feet, but before they could speak, the judge intervened. "Mr. Morinville, once again, matters of that nature have no bearing."

After the Peaveys sat, Etienne resumed. "If you don't put that boy away, there's gonna be some howling. Just think what could happen. Sam lost all kinds of pints of blood. There's little kids at school. Sam's lucky to be here now."

"Yes, we are aware of that," said the judge. "But can you help us understand something? If you've known the boy for a while, maybe you've observed incidents that could shed light on whether there is a pattern of bad behavior or if this was a onetime incident precipitated by unusual anger."

"I was just gonna say," said Etienne. "We found animals, chickens and cats and once a dog that—"

Now Leah couldn't hold back. "Wait a minute," she began, but Langerud shook his head.

"I'm telling you, there's all kinds of things been happening that just aren't right," said Etienne, snapping his chin downward in emphasis.

"I think that will do," said the judge. "You may return to your seat, Mr. Morinville. Mr. Peavey, do you wish to say something?"

"Yes," said Harold, forgetting to stand. "Most of what Etienne says just isn't so."

"That's what he says," cried Etienne, who, only halfway back, spun around. "Their kid tried to kill my Sam, and that's in the facts no matter what's claimed."

For the first time, the judge rapped his gavel, startling everybody, in particular the bailiff, who had been transfixed with Etienne's claims. "How about you, Mrs. Peavey. Would you like to speak?"

Leah opened her mouth and tried to swallow.

"Mrs. Peavey?"

"I just don't understand. My son, Richie Lee, he's a good boy. Every mother would know." She brought her handkerchief to her eyes, regretting her own words, knowing they meant nothing. She turned slightly and spoke as if to the framed picture of President Eisenhower on the wall. "I want to apologize to Mrs. Morinville and to her husband. We're all just farm folks."

Silence overtook the courtroom for a full minute.

"Will that be all?" asked the judge.

Leah nodded and wiped her eyes.

"Counsels, please approach the bench."

Leah's chin slipped to her chest. Harold rested his elbows on his knees, his hands clasped as he studied the floor.

The lawyers were arguing, speaking over each other's claims. Leah picked up a few words: violence potential, irrationality, case precedent, normal prerogative.

Quiet descended over the courtroom. Just as the lawyers took places, the main door creaked open. Someone had entered. All heads swiveled around again as Aunt Dolores entered and waved hopefully at the Peaveys before seating herself.

The judge waited as Dolores shimmied around on the wooden pew making herself comfortable. Satisfied she was only a spectator, he sighed deeply. "I want the boy here. In my chambers, tomorrow at nine thirty."

The lawyers looked at each other. Langerud spoke. "Richard, you mean."

The judge glared at Langerud. "Yes. The son. The reason we're here."

Both lawyers were sweaty, frantic, eager to speak. Someone flushed a toilet in the nearby restroom, and the ancient pipes clanked and rattled.

The prosecutor got up. "Your Honor, in the interests of the state—I know of no precedent."

The judge pivoted in his chair. "No. And neither do I."

* * * * *

"Richard, do you know who I am?"

The judge sat beside Richie Lee on the sofa. His tie was loose. His robe that looked like a dress hung in the closet. Richie Lee didn't like being called Richard. The judge smelled like soap.

"Richard? Who am I?"

"The judge."

"That's right. Can you tell me what a judge does?"

Richie Lee thought about it for a long time but couldn't think of anything. The judge made loud breathing noises, like fat people.

"What does a judge do, Richard?"

"He makes boys go to reform school."

This was the biggest sofa he'd ever seen. Long and smooth with a hump. It was like a fort. Once Mom made a fort with the clothes rack and a blanket. From inside, he had watched his mother's feet and imagined he would stay there forever.

"Do you like to pretend, Richard?"

The boy's shoes, tied in flowing double bows, dangled over the front of the sofa. He clapped the edges of his soles together. The telephone on the desk rang one time. The books looked all the same. "I don't know," he said. Today was Friday, chocolate milk day at school.

The judge touched his mouth with his hand like Daddy did when he burped.

"You're sure lucky, Richard. You have a wonderful father and mother."

The boy blinked. People always said that.

The judge grunted as he leaned over to pull his sock up. Coins and keys jingled in his pockets. "I wonder, do you ever get mad at your mother or father?"

"No," said the boy.

"Really?" said the judge. "I thought everybody got mad sometimes. Even old codgers like me."

The boy bit his lip, wondering what codgers were.

The judge stood, stretching and yawning. The coins shifted. "I like seeing my grandson. But he lives such a long ways away I have to pretend we're having a nice visit. Do you ever pretend that you're someplace else, Richard?"

"I don't know," said the boy.

* * * * *

Leah departed the courtroom, counting on Harold to break the news to Richie Lee that instead of coming home to the farm, he was to be placed in the state reform school. Rather than drive the two blocks to the hospital, Harold left the pickup at the courthouse and walked, taking the long way through the alley to avoid Useless Johnston, who stood by a light pole digging in his ear with his little finger.

Passing the newspaper office, he skipped over a crack in the concrete. A few feet on, he noticed that the license plate holder on Mr. Mott's front bumper was missing a bolt. In the vacant lot next to the Presbyterian church, sprouts of weeds poked up through the feathery-smelling soil.

He recalled that stately evergreens once swayed in the wind on the north side of the hospital and speculated as to why they'd been cut down. For years, before the war, a small gazebo housing a statue of the Virgin Mary stood in the backyard of the priest's residence. He decided he'd like to learn what became of it.

By the time he reached the door to the hospital, Harold had almost willed himself into believing that none of this had anything to do with him.

# THE THINGS YOU LEARN

## 1 | Castle and Bee Stings

Bertie Breen knew there would be hell to pay if he didn't finish patching the granary roof. But the day came up cool and clear, perfect for riding, and he hadn't had a chance to exercise Alouette in all the weeks since Ma took Sam Morinville on as the hired man. When younger, Bertie rode the horse bareback around the pasture close to home. Now, however, with Sam away at the cattle auction in Mylo, he looked forward to the chance to explore the dense woods and hills to the north, areas that Ma always warned him to stay away from.

The horse, a bay with black points and a sweet disposition, had belonged to Bertie's father, and she was getting older. Bareback put more strain on both horse and rider so, after grooming her down with the dandy brush and currycomb, he draped the blanket over her back, careful that the hair lay flat, then hefted up the saddle and adjusted the cinch.

After a couple hours of wandering with occasional stops to feast on blueberries, which grew more profusely the farther Bertie traveled, Alouette began acting skittish, grinding her teeth and rearing her head. When she favored her right front hoof, Bertie dismounted to check. Lacking a pick, he poked around an ash tree looking for a branch to whittle down to the proper size to clean mud out of the hoof. As he rummaged through the brush, Alouette pulled her reins and trotted down a small ravine that bisected two particularly high hills. At the base of the hill on the left, a patch of bluestem and sedge sprouted, attracting Alouette's desire to graze. But no, she continued even when Bertie whistled, then disappeared into a stand of hawthorn. Trotting easily after her on his long legs, Bertie followed the ravine to its end in a small creek, hopped over it and stumbled on a rock before spotting the horse standing patiently in a clearing as if waiting for him.

Suddenly the switchgrass parted as an animal leaped past a clump of ferns and bounded toward the woods, causing Alouette to rear up in fright. Bertie at first took it for a small deer but recognized it as a goat when he saw its backside. His eyes fell on a stone wall, mossy and overgrown so heavily with vegetation that it might have been an outgrowth of nature. Pulling Alouette by the reins, he pushed through the grass for a closer look and found that the wall was the most noticeable part of a dwelling. Pushing aside concealing clumps of hazelnut and chokecherry, he saw openings for a door and a rough slit for a window.

Inside, he discovered a square table constructed of split logs lashed together with vines. A lower table or bed lay partially covered by a section of collapsed roof. Bracing himself, he boosted the damaged roof up for a better look, then let it drop. There on the floor lay an assortment of yellowing bones. They were too scattered to conform to the shape of any animal he recognized, but when he knelt for a closer look, he recognized what he'd found.

A human skull lay on its side with its vacant eyeholes pointed toward the door.

Startled, he shrank back and withdrew to compose himself. Alouette, sensing his uneasiness, shied away. He caught her, mounted and, quickly as he dared, urged her across the creek and up the ravine the way they'd come.

On the ride home he thought about what he'd found. Someone must have been murdered right there a few miles from home. In fact, he'd heard of another person, Sam Morinville's older brother, who had been shot and killed a long time ago. Maybe the murderer was the same person.

Of course it was important to tell someone. But now his mother lay sick in bed again, and he barely spoke to Sam. The site might lie across the line in Canada, and he had no understanding of how or who to notify. As he came within sight of the barn, comforted by the sound and sensation of Alouette's steady trot, he began to rethink the discovery. He liked the feeling of having his own secret. Everyone around him knew every single thing about him—that the girl he called sister wasn't really part of the family, that some people spoke of his mother as having "nerve troubles" and that his dad had died years before.

What if the person in the hut hadn't been murdered? And what if the death happened long ago—would it matter to anyone now? He imagined the hut as it once was, and immediately his mind churned over what might be involved in restoring it. First it needed a roof and proper door. If the vegetation went untouched, the place could remain unknown to anyone else even with the old road to the east being widened and graded. But what about the bones—he shuddered at the thought. But they could be gotten rid of. He knew how to do that. And that knowledge reminded him that he did have a secret after all.

The details had mostly been erased from his youthful memory. Bertie hadn't seen the dogs for a while, but every now and then a bone turned up loose in the soil, sickening him that it might have belonged to his uncle.

\* \* \* \* \*

Over the next year, on days when he could escape Sam's growing expectations for help around the farm, Bertie did indeed make repairs to his *castle*—as he thought of it, roping materials to the back of Alouette. Fortunately, the horse remembered the way, for the site lay so secluded and sheltered by the hills that Bertie himself would have had difficulty finding it again. No wonder he'd never heard of it though it couldn't be more than three or four miles distant in a straight line from the farm.

The first task, which once accomplished made everything else easier, was to tend to the bones. Using the good spade and hoping that Sam wouldn't develop a sudden need for it, he dug a hole in the rooty, rocky soil near a thicket of wild rose bushes. He then slipped his fingers into a pair of old work gloves—one of which had a hole where the thumb had been, requiring that he wedge his own thumb against his pointer finger to avoid touching bone. Surprised at the lightness of the bones, he lifted each one as if it were delicate glass and slipped it into a potato sack.

Relieved at how easy that part was, he laid the bag into the uneven hole and hurriedly covered it. He was aware of the custom of praying at a burial, but he knew no prayers. As a substitute, he stumbled through the Pledge of Allegiance.

While Alouette grazed in the clover patch, Bertie puttered around the castle, fixing and tidying. The first time it rained on his flimsy roof, the moss absorbed so much water that the whole thing collapsed. Eventually, he fashioned limbs from scrub pines. Tar from the pines helped bind the branches to keep out the rain while the green needles served as camouflage. A door confounded him, so he made do with hanging a canvas over the opening and weighting it down with rocks to keep the wind out. A similar arrangement covered the window.

Though the day might be far-off, he envisioned converting the hut into a home in the woods where he might live like Daniel Boone. He would hunt and fish for food, draw water from a spring, make his own clothes. The hut would at least provide a temporary escape from Sam, who ordered him around the farm like Bertie were the hired man instead of the other way around. If Ma never got over her sickness or if Sam never found a job somewhere else, he could bring Vickie to the hut, and they could stay until it was safe to come out.

But he had to be careful. As it was now in the middle of summer, Sam's need for help left him little time to work on the hut or to see to other matters he liked, such as tending to his bees.

Of course, all his plans would be ruined if Sam found out about the castle. For now, he dared tell no one, not even Vickie, who he shared everything with.

\* \* \* \* \*

Just past the peak heat of a July day, he stood against the north wall gazing at the popcorn clouds rolling over the hills from the west, hoping they carried rain so they couldn't hay tomorrow. This was his first chance for a visit to the castle in ten days, and he'd missed it. He chewed on the stem of the pipe he'd fashioned from a corncob and a willow shoot. A handful of fat, warm drops hit the canvas over the window with a reassuring splat, a sound that, combined with the aroma of sap and the faint swampy smell from the lake, awarded him a rare sense of contentment.

He set the rocks in place and started home.

As he neared the house, the old weather vane came into view. Atop it rested the rooster, rusted into place with its beak pointing slightly to the west rather than true north. The house and farm might be run-down these days, but the weather vane still granted it a distinction. You could see it from a distance, and folks identified the place by its existence. Bertie's mother, who seldom talked of the past, once mentioned that the iron rooster was the first thing she saw when she came to live there.

He came around the corner to find Sam on the step, smoking a roll-your-own. By this time of day Sam grew sulky from his trips to the outhouse to swig from his bottle of whiskey. He sat motionless as a stump on the middle of the step like he was daring Bertie to squeeze to the side to get around him.

Sam spoke with his hooded eyes fixed on the fiery end of his cigarette. "Where you been? I told you I want to start cutting hay."

"Checking the combs."

"Yeah? I don't see no honey."

"Bees quit making honey when it gets real hot."

Sam was tall and thick-shouldered with black hair growing to the base of his neck. Bertie knew he was trying to look like a fierce Indian from storybooks, but with his white man's plaid work shirt, his missing tooth and his habit of picking his nose, he didn't look like Indians in any book Bertie had seen. He waited for Sam to move so he could go in and wash up.

"How'd you get them burrs on your trousers? There's no cockleburs in the field where you got them hives."

Bertie lifted a foot and brushed his pant leg. "I was up higher looking for cranberries."

"It's too early for cranberries."

It wasn't Sam's way to speak lacking a reason, and Bertie knew he sure didn't fret too much over cranberries or honey. In fact, he never went near the hives for fear of being stung. He concentrated on picking a burr from the back of his pants, knowing Sam was trying to steer him into a corner.

The tall form of his mother loomed in the doorway, her eyes offering a vacant, frightened look that had become familiar. The smoky smell of frying salt pork filled the air.

"Supper's ready," she said. "Bertie, go tell Vickie to put her fiddle down and come get something to eat."

Sam grunted as he stood. He flipped his cigarette stub in the direction of a hen, who jerked her rusty head toward the smoldering white butt. "Think you're gettin' away with something, don't you?" he said.

Bertie left the comment hanging.

\* \* \* \* \*

That night, wanting a distraction from Sam's disturbing words, Bertie dragged out the old radio from underneath his bed. He wired in the dry cell battery and turned it on. He waited as it came to life, smelling the faint burn of dust as the tubes heated. The dial listed settings for Berlin, London, Manila and other distant places offering mysterious sounds of incomprehensible languages. Occasional strings of words buried in static rose and fell like bursts of rain in a thunderstorm.

The old Philco with its cherrywood case and cloth-covered speaker came from the Breens' relatives the Peaveys, where it had gathered dust after the REA reached their farm. Bertie remembered a time when he and Vickie looked forward to rare visits to the Peaveys. Compared to his family, they seemed rich. They even owned a television set. In the fall, Richie Lee Peavey always stepped up on the school bus with new shoes and bright blue overalls still stiff from the store.

That was all before Sam Morinville came to work for the Breens and before Richie Lee got sent away to reform school for stabbing Sam on the bus, an incident that Bertie blamed himself for. If only he hadn't stayed home to put up storm windows that day. Sam loved to pick on the little kids, especially Richie Lee, but left him alone when Bertie was there.

He wanted to listen to Jack Brickhouse announcing the baseball game from Chicago a thousand miles away. He supposed that when the announcer was young, kids called him Jack Brick Shithouse. Smiling at the thought, he swiveled the radio this way and that, trying to pick up the signal, but got only static. An antenna was what he needed. Maybe he could take some wire and hook it to the weather vane on the roof, except Sam would see it and rip it down.

\* \* \* \* \*

As soon as the dew burned off the next day, Sam and Bertie set out to pick bales. Of the many disagreeable chores on the Breen family's little farm by Dark

Lake, Bertie considered haying the worst, coming always when the hot summer air felt sticky as cotton candy and dust rose in billows of invisible particles that lodged inside your shirt and behind your eyelids. Insects of every kind—grasshoppers, horseflies, yellow jackets—stirred by the clattering baler, flew about in chaos before landing in your hair, your eyes or your open mouth if you breathed in at the wrong time.

Shaded by his cowboy hat, Sam drove the tractor pulling the baler while Bertie looked for snags as the teeth scooped the windrows of hay, guiding them toward the hidden mechanism that turned them into bales and expelled them through an opening that made it seem like the baler was giving birth. In its wake, a thousand smells filled the thick air—grease from gears, exhaust from the tractor, the never-settling dust, hay on the verge of rotting and the unforgettable sweat-and-whiskey stink of Sam Morinville.

At some point, based apparently on Sam's whim, they muscled the baler to the stubble side and replaced it with the hay wagon. Again, Sam perched on the throne of the tractor like a king, looking back only to drool tobacco juice over the power drive. Bertie followed the wagon, loading the bales half as heavy as he was while watching for garter snakes startled at losing their hiding place.

They finished the third load as Fawn and Vickie, dressed identically in bib overalls, appeared with the noon meal. Sam shut down the clatter of the tractor, and in the abrupt calm the air felt stagnant. Sam climbed down heavily, lurching as his feet hit the earth, while Fawn brushed aside loose stems of foxtail and dirt to form a counter on the end of the wagon where she set out the food—bread with apple butter, pickled beets, two hard-boiled eggs each and a quart jar of grape nectar.

With one hand, Sam gulped down half the nectar, wiped his mouth with his arm and set the jar down, glaring at Fawn. "This stuff's warm," he said.

"The last of the ice melted last week," said Bertie, wanting to protect his mother.

"I know when the ice melted," said Sam, setting the jar on the wagon so hard most of the remaining contents sloshed out.

While the two others ate, Fawn and Vickie waited. They would take their dinner at the house. A stone lying in the dust caught Vickie's attention.

"Look what I found," she cried, picking it up. "An arrowhead."

Bertie turned the triangular stone over in his palm, studying it intently. He passed it to his mother, who scratched at it with her thumbnail and handed it back it to Vickie. "I bet it is," said the girl.

Through this exchange, Sam silently peeled a boiled egg—first the shell, then the skin. His presence hung awkwardly over the other three. Despite fitting most people's perception of an Indian, he feigned disinterest in the conversation about the arrowhead. To do otherwise risked solidifying his image, undermining his position in the family. Even Vickie understood this and refrained from involving him in the discussion.

Sam stuffed his egg in his mouth whole and chewed in his odd sideways manner, like a giraffe. After swallowing, he wiped his mouth, peered into the wicker basket, then looked up at Fawn. "Did you bring some of them marshmallow things?" he asked.

"They're all gone."

"Huh? Well, I ain't full. How about graham crackers?"

Fawn lifted the towel, pretending to examine the basket's contents.

"There were plenty the other day," growled Sam.

Fawn put a hand to her throat. "Vickie can run and bring more bread."

"I'll get it myself," said Sam. "I gotta use the can and I want to see what else there is." With his slogging head-down walk, he trekked across the field, watched by Bertie. Maybe Sam needed the toilet, but more likely he was after his bottle.

Fawn and Vickie left quickly with the basket, avoiding Sam as he came striding heavy-heeled across the field straight for Bertie.

"Now I know what you been doing," he said, catching his breath.

"What do you mean?"

"You got a hidey-hole somewheres where you keep the food you're swiping."

"What?"

"You heard me. I just looked. There's all kinds of stuff missing, including my breakfast food. A whole box of Cheerios gone. Either you or the girl got into them and I'm saying it was you."

"I never took no Cheerios."

Both Bertie and Vickie loved the sweet little donuts that crunched between the teeth, but Cheerios came from town and cost thirty-nine cents. While all else made do with dry bread softened in warm milk, Sam ate store-bought cereal mixed with fresh cream while spooning sugar into his coffee in such heaps that it lay on the bottom of the cup like brown sludge in the hogpen. And while Bertie occasionally snuck a small handful of Prince Albert from the can Sam kept in the icebox, he dared not touch the Cheerios, and he said so.

"You think you got to steal other people's food to eat? Go someplace else. See if they feed you better."

Sam stood with his back to the sun, making Bertie squint to see into his face. "I do my share. You can ask Ma."

"I don't need to ask nobody. Every time I need help, you're riding that nag of a mare around playing cowboys. Last time I butchered, you run off all day and your mother had to help."

That was true about butchering, a grisly task that Bertie lacked the heart to participate in. "Ma told me I didn't have to," he said.

"I'm the one that decides who does what," said Sam, jabbing his thumb into his chest. Pearls of sweat formed on his face below his hat.

"I don't have to listen to you. You don't belong to this family," said Bertie, turning away in hopes of ending the conversation.

But Sam refused to allow it to end on its own. Grabbing Bertie's right arm, he pulled and twisted it up behind Bertie's neck. "Anytime I felt like it, I could bust your arm and wring your neck like a rooster, and you better not expect your old lady's gonna do anything about it." He spoke into Bertie's ear, his breath smelling of whiskey. He held the position for a minute before releasing Bertie toward the hay wagon with a shove.

As Bertie rubbed his arm and shoulder, Sam climbed up on the tractor seat and adjusted his hat. He dug in his teeth with a toothpick, pulled out a particle and wiped it on his pants. He fingered the outline of the round can of Copenhagen showing through his bib pocket. Extracting it, he twisted the lid and grabbed a pinch in the crook of his pointer finger. "Now get the hell to work," he said.

But before they completed one circle of the field, the tractor lurched to the right like a runner losing a shoe. Cursing, Sam lumbered from the seat and bent over the front wheels. The bearing had gone out again.

"Go tell her to make her list and get ready to go to town," he ordered, checking the sun overhead. "And hurry up."

Bertie knew that Sam's intentions would upset his mother. Not only did Fawn dislike going to town, but Sam would dig into her egg money to replace the items he claimed were missing from his personal hoard—cans of sweet fruit cocktail, olives from which the stones had been removed and perfect blocks of salty cheese.

As usual, Vickie pleaded to go along, and as usual when Sam was in a foul mood, permission was refused.

In minutes, Fawn and Sam were off, she with her checkered scarf tied under her chin, Sam with his outsize cowboy hat, bumping along in the dusty pickup with its missing back window.

With the adults away, Bertie looked forward to unexpected free time. After haying would come harvest, and time would be scarcer than ever. He wished they could hire custom combiners like other farmers in the area, but the farm was too small for that.

He better not leave Vickie alone for the time it took to saddle up Alouette and visit the castle, but he could check his hives and maybe take advantage of the late hatch to try the lake for northerns. First though, he wanted to try rigging an antenna for the radio just to see. He picked up the coil of fencing wire by the shed wall when Vickie appeared at the door.

"Whatcha doing?" she asked. She had on a pair of Bertie's old coveralls over a ragged shirt. She was outgrowing them, but they'd have to last until fall.

"Nothing," said Bertie.

"What's that wire for?"

"It's for none of your business, that's what for." Ever since Vickie heard about the radio, she begged him to let her try to tune in CBC so she could listen to that fancy music she liked.

"Aren't you supposed to peel some spuds?" he asked.

"The bin's empty."

"There was plenty a couple days ago."

"Go look for yourself."

"There's more in the cellar."

"There's spiders down there."

Bertie pulled off a long length of wire and snipped it cleanly with the cutters. "I'll get some potatoes for you. Just hold your horses."

"You don't have to get mad," said Vickie. "Besides, I heard Sam tell you to empty the rain barrel and clean the stalls."

"I got news. Sam's not my boss."

"He tells you what to do."

Bertie looped the wire over his shoulder. "He just works here. It's Ma that's the true boss. Then comes me and then you."

"I can't stand Sam," said Vickie. "Yuck! The way he spits in his jar and then brown drool catches on his chin. Ew!" Her large, cupped ears reddened. "I wish the Able gang would catch him."

"How do you know about the Ables?"

"I know lots of things."

"You're just extra mad 'cuz Sam threatened to smash your fiddle."

"It's a vi-o-*lin*," corrected Vickie, emphasizing each syllable.

"At least I don't call it a squawk box like Sam does."

In fact, Bertie was rather proud of the violin. Vickie had treasured it since she was a baby though the thing amounted to no more than a couple pieces of poorly glued wood. At a barn dance, Bertie had listened to a real fiddler and liked the jigs that he played. Before then, he hadn't realized that a bow was required to produce music. Eventually he found the bow in the attic along with the missing strings. After much experimentation—including painting the body green, Vickie's favorite color, which pleased her but rendered it mute, leading to hours of sanding—he'd produced something that at least looked like a violin. Vickie considered it proof of her brother's ingenuity, and with no instruction, managed to coax some passable tunes from the contraption.

"Maybe Ma will fire him," said Bertie. "Actually, I could fire him anytime if I wanted."

Both knew the wishful folly of that statement.

"Bertie, would you give me some money if I wanted?" said Vickie.

"Heck, no. Get your own. Besides, what makes you think I got money to buy you a new fiddle or whatever you want to call it."

Bertie knew what prompted the question. Sam's pregnant sister Rebecca had come by with her boyfriend Vernal, who waited in the car while she went inside to hit Sam up for a loan. She barely got the words out before Sam bulled his way outside threatening to beat the hell out of Vernal, who locked the doors when he saw him coming.

Vickie considered her brother's reply. "You'll never catch me having a baby," she said.

"And how do you know that?"

"Because I hate boys." She ran her fingers over the surface of the grindstone.

"Keep your hands off stuff before you get hurt," said Bertie.

"I won't get hurt," said Vickie. "Anyway, you know what?"

"What?"

"I saw Sam kiss Mama."

"What? You never saw no such thing," said Bertie. "Who would let him kiss them?" He wrinkled his nose in disgust.

"I saw it with my own eyes right in the kitchen," said Vickie. "Mama was pumping water at the sink, and Sam come up behind her."

"Well, that's not the same," said Bertie. "What did she do then?"

Vickie hesitated, searching for the right words. "She gave him a hug kind of."

"Now I know you're making up stories. Then what?"

"Nothing. Sam saw me and got real mad and told me to quit sneaking up on him."

After gathering a dozen potatoes for Vickie, Bertie decided he'd fool with his radio another day. Right now he wanted to walk around the lake to check his beehives. As long as he was busy raking mud and manure out of the stalls when Ma and Sam got back, he wouldn't be in trouble.

As he reached the woods, something yellow on the ground by a cranberry bush captured his attention. An empty Cheerios box, still stiff and dry. He stood motionless, afraid to touch the box, when he noticed the absence of bird calls. He checked the sky for a hawk on the hunt. A breeze fluttered the aspen. Confounded, he let the box lie and carried on toward the hives.

Bertie kept only four hives, down from the sixteen he started with, having found that other chores left him no time to tend to so many. Even at that, after keeping some honey for the family along with a jar for the Peaveys as a Christmas gift, he had saved almost eight dollars to buy a Big Ben pocket watch like the one Harold Peavey carried. He hid his savings—a five, two ones and change—in an old sock. Then, one rainy Saturday while gathering things to go to town, he found his stash missing—sock, silver, bills and all. It didn't take Dick Tracy to know that Sam swiped it, but Bertie never bothered to accuse him, knowing the row that followed would upset Ma.

The hives were set on the northwest corner of the pasture across from a damp meadow owned by the state game reserve that grew abundant with wild rose, willow and untended grass. As he came closer, Bertie knew by the loud buzzing that something had disturbed the bees. The top two supers on one of the hives lay leaning on the lower combs. He regretted not having brought his gloves, but he disliked the lack of feeling in his fingers and found that if he scraped a fingernail briefly over a sting, he could gouge out the stinger before the venom soaked in. His face was another matter. His breath attracted the bees. A sting in the area of his nose or mouth left him hurting for hours. To prevent this, he safety-pinned a cheesecloth veil to his straw hat and draped it over his face.

Thank goodness the bees hadn't swarmed, a possible outcome of the hives being disturbed. That happens and there go your bees. He set the supers back in place, trying to determine what went wrong. Raccoons or possums would make more of a mess, as would other animals. This looked like the action of humans.

At once, he checked the other three hives and found them intact down to the brood combs. He pulled a few leaf shreds and grass stems from a super and replaced the lid.

## 2 | Eating Hoppers

On the hike back to the house, Bertie puzzled over what he'd found. The disturbed hives could be attributed to animals after all, but not the Cheerios and the missing potatoes. Someone would have had to have gotten into the house for those. Moreover, the way Sam talked suggested to Bertie that this had been going on for several days. The occasional hobo that came by never hung around that long. There was the Able family that everyone considered criminals, but they wouldn't have bothered with a few spuds and a box of cereal.

Bertie knew he should report what he'd found to Sam and let him worry about it. But Sam had a way of ridiculing any idea Bertie had, and in this case, he'd be more likely to accuse Bertie of trying to shift blame on someone or something else. Besides, Bertie had to admit to himself that the situation represented a break in the endless repetition and boredom of life on an isolated farm. He decided he would wait and try to learn more.

After two days and nights with nothing more happening, Bertie began to believe it had been only a prowler or hobo who had moved on in search of better pickings. But he wanted to be sure. After lying in bed listening for the sounds of the house to fade, he tiptoed downstairs carrying his shoes, staying to the side to avoid the squeaky boards. He sat on the step tying his laces. A car drove by throwing up a clatter of gravel which shortly settled to quiet. Growing up without the instant light provided by electricity, he knew how to make his way easily around in the night.

He followed the cow path past the barn. A swishing to his right startled him. Raccoons. No mistaking their wild smell of old pee and strange skittering speech. He intended to return to the place he'd discovered the empty cereal box, that being the only clue he had as to the presence of someone else. If he found nothing there, he'd follow his private shortcut in the direction of the castle, though he knew that unless he took Alouette he'd never make it all the way on foot.

But before he reached the hill on the far side of the hives, another noise, something moving through brush carelessly and unnaturally, reached him. No animal moved that way. At that instant, his unhappy house with Sam lording over it seemed welcoming. He flexed his knees like an athlete, ready to run.

"Bertie?"

He whirled around, trying to locate the source of the voice, muffled and soft.

"Bertie, it's me."

Twigs cracked, grass parted and a figure, short and stocky, emerged.

"Who is it?" Bertie demanded.

"Richie Lee."

"Who?"

"Richie Lee Peavey. Don't you know me no more?"

"Richie Lee?" The name failed to match the person before him. The distant cousin he'd known had grown, stretched out. Only the roundish face of his mother suggested his origins.

"Yes."

"What are you doing here—aren't you in reform school?"

"I ran away," said Richie Lee.

"You did? Do your folks know whereabouts you are?"

Richie Lee shook his head. "Nobody knows. Except you now. I been sleeping in that stone house up a ways. In the daytime, I hide out in the woods down here closer to the house."

Bertie lowered his voice. "How long you been here, Richie Lee?"

"I think it was Wednesday. I run away on Sunday."

"Huh? Don't they got fences down there?"

"They ain't nothing to get over. If you go to chapel, you get an hour free. That's when I lit out."

"How did you find out about the stone house?"

"I seen you and Alouette, and you looked like you was going somewhere so I followed. It was after I slept in the hayloft the first night and saw Sam Morinville pitching hay."

"But what do you have for food and stuff?"

"I ate chokecherries till I got the diarrheas. I tried to catch a goat and milk it, but they're too wild. And then I snuck in your house and took some spuds and a box of cereal. And some crackers was all." Richie Lee's voice broke. "I never dared go back to the house after I seen Sam Morinville. What's he here for anyways?"

"He's our hired man."

"No!" said Richie Lee. "Since when?"

"Ever since last year. You just can't find a hired man no more."

"And he lives here then?"

"Yep."

"It's 'cuz of him I wound up in reform school."

"I know," replied Bertie.

As if drained of words, the boys assumed an uncomfortable silence.

"That's all you had to eat since Wednesday, the Cheerios and stuff?" said Bertie.

"I tried to get some honey, but the bees stung me bad. Right now I could chew bark off the trees. That's how come I gave in and called out to you. You don't suppose you could find something for me to eat, do you? I'd thank you lots." He looked at Bertie, pleading.

Never before had Bertie known his cousin Richie Lee to demonstrate manners. Maybe reform school taught him that. "It won't be much, and it'll be a while."

Bertie took barely two steps when Richie Lee called. "Bertie, you're coming back, ain't you?"

"I'll be back," he said. "Keep close to this spot but stay back in the brush."

\* \* \* \* \*

By Bertie's return, the emergence of dawn cast its pale light, and he could see Richie Lee more clearly. His clothes, a gray, long-sleeved cotton shirt and striped overalls, were stained green and thick with nettles. His hair resembled winter stubble.

Bertie handed over two slices of buttered bread wrapped in waxed paper. "Sorry, this is all I could get my hands on so quick."

Richie Lee crammed one slice in his mouth, then folded the other and wrapped it in a dirty cloth. Wiping his face, he spoke. "You grew a lot, Bertie. Look at you."

"So did you," said Bertie. "But tell me, how come you run away anyhow? You didn't have that much longer to stay."

"I don't know. I just saw the chance and there I went. Who cares? I done it and I'm never going back. Know what they do to kids they catch?"

Bertie had only the vaguest idea. Richie Lee was quick to enlarge on it, claiming that such boys were stripped naked and, once a day for a week, plunged into a horse trough of water into which blocks of ice had been placed.

"That's bad all right," said Bertie, doubting the story. Richie Lee had been known to make things up. "Still, you got to get that straightened out before you go home."

"I ain't going home."

"Why do you say that?"

"My dad, he don't want me. He as much as told the judge I belonged in reform school. Anyway, he's not my true dad."

Richie Lee had said that before, and Bertie found it upsetting, but then Richie Lee said a lot of things that were questionable. Bertie thought of his own father and his favorite memory when his dad pretended to examine Bertie's ears while explaining that the family ate so much rabbit stew that he wouldn't be surprised if their ears grew out.

"But what do you suppose you'll do now?"

Richie Lee shrugged. "All I know is I'm just glad to get away."

"Tell me how you made it clear up from Mandan. Who helped you?"

"Nobody helped me," said Richie Lee indignantly. "Except once, I mean," he added sheepishly.

He explained that he got lost in Minot and had to get directions at a gas station. He went on to say that most runaways soon found themselves back in Mandan because they made their way directly to wherever they came from. Sometimes the authorities reached their homes before the boys got there. Richie Lee himself intended to choose a different direction, but each move just seemed to take him north. He first snuck onto the back of a truck loaded with two-by-fours going to Minot, and then hitched a ride with a plumber on his way to Dunseith.

"But weren't you afraid somebody would spot you when you got close to home?" asked Bertie.

"Once I reached the reservation, I knew I could pass for Indian since everybody's on foot there."

Bertie chuckled at the thought that Richie Lee, with his short, light hair and pale skin, could be mistaken for an Indian. "But then what made you come to our place?"

"I didn't know where to go. I never meant to stay till I seen you going to the place made out of rocks. How long's that been there?"

"Who knows?" said Bertie. "The way it's tucked kind of under those two hills, it's likely nobody but me and you know about it. Just so Sam never finds out."

The sun came up full, and Bertie's chores awaited. He promised to return later with food while pondering where it would come from. Maybe he'd have to eat less himself and share.

* * * * *

No one questioned him when he went out at sunset to check his hives or take Alouette for a ride. The boys agreed to meet roughly halfway to the hut near a prominent oak with a thick horizontal limb that they referred to as the hanging tree. Here, Bertie handed over scraps of food—stale bread, late-season vegetables from the garden, half-rotten apples and undersized potatoes that might not be missed. As they shared a smidgen of strong tobacco in Bertie's corncob pipe, Richie Lee related his stories of reform school.

"I know how to make whiskey," he said.

"What? You do not."

"Yes, sir," insisted Richie Lee.

"Well, it's not really whiskey," he admitted after a minute. "But it makes you drunk. You mix up sugar and potato peelings, that sort of stuff, and let it set for a while. They call it rat piss."

"Sam keeps a bottle of whiskey out in the crapper," said Bertie. "First thing every morning, he goes and has a shot. You can smell it on him."

"Your ma, she don't mind?"

Bertie raised his hand to shush Richie Lee. They listened. "Must be a deer," said Bertie.

"Know what else?" said Richie Lee, enthused. "I can make a shiv from a comb—a shiv, that's a knife. You'd be surprised at the things you learn. Did you know you can eat grasshoppers? The guys from Fargo, they're afraid to."

Bertie considered this. "What's it like living where there's all those rascals you got to keep an eye on?"

"It depends. Like I say, them from big towns are the ones to look out for. I got so I'd keep my mouth shut in class even when I know the right answer because some of them, they don't like it when you show off."

"Do they ever let you go anyplace like a store or ball game?"

"Not so much," said Richie Lee, delighted to be treated as a source of information. "You can see the highway from the upstairs at Dorm A. It seems like there's a million cars go by every day. The airport's close, and the planes come right over the top of you. You see that and it makes you want to bust out all the more."

Bertie picked up a crooked oak limb and jabbed it at the ground, snapping it. "I'd like to bust out of here," he said. "Get away from Sam."

"Maybe you could live in the stone place."

"I thought of that. I'm not so sure now."

"Just don't wind up where I did," said Richie Lee.

Bertie nodded. "Did you know I quit school? I never went but half the time, and I couldn't see any sense in it if I was gonna stay on the farm, but now I might change my mind. Even if Sam wasn't here, the place isn't much good. This land in the hills, you can't grow stuff. All rock and roots."

The two talked on through the night, of hound dogs, jackknives, race cars, kids they did or didn't like, the strange ways of girls. They speculated on why an Indian would wear a cowboy hat and even discussed the pending election, agreeing they hoped Kennedy would win.

By the time Bertie made his way back to the house, sleepers were up and smoke from the cookstove rose above the kitchen.

Sam leaned against the doorframe with his thumbs hooked in his belt loops. "Must be something awful interesting going on for you to be up so early."

At first Bertie ignored the comment, then turned back. "Not interesting enough to get you out of bed."

Sam snorted contemptuously and shambled toward the outhouse.

On this hot, muggy day, the horseflies drove the cows mad. The stench of decay rose from the slough and the well water was going bad from lack of rain, leaving a coating on the mouth like metal. Everyone was cranky except Sam, who went about with a rare smile on his face.

By noon, Bertie convinced himself that Sam knew something. He spoke with a kind of confident pride. *Hand me them tin snips. Go see if she's got dinner ready.*

Bertie was scrubbing the bowl of the cream separator when he came by. "Going out again tonight?"

Bertie concentrated on using his fingernail to peel a line of scum from the rim.

"What's your trouble?" said Sam. "Your tongue broke?"

Bertie spoke with his head down. "Sure, I'm gonna see my girl. She lives up in a tree."

Sam angled his chin downward to drool tobacco juice exactly between the tips of his boots. "Like you'd know what to do with a girl."

"I know plenty," said Bertie quietly.

"Shoo," said Sam. "Tell me one thing you know."

"I know you better let Ma alone."

"What?" said Sam, stepping closer.

"I said stay away from my mother. Go find yourself a squaw."

"You little shit," he said. "If not for the old lady, I'd have the sheriff after you and don't forget it."

Bertie let that go. Not so long ago, he'd have laughed out loud at Sam mentioning the sheriff, who was about the last person he'd want to see.

\* \* \* \* \*

That afternoon, as soon as he could slip away, Bertie set out for the woods. He arrived at the hanging tree and whistled sharply. Richie Lee emerged from the brush, looking thin and dirty in the bright light.

"I think Sam knows," said Bertie.

"Huh? What did he say?"

"He talked that he could get the sheriff, but it's more how he acts. The thing is, you got to stay away from the castle for now."

Richie Lee pulled on his lower lip. "Where can I sleep then?"

"Take the blanket and bed down in the sedge grass."

"I don't want to sleep in no grass. What if it rains?"

"It's not supposed to rain for a while. I don't see any difference from a regular bed," said Bertie, trying to convince himself. "You got any ideas of your own?"

"Why don't we both run away somewheres?"

"Don't be stupid."

"No, really. What about if we both took off?"

"And go where?"

"Out west. Kentucky or Montana maybe. One kid at school run away out there, and they never found him. If we were quick, we could set out tonight."

Bertie glared at Richie Lee for a long minute. "Listen to me," he said sternly. "We wouldn't get two miles. If you're scared of sleeping outside, try the haymow, but don't blame me if you get caught."

As he saw the tears form in the younger boy's eyes, Bertie himself felt like crying. He saw nothing good coming. He could never turn Richie Lee in even if for his own good. Keeping him fed and safe would only get more dangerous. And if the boy were discovered, he would for sure bring Bertie into it. Whatever came about, dreams of making any kind of home in the hut were gone.

Hurrying back, Bertie smelled smoke to the southwest. Nobody would be burning brush this time of year. He made his way in that direction, crossed the barbed wire fence of the pasture and climbed the slight rise leading to the game reserve. The smoke rose straight into the blue sky. Bertie knew its source at once. Before him sat his hives, each one aflame. He darted toward them but halted a few feet short, seeing that the fires were dying on their own.

Over the rocky pasture his feet flew, across the fence and through the creek, never pausing. The barn door looked barred, and the cows bunched about the yard. The shop entrance was bolted from the outside. He raced to the house, scattering the chickens, screaming Sam's name. He swung open the storm door, pushed through the kitchen door and found no one. He took the stairs two at a time, his pounding steps shaking the house. His mother's door was closed, but he turned the knob and shoved it open.

Sam sat on the edge of the bed, hair mussed, barefoot, pulling his underwear up over his knees. On the opposite side of the bed stood Bertie's mother, the flowery summer bedspread wrapped around her.

"Albert," she said.

"What the hell! Don't you knock for crying out loud?" said Sam, reaching for his trousers.

Bertie's eyes went from one to the other. "My hives," he said.

"What about 'em?" said Sam, back in command now that his pants were properly fastened.

"You set fire to my hives. They're all burnt up," said Bertie.

His mother pulled the bedspread tighter.

Bertie backed away toward the door, glaring at Sam. "You had no cause to do that."

"I told you bees don't belong there. I wasn't even close and got stung three times."

"That's your own fault. And I bought those bees with my money. You have to pay me back."

"Get out of here," ordered Sam.

* * * * *

Bertie walked outside and sat in the old swing his dad rigged from a bough long ago. It hung so low to the ground that a tall person like Bertie had to sit with his knees touching his chin. He listened to the cooing of the pigeons, a sound that once soothed him but now felt mocking. Over in the calf pen, flies buzzed about. Never had manure smelled so putrid, or the sagging, rusty barbed wire surrounding the pasture looked so ugly.

In a while, he heard the rise and fall of voices in the house—Sam's low grumbling, his mother's muted responses, Vickie's adolescent babble.

The image persisted. Sam grunting as he struggled with his pants, his thick, brown thighs bared. His mother's hollow look, her face as expressionless as a window.

## 3 | Infinite Directions

"Bertie, get up."

It was Vickie, her voice carrying an unusual tone of authority.

"What time is it?"

"Mama said to come quick."

Bertie sat up, hearing the murmur of voices in the kitchen. He pulled on his pants and shirt, leaving his feet bare. He opened his door into a wave of heat from the cookstove and tiptoed to the kitchen to protect his feet from cracks in the linoleum.

At the table, his finger curled around the handle of a coffee cup, sat Sheriff Dale Aingher. His hat rested on a chair. "Well, well," said the sheriff. "You're sleeping late for a farm boy."

Bertie offered a hesitant smile.

"The sheriff has some questions for you," said his mother in a pleasant voice.

With his mouth still dry from sleep, Bertie swallowed and took a chair across from the sheriff.

Aingher tapped a foot on the floor and leaned toward Bertie.

"It's about the Peavey boy. We got a report he's missing from the school in Mandan. Did you know that?"

Before Bertie could answer, his mother came to his rescue. With her hair brushed and a clean apron, she looked like a brand-new person from a day earlier. "Richie Lee's younger than Bertie," she said.

"We're looking after his best interest," said the sheriff. "These days it's not safe for a kid that age out on his own."

Bertie tried to sit still. He had to pee something awful.

The sheriff leaned back in his chair and stuck out his feet. Bertie smelled the polish on his boots. "Sam Morinville says you like to wander around the hills. You haven't spotted anything different, have you?"

Bertie squeezed his hands out of sight under the table to keep them from shaking.

"Anything at all would help," added Aingher. "Something that don't belong, signs that someone's come through."

"Not that I can think of," said Bertie.

The sheriff held his gaze for a minute. "Yes. Well, I thank you for the time. You know how to get hold of us," he said, reaching for his hat.

Bertie stood beside his mother as the sedan pulled slowly out of the farmyard, barely bothering the chickens pecking in the dirt.

"That's a shame," said his mother.

Bertie, aware any reply would firm up his lie, held his tongue.

"But thank goodness," his mother added. "When I saw the sheriff's car, I thought they'd found out."

"Found out what?" asked Bertie, alarmed all over again.

His mother turned and wiped her hands on her apron. Sweat glistened on her forehead. "Just the other day, Sam and I were talking about your Uncle Foss. Sam said he thought there could still be throwbacks over that business. Next thing I know, the sheriff pulls up."

Bertie looked at his mother. "You told Sam about Uncle Foss? You said it was our secret."

His mother rested her hand on Bertie's shoulder, engulfing him in the strong aroma of Ivory soap. "Well, Sam's like family. Anyway, it was so long ago."

"But, Mama," he said, reverting to the word he'd not called her in a long time. For a second, he wanted to tell her the complete story, believing only she who was his only living blood relative had the power to fix matters. But in that same second, he saw in her a rare look of serenity. It was better to let her be and tend to all the messes as best he could. Single-handedly. Sometimes he longed to grab on and ride the clouds away, caring not where they might take him.

\* \* \* \* \*

Bertie spent the morning nailing plywood over the rotting floor of the henhouse to keep out weasels, glad to be occupied by himself so he could think. He should have put a stop to Richie Lee staying in the hut as soon as he found him.

The situation got worse as time went by. And now Richie Lee had the foolish idea for Bertie to run away with him, like it wasn't job enough looking after him now. When he came in for dinner, sick to his stomach from the smell, his mother had news for him.

"Harold Peavey sent word he needs to see you," she said.

Bertie wiped his feet on the rag rug, trying to appear calm. "Harold? Did he say what it's about?"

It took his mother forever to speak. First, she jabbed a fork into the boiling potatoes to make sure they were done, then looked around for a pot holder before bunching up her apron and sliding the saucepan away from the burner.

"Ma, did you hear me? What did Harold want?"

"Hmm? Oh." She looked at him like she'd just noticed his presence. "He needs you to do his chores so he can help the custom combiners. They're short of hands."

His mother went on to explain that Bertie would stay with the Peaveys during the estimated five or six days they needed him, and that Harold would pay him five dollars a day.

"Five a day? But what about our own crops?"

His mother dumped the potatoes into a serving bowl and stood back as the steam cleared. "Sam says the barley's not ripe yet. Vickie can help with our chores."

"How soon would I start?"

"The crew's there now. He'll be over to pick you up in a little while."

Bertie knew he had no real choice. The Peaveys had been good to his family, and twenty-five dollars, maybe more, was more money than he'd ever had in life. But what about Richie Lee? He couldn't just leave him up there in the woods alone like an orphan lamb, and he didn't dare tell anyone because everybody along with Sheriff Aingher and Richie Lee's folks would wonder why Bertie hadn't said something earlier. But what if something happened to Richie Lee? Like if he broke a leg or got so hungry he ate poisonous mushrooms? It would be Bertie's fault.

His thoughts were interrupted by the slam of the screen door as Vickie entered with her new kitten in her arms. "Mama, Ollie's hungry," she said.

"You know where the milk is, but take him outside first. You know how Sam is about cats."

"But, Mama—"

"No buts. Go. And quit giving him so much milk. It just goes to waste."

Bertie waited as Vickie, with her squirming kitten, followed orders. "Ma, do you think Harold knows anything about Richie Lee?"

"What? Of course not. You better get your stuff ready. He'll be here before you know it."

Bertie downed his meal, knowing how much Richie Lee would love a helping of boiled baloney and buttered potatoes. If only there were some way to get food for him at least until Bertie was through at Peaveys. He gathered his overalls and barn boots from the porch and looked outside, expecting to see Harold's pickup pull into the yard. No sign of him, but there was Vickie teasing her kitten with a piece of rhubarb.

"Vickie," he said, approaching her. "How would you like to make a whole dollar?"

The girl frowned at him. "Doing what?"

"Well," said Bertie, unsure if this was a good idea. "I can't tell you here. We need to get away from the house."

That awoke the girl's curiosity. "How come?"

"So nobody hears," he said, glancing over his shoulder. "We'll go over by the pasture and pretend we're looking for Juneberries. Leave Ollie. We have to go fast before Harold gets here."

"Do you think they'll ever find Richie Lee?" said Bertie as they crossed the yard.

"I hope not," said the girl, skipping to keep up with her longer-legged brother.

Surprised at the answer, Bertie questioned her further. "You know why they sent him to reform school, don't you?" asked Bertie, watching for a reaction.

"Mama said he got in trouble 'cuz of Sam," Vickie answered.

"But you don't think if Richie Lee did harm he ought to take his punishment?"

Vickie looked up, her suspicions aroused. Never in her recollection had her brother sought an opinion from her. "No, I told you I don't want them to catch him 'cuz the reform school has guards that spank you all the time."

"That's right. Even if you didn't do nothing," said Bertie.

Vickie thought about this. "Do girls have to go to reform school?"

"Sometimes, but they got a different one for them. It's not so mean."

They reached the far border of the pasture and entered an area that had been clear-cut for firewood years before, though saplings grew there now. "Vickie, do you think you can keep a secret?"

"A secret? What is it?" she said, not quite successfully stepping over a cow pie.

"First you have to be sure you can keep it."

"I can keep it. Tell me," she said excitedly.

Bertie began with the discovery of the stone house and how he cleaned it out and fixed the leaky roof, omitting the part about the bones. Vickie made no comment until he mentioned the bed and the chair that he'd made with tree limbs and twine.

"But whereabouts is it?" she asked.

"North a ways."

"Which way's north?"

Bertie hesitated a minute and pointed to the east. "It takes a long time to get there unless you take a shortcut through the woods. Anyway, this is good. We can talk now."

"Is it like a playhouse?" asked Vickie, staring in the direction her brother pointed.

"More than a playhouse. Someone could live there if they had food to eat."

"I wouldn't want to live there if it didn't have a door and stuff," said Vickie.

"It wouldn't be so bad. Someone's staying there right now," said Bertie.

Vickie's eyes lit up. "Really? Who?"

"Richie Lee Peavey."

"Richie Lee?" The words burst from the girl's mouth. "Can we visit him?"

"No, not now," said Bertie, wanting to dampen Vickie's excitement. "Don't forget, this is a secret. *You cannot tell!*"

"I won't. You don't have to get mad. When can we go there? I want to see the little house."

"You'll have plenty of chances after tomorrow," said Richie Lee.

Bertie used plain words in describing how Vickie would supply Richie Lee with food while Bertie worked at Peaveys. She must see to it not to take any of Sam's favorite foods or take too much of any one thing. She would follow an established pattern. Every two days she would hide the food under the dead tree behind the barn, and Richie Lee could pick it up at his own leisure.

"I wonder when I could drop it off," said Vickie, warming to the strategy. "Maybe right after dinner when Sam goes to the outhouse for half an hour and Mama lays down on the couch."

"That's a good idea," said Bertie. "That way if Richie Lee gets caught you wouldn't get blamed."

"When will you pay me the dollar?" asked Vickie.

"When I get back from Peaveys."

Vickie looked to be considering something. "You should give me at least a dollar and a half."

"I'll make it two as long as you don't let yourself get seen."

"And you have to teach me how to ride Alouette."

Bertie sighed. "OK. Come on, let's get back."

They arrived at the house just as Harold pulled into the yard.

Harold, who looked older since Bertie had seen him, put him at ease by shaking his hand just like they were equals. During the few minutes that Harold stood in the yard speaking to Bertie's mother, Bertie worried what might happen if Richie Lee were watching from the woods. Maybe at the sight of his father he would burst into the open, begging to be taken home.

While the combiners and Harold began harvesting the next day, Bertie took on the chores. How easy it felt compared to the backbreaking labor required at home. The gleaming stainless steel milking machine not only cut milking time in half but spared the aching muscles in his arms and hands that came with the endless squeezing and pulling needed before the invention of the modern device. When pulling the manure spreader, he marveled at how easy the big John Deere 620 was to shift and how powerful it felt in his control. When not in the field, he slept in Richie Lee's old bed and took his place at the table. Richie Lee's mother prepared filling meals topped off with fruit pie for dessert every night. The house carried a fresh, scrubbed smell. Outside, the farmyard looked green and neat. The morning mist carried the sweet smell of clover. Why would Richie Lee not want to come back to such comforts?

One rainy afternoon when they couldn't get in the field, the custom combiners hung out in the barn killing time. They were a cheerful bunch, easygoing and suntanned, speaking in deep Texas drawls as they draped themselves over hay bales and told their humorous stories of the odd people they met on their travels through Oklahoma and on up through the Dakotas bringing in the wheat crop. Listening to their tales, such as the one about the farmer who locked his daughter away to keep her from the predatory strangers only to have her sneak out the window, made Bertie envy their carefree lives.

But as the days passed, his concerns about Richie Lee grew. One day in the house filling his water jar, he overheard Leah on the phone asking someone for news about her son. He could barely keep from crying out: *Wait!* I know where he is.

The days passed. Once seated in the pickup for the ride home, Bertie accepted two small white envelopes, one with his name on it containing three ten-dollar bills that included the extra five for the rainy day. "The other envelope's for your mother," said Harold.

Only later did Bertie understand that Harold had planned to give him ten dollars a day, rather than five, but knew that if the entire earnings were turned over to Bertie, Sam would soon have his hands on it.

Back at his own place, Bertie looked around, noticing as if for the first time the trash heap behind the granary, the two hulks of cars with windows out and tires gone flat, pieces of rusty fencing—all the sorry signs of the life that lay ahead of him.

At the first good chance he had, he saddled Alouette and rode north toward the castle, eager to share a proposal he'd come up with. Richie Lee emerged to meet him, holding the reins so Bertie could dismount.

"Say, you look like you done OK with me gone," said Bertie, taking note of Richie Lee's clean overalls, probably a pair he'd outgrown.

"That Vickie, she's a peach," said Richie Lee, smiling. "Once she come all the way by herself to play me some songs on her fiddle."

"So, you showed her how to get here?"

"She wanted to see. Come look at what else she brung."

Richie Lee bubbled with pleasure as he led Bertie inside the hut. Along one wall lay blankets and a pillow resting on a mattress made of straw stuffed into feed bags. On the far side, a shelf constructed from a wide board and flat rocks held potatoes, rice, even a folded waxed paper of salt and pepper and a fruit jar filled with Cheerios.

Bertie scanned the abundant accumulation of supplies and frowned. He selected a can of fruit cocktail and studied the label. "Store-bought," he said quietly to himself. Outside, a flock of Canada geese passed overhead, their determined calls filling the air.

"Know what?" said Richie Lee. "Vickie's got it figured how to make it through the winter."

"Is that so," said Bertie, only half listening.

"First, we mix grass and mud to stuff up the cracks. And if the fireplace don't work, I know a way to keep warm. I seen down in Mandan in the leatherworks they got a little stove so small you could put two of them in a bushel basket. And all we need is a few old boards to make a decent door."

Bertie let Richie Lee go on for a minute before interrupting him.

"Richie Lee, listen," he began. "This seems easy when all you got to do is wait for someone to bring what you want like in a café. You remember how high the snow drifts get up here in the trees, don't you?" Bertie eyed his cousin sternly. "I told her not to take stuff that would get noticed," he said, picking up a half-full bag of dried beans. "It was my fault really, but now we're in a fix and we got just three days before it gets worse."

"How come?" asked Richie Lee.

"Just about every Saturday, Ma and Sam make a special trip to town for supplies. Sam helps make a list to decide if we really need something or not. Today's Wednesday. Early Saturday morning they're going to see how much is missing."

"But how would they know what came of it?"

Bertie hefted the bag in his hands. "Sam's not that dumb. Pretty likely he's seen how funny Vickie's been acting. It won't take long."

Richie Lee bit on his thumb. "Then I better run away again," he said.

Despite all, Bertie felt an unfamiliar surge of pity for the boy. "No, I had time to think it all out a little at your folks' place after I got to visiting with the custom combiners. They're looking for hands, and there's plenty to do even for someone your age, and there's no questions asked. And it might not be a bad idea for me to go too, like you wanted."

As Richie Lee listened, suddenly more attentive, Bertie laid out his plan. They would take off in the night and catch up with the combiners around Granville. Nobody's gonna think anything of a couple of boys thumbing around this time of year. Finding the crew should be easy. Just check the bars on a Saturday night.

Bertie downplayed one detail—his intention to go off on his own eventually. He didn't want to go into that, he explained. He just wanted to see more of the country. But Richie Lee could stay with the combiners all the way down to Texas. More than likely—here Bertie fudged a little—one of the crew would invite him to stay the winter with his family.

"If you wound up on a ranch, you could have your own horse," he added, hoping for a positive reaction. He sensed his cousin's curiosity growing, his mind perhaps dwelling on the joys of exploring the hills of Texas astride a beautiful palomino. As he went over the details, Bertie began to like his brainchild more all the time. Richie Lee, listening closely, had questions. How far away was Texas? ("A long ways. Maybe a thousand miles.") What was it like? ("Summer all the time.") How much money would he make? ("Lots depending on crops.")

"But what if somebody finds out?"

Bertie couldn't let this fall apart now. A small fib wouldn't hurt. "From what those fellas were saying, Texas is still wide-open country and nobody much worries where you been or what you done. And then, naturally, you'd be far away from what all's going on around here."

"You would stay there too?"

"For a while."

Richie Lee looked away. "Bertie, what was it like over at home?"

"At your folks? Everybody's pretty busy at harvest."

"Did they talk about me much?"

"Of course. They miss you terrible."

Richie Lee sniffed and bit his lower lip.

As Bertie studied the boy, he saw not an innocent kid who'd taken missteps, but an out-and-out dependent and helpless baby who should never have come loose of his mama's apron strings.

"Richie Lee, you got two choices: either do exactly what I say or go back to your folks right now. You get what I mean?"

"Yeah," he muttered.

"All right then. For now, you stay out of sight. Be ready to go tomorrow night. We'll be facing plenty of walking, so just take what you're wearing and what you can carry in food."

All the way home, Bertie fretted. He had to say something to Ma. He couldn't just pull out. He could tell right off that she was sick again. When he gave her the envelope with the money from Harold, she looked at it like it was full of dead worms. Later he found the envelope on the kitchen floor, unopened. He also worried whether Vickie might accidentally tell something that would give the whole thing away.

More than likely, nothing but more danger lay ahead, but a bad plan was better than no plan at all.

\* \* \* \* \*

In the morning, Bertie found that in his absence the stalls had not been mucked out, nor the separator cleaned, nor the hay cribs filled. By noon, he was sweaty and filthy. He headed for the stock tank to clean up, recalling his dad plunging him into the tank to cool off on days like this. Removing his shirt and pinching his nostrils, he lowered his head into the tank. As he straightened up, he heard the familiar, distressed voice of his sister breaking the oppressive muteness of the summer day. He opened his eyes.

Sam, with one hand grasping a belt loop of Richie Lee's pants, was leading the stumbling and weeping boy across the barnyard like a stray calf. Right behind them came Vickie, red-faced and sobbing, her words garbled. Hens fluttered to the side, and the commotion brought Bertie's mother from the house, the screen door banging behind. When Vickie spotted her, she charged up the steps and threw her small arms around her legs.

"What is it?" asked her mother, leaning to comfort her. "Who's that boy?"

"Ask him," said Sam, gesturing with his thumb toward Bertie, who approached unhurriedly, his shirt dragging in the dust.

"It's Richie Lee. I been hiding him out. It wasn't Vickie."

"Bertie, Sam made me tell," cried Vickie.

Her mother tugged her housedress around herself. "He's been here on our farm?"

"He didn't have no place to go," Bertie replied.

"He'll have a place now," said Sam. "Same one he ran away from."

"But where did you find him?" asked Fawn.

"He was in a kinda cave up north," said Sam.

"It's not a cave," said Bertie. "It's an old house made with stones."

"Quite the hideout, all fixed up and stocked with food straight out of our kitchen," said Sam, looking directly at Fawn. "What have I been saying all along?"

She gazed toward the distant woods. "A stone house?"

"You know about it, Ma?" said Bertie.

His mother stiffened and went silent.

Sam leaped in impatiently, turning to Bertie. "I thought you told the sheriff you never seen him. And you just come from his parents. I bet you never said anything to them neither."

Hearing a reference to his parents, Richie Lee tried to lunge away. Sam delivered a hard jerk on the strap, causing the boy to cry out.

"Quit hurting him," screamed Vickie.

"Not only did he lie, he harbored a criminal, which is not legal in North Dakota," said Sam.

Despite all, Bertie smirked at Sam's attempt to sound like a fancy lawyer. "Richie Lee's not a criminal," he said.

"Is that a fact?" answered Sam. "I still got a knife scar to prove it if you want to argue about that. First thing in the morning, we're taking them both to town and we'll see who's a criminal. Fawn, get me the roll of baling twine out of the shed."

"You mean to tie them up? You don't need to do that," said Fawn. "Bertie could have run off before if he wanted."

"I said get me the twine," replied Sam.

At this, Vickie renewed her cries of protest. After following Sam's order, her mother took Vickie by the arm and pulled her into the house. With neither boy offering resistance, Sam bound their wrists and herded them into the porch, where he tied their ankles together. When finished, he tested each knot with a good tug and stepped back, satisfied.

*****

Outside, a thin line of clouds accented by moonlight appeared. In the kitchen, Bertie's mother and Sam talked—Ma in a muted, hard-to-hear tone, Sam in short, angry sentences. Now and then, an outburst or a footstep caused Richie Lee to shy away from the sound and pull on the restraints, rubbing the skin raw where the twine bit deep.

After a long time, the lights dimmed and silence came over the house.

"Bertie?" Richie Lee spoke softly.

"Yeah."

"What will happen to me?"

"You heard Sam as well as I did," said Bertie.

He reviewed the changed situation. He had no doubt what lay in store for Richie Lee, but how about himself?

For him, the worst punishment was in his head. He saw it in his mother's face when she grasped that he had fibbed to the sheriff. It was the way his sister looked at him, expecting him to do something when Sam was hurting Richie Lee. Someday, maybe when Sam was gone and Ma got better, he'd make it up to them.

He had friends who poached deer or snipped wire fences just to be a nuisance. Bertie had never even shook a gumball out of the penny machine at Ralph's gas station. The penalty for helping out a runaway kid couldn't be too harsh. Billy Crowfoot from the reservation, who every Saturday got taken in for being drunk, was made to gather trash or paint the walls inside the jail.

On the other hand, prison was where they sent people like the Ables, or those who robbed banks or killed their wives with an ax. At least that's what he thought. But then, what did he know about matters of the grown-up world? He began to worry a little more. Maybe Sam would tell things in a way that made them sound worse. Or Richie Lee might tell lies to help himself out. It could be Harold and Leah Peavey had it in for him for not letting them know where their son was.

He sank into a light sleep with his head resting on his knees. He came awake to jostling movement and whispering. Vickie was picking at the tangled knots binding Richie Lee's wrists.

"Get a knife then," said Richie Lee.

Bertie tried to clear his thoughts as Vickie stole through the open door to the kitchen. He heard a drawer open followed by silverware clanking. Any second he expected menacing footsteps tromping down the stairs.

"Be quiet!" hissed Richie Lee in a voice as disruptive as the noise Vickie was making.

Gratified at first, Bertie quickly saw her daring attempt at freeing the boys as the beginning of even more dilemmas. Trying to go anywhere burdened with Richie Lee would be impossible now. And there was no telling what was in store for Vickie at the hands of Sam, considering that in her unpredictability, Ma would not stand in the way.

Vickie tried ineptly to saw through the twine holding Richie Lee's wrists. When she made no progress, she turned the knife over to Bertie, who managed to free himself and then Richie Lee.

"Vickie, listen," said Bertie, rising to his feet, stiff from confinement. "You are a brave girl, but you know you're in hot water if anybody figures out what you did. As soon as we're gone, put the knife back in the drawer and go up to bed. Pretend you're asleep. They'll think we got ourselves loose."

"I want to come with you," said Vickie.

"I'm sorry," said Bertie. "You can't."

"Come on, hurry up," called Richie Lee, who was already at the porch door.

"Sh!" said Bertie. "Someone's coming."

All three turned toward the door as it swung open, squeaking on its hinges. Behind it stood Bertie and Vickie's mother, a flickering and fading flashlight in one hand, the .22 single shot rifle dangling dangerously in the other.

"You kids," she said, shaking her head.

Bertie looked at his mother in amazement. She'd put on her Sunday outfit, a dark brown dress with puffy sleeves. Her hair, which usually hung in fuzzy strings when she awoke, was brushed and held back over her ears by bobby pins. She'd even put on lipstick, though a slight smear bright as ketchup showed at the corner of one lip. Yet, to Bertie, her angelic appearance contrasted mightily with his awareness that this was the only time he'd ever seen her with a gun.

In the dim light, Richie Lee reached for the door latch. Immediately, the muzzle of the rifle was directed at him.

"Get down on the floor like before," said his mother. Richie Lee looked at Bertie for help, but abruptly changed his mind.

"Ma?" said Bertie. But before he could say another word, his mother leveled the gun at his chest.

His mother raised herself to her full height. "This might be the last time I tell you what to do, but I'm still your mother. Now take that rope and tie Richie Lee back up exactly the way he was except leave his feet free."

Vickie fell into whimpering. A glance from her mother hushed her.

"Go on." Bertie's mother's voice carried greater authority than he recalled since he was a small boy. He did as ordered, splicing the pieces and taking care that the binding wasn't too tight.

"All right, Son," she said. "Us three are going to sit quiet, and then in a half hour, I'm waking Sam."

She lowered the gun. "This is best. Never mind about Sam. It's my own doing, and I'll see it through one way or the other. Anyhow, he'll be satisfied if he's got Richie Lee to turn in, and truth is, you being gone might settle him down."

\* \* \* \* \*

Outside, the moonlight cast faint shadows across the outline of the barn, exaggerating its tilt from the north winds of all those years. Bertie surveyed the farmyard and the fields beyond, picturing the quaking aspen that would in a few weeks blaze the crest with orange and yellow.

He debated about bringing Alouette, but that would be foolish. Vickie would see after her.

One duty was left. He hurried to the outhouse. Standing on the seat, he reached up among the rafters and felt for Sam's bottle. He held it to the dim light and found it about a quarter full. He unscrewed the cap and poured half of the contents into the toilet pit. Then he unzipped his pants, urinated carefully into the bottle and replaced it in its hiding place.

His instinct told him to set out through the woods, but that would be where they'd look for him first. He made for the road, his spirits growing lighter. He continued on, paused and looked back. The outline of the only real home he'd ever lived in grew faint. A few more steps and only the ancient, off-kilter weather vane on the roof stayed in sight, glinting in the moonlight, beckoning him to go, to choose any one of the infinite directions in the world.

# IN THE NEIGHBORHOOD

Though reluctant, Dolores eventually allowed Max to drive her down to Minot, where she saw the same doctor, not so young anymore, who had assured her years ago that the pain she'd developed was not cancer of the pancreas but a fractured pelvis. This time the news was unwelcome.

Cancer indeed, inoperable and spreading like ink on a tablecloth. With Max yapping all the way home about getting her in the VA, by god, where the doctors knew how to deal with ailments like this, Dolores made her plans.

They reached home late on a Wednesday, and she spent Thursday morning at the table writing notes on her good cards with the watercolor flowers. One was addressed to her niece by marriage Leah Peavey, and one to the man who, of her many husbands, had stuck by her the longest, Max Plummer, the former sailor—and still proud of it. In the afternoon, she hung up her favorite dress to air, the one she called her Alice Blue Gown. She dug out her Carmen Miranda hat and tried it on. The hat looked like a fruit salad and made a horrible mismatch with the dress, but Dolores decided she'd wear it anyway as one last thumb in the eye of the town's abundance of persnickety bloviators.

That evening after Max left for his Legion meeting, she put on the dress, its silk shoulders still making her feel as if she were drifting like a sapphire balloon on a breeze, and then the hat. In the living room, she slipped her favorite Perry Como record, the one picturing Perry with too much grease in his hair, from its jacket and spindled it on to the turntable. While sipping a glass of gin and lemonade, her drink of choice for all occasions, she listened to the soft sounds of "Fly Me to the Moon."

When the song ended, she set the mostly full glass aside, a terrible waste but nothing agreed with her stomach anymore. She hoisted herself painfully on a chair so she could reach the top closet shelf for Max's revolver and checked to see that it was loaded, which it naturally was. Stepping outside into the warm fall evening, Dolores seated herself in a plastic lawn chair that provided her a view of her rose garden, placed one hand over the hat to keep it secure and with the other, shot herself through the mouth.

\* \* \* \* \*

Leah Peavey received the news shortly before noon the next day when Max phoned her at the farm. Stunned, she thanked him politely, set the phone down and let out a screech that brought Harold from the garden where he'd been stretching chicken wire over the peavines. Certain that she'd gotten bad news about Richie Lee being back in reform school, Harold stood before her, stooping slightly maybe to help absorb the blow.

"What is it?"

"Dolores died," said Leah, cupping the phone to her chest. "She committed suicide."

"What?" Harold took a minute.

"She shot herself," said Leah, collapsing into tears. "Max found her in the yard. Why did she do that?"

Harold reached tentatively for his wife, then changed his mind and pulled his gloves off one finger at a time. "Something or other must of come over her," he said.

Leah pursed her lips in determination and returned the receiver to its cradle.

\* \* \* \* \*

Despite their difference in ages and worldly-wise outlooks, Dolores had gotten close to Leah while married to Leah's Uncle Orville. The friendship continued after Orville's death and even deepened after Dolores went on to marry again.

To Leah, Dolores represented all the adventure and daring that life had denied her. Dolores had been glamorous and sophisticated, proud of her checkered past and willing to brag about it. In comparison, Leah saw herself as fat and uninformed, stuck on a dirt farm in the hills and in a marriage to a stodgy man years older than herself whose idea of fun was staying up till ten on a Saturday night to watch Jackie Gleason.

\* \* \* \* \*

The late Dolores's love of the unconventional extended one step beyond her earthly life. During the brief years of her last marriage, knowing smugly, as she knew all else, that she would predecease this husband, she reminded him on a monthly basis that she intended to be cremated. No one in all of Chippewa County had ever heard of such a thing. Why, it wasn't like they lacked full-sized grave space, observed the mail carrier, Howard, to Leah. But cremation it would be or nothing, so Mr. Murray, the funeral director in Rolland, was forced to send Dolores all the way to Fargo on the train, and two days later upon its return, accept for a much lower freight tab what was left of her.

Now the urn sat on a long folding table in the Legion hall, looking like the trophy the basketball team had brought home from Minot the year Leah graduated from eighth grade. She gazed at it, feeling lonelier than ever.

Max, maybe sensing a certain achievement in becoming the last spouse in a long line, scurried around in his navy dress uniform, now two sizes too small, reminding Leah of the kid on the Cracker Jack box. At the poorly attended service, a few folks got up and said what they could about Dolores, how she nurtured a pretty rose garden and always offered a nice friendly smile—the first compliment being questionable and the latter not true at all. To a person, they stumbled near the end of their words, no doubt conjecturing how far they ought to go in praise of a trollop who'd been married seven times.

On the way out, Max gave Harold a brisk handshake before offering Leah a practiced hug that felt to her like the man was made of sticks. He handed her a small sealed envelope.

"Dolores left this for you," he said, and turned toward the next mourner.

\* \* \* \* \*

Back home, a fresh sense of remorse descended on Leah as she stood over the kitchen counter slicing peaches for a cobbler. Although they visited infrequently, she considered Dolores her only friend. The ancient feud with her closest neighbors the Morinvilles smoldered on, meaning, among other things, that she lacked anyone with whom to share the small pleasure of exchanging country housewife gossip. And now, in contrast to the way they felt at first when Richie Lee got in this mess, the distance between herself and her husband increased, like a boat sliding gradually away from shore—though Harold would never admit to such a sentiment. As usual, she had to study him like a jigsaw puzzle while the correct picture formed. At the same time, the things that annoyed her about him took on greater prominence—his habit of stepping inside to remove his barn shoes instead of taking them off in the porch, the way he brushed the curtain aside to check the weather every morning, even the sight of his doughy forehead under his cap where the sun couldn't reach it.

In an absurd impulse born of habit, Leah found herself wanting to dial the phone to tell Dolores the news. The news that Dolores had died. In despair, she shoved the cobbler into the fridge without bothering to cover it. That's when she remembered the note.

She poured coffee left over from breakfast and pulled a chair up to the kitchen table. She held the envelope to her nose, imagining she could smell Dolores herself, a mix of tobacco smoke, expensive perfume and cheap gin. She unfolded the crisp paper, expecting a rambling discourse on life and the advice that Dolores was so full of—lose weight, dump Harold, go to business school, change her lipstick. She sighed, then grinned at the two sentences:

*Go blow your nose. Make sure Max prunes the roses.*

That was it. She turned the flowered page over. Nothing. Not even a signature. She sniffed. Realizing that she did have a runny nose, she chortled like a schoolgirl before breaking out into howling sobs that convulsed her body, leaving her short of breath and slumped in the chair with her legs splayed and head back. Then she got up and blew her nose before dumping the cold coffee, rinsing the pot and starting a fresh batch.

While it gurgled, she gazed out the window toward the barn. There was Harold, making his way to the machine shed, stepping carefully, a plodder, an average man. A car drove past on the road, bouncing through the potholes, and he looked up briefly to see who it was and that it presented no threat to his small world before returning to the business of his day.

Leah also saw the car. The once-pretty Rebecca Morinville on her way to visit her mother. Several years of age had separated them, but in the loneliness of farm life and as the only daughters in their families, the two had forged a brief friendship—two giggling girls, all arms and bruised legs, spying on Rebecca's brothers. But then the conflicts between the families arose, and not just over fence lines and escaped cattle. On two occasions, blood had been spilled, ending the friendship.

Reflecting on Rebecca's own situation—she'd had a baby by a young man who was, as people liked to say, "not from around here"—Leah had an idea. If she finished the cobbler, she could take it over to Morinvilles on the pretense of wanting to see Rebecca's baby. From there, a thaw in neighborly relations might begin. Just in case she lost her nerve, she set the oven on preheat, turning it up to 375 to save a little time.

Though it required but a few minutes to walk over, Leah took the pickup. She rested the cobbler beside her on the seat, aware that Harold would wonder what she was up to, think about it for fifteen seconds and then go back to work.

The Morinville place looked like it always had except for a handsome metal grain bin standing in place of the old granary. The unpainted barn was beginning to sag. Etienne Morinville had for a number of years abandoned livestock in favor of using his acreage to grow wheat, but as time passed, he evidently felt it was cheaper to raise his own food after all, and now chickens ran about pecking the dirt and the stench of hogs permeated the air.

Leah gathered herself, sensing she was being observed from every curtained window. On a farm, you sensed from the way the air shifted that a car had pulled up. While she waited, unsure of herself now, the porch door opened and Rebecca emerged all in a dither with a cigarette dangling from her lips, lugging a red-faced, bawling little boy by the arm. Barely acknowledging Leah, she plopped the boy into her car and got in beside him. The car wheeled around on the patchy grass and was gone.

As a bewildered Leah sat there, Ida Florence emerged, toweling her hands and squinting into the morning sun. The two women met occasionally in a store or on the road but exchanged only distant nods. Leah cranked her car window down.

"Good morning," she said, unsure how to address the woman she had always thought of as "Mrs. Morinville," since now, even with a generation difference, they were equals—mothers and wives trying to get along in a troublesome world.

"I was in the neighborhood and thought I'd stop by," said Leah, realizing how foolish that must sound considering she'd been in the neighborhood all her life.

Ida Florence peered into the car. Stout and gray now, she bore little resemblance to the woman Leah remembered in her youth.

"Do you want to come in?" asked Ida Florence, her country manners overcoming her agitation at what must have been a quarrel with her daughter.

"Just for a minute. I don't mean to interrupt anything," said Leah. In her nervousness, she grabbed the peach cobbler by the overheated, slightly burned bottom and nearly spilled the whole thing on her lap.

Breathing hard from the effort, she climbed the steep steps with her pastry dish held by the handles. As she entered, she was struck by the similarity of the house to her own. Two stories with an attached porch which, like hers, had a loose screen that allowed entry of insects at will. In the kitchen, the faint, smoky aroma of fried bacon hung in the air. On the wall hung a calendar displaying a portrait of the Virgin Mary.

As she pulled out a chair, Leah heard a door close quietly and footsteps thumping toward the back entrance. Maybe from Etienne hastening out of sight. She centered the cobbler on the tabletop and sat, trying to keep from looking like she was inspecting the concentration of clutter surrounding her. Mail, cups, folded paper bags, a small pulley with belt attached, a slick yellow drugstore envelope stuffed with photographs, a can of ground coffee, a glass jar full of clamshells, and other detritus occupied every space. Ida Florence used a husky forearm to clear a space on the table. She poured coffee into two cups, set out a bowl of sugar and reached into the fridge to retrieve the can of Carnation with two knife punctures in the lid. "Do you take cream?" she asked.

"Oh, don't go to any bother," said Leah, who in fact drank her coffee black but, not wishing to offend her hostess, dribbled a generous portion from the familiar red container. She waited as Ida Florence eased into a chair, then pushed the peach cobbler toward her.

"Why, what's this?" said Ida Florence, pretending to have just become aware of it though it was as conspicuous as a barking dog.

"It's supposed to be peach cobbler. I hope it turned out." To her horror, Leah spotted a long black hair wedged between one side of the glass and its contents.

"It looks delicious," said Ida Florence. "Do you want to try some?"

"Oh no, it's for your family," said Leah. "I'm trying to watch my weight." She smiled self-consciously. In truth, she could have dug into the sweet, gooey dish with both hands.

The women sipped from their cups and scrutinized the cobbler. A buzzing fly descended like a helicopter from the ceiling and alighted on it. Both women looked away before Ida Florence shooed it off, saying, "The flies are a nuisance this year. I sprayed so much DDT in the house Rebecca claimed she couldn't breathe."

"They say DDT's not good for babies," replied Leah. She detected a disturbed expression on Ida Florence's flat face.

"Yes, well they say that flies aren't good for them either."

Now she'd done it. She'd gone and insulted the older woman. She must sound like Dolores. The thought made her pause. "Did you hear that my Aunt Dolores passed away?"

Ida Florence nodded. "Someone said she shot herself to death."

Jolted by the bluntness, Leah struggled to find her poise. She lifted her cup to her mouth before realizing she had drained it completely. "She had cancer bad," she said.

"Know what? Me, I'd do the same thing," said Ida Florence. "What's the sense in staying alive if all you're going to do is have pain and be a bother to everybody?"

Leah lacked a response to such a declaration. "How's Sam making out these days?" she asked.

"Pretty good, far as we know," said Ida Florence, reaching for the percolator. "More coffee?"

Leah wanted more but declined the offer in her nervousness. The least she could do was shift conversation away from Sam, a true scalawag and likely a source of great shame to his mother. "I saw in the paper that Casey won a 4-H prize."

"Yes, he did," said Ida Florence, brightening. "He made a map showing every farm between here and Rolland. It took him over a month." Then, as if to return the favor, she asked, "How is Richard getting along?"

This was getting worse. Leah had led them into the quagmire of discussing children, having vowed to avoid it considering the trials both families had endured with their kids. For one thing, Ida Florence could barely know Richie Lee, the boy having been born after the feud began. But then again, the woman had good reason to dislike him given that he was in reform school because he had attacked Sam, causing him to require surgery. "Better after they got him back to Mandan," replied Leah.

Still not content, Ida Florence sent out another probe. "When does he get out?"

"Not till he's eighteen unless something happens, which isn't likely."

"The poor boy will be grown up," said Ida Florence.

In the simmering air, Leah paused to appraise the meaning of that remark. The history was long for the two families. They'd not touched on Freddy, Ida Florence's eldest child, now long-dead, who had been the object of Leah's adolescent romantic interest. How regretful that he represented the strongest connection binding the two women.

Yet that wasn't entirely true considering that they were both mothers of trying children.

The scrape of the porch door broke the silence. "Ida Florence?" It was Etienne.

Ida Florence went to the porch while Leah tried not to hear the conversation with its murmurs and raised voices.

Ida Florence returned. "Etienne says he needs me in the barn," she said, her eyes down.

Leah vaulted from her chair. "That's fine. I better get back and start supper."

"Yes," said the older woman, backing away.

Sensing Ida Florence's uneasiness, Leah hurried to the pickup. She hit the ignition just as Ida Florence came heavily down the steps with her hands in the air.

"What about your dish?" she called.

Leah looked at her. The brightness of the afternoon sky brought out the lines in her forehead. "I don't much use that one anymore."

"Then what do you want me to do with it?"

"It doesn't matter. Send it over with Casey."

"I could put it in my own dish and wash yours."

"There's no hurry."

Ida Florence glanced toward the barn, where Etienne stood staring toward the women, his belly straining his suspenders.

"I could bring it over myself then," offered Ida Florence, lowering her voice.

"You don't need to bother," said Leah. "I mean, of course you're welcome to visit any time."

"I forgot to thank you," said Ida Florence, looking past the pickup to Etienne, who was walking toward them.

"You're welcome," answered Leah automatically, rolling up her window. She then realized that she hadn't thanked Ida Florence for the coffee, but by now the woman had turned away. She disappeared into the barn with her husband.

In despair at the awkward, graceless parting, she slammed the transmission into reverse but failed to disengage the clutch, causing the gears to give off a frightening metallic shriek and the engine to quit. She hit the starter and pumped the accelerator, but the engine wouldn't catch. If she kept trying, the battery would die. Close to tears by now, she could think of nothing to do but walk home, which would upset Harold at having to retrieve the car.

A tapping sounded at her window. It was Ida Florence. "Etienne says you flooded it. You got to wait a few minutes before you try it again."

At home finally, Leah went straight to the pantry and reached high behind the tall cardboard boxes of saltines, graham crackers and oatmeal to where she kept her stash of whipped, fluffy Duncan Hines frosting. She opened a can, marveling at the pure, white, satiny texture. She imagined the coolness on her tongue, the easy way the rich, sugary emulsion would slide down her throat. Such a well-deserved treat it would make after a trying afternoon.

She brought the can to her nose, savored the aroma for a minute and smiled in contentment. Then she dropped it in the garbage pail and covered it with potato peelings.

# A NEWFOUND GRIP

## 1 | Gift from Heaven

Richie Lee Peavey made his way excitedly along the well-trod dirt path connecting the dorms and the Administration Building, ignoring the concrete sidewalk. Told by his counselor that the superintendent wanted to see him, he believed he knew why: his application for an early release had come through.

True, he feared the opposite. It seemed like every week or two somebody fouled him too hard on the basketball court or tried to step ahead of him in the cafeteria breakfast line. To teach them a lesson, Richie Lee threw a bowl of oatmeal in their face or, if a monitor was close by, waited till he got the guy alone in the hallway.

Despite Richie Lee's protests that the offenders had it coming, he soon found his name appearing once again on the dreaded report—the half-page sheet describing the particulars of punishable incidents with which he'd soon be presented.

> Richard Peavey, Unit 1 D, 2/14/64:
>
> Went to laundry room following accounts of two boys fighting and observed above person striking Thomas Gustafson (same unit) with his fists about the head and eyes. Injuries: Peavey none. Gustafson bruise and small cut on cheek.

Such papers filled the overstuffed manila file that always lay on the superintendent's desk when Richie Lee was brought in, open and ready to bare its unfortunate secrets. This time, however, there hadn't been a statement on him for a good three months. From the plump, harassed boy he'd been when the misdeed came about, he'd grown into a wiry teenager, a little touchy but smart enough to look the other way.

He took the steps two at a time directly into the supe's outer office, the air, as always, rich with the smell of floor wax. Miss McMullen, the receptionist, a thin woman with no boobs to speak of, recognized him and told him to take a seat.

For once, no other boys waited in the area, slumping on the hard metal chairs, heads down, arms folded. There was, however, one other person there, a soldier of some kind, his shoes shiny, uniform trim, cap resting bill out and centered on his lap. Richie Lee looked at him warily, not wanting to catch his eye. In fact, people in uniform set him on edge. He had no notion how to talk to someone with such showy authority. He chose a seat a distance away from the soldier so that they couldn't converse, but before he got settled, Miss McMullen told him he could go on in.

Superintendent Sanford, a ruddy, red-haired man wearing his customary white shirt and bow tie, waited with his hands on a desk cluttered with an overflowing ashtray, stacks of papers and, for some reason, a pair of boxing gloves.

"Hello, Richard," he said. "How are you?"

"Fine." The office always smelled of tobacco smoke, triggering in Richie Lee a craving for a cigarette.

"Richard," said Sanford, who believed in getting to the point without delay. "The board forwarded its decision on your application. I have to tell you it was not granted."

Richie Lee swallowed and took a half step backward as if the words had struck him in the chest. "Not granted?"

Sanford wet his thumb and leafed through some pages. "You can figure it out. You know the rules. Look at your history." He paused to let that sink in. "On top of the running away, it's a pretty spotty record."

"But they said you could be considered to get out any time after you were sixteen, and my account's clean since last fall."

The superintendent pressed his hands together in a praying gesture and sat straighter in his chair, which made a squeaking noise. "And that's to your credit. However, you must bear in mind that you received clear warning that such is only supportive and that the final word comes from the board."

"But I even told my folks I'd be getting out for sure."

"They'll be receiving a letter of explanation," said Mr. Sanford, bracing for a protest.

But Richie Lee, his powers of concentration focused on keeping from crying, had nothing more to say.

"I won't pretend that I don't know how unhappy you've been during your time here," said the superintendent. "It's a rare boy who is content. As you've been reminded many times, this is not the Good Ship Lollipop."

Sanford grinned at his favorite saying, one that Richie Lee heard so often it almost made him gag. Then the supe surprised him by rising from his chair. "However," he said, clearing his throat importantly. "I've been studying your case, and there just might be a road out of here after all."

Richie Lee waited for more, suspicious.

"If you're willing to listen." Sanford stuck his head out the office door. "Major?" he called.

The door opened wider and the soldier Richie Lee had seen strode in, sharp and erect as a flagpole. Following a hand-crushing shake and a barked how-do-you-do, all three were seated around the desk.

Sanford spoke first. "Major Dawes has a few things of interest for you, Richard, so I'll let him do the talking."

"Richard," the major began. "A smart man like you knows what's going on in the world, but bear with me and I'll try to shed a little more light on it."

Despite his earlier impression, Richie Lee liked this army person at once. He smiled a lot as he talked. And he called Richie Lee a man! He spoke with a low, gravelly voice, like a person who doesn't scare easy. Then, to Richie Lee's astonishment, he pulled a pack of Camels from his breast pocket and offered one. Richie Lee was about to take it when the supe's chair squeaked slightly.

Major Dawes explained that he was a recruiting officer for the army of the United States of America, which now faced threats from many directions. In the long history of the great nation, we had never failed to come to the aid of a friend. Just now, it looked like the Soviet Communists and the Chinese were moving in on a country called Vietnam, with which we had a long friendship. How and why that came to be was for another time. What was important now was to recognize that action was required. The president of the United States, Lyndon Johnson, had sent out a call for young men to help by joining our army, which was being stretched to the limits.

Richie Lee sat patiently through this update. Of course, he knew from television about the fighting in that Vietnam place, but had no awareness of the urgency. Major Dawes pointed out that if we failed in our responsibility to stop the Commies over there, the day would arrive when we'd find ourselves battling them not only on the beaches of California but on the farms and fields of North Dakota! Richie Lee thought of guys he knew like Dale Aingher Jr., the sheriff's son, who joined the army. It sounded strange, and he couldn't quite picture Dale with a rifle standing guard over Richie Lee's own dad's dairy cows. He wished the major would get to the part involving him.

"I'll tell you something about the army, Dick." The major paused. "Is that what they call you—Dick? Uncle Sam's army has a policy that says we don't trouble any on what you done or where you come from." Dawes turned briefly toward

Sanford as if looking for agreement. "We in the army believe that your past is your own business. A man comes into the army, he gets a clean slate. And that's God's truth."

In the pause that followed, Sanford spoke up. "Richard, Major Dawes wants to give you another chance."

"Absolutely," said the major. "My friend Mr. Stanford hit it on the head. Dick, how would you like the opportunity to get out of the school here a year ahead of time?"

Richie Lee looked from one man to the other, scarcely daring to believe what he was hearing. "I'd like it for sure."

"I thought you might be interested," said Dawes. "I know your background, and talking here like we are, I came to the decision that a man like you would be a credit to our military forces. As you know, you can't sign up till you're eighteen ordinarily. But—" Dawes raised his pinky and his index finger in the air, an odd gesture. "We've been coordinating with Mr. Stanford here on a brand-new arrangement that might suit men like you just fine."

The supe frowned and looked uncomfortable, maybe at the mispronunciation of his name. "And you will be allowed to finish your high school education," he said.

"Of course!" boomed Dawes. "Absolutely."

The mention of education and it being allowed was a setback for Richie Lee. Now he was sorry he hadn't accepted the earlier offer of a smoke. "How would I go about all that?"

"I'm glad you brought that up," said Dawes. "All you got to do is sign a pledge for us. Then, when the paperwork is over, which might take a while—not too long in case you're worried—you pack up and say goodbye to the institution here. You're free to do what you like the rest of the time. I was you, I might consider a little sightseeing. You ever been to Mexico, Dick?"

"I don't get what you mean by pledge," said Richie Lee, careful to keep his tone pleasant and conversational lest he frighten this gift from heaven away.

"You know, it's like when you pledge allegiance to the flag." The major looked to Sanford for help.

"It's like a promise," said the superintendent.

"Exactly!" said Dawes. "You promise you will sign up with our armed forces on your eighteenth birthday after you've had that year or so to run with your friends and enjoy life. You know, see your folks and catch up on all the things you been deprived of all this time. How's that sound to you, Dick?"

Richie Lee looked at the superintendent, who clasped his hands behind his head and smiled pleasantly.

"Gosh," said Richie Lee. "How long would I be in the army?"

Dawes lit another cigarette, this time not offering one to Richie Lee. "The enlistment now is just for two years. Course if you do well, you're free to sign again. Myself, that's what I did, and they sent me to OCS. That's for officer training. What kind of things are you interested in, Dick? Do you like to tinker with automobile engines maybe?" He exhaled a blinding cloud of smoke.

"In shop, me and this other guy built a transistor radio," said Richie Lee.

"Electronics!" said the major in a booming *bingo!* voice. "Did you know the army can train you in that field for free? When you come out you can get a job anywhere you want."

"I think I heard about that," said Richie Lee, not wanting to sound entirely ignorant of army ways.

Dawes nodded sharply. "I won't go too far into all the other advantages like insurance and health needs. There's army dentists that fix your teeth if you ever need it, and of course you get a clothing allowance, not to mention housing and food. All courtesy of Uncle Sam."

Richie Lee's demeanor sagged slightly. Dawes caught it immediately. The fixing your teeth bit was a blunder. He leaned in toward Richie Lee. "Once a month is payday," he said in a conspiratorial whisper. "And that money is yours to spend like you want." He glanced at Sanford and lowered his voice a couple more notches. "Girls, I will tell you from experience, they like a man in a uniform if you catch my drift."

With that, the major's voice returned to its room-filling volume. "But tell me, Dick, is this something you think you have a feel for?"

"Well, yeah, I think so," said Richie Lee, his tone just a cut less enthusiastic.

Here, Sanford broke in to offer his sole piece of advice for the day. "I wouldn't make a decision at the moment," he said. "You do need to consider from all sides. I know Major Dawes won't mind my mentioning that the military is not the Good Ship Lollipop."

Dawes apparently thought this was quite funny. "No, sir. No, sir," he repeated, grinning and shaking his head. "But listen. I know where to find you, Dick. Tell you what. I'll come back and visit with you next, let's see, next Friday. That's ten days. A word to the wise, though." Dawes paused and winked. "The army has what they call quotas. Now as we speak, there's openings in this jurisdiction, but you never know. All I'm saying is, I wouldn't dilly doodle about making up my mind."

But Richie Lee had already firmly made up his mind. When he shook hands again with the major it was with a newfound grip of gratitude.

## 2 | Long Distance

One hundred and fifty miles straight north, Leah Peavey, after grocery shopping, lingered in town for Bank Night, the prize having risen to over $200. She smiled at the memory of eating brownies at Dolores's until it was time to go down to the theater for the drawing. The potential winner had but two minutes to speak up, and Leah always worried they would miss the announcement.

"I'm not going out of this house for any amount of money till I get my lipstick on right," Dolores would say, cackling.

\* \* \* \* \*

Again, her name was not drawn. She checked the clock on the dashboard. Harold would wonder what was keeping her, but he'd prefer a late supper over trying to fix food for himself.

Slowed by a light snowfall, she reached home to find him in his easy chair with his eyelids down, his hands resting over the arms and his feet planted squarely on the floor. Leah knew by his posture that he wasn't asleep and by the angle of his chin that something bothered him. The quieter he was, the more he had to say, but first you had to get him going. He opened his eyes at the sound of his wife's footsteps. "Still snowing out?"

"It's letting up." The hangers in the hall closet jangled as Leah fumbled with her coat. "Mail come?"

Harold turned his shoulders and head in one motion and pointed to the kitchen. He was taking on the stiff gestures of an older man. "It's there on the table."

"Anything from Richie Lee?"

Waiting for a response, Leah at first thought he didn't hear her.

"Not from him," said her husband.

"What do you mean?"

"It's that brown envelope. You can read it."

"I know I can read it," said Leah, rubbing her hands vigorously. "But I want you to tell me."

Harold straightened up on the chair. "It didn't say much. It's mostly forms."

Leah took up the letter, holding it to the light. "Who is this Gene Dawes?"

"He's an army recruiter."

"Recruiter? What's that all about?"

"Keep going."

Leah read the letter to completion. "So, Richie Lee could get out in a few weeks?"

"Well, yeah, but after that he goes into the army," said Harold.

"But he'd be home first." Trying to suppress her excitement, Leah read the letter again from start to finish.

"Did you see here on the third page it says he needs parental permission since he's not eighteen? How does that work exactly?"

"It tells on one of those forms, the last one." Harold's voice took on a tone of annoyance. He disliked having to clarify things that were obvious.

"Oh. I see. There's two spaces."

"That's right," said Harold, rising from his chair. "One for each of us."

"Then, we both have to sign or else they won't let him?"

"That's how I read it."

\* \* \* \* \*

Leah retreated to the kitchen while her husband went outside to clear the steps and check that the barn and henhouse doors were sealed against the increasing snow. Leah knew that all those doors were solidly secured and that no human was likely to soon need a cleared path to their own door, but this was her husband's way of dealing with any hindrance—put his back into an unrelated task and trust that a solution for the original dilemma would enter his head.

She took four large potatoes from the bin and filled a saucepan with salted water. She opened the fridge door and realized she'd forgotten to take the pork chops from the freezer. And they'd used up the last jar of peas, Harold's favorite vegetable. She took up the letter and stood studying it as her husband returned, stomping his feet.

"I see here that he gets to choose what kind of training he wants," said Leah.

"Well, I would expect that."

"And he can get his high school diploma, too," she added, wondering how far she could take this.

"But can't you see what they're trying to pull?" said Harold. He grabbed a knife from the drawer and picked up a potato. "You see, those people like this Dawes, they got an allocation they got to make." He stood with the potato in one hand and the knife in the other, looking like he was trying to form a connection between the objects.

"Gimme that," said Leah. "That's a butcher knife. You'll waste half the spud." She untied her apron. "It's gonna be midnight till we eat at the rate we're going. Why don't I just boil up a pot of oatmeal or open a can of Spam?"

Harold, who liked full meals of meat, potatoes and vegetables, looked away sadly. "That's fine," he said. He looked for a place to set the potato down. "I just don't see what business the school has letting a United States Army recruiter in to talk to those kids. That's not right. You never know what a boy like Richie Lee will be thinking."

"I can tell you that," said Leah, setting a saucepan of water on the stove. "He's thinking what he always has, that he'll do just about anything to get out of that place. You ask me, I still don't see that they're doing him much good."

"I wouldn't say that. Last we heard he was doing a lot better, compared."

"That's only because he thinks he has a chance to get a good behavior release," said Leah.

"All we can do is wait and see," said Harold.

Such a response infuriated Leah, who knew it meant that her husband sought to end the conversation. "Wait for what? He's gonna be as anxious as a mother hen fussing over what's to happen." She fixed her gaze on the pan of water, as if willing it to boil.

"But I can't help but figure he hasn't thought it all through," said Harold. "He can't see the price he'll have to pay eventually. I bet he expects we'll sign the papers and that'll be it. I ought to talk to him."

"Well, then why don't you?" suggested Leah. "We got a phone now, you know."

Harold, who was almost forty before he enjoyed access to his own telephone, still retained the Depression-era aversion to long distance. "Listen to that wind. The lines will be down for sure."

Leah, convinced her husband was stalling, reached for the phone on the wall. Sure as heck, the weak tick and buzz of a sound going nowhere greeted her.

\* \* \* \* \*

Two days passed with snow continuing to pile up when the unexpected jangling of the phone startled her. The wavering voice of an operator advised that Richie Lee Peavey was calling collect. Leah delivered a quick hello and told her son to hold the line while she went to fetch his dad. Stepping outside without overshoes, she saw it would take her forever to get through the drifts to the barn, so she opened the pickup door and leaned on the horn. She waited, knowing the barn door would open unhurriedly and instead of responding to the noise, Harold would stare toward the house for a long, wasted minute while she hit the horn again before he came to see what she wanted.

Through the staticky and dim connection, Leah grasped Richie Lee's question. Had they gotten the letter from Major Dawes? She said that yes, they had.

"I said you were supposed to get a letter by now," said Richie Lee.

"Yes, yes, we did," said Leah, raising her voice. "We got the letter. Is it snowing down there?"

Leah made out only one word in her son's reply: "snow."

She heard Harold on the porch. He took the receiver. "Hello? Son?" He tried again. "Richie Lee?" He lowered the black receiver and frowned at it. "It's dead," he said.

"Then hang up and call him back," said Leah.

Harold leaned over the cradle and, with a dirty finger poised in the air, studied the dial, his movements exasperatingly slow. A puddle of meltwater formed at his feet.

"Just dial zero," prompted Leah. "You know what to—oh, let me have it."

Harold stood rubbing his hands as if trying to rid them of the feel of the telephone as Leah tried unsuccessfully to get through.

"What did he say before the line went bad?" asked Harold.

"He didn't say anything because I wasted all that time trying to get you to come in from the barn."

"Well, for crying out loud," said Harold.

\* \* \* \* \*

After her husband went back to the barn, Leah couldn't keep herself from attempting a call again. When she heard the sound of a motor turning over, she used her hand to wipe a clear space on the window. She saw nothing through the blowing snow.

The shovel clunked against the porch wall and Harold entered.

"What are you doing out there?" asked Leah.

"Warming up the pickup."

"What for?"

"I'm going to Mandan and talk sense into that kid," said Harold.

"Now?"

Harold worked his gloves off. "Sunday's the only visiting day."

"In this weather?"

"I heard a car go by. If I can get out of the yard, I'll be OK. I can chain up if I have to."

Leah recognized a determination that she knew well—the sense of a plan so precisely constructed it was essentially half carried out. Her husband was way ahead of her.

Maddeningly slow, Harold pulled down gloves, a scarf and his good cap from the closet shelf.

Leah persisted. "I don't see what you hope to accomplish," she said.

He wasn't listening. The man had declared that he was driving to Mandan so drive to Mandan he would.

She looked about in frustration. Her eyes settled on the hopeless telephone. "We can keep trying to get through. Otherwise, you can at least wait till morning to go. Do the chores early and you'll get there in plenty of time for visiting hours."

To her surprise, he hesitated. She could read his thoughts. He didn't like having his strategies interfered with, but a small concession would make everybody feel better. "I'll think it over," he said, which Leah knew was equivalent to consent.

She watched as he geared up. For a suitcase he was taking the old canvas bag that used to hold the croquet mallets somebody gave them until Richie Lee left them outside over the winter and the handles warped. He packed one pair of long underwear, a shirt, heavy socks and the blue cardigan that he'd never worn because it had to be dry-cleaned. Other than that, he would make do with what he was wearing. Naturally, he would not spend the night in a hotel. Not only was the five or six dollars unreasonable for just a bed but finding a place and figuring out how to check in made it not worth the fuss. The few times they traveled more than a few hours away, the Peaveys stayed with relatives. If by himself, Harold's habit was to keep driving and take periodic naps sitting up behind the wheel.

"You'll need something to eat on the way. I'll make sandwiches from the leftover ham," she said.

"Fine. Then why don't you go on to bed," suggested Harold. "I want to listen for the forecast."

Harold turned the bag upright and knotted the cord to close it. Fully charged now, he looked eager to get on.

\* \* \* \* \*

Leah awoke at six and, to no surprise, found the other side of the bed cold. Tugging her robe over her broad back, she hurried downstairs. She felt the coffeepot with her hand. Still warm. At least he'd gotten some sleep. The sky outside was gray with light snow still falling. As she reheated the coffee, she found that she had to keep reminding herself that her husband was not safely in the barn but straining to see through the windshield of an old pickup bumping through snowdrifts, no doubt one of the few vehicles on the road in the entire state.

She washed her face and dressed. After eating several slices of buttered toast with rhubarb jam, she fried two eggs, supposing the extra calories would be burned up against the cold. She washed, dried and put away the dishes. She considered doing a load of laundry but dropped the notion since she was almost out of Oxydol. She thought she heard someone at the door. She listened carefully. It must be the wind. But there it was again, a persistent and alarming rap. Something must have happened to Harold.

Two people, one rather stout, stood on the step, not having sense to come in to the inner door and knock so as to be heard.

She turned on the porch light and they entered. Peering beneath various scarves and a thick coat, Leah recognized Ida Florence Morinville. The other, a lean and younger person, was her son Casey, grown nearly to a man. He spoke first.

"Morning, Mrs. Peavey," he said, removing his stocking cap. "Sorry to bother you."

"Come in," said Leah, confused but glad that she'd cleaned the kitchen.

"We can't stay," said Ida Florence. "We need to borrow chains if we could. And while we're here, let me return this." From inside her coat she produced the baking dish she'd had since the previous summer.

With Casey doing most of the explaining, they filled Leah in as to what happened. Early in the morning, they'd heard tires whining and an engine revving, typical of a vehicle stuck in snow. It was Harold, who'd slid off the road barely a quarter mile into his trip. Having left his tire chains behind, he was trying to maneuver himself back onto the road. Casey brought tire chains and a shovel, and shortly, Harold was back on his way with the Morinville chains on his pickup. Now, a couple hours later, Etienne Morinville said he wanted to go to town to pick up medicine and special feed for a sick cow and needed chains for his pickup.

Ida Florence shook her head. "I told him two days ago to get ready for the storm."

With Leah's permission, Casey went to the shop for the chains, leaving the women shivering and awkward in the cold porch.

"I have coffee," said Leah.

"No, don't bother," said Ida Florence.

"It's already made," said Leah, trying to forget the painful twenty minutes in the Morinville kitchen from the summer before when she'd brought peach cobbler over as part of a misguided attempt at making peace following years of acrimony between the neighbors.

Inside, Leah patted a chair for her neighbor to sit.

"Casey tells me your husband never mentioned where he was headed," said Ida Florence.

"Oh, he got it in his mind to drive down and talk to Richie Lee," said Leah, her hand shaking as she poured coffee into one of her good cups.

Ida Florence looked down, ill at ease, her feet planted flat on the floor, her knees at forty-five-degree angles.

"They'll let him out a year early if he agrees to join the army," explained Leah.

Ida Florence gazed blankly at her coffee. Leah felt compelled to push the one-way conversation forward.

"Both parents have to sign for him to go, and I know Harold will want him to stay in school."

Ida Florence frowned. "Casey, he hopes to get one of those scholarships that pays for college."

"Good for him," said Leah, though she couldn't deny a feeling of resentment. *College.* How far away such a vision lay for her own son.

The wind rattled the house and a flurry of snow, dislodged from the roof, drifted across the window, momentarily dimming the kitchen.

"Since you just got the one boy, maybe eventually he'll come back and take over the farm," said Ida Florence.

"Richie Lee never went in much for farm life," said Leah. "I expect when he's out of reform school he'll head down to Fargo or maybe Minneapolis and look for a job. The only way I'll ever have him around anymore is for him to get that year off before he goes in the service."

Ida Florence crossed her arms over her chest. "I'll tell you," she said, lunging forward in emphasis. "Once they've gone out in the world it's never the same. Oh, they come back to visit or because they got nowhere to go. But they're not connected to you anymore. Rebecca, she don't even call, and we just fight when she does visit. Since he went to work at the Breen place, Sam don't even stop when he drives past on his way to town. To have them living under your roof, to make their favorite pie, to see them safe in bed every night for a year? I was you, I'd take that in a second."

"I know. I would if it were my choice," said Leah.

Ida Florence straightened herself up on the chair. "Then how come you don't make it your choice?" she asked.

## 3 | Bouquet of Tiny Flowers

Harold knew he'd get more traction with the car than the pickup, but the pickup lent better clearance. He'd thrown four bales in the bed to add weight to the drive wheels, checked the spare air and grabbed a long-handled spade, but chose not to take the chains as getting them on and off was a bother.

He intended to set out west on Highway 43, though it was ten miles of gravel, and then catch 3 going south. But, not out of sight of the lights from his own place, he hit that narrow part by the Morinville turnoff, and the mound-ed dirt from the last time they bladed hooked the right front wheel and into the ditch he went.

After freeing himself with the help of young Casey Morinville, he drove all day through the steady, drifting snow, compensating for the wind from the west, using his hankie to clear a spot on the windshield that the defroster couldn't handle. As he tired, he began having doubts, wishing he were home. Right now, he would be enjoying those moments after a good supper, drinking his coffee and listening to the wind, content in the knowledge that the cows were milked, fed and bedded down in fresh straw.

After a short snooze outside the McKenzie Standard gas station, he turned west on Highway 10. Passing the imposing capital building at Bismarck, he continued the few short miles across the river to Mandan.

\* \* \* \* \*

Richie Lee entered the otherwise empty visiting room accompanied by a counselor, who, Harold knew at once, was the price of an unannounced visit. At once, his son's reaction bothered Harold. Though he couldn't have had a warning, Richie Lee behaved just like he'd been expecting to see his father there on the couch with his winter coat folded over his lap, as out of place as a clown at a funeral.

The counselor, a young, square-chinned man with a crew cut, made a beeline toward the opposite side of the room and buried his nose in a *Sports Illustrated*.

"Richie Lee, I came down to talk to you about this army thing."

The boy rolled his eyes and sagged back in his chair.

"Son, do you know much about the army?"

The reply came quick as a shot. "Do you?"

Harold had known this wouldn't be a snap. "I might claim to have some idea."

The counselor looked up.

Harold shifted his feet. His thighs sweated under the coat. "Back then, a younger man like me who was poor…"

He paused. The only thing Leah told him was to keep from getting preachy. "When I was a kid there used to be a lot of boys who came back from the first war in awful shape."

"They let boys in the war?"

Harold took in a slow breath to summon his patience. "No, I don't mean schoolboys. They just called them boys. Anyway, one of them lost both eyes and got his face messed up."

For once, Richie Lee disclosed some interest. "How do you mean?"

"He just looked like his face was all just gone, even the nose and lips."

"He must've got too close to the A-bomb," said Richie Lee.

"No, no, this was the first war," said Harold, barely able to suppress his annoyance. "It was poison gas. It's supposed to be illegal, but you see, when it comes to war, there's no rules like in a football game. Now you take—"

Harold stopped again. He'd intended to relate to Richie Lee the news that sheriff Dale Aingher's well-liked son Dale Jr. had been severely wounded in Vietnam. The young man had either lost a leg or been paralyzed from the waist down—the story wasn't clear. In high school, he was a small but quick football player with the Rolland Bulldogs who dreamed of playing for University of North Dakota. But at the urging of his father, he joined the army, hoping to put on muscle and, after two years, be big enough to play college ball.

"Well, never mind that," said Harold. "Richie Lee, what I come to tell you is that I don't want to see you make a mistake."

Richie Lee shifted uncomfortably on the sofa. The radiator hissed and clanked.

"I'm saying we don't want you to do this, agree to join the army. You got nothing to gain."

"So you won't sign the paper," said Richie Lee.

"It's what's best, that's all."

Father and son retreated into a dejected uncommunicativeness. Richie Lee toyed with the seam of his overalls while his dad reflected on the power of a piece of paper—a few scratches of a pen and somebody's world changes.

"But what I wish is that you come to your own decision. You'd feel a lot better, I guarantee." Harold immediately regretted his words, guessing that the fine point would likely escape the boy.

Richie Lee had a ready response. "After I'm eighteen I could get drafted anyway. What's the difference?"

"Well, that's not so," said Harold. "You stay here, get your high school diploma, then you go to college. They aren't drafting boys out of college."

Richie Lee snorted and looked at the counselor. "They made me take one of those tests to see how you'd do in college. I never even finished it before the bell went off. Anyway, Major Dawes said it's just a question of time till everyone gets drafted."

"He doesn't know that," said Harold. "There's trade schools."

"The army can teach me a trade for free."

"I wouldn't call that free," said Harold. He was running out of argument. It was time to press the matter. He slid his glasses off and squeezed the bridge of his nose.

"Son," he began, staring at the ancient boarded-up fireplace across the room. "I want to let you in on something that took place before you were born."

"I know about it," snapped Richie Lee.

Harold was stunned. "You don't know the whole story."

"I know you said you wouldn't go in the army so they sent you to prison."

The counselor looked toward them, alert to something that caught his attention. Richie Lee called to him, "Mr. James, how much time I got left?"

James checked his watch. "Twelve minutes."

Because they were seated side by side, Harold had to twist his neck around to face the boy. He rolled his shoulders, trying to get the kinks out. "That wasn't all," he said. "I got home and folks I knew all my life wouldn't speak to me. I even got my nose broke out of the deal by some guys I grew up with." He touched his nose as if to indicate where it was broken. "All of that for standing up for what I believed."

"You think I don't want the same?" said Richie Lee.

"Sure, that's part of it, but you mostly want to get free of this place. Isn't that so?"

"I made it out once and it didn't turn out so good," said Richie Lee. "But do you want to know the real reason I want to go in the army?"

"Yes, I would."

"A long time ago, I asked Ma how come you were different. You weren't like other dads. She said you were ashamed of what you done."

"Just a minute on that one," said Harold.

"No, listen," countered the boy. "All you ever wanted to do as far back as I know was stay home. You don't belong to no Lions clubs or stuff. You never go bowling or play golf. You don't even go to the bar on Saturday night like everybody else. You got no friends because you got nothing to talk about with anybody. I'm not gonna be like that. I don't want to be ashamed."

The counselor rolled up his magazine and stood. Harold looked at his son. For all the world, he knew there was nothing more to say.

* * * * *

Leah concluded it had not gone well by the way the pickup pulled into the yard, slow and careful. Harold let it come to a stop crooked in the ruts of the driveway. For a minute, he sat, then stepped out.

He averted his eyes as he entered the house and took his time hanging up his coat.

"You made it OK," said Leah.

"Yeah."

When he offered no more, she let him be. His habit was to fall into an unshakeable reticence for an hour or so, then, like an old plow horse left out to pasture, come around and find his way home.

"Are you hungry?"

"Hmm? A little." He lowered himself into the easy chair. It creaked as it accepted his weight.

"I could scramble some eggs."

"Don't go to any bother."

He planted his open palms carefully on the armrests, then, as if carrying out the most difficult thing he'd ever done, raised himself from the chair and wobbled toward the bathroom, bare elbows pointing backward, broad back bent.

"I'll get some eggs." Leah pulled on her parka with its many handy pockets for working around the farm. Outside, the late winter sun slipped behind the hills past the Morinville place. She followed the icy, narrow path toward the henhouse, where warning clucks sounded from within.

She stood for a while gazing at the oak where Harold once set up the rickety stepladder to rig a tire swing from the stoutest limb. He hadn't realized that Richie Lee had followed up the ladder behind him, and when he started down, they both tumbled to the ground in a heap. Neither was hurt, and a laughing Richie Lee begged to do it again.

To the north where she maintained the garden patch her mother tended so many years ago, she once found Richie Lee breaking apart a red pepper. Within seconds, the tender skin on his little fingers was on fire, setting him to crying pitifully before she soothed the condition with a paste of baking soda and milk. Another time, he presented her with a bouquet of tiny flowers—blossoms from her tomato plants.

And then events exploded, one after another, beyond her reach. Richie Lee's difficulties at school, the distancing from his dad followed by the boy being snatched away and sent to Mandan. And finally, the shock of Aunt Dolores's death.

The cold penetrated her parka, and she started inside before remembering what she came for. "Oh, the hell with it," she said under her breath.

Back in the house, her husband stood by the window, silent as a rock. He must have been watching her.

"Harold?"

He turned. "Yeah?"

"Harold," she said. "I'm only going to ask you this one time."

She waited for a response. Here was a man who would always accomplish with his hands what he could not do with his mouth.

"You don't need to ask," he said.

# PARTY LINES

As Etienne and Casey Morinville rushed to move wheat from the grain bin to reach town before the elevator closed, a change in pitch of the auger motor attracted Ida Florence's attention. She slid the kitchen curtain aside. Casey stood atop the ladder leading to the trapdoor while Etienne shouted orders from the ground. Ida Florence turned back to peeling potatoes. When the noise turned into a piercing whine, she looked out again to see her husband scrambling up the ladder, moving too fast for a man of his size and age. She hurried outside just as Etienne's shoulders and arms disappeared through the trapdoor.

Swaying with each arduous breath, apron fluttering, she staggered as fast as her bulk allowed. After calling and hearing no reply, she seized a crescent wrench lying beside the auger and pounded on the side of the bin. She heard nothing in return other than the labored churning of the auger, which was giving off a smell of hot oil. She put a foot on the ladder but stopped at the first rung and headed back to the house, trying to decide who to call.

\* \* \* \* \*

When the phone jangled in her kitchen, Leah only half listened. Since Dolores died, no one called to chat, and anyway, with numerous families sharing the party line, the thing never quit ringing. But it was her own signal, four shorts and a long. She picked it up and heard a gasping Ida Florence Morinville.

"Please, can you help? They fell in the grain bin, Etienne and Casey."

"What? Oh no." Stunned, Leah tried to gather her wits. Everyone acquainted with a farm knew what that meant. "I'll get Harold," she said.

In the two-minute ride to the Morinvilles, Harold surmised what they'd done. One or the other, probably the boy, had entered the bin from the top to dislodge the crust that tends to form over the top of wet grain. Anyone walking on the surface risked falling through and becoming trapped.

Harold steered the pickup across the bumpy yard to the gentle rise where the bin sat, skidding to a stop next to Etienne's hitch wagon. He leaped out, not bothering to close his door, and grabbed a coil of rope from his truck bed. Ida Florence stood beside the ladder shifting her weight from one foot to the other like a child having to pee. Harold reached the top of the ladder and peered into the dust-filled air. Etienne, after climbing in to rescue his son, who was now submerged underneath hundreds of pounds of wheat, had fallen near the side wall, where he slowed his descent by clawing at the nuts along the vertical seams. Though momentarily safe from suffocation, he'd come to a stop out of reach from above but buried up to his chin. He couldn't move his limbs against the tremendous pressure of the grain, but by wiggling his head he managed to dislodge enough kernels to allow occasional frantic and dust-filled breaths before the slippery mass filled in again. Now, as Harold leaned in with a flashlight, the grain quietly shifted.

Harold leaped down the old ladder, scraping a shin on one of the splintery rungs. Scanning the area, he spotted a short, weathered one-by-six with a rusting nail in it from the pile of scrap lumber remaining from the old granary. Urging Leah up the ladder, he handed the board to her while explaining what he wanted her to do, then rushed to the auger inlet to try to clear an escape route.

With her upper arms hooked over the opening of the bin, Leah extended the board cautiously toward Etienne. It barely reached his face, but by tamping and twisting it, she nudged just enough of the slippery wheat away from his mouth so that he could breathe. As she worked awkwardly from above, she accidentally scraped his chin with the nail. He let out a cry and rolled his eyes upward. Leah pulled the board back, seeing a fury that Etienne's frightened eyes could not hide. For an instant, Leah willed the man to sink into the silent grain, never to be seen again.

Just then, Harold realized to his alarm that the auger was still running, the little gasoline engine determinedly put-putting. For a second, he thought about letting it be in hopes it might help clear the bin—but no, the auger was too clogged to do any good. He hit the off switch. The engine went silent, and the screw stopped. The shield covering the power shaft was missing, and Harold stuck his arm in as far as he could reach, trying to determine how densely packed the grain was along the inlet screen. He felt something wet and pulled his arm out. His hand was coated in blood. He wiped it on his pants, conscious of Ida Florence hovering behind him.

"We need a cutting torch," he said.

The woman frowned in doubt.

"Is the machine shed locked?"

She looked toward the little flat-roofed building. "It shouldn't be."

Harold checked his watch. Ten minutes since the call came. He knew Ida Florence had also called Rolland for help, but by the time the undermanned volunteer fire department made its way to the farm with whatever equipment they owned, it would be too late.

"Leah, what can you see?" he called. Her garbled response was unintelligible.

He ran for the shed and threw the door open to the oily, damp air. As his eyes adjusted he spotted a rusty oxygen tank but no hose or cutting tips. A double-bitted ax rested against the workbench. Back at the bin, he took aim at the wall. The ax clanged against the steel. A crease formed. He struck again, aiming for the same spot, but missed. A smaller crease showed. Again, he swung with all his strength. Another blow, another. Nothing. He let the ax fall at his feet and wiped his forehead in frustration. The precious grain, whose accumulation meant life to the farmer, was about to smother him.

"Leah, come down," he barked.

She turned. "What?"

"Get down," he called louder, limping on his sore leg to the pickup.

Studying the lines of bolts, he selected his spot, midpoint in a panel where there'd be no brace, and opposite from where Etienne struggled to breathe. Calling for both women to stand clear, he started the engine, and after backing up to adjust the angle, he centered the hood ornament on his target. He shifted into low and hit the accelerator.

The booming impact produced an explosion of dust, the windshield cracked and the truck stalled. Ahead, a small dent appeared at the height of the truck bumper. He restarted the engine, muscled it into reverse and drove forward again. The sound was just as loud as before, but he sensed a little give this time.

"Wait, stop, please!" cried Ida Florence. "You'll kill them both."

From the corner of his eye, Harold glimpsed his wife tugging on Ida Florence's arm. He drove into the bin a third time. The wall caved in noticeably, and the bottom section of curved steel sheared off the bolts on the concrete foundation. But still the thing held its shape, its contents intact.

For the fourth attempt, he backed up an extra ten yards and this time hooked himself into his seat belt, which he'd never used since buying the truck. An instant before impact, he glanced at the speedometer. The needle quivered near forty. The wall of the bin, freed from its anchors, repositioned itself in and upward, shaking, and the edge came to rest on the hood of the pickup three feet from the steering wheel. Engulfed in dust, the wind squeezed out of him by the seat belt, Harold wasn't sure what had happened. With a good part of the bin resting on the hood and the front wheels buried in wheat, the truck was as immovable as a boulder. He tried his door. It wouldn't budge. He slithered his way to the other side and staggered out, stepping into a surge of flowing wheat that almost carried him off his feet before spreading and coming to rest.

At once, Leah fell to her knees, tunneling into the freed grain and raising more dust. Harold joined her, forming a scoop with his arms and pulling the grain toward him, only to have the cleared space refill. Leah felt a shirtsleeve and tugged. Harold thrust both hands in beside hers. Probing, he touched an object that didn't belong. He pulled on it until it came loose, and the brim of a straw hat emerged. Finally, the boy's shoulders and head appeared. With a powerful heave, Harold pulled him free. The lower left leg and shoeless foot appeared mangled. Blood oozed through the dirty wound. With Harold's help, Leah ripped the boy's shirt from his back and wrapped it tightly around the gash.

From the left came a shout from Ida Florence. She'd located Etienne. Harold worked to free the bulky body, seeing at once that the chest revealed no visible movement. Immediately, Ida Florence elbowed Harold aside and pounced on her husband, using the hem of her housedress to wipe away grain dust and dirt from his face.

"Let me get him out in the air," Harold said.

Seeing that Ida Florence was hindering Harold's efforts, Leah ran over to help, leaving Casey on the ground against the pickup, his head between his knees, drawing one great breath after another.

They pulled Etienne into the little swale of cool grass adjoining the potato patch, and Harold straddled his hips with his knees and began the artificial respiration he'd seen performed once or twice in movies. As he forced the heels of his hands into the soft abdomen, he felt a resistance.

"Wait," said Leah. Grabbing for Etienne's chin and forcing his mouth open, she wedged two fingers in and extracted a loose wad of moist grain.

But still the man's chest displayed only a quiver of movement. Harold resumed the rhythmic compression, counting silently to himself as Ida Florence stood by with her hand over her mouth, whimpering quietly. Detecting no response, Harold increased the pressure. With his upper arms wearing out, he leaned in to exert his weight, doubting he was getting anywhere. On the fourth push, a congealed lump of grain and dirt the size of a meatball flew from Etienne's mouth, followed by a straining noise like someone vomiting. Harold eased the pressure, expecting breaths to follow. None did. He and his wife looked at each other.

Then a long, hoarse cry emerged from his throat just as a distant siren sounded and the fire truck and makeshift ambulance from Rolland bounced across the yard. At the arrival of the vehicles, Ida Florence, in her anguish, dashed toward them and was nearly run down by the ambulance.

Tom Keegan, the volunteer fire chief, hurried to unstrap the oxygen tank from the truck. A younger, long-haired fellow that Harold didn't know knelt beside him and felt for Etienne's wrist.

"He just now took some breaths," said Harold.

The young man wore a long-sleeved light blue shirt. *Hank* was embroidered in red on the pocket. He raised Etienne's right eyelid.

"How long was he buried in there?" asked Hank.

"Been a while. Maybe twenty minutes, half hour."

Hank frowned and stepped back to make room for Keegan with the oxygen tank.

"He's breathing, right?" said Harold.

Hank ignored him as he thrust the heel of his hand sharply into Etienne's abdomen to clear an air passage.

While a third attendant saw to Casey's injuries, Harold felt suddenly useless. He lifted up a section of corrugated steel and stood gaping at the wreck of the pickup and grain bin. From a distance, it resembled an unlikely accident, a drunk running his truck into a bin full of good wheat.

With the accident victims loaded into the ambulance and Ida Florence riding along beside the driver, the emergency vehicles pulled away, consigning the Peaveys to a state of bewildering inactivity. Harold spotted a shiny object protruding from the pile of grain. He dug it out and examined it. It was the hood ornament from his pickup. He set it gently back in place, but it slid off to the ground. He shrugged his shoulders and headed for the barn to look for a snow shovel. Quietly, he began moving grain away from the wheels of the pickup.

"What are you trying to do now?" asked Leah.

"Dig the truck out."

Leah watched her husband, his strong shoulder muscles working in patterned movements under his sweaty shirt, the lowering sun scorching the weathered skin of his neck. "Oh, don't worry about it for now," she said.

After a couple more half-hearted scoops to think it over, Harold wiped his forehead with the heel of his hand and thrust the shovel into the mound of grain.

The couple looked about the buildings, hills and poplar trees—items glimpsed a million times from a quarter mile away but which they had not come within ten feet of more than two or three times in nearly twenty years. Even now they felt like they were trespassing.

Side by side, they crossed the field, with Harold adjusting his steps to accommodate the slower pace of his wife. Stepping around the clumps of sow thistle and foxtail, husband and wife approached their vegetable garden, where the satisfying sight of plump tomatoes, yellowing squash and neat rows of green peas with their good sweet smell served to remind them of one more small reward in the lonely farm life they had chosen. As they crossed the yard to the house, swarms of grasshoppers and blister beetles took flight, only to resettle when the stirring passed.

# EVERYTHING FLOWS AWAY AND DOWN

## 1 | My Own Farm

Bertie Breen thanked the mail carrier, Howard Mitchell, for the lift and paused to survey the farmyard. The gray siding of the house could do with a painting, and the porch still leaned to the south. Jimsonweed and pigweed invaded the pasture where he learned to ride Alouette. Next to the barn, the old pickup with the busted-out back window rested on its rims. In its place in the driveway sat a Ford half-ton pickup, blue and glossy-new, with chrome wheels and bumper to match.

On the way up, Howard didn't have much to say when Bertie asked how things looked on the old farm, only that things looked OK. But when Bertie questioned aloud whether Sam Morinville was still around, Howard became more definite, playing a finger on top of the steering wheel. "Ohhh yeah," he said.

Bertie crossed the patchy yard quickly and circled the house to the kitchen door. He tapped softly and stepped in.

"Hello, Ma."

"Oh. Bertie," she said, rotating her head sluggishly, as if her neck was causing her great discomfort. "I was just thinking about watermelon."

Taken aback at first, Bertie knew the custom would be to embrace her, but her position at the table made a hug awkward. He forced his face muscles into a smile as bogus as if someone had slapped his face, noting at once the return of an identical grin. This was not starting well. But at least it was an improvement on his departure five years earlier when his last view of his mother was one of her pointing a gun at his chest.

Now his mother sat hunched in her wooden chair so the slanting sun illuminated only the top of her thin body, making her look smaller than he always thought of her.

"Did you get my letter that I was on the way home?" he said.

"Letter?"

"I wrote a couple weeks ago. Didn't it come?"

"Sam, he gets the mail," said his mother.

"Things must be good for Sam. I see that rig out there."

His mother held a magazine on her lap. As she gazed at her son, she rolled the corner of a page tightly around her index finger. Her eyes revealed the desperate look of someone overburdened with thoughts.

"Maybe you can take me to the doctor," she said, her twiglike fingers pattering the paper.

"You're not feeling good? Sure," said Bertie.

With great strain, his mother stood and went to the window, favoring her right side. Her housedress hung loosely on her long frame. She pulled aside the curtain, blinking against the sunlight.

"Do you know who I mean?"

"The doctor? Not for sure," said Bertie. "Is Vickie around?"

"After I take my nap," said his mother, then picked up her magazine and burst into laughter.

Discouraged that she looked as troubled as ever, Bertie smiled weakly and made for the door. "I guess I'll go find her," he said, ashamed of his eagerness to escape his mother's presence.

\* \* \* \* \*

Also, Bertie couldn't wait to check on his horse, Alouette. She'd be aging, but horses lived a long time. That meant going to the barn though, and he wasn't ready to run into Sam. To avoid that, he hoofed it up the hill north of the house to have a look around. From the top of an alder, a crow squawked at him, warning him off and making him feel like an intruder. At the crest, now overgrown with bottlebrush and wild rye, he gazed across the farmyard. Despite all, it was good to be home. The morning breeze passing over the barn stirred pleasant sensations—the sweet smell of fresh alfalfa, the bawling of a calf.

He saw his sister lolling on the step leading into the porch and smoking a cigarette—an unsettling sight. But then again, he'd taken it up at age thirteen.

"Vickie," he called, sensing she hadn't spotted him as he emerged from the side of the porch.

Chin in hand, she rotated her head dreamily toward the voice and, as if jolted from a trance, twisted about and reached for him, her smoldering cigarette wedged between her fingers.

"Bertie!" she cried. "Nobody told me you were coming home."

It felt less than right to seat himself beside her—the step lacked that much width—but with a brief smile she scooted over to the edge to accommodate him.

Then, watching her casually puffing on the cig, he could think of absolutely nothing to say. "You changed," he said finally.

That was true. A gawky preadolescent full of curiosity when Bertie ran away, she'd become a young lady, edging toward chubbiness but still displaying the prominent ears framing a heart-shaped face, full pouty lips and fetching eyes that were alert though slightly discontented.

"So did you. You're so tall. You let your hair grow out."

"Yeah. But don't mistake me for one of them hippies."

"I don't see what's all that bad about hippies."

"Is that so? Anyway, let me count. You're a junior now?"

"Sophomore. I quit for a year."

"That was a mistake."

"Yeah? You never went at all," said Vickie.

Bertie grinned, stretching his long legs from the step. "You got me there."

Behind them, the door opened, and their mother appeared carrying the dishpan full of dirty water. Stepping between the two, she heaved the water into the air. It hit the ground with a sharp splat, scattering the chickens, which instantly scampered back to see what tidbits of food might have materialized.

"Vickie," said Bertie when their mother went back in. "Is Ma OK?"

The girl twisted around and leveled her eyes. "Nope. Not really."

The directness of the reply unsettled Bertie. "You mean like before? Or is she worse?"

"Quite often she stays in bed all day. Lots of times she seems like she doesn't hear what you're saying or else she just doesn't want to talk. It's worse when she doesn't take her pills."

"How come she doesn't take her pills?"

"Sam says they're too expensive to buy every month."

Bertie frowned. "Sam says? Well, Ma wants me to take her to the doctor. We'll see what Sam says about that."

Vickie tossed her cigarette into the mud created by the kitchen slops. "Oh, Mama's always after someone to take her to the doctor. Half an hour later, when you're all set, she'll want to know where you're going. Besides, Sam handles all the bills and money."

"That's what I figured," said Bertie. He studied his hands briefly. "I gotta ask you one more question that's sort of tough. Does Sam still—you know—sleep upstairs?"

Vickie shot her brother a quick look resembling a reprimand. "You mean does he sleep with Mama? Yeah, that is, when he doesn't fall asleep in the easy chair, which is most of the time. Then on nights when he gets back from town late, he just sleeps in his pickup."

"Sounds like he hasn't changed. But I want to know, are you still playing the fiddle?"

Vickie smiled, pleased that he asked. "Yes, I'm in band at school."

"I had it in mind that you were getting pretty good around the time I left."

"Actually, I'm the only violinist in the band, which isn't so great."

"But you don't use that old violin me and you fixed."

"No, Sam got rid of it."

"What? Oh no. How come?"

"Well, when I practiced in the house it gave him a sick headache. So when he was around, I went out to the woods or the barn. Then he claimed it made the milk go down. It ended up with him grabbing the violin and hitting it against a stanchion. The fingerboard broke off and the strings pulled away and that was it." She lit another cigarette, exhaling a long jet of smoke.

"So you got a new one then?" asked Bertie.

"Of course not, silly. You think Sam would spring for that? The school bought one for me."

The two moved into the kitchen, where the coffeepot rattled on the stove, grounds and water boiling over. "Mama left Sam's coffee on," she said. As she reached for a towel, the gesture pulled her shirttail to the side, revealing a small ball-peen hammer fitted into a loop in her jeans. Promptly, she tugged the shirt down to cover it. "Sam must be done with chores," she said. "I'm going upstairs to check on Mama."

Bertie helped himself to a half cup of the scorched mixture and sat down.

The porch boards creaked, the door opened and in came Sam, carrying a wad of circulars and letters from the mailbox. He was about to drop the bundle in front of Bertie, then changed his mind and set it on the sideboard.

"Hello, Sam," said Bertie.

Sam offered a sullen glance and turned his back to sort through the mail, his big hands clumsy at the delicate task. He'd put on weight since Bertie left, but otherwise looked the same—still wearing the same dirty cowboy hat that Bertie knew so well, causing him to speculate whether Sam had bothered to take it off in the intervening years.

"When did *you* get here?" said Sam, his concentration fixed on a brown envelope.

"Just a bit ago," said Bertie, knowing Sam would not have missed his arrival. "How you been?"

Sam grunted and reached for the butter knife on the counter, thrusting it into a corner of the envelope.

"Get anything interesting?" asked Bertie.

Sam turned his head cautiously, maybe trying to catch Bertie's tone. "What do you care about the mail?"

Bertie squeezed his coffee mug to keep his hand from shaking. "I don't unless there's something in there with Ma's name on. Like a money order, say."

Sam stood erect, his thumb and pointer finger grasping the envelope. "I'm giving you one week," he said, waggling the envelope. "After that, I want you off this place."

"You trying to kick me off my own farm?" said Bertie.

"Your farm?"

"It ain't yours, that's for sure."

"You're here after next Wednesday and we'll sure in hell see whose farm it is."

Bertie rose too hastily, knocking his chair over backward. Flustered, he set it back in place.

"Watch it there," said Sam, offering a sneering, gap-toothed grin.

\* \* \* \* \*

Angry with himself that he hadn't been back half an hour before locking horns with Sam, Bertie left the house to check on the horse. This time of day, she would have been pastured, but only a few cows meandered around. When he found her old stall filled with stacked bales and the old generator, he rushed toward the house, scattering the chickens.

Vickie was alone in the kitchen, breaking eggs into a bowl.

"Where's Sam?"

"I don't know. Check the outhouse," said Vickie, concentrating on her eggs.

"What happened to Alouette?"

"The horse?"

"Yeah."

"She pulled up lame. Sam said it wasn't worth it to have her looked at so he had the rendering plant in Devils Lake come and get her."

"What? I can't believe Ma would let him do that."

Vickie opened the fridge, needing two hands since the catch was broken, and took out the pitcher of milk. "You think Sam would bother to ask? First thing we knew, the truck pulled in and hauled her off."

"Vickie, Dad raised that horse from a colt."

The girl shrugged.

"I don't get you," said Bertie. "Doesn't it bother you the way Sam is?"

Vickie took a long time in replying, like maybe the question had never occurred to her. "What do you expect me to do? Put my hands over my ears like Mama does when Sam's drunk so she doesn't have to hear herself screaming? That wasn't my horse to worry about."

"You're a strange one, aren't you?" said Bertie.

Vickie dribbled the egg mixture from the bowl into a frying pan. "Things changed when you left. Mama was sick, and I knew Sam wouldn't watch out for me."

Bertie felt a growing admiration for the girl, the sister he felt he'd never really paid attention to. That was one more matter he intended to make up for once he got settled in. "Does that have to do with the hammer you always got with you?"

"What do you think? Sit down and eat some scrambled eggs."

"What about the others?"

"I'll bring some to Mama. Around here, we eat when we're hungry. By the way, I suppose you want your old room back."

"Keep it for now," said Bertie. "I'll sleep on the couch."

\* \* \* \* \*

Bertie spent that night restless in the living room, where the single change from years before was a small television resting unplugged on the floor. A little after six, he awoke to a commotion upstairs and hurried outside before Sam came down. He planned to go to town and see about finding work but knew better than to ask Sam for the use of his pickup. He'd have to hitch. He cut through the woods toward the road, stopping to pee beside the pond bordering the hayfield. Beavers had been at work on the birch. The gentle beauty of the greenish water reflecting the willows behind it lifted his spirits. The low wooded hills in the distance were so unlike the overwhelming spectacle of Alaska, with its towering mountains, or the endless dusty flats of Oklahoma.

With light traffic, it was nearly noon before a pickup slowed and pulled to the side. He was finally in luck. The driver wore a clean plaid shirt and spotless overalls, which meant he was on the way to town.

"Say, you're Harlan Maas, right?"

"Yup."

"I'm a Breen. Albert. They call me Bertie."

The cab carried the usual farm vehicle smell of age—manure, rotting leather, mildew. Bertie rolled his window halfway down. "I know your boy Bobby. He was two years ahead of me in school."

Harlan pulled a tattered pack of Chesterfields from his shirt pocket. He pushed in the lighter and waited for it to pop out.

Bertie smiled. Harlan was a typical person from the bush—cautious and quiet. The man had probably known Bertie since he was a baby, but time had formed a barrier, requiring that their acquaintanceship be reestablished.

A dusty green Plymouth approached from the other direction. Harlan lifted a single finger a quarter inch in greeting as the two vehicles passed.

"How is Bobby these days?"

"Good, from what we hear."

"He's not with you on the farm then?"

"Bobby? No, he went in the service."

"Is that so? Army?"

"Yeah. Army."

Bertie looked away as the ditch slid by, bright flashes of old beer bottles patterning the dusty weeds.

The pickup swerved slightly to the left, and Harlan corrected. "Tie-rod," he said, dropping a long ash on the floor. "Say, wasn't it you that was up in Alaska?"

"That's right. I just got home."

"What brung you back?"

"You heard about that big quake they had? It caused a tidal wave that hit town and wrecked the boat I was fishing on. Drug it a quarter mile up on shore."

Bertie loved telling the story of his fishing boat's fate and waited for a reaction. Harlan pulled on his bushy, white moustache and drove on.

"The truth is, I was missing home. The hills is in my blood, I guess. And then my ma, she's not been feeling too good."

Harlan took a while digesting this information. They passed the Peavey farm where Bertie's relatives lived, reminding him that he had an obligation to call on them. The pickup slowed for the turn south at the crossroads. Harlan cranked the wheel to the right and let it correct itself. "Then you gonna farm, are you?"

Now it was Bertie's turn to be closemouthed. "I'm not too sure. I'd like to eventually."

They bounced along for another mile while Bertie explained that, with things on his family's farm being unsettled at the moment, he intended to check in town for work before he decided on something particular. "You don't happen to know who might need somebody?"

Harlan wrinkled his mouth as if he found the thought distasteful. "I couldn't say."

\* \* \* \* \*

When they reached town, Harlan let Bertie off by Staggs Hardware and told him to look for the pickup in two or three hours if he wanted a ride back home.

Bertie waited around in Staggs, noticing how the air around the gun section smelled of firearm lubricant, which always reminded him of the fingernail polish remover that sat unused in his grandma's old dresser. When he got up the courage to ask a clerk if there might be a job available, maybe in the tool department, he was told that the manager had quit suddenly and left town, so for the time being the hiring was on hold.

At the Standard Station, he was turned down with a shake of the head by Ralph, who was sweating over a tire that wouldn't come loose from the rim.

"Breen," said Mr. Orson at the dairy. "Breen. You're from up in the bush then?"

Bertie admitted that he was.

Mr. Orson, a pleasant, careful man who stood a foot shorter than Bertie, scratched his head under his white paper hat. "Aren't you some relation to Harold Peavey?"

"My dad was related to Mrs. Peavey," said Bertie, his hopes rising.

"I hired Harold here way back before the war. A good man. I felt bad when he got into that trouble."

Before Bertie could come up with a suitable reply, Mr. Orson checked his watch. "You tell Harold hello next time you see him."

At the lumberyard, the TV repair shop and the auto parts store, he was asked about his schooling and told that most businesses had policies of not hiring people who lacked a twelfth-grade diploma. What a high school education had to do with nailing shingles, wheeling cement or twisting in replacement headlights, Bertie had no idea and didn't want to know.

\* \* \* \* \*

When he saw no sign of Harlan's old Ford, Bertie set out for the highway to thumb it back home. Then, at the end of Main Street, he spotted the rig outside Milo's Bar. He hesitated, not wanting Harlan to think he was pestering him to hurry. He leaned against the front fender of the pickup and lit a cigarette.

Four cigarettes later, the door to the bar flew open and Harlan emerged through the twang of guitar music. He halted unsteadily when his gaze fell on Bertie. "There he is," he said.

Harlan's sleeves were rolled up to the elbow, exposing wiry arms. He groped in his pants pocket, bringing attention to a wet spot on his crotch, and fisted out a handful of coins and bills that he peered at. Trying the other pocket, he found what he was looking for.

"You take the wheel till we get out a ways," he said, dangling the keys inches from Bertie's face.

Harlan's Ford had a stick on the floor, and when Bertie tried third gear, the transmission let out a screech that disconcerted him but to which Harlan paid no heed. The pickup rolled jerkily to the end of Main and then north on 43 toward the Canadian border and home. Bertie downshifted to pass a wagon hauling bales, and the change in engine pitch roused Harlan, whose chin had sunk to his chest. He stretched, yawned and startled Bertie by breaking out in song, his voice perfectly in tune as he sang "Green, Green Grass of Home."

With a thumb and finger Harlan tugged at the loose skin of his throat. "Sam Morinville," he said, as if in answer to some problem whirling in his head.

Bertie sensed this was the opening of a conversation that would provide him with useful information and he listened eagerly, not wanting to break the spell. Despite the hours in Milo's Bar having clearly animated Harlan's tongue, nothing more was forthcoming, and they rode in silence. Then a mile or two on, Harlan sat up and jabbed his thumb toward a dirt road to the south. "Down there's the old Able place."

Bertie looked. "I knew it was one of these roads along here, but we were always told not to go near the Ables."

"Quite a bunch they are," said Harlan.

"You know," said Bertie, steering around a pothole, "I been hearing about them all my life now and I never did learn what it was that gave them such a reputation exactly."

Harlan cupped one knee in his hands and leaned back on the seat. "Well, sir, they got into bootleggin' during prohibition. Good shine they made, never used bread yeast and never bothered with the last of the wash neither. They had stills under every tree, each one capable of a ten-gallon run. They had regular routes running as far as Bismarck."

"You seem to know a lot about it," said Bertie, smiling.

"Not me, but my uncle, he ran his share," said Harlan, missing the gentle jibe. "Made enough to quit and buy himself a gas station out west."

"Is that so?"

"But speaking of the Ables, they never hung on to the money, so now they're as bad off as the rest of us except they get by poaching deer and running so damn many traplines they's not a fur animal to be found no more. Lately I heard they're pickin' buttonweed and selling it for marijuana dope on the reservation."

"And how come they never got clamped down on?"

"I couldn't say," said Harlan, fumbling for a cigarette. "One of the twins did do time for auto theft a ways back. Some believe Sheriff Aingher is in cahoots with them. What they are is one of them outfits that don't want no gover-ment snoopin' around. When REA come through, they tried running wires from the poles to their place, and young Pete got electrocuted. Fried him like a walleye. That's why they got the generator even if it prob'ly costs more in fuel."

They passed Loon Lake as the sun dropped over the horizon, casting the lake in a blaze of orange. "They ever bother you, the Ables?"

"Not so much since Four-finger Maggie died. Me and him go way back. Oh, once in a while they come along with a Turtle Mountain credit card."

"A what?"

"You know. A ten-gallon cream can and a siphon hose."

"That's a good one," said Bertie, chuckling.

"I'll tell you what though," said Harlan. "Folks that lived in the bush long as I have know it's not smart to get on the wrong side of the Ables. Stories go back about how somebody that done them wrong might just disappear, you know, like on television."

Bertie doubted that. "But doesn't the law know to suspect them? Seems like that would be the first place to check into."

"That's just the thing," said Harlan. "The law, it's as happy to be rid of some. Like in that Mafia, if the gangsters just shoot each other, nobody gets too excited."

"How come I never heard about that when I was growing up?" asked Bertie.

"Beats me," said Harlan, turning his hands palms up. "Probably because it's been a while since any big to-do come about. Then too with how things have changed on the reservation. Things never was on their side from the start, so…" Harlan's voice trailed off.

Bertie slowed as they came to a hill marking the turnoff to Hooker Lake. Just over the crest, a station wagon with Minnesota plates was pulled over to the side. Two people stood by the car, their hands shading their eyes as they gazed off into the distant woods. Harlan craned his head around trying to get a good look. "Wonder what they're up to," he said.

The turn in the conversation left both men with no place to go, and they rode silently for a way before Harlan burped softly. "You find anything in town?"

"Nope."

"I doubted you would," said Harlan. "There just ain't nothin' here for young people startin' out. You take my farm. That Jasper my daughter married never put in a day's honest labor in his life, and him and her got three little ones already. The wife brung them in so's the grandkids can have something to eat besides jam sandwiches and pop. Well, Bobby seen there was no room for him on the farm, so he went down to Wahpeton to learn diesel."

Harlan shook his head. "But he never took to school learning, so he come back just like you figuring to get a job in town. Six months later he was in the army."

Bertie thought about that. "Well, I seen a lot of the world and I don't need to see no more. I'm gonna starve, I'd rather do it with my own kind."

Harlan rubbed his eyes with both fists. "I been here all my life, and I'll be sixty in December. But the fact is there's changes that can't be fought. It's like a stream of water sweeping through, and it's having its way with the people and the country. Slow down, here comes your turnoff."

Grabbing the bag of groceries he bought in town, Bertie got out and held the door while Harlan came around from the other side. "Thanks," he said.

"You betcha," said the man, blinking as if to clear his vision.

Up went his window, and the pickup crawled away. Bertie watched as it rounded the curve, one taillight flickering on and off.

*****

As he neared the house, Bertie spotted the silhouetted bulk of Sam filling the kitchen window, arm slicing the air, chin scissoring. Just beyond him stood the gaunt form of Bertie's mother, elbows pinching her ribs, head bowed like she was trying to shrink into herself.

At the sound of the door opening, all eyes turned toward Bertie. He set the bag of groceries on the counter.

"What's that supposed to be?" said Sam.

"Just some coffee and stuff. I seen it's getting low."

Sam peered at the paper bag, trying to conceal his curiosity. "Well, put it away whatever it is." With that, he left the room and went upstairs, his booted feet scraping the floorboards.

"I got some of those plums Vickie likes," said Bertie. "Where do you want 'em?"

His mother either didn't hear or chose to overlook the question. He turned to the refrigerator, struggling to open the door. "It looks like you could use a hand here," he said. "The barn needs fixing up. It's starting to lean."

"That barn's been leaning since you were a baby," said Fawn.

The ceiling joists groaned under the pressure of feet, and Bertie dropped his voice. "Ma, I was thinking it's time for me to come home to stay, but I checked in town for jobs and there's nothing. It would be good to help out around here, but Sam, he just don't like me."

"Sam has it hard being Indian."

"It's not being Indian that's his problem. Being Sam is what's wrong with that fella. I bet you a dime to a donut he took the money I been sending and that's how he paid for that fancy truck."

"You can't run a farm with no truck."

Bertie thought about the pitiful, limping vehicle that Harlan Maas got by with but let the point go. "In so many words he told me I'm not welcome here."

Receiving no reaction, Bertie watched his mother pick items one by one from the grocery bag. When she came to the can of coffee, she traced a finger over the letters on the red label, mouthing them silently: "F-o-l…"

"I got to go to the doctor," she said, returning the coffee to the bag.

"All right," answered Bertie. "Just let me know when you're ready."

\* \* \* \* \*

Bertie could tell Sam had seen him coming around the corner of the barn by the water tank—the very tank they found Bertie's father in when Bertie was a small boy. Just the same, Sam pretended like he didn't hear him. He held a pipe wrench in his left hand as he knelt over the pump. He leaned back on his heels. "What do you want?" he said after a proper wait.

"I'm seeing if you need a hand."

Sam let go a snort of contempt. "Nope."

"I'm not a kid anymore. I learned a lot when I was crewing on a boat."

"Is that so?"

"But that don't mean I forgot my way around a farm."

Sam tapped the pump housing with the wrench like a judge with his gavel and took a breath. "Where were you when I was pulling that breached calf? Or when the mower broke down, and we lost half a field of alfalfa? There were a hundred times I needed help and now that Vickie's big enough to drive the truck and run errands you come along with your high-hat Alaska stories all ready to take over. Who do you think you are?"

"Just a guy coming home to find out if he's welcome," answered Bertie. "Like I said before, what makes you think you got a right to lord over me here?" Bertie knew he had the momentum and he didn't want it broken, but Sam fixed his eyes on his task, gripping the wrench menacingly in his fist.

"Go find something to do. Can't you see I'm busy?"

\* \* \* \* \*

Bertie chewed over hiking up to have a look at the old log and stone hut that he used to call his castle, but it would take a while and it looked like rain. He spent the remainder of the day picking up old shingles, kicking at rotting fence posts and worrying over his mother. He sighted her from time to time sitting on the edge of the wicker chair on the porch with the door open, like she was waiting for a visitor who would never arrive. Vickie had told him that when she took on this half-awake condition, everything on the farm seemed to slow down. Now Bertie saw what she meant. Even the air felt static and heavy. The chickens pecked around indifferently.

Long after sunset, he came quietly into the empty kitchen with its bare shelves, cracked windowpanes and the pitiful, smoky cookstove that was old in his grandmother's day. He made himself a sandwich with the heel of the bread and the jar of honey. After tidying up, he pumped a glass of water and shuffled into the gloomy living room, where he sat on the easy chair, possibly fifty years old by now, and stared at the shadows fluttering across the ceiling like ghosts.

"Bertie!" He opened his eyes to see Vickie shaking his shoulder. His neck hurt from the chair. His mouth felt dry.

"Bertie, Mama's gone."

"Gone? Where?"

"I don't know. She's not in bed."

As Bertie rubbed his neck, Vickie explained that their mother, when she could not sleep or became disturbed in the night, often wandered outside. Usually, but not always, Vickie knew when something was amiss by the sound of the porch door closing or the livestock growing restless, easy sounds to pick up in the total stillness of the country night. The results were unpredictable. Sometimes their mother curled up in the tall grass to be found with her eyes open. Once she walked to the marsh a mile away.

"What does Sam do when that happens?" asked Bertie as they headed outside.

"He doesn't even know she's gone," said Vickie. "Like right now. I heard him snoring in bed." She traced the weak beam of her flashlight about the area—the outhouse, the garden, the line of cottonwoods near the road. They checked the latch on the barn door, setting the calves into a contagious bawling, believing they were about to be fed.

"When we get to the pasture fence we'll split up. You go left," said Vickie.

After half an hour or more of searching and calling, Vickie came upon their mother on her haunches, intently examining a post. Vickie waved the flashlight in the air as a signal to Bertie. As they tried to coax their mother to her feet, they found that her robe was snagged on the barbs of the wire fence, and that she bled from scratches on her arms and hands.

"Ma, come on, let's get you to the house," said Bertie, using Vickie's flashlight to examine her injuries.

The woman raised a hand to shield the flashlight beam from her eyes.

"Look. She's barefoot—her feet are cut too," said Bertie.

"Mama, where's your shoes?" demanded Vickie.

She went to her knees. "Mama? Mama, look at me."

"What is it?" asked Bertie.

"She's acting like she took too many pills. Mama?"

"Can you walk, Ma?" asked Bertie. "Here, give me your arm."

With Vickie on the other arm, the two tried to lift their mother to her feet, but her body went limp.

"Why don't we wake Sam to help," said Bertie.

"By the time we get him up and moving we'll all be soaked," said Vickie. "Feel that? It's starting to rain."

"Does he leave the keys in the pickup?" asked Bertie.

"I don't know," said Vickie. "You can go see but watch it. That ugly pickup is his pride and joy. He parks it on that little rise outside the house so he can see it from the upstairs bedroom."

As they talked, their mother wrapped her long arms about herself and levered her knees up.

"Are you cold, Ma?" asked Bertie. "Here." He pulled his shirt up over his head and draped it loosely over his mother's shoulders.

The rain diminished as he hurried away, bare-chested. To his surprise, he found the pickup unlocked. He opened the door and the interior light washed over him as bright as a flashbulb. He pulled the door closed too quickly. The sharp noise echoed against the barn.

In contrast to the shiny exterior, the cab of the pickup was filthy, smelling of Sam's odor of whiskey, tobacco and old food. The engine turned over easily but would not catch. When it came to life it was with a roar that must have sounded like thunder in the nearby house. Bertie shifted to reverse and released the clutch only long enough to nudge the truck from its stationary position. Leaving the engine in idle speed, he allowed it to roll down the long incline past the clothesline before braking and heading back over the lumpy ground toward the far side of the pasture where his mother and Vickie waited.

With difficulty they managed to coax their mother into the cab, where she stretched her long body across the passenger seat with her head resting on Bertie's shoulder. Vickie, with no room remaining, climbed into the bed of the pickup. During the slow, bumpy trip back toward the house, their mother revived slightly, inquiring of Bertie where they were going and bracing herself with one hand on the dashboard.

What she didn't notice, but her son did, were the number of lights on. In the back, Vickie banged her knuckles on the window, pointing toward the house.

Bertie eased the pickup to a stop in its parking spot just as Sam charged out of the porch, kicking the screen open. He too was naked from the waist up, resembling one of the fake TV wrestlers, the waistband of his shorts stretched tight over his swollen belly.

"What the hell is this?" he demanded.

"Come and help," said Bertie as he opened his door. "Ma's hurt." But before he could get his feet planted on the ground, Sam stood before him, anger twisting his face.

"You don't never touch my truck," he said, bringing a fist back.

Bertie's mind flew to the times that he'd quarreled with Sam growing up. It was a good thing they'd never come to blows, for Bertie had been a string bean of a kid, easily outmatched by Sam's size. But over the years, he'd filled out. In Alaska, where his muscles swelled from the strenuous duties of a deckhand aboard salmon seiners, he'd held his own in bar brawls and believed that now he could at least defend himself. However, the instant he tried to deflect the punch, he knew he was in trouble.

The blow struck square on Bertie's nose, stunning him and overwhelming his senses with the smell of Sam's musky, unbathed odor, worsened by the man's sour breath from his interrupted sleep. To protect himself, Bertie brought his arms up over his face. While Sam was overweight, he still had the breadth and strength of an ox. Abandoning her mother, Vickie tried to intervene by clutching Sam's arm. He shook her off with one swipe, but the distraction allowed Bertie to scramble out of his reach. Temporarily free, but nearly blinded by flashes of white light, Bertie stumbled in the direction of the porch steps, where his mother had retreated, shrieking pitifully.

He got as far as the front of the pickup before Sam grabbed him. In one fierce motion, he swung him around and slammed him down against the hood, which gave the inch or two needed to save Bertie from broken ribs. As he twisted away from Sam, he felt the vehicle move. He'd left it in neutral, and the push it received from his weight dislodged it, sending it rolling gently down the slope.

Like maybe he was trying to decide, Sam turned his eyes first toward Bertie, who stood with his chest heaving, then to his pickup, glinting in the moonlight and moving away from him as it gained speed. The vehicle veered toward the clothesline, its right rear taillight striking one of the sturdy metal posts, shattering the lens and scraping the blue paint from the fender. The indirect blow diverted the vehicle away from the path it had taken toward the harmless, soft soil of the garden and into a curved route that carried it toward the barbwire fence adjoining the pasture. There it took out a post, smashing the fancy chrome grille, and, before becoming mired in wet manure, broke through the fence, picking up parallel scratches back to front and creating a metallic screech that caused Fawn to cover her ears.

As Bertie stood, bent from the waist and wiping his face with the back of his wrist, Sam, with exaggerated deliberation, pointed at him.

"I ever catch you on this place again, I'll kill you," he said.

Then, barefoot and in his shorts, he hobbled down through the scattered weeds and chicken droppings that made up the yard to minister to his pickup.

"Hurry up. Go get your things while I take Mama inside," ordered Vickie.

Disoriented and confused, Bertie ignored her.

"Hurry up! Didn't you hear what he said?" said Vickie.

Inside at the sink, his mind cleared. He pumped water furiously to bathe his face. Waves of pain blinded him. He felt his nose lying flat against his cheek. From outside came the shrill scream of tires spinning uselessly in mud.

"Are you hurt bad? Let me look at you," said Vickie, descending the stairs.

She stood on tiptoe peering into Bertie's face, spreading an eyelid open with her fingers. "What about Ma?" he asked.

"She's not hurt bad, just upset," said Vickie. "Wash your eyes out better. But hurry up. You got to get away from here."

"The hell," said Bertie, wincing. "I live here."

"Not now you don't," said his sister.

"I got nowhere else to go, and I can't go anywhere leaving you and Ma with him," argued Bertie.

"We managed before and we will again," said Vickie. "Just get. Think about it. If he does something to you, he'll do the same to us."

"Then I won't let him do anything," said Bertie, toweling his face and examining the blood left on the towel.

Vickie tore the towel from his hands. "Please go. The longer it takes to get unstuck, the madder he's gonna be. I know him better than you." She shoved the bag of spare garments she'd gathered into his chest.

Still protesting, Bertie let himself be steered out the back door and toward the woods, knowing his sister would watch until he disappeared from sight. As he circled the hill behind the house, the gentle rain resumed. He rested under an alder, waiting for the lights in the house to dim, then set out walking. By the time he reached the highway the rain had eased. He accelerated his pace, following the road but taking to the ditch when the rare car happened along. As the light grew in the east, his nose quit bleeding, but all else, mind and body, ached like never before.

## 2 | The Price of a Lie

Bertie reached the turnoff to Peaveys in the full sun of midday, hurting, miserable and tired enough to bed down in a chicken coop. When he saw the back of the grain truck sticking out of the machine shed, he knew he'd find Harold at work under the hood, and he was right.

Harold, who'd turned considerably grayer in five years, grasped Bertie's hand and looked intently into his face. "Whoa," he said. "What the heck did you run into?"

"Me and Sam got in a fight."

Harold raised his cap and wiped his forehead. "You better come inside. How'd you get here anyway? You walk?"

Bertie hadn't seen Harold and Leah since his return. As Harold led him inside, he remembered that he thought of the Peaveys as rich. Now as he looked around at the old furniture and older kitchen stove, he realized that they were not a whole bunch wealthier, but tidier, more organized than his family. The windows all sparkled and the table was covered with an ironed cloth held in place by a vase full of yellow flowers.

Hearing footsteps, Leah came to the door. "Bertie Breen, is that you? Good lord, what did you get yourself into?" She touched Bertie gently on the cheek. "We better take you in for stitches."

Bertie pulled away. "No," he said quietly. "I don't need that."

"He came on foot all the way from Fawn's," said Harold.

Leah leaned toward Bertie. "I guess he won't bleed to death, but he's gonna have a crooked nose."

As Bertie dabbed iodine on his cuts, the other two talked in low voices. He joined them at the kitchen table, where all farm families conferred when any serious matter was at hand.

"We never even heard you were back," said Harold. "Are you here to stay?"

"I had that in mind, yeah," said Bertie.

"How did you and Sam get into such a tussle?"

"I don't know. I just been back a couple days. Before I could even say hello, Sam made me know I wasn't welcome. He even told me I had to get out in a week."

Bertie waited for a reaction.

"Anyway, what started the fight wasn't about that." He went on to explain about his mother disappearing in the night and how he and Vickie used Sam's pickup without permission.

Leah broke in. "Is your mother all right?"

"Oh, yeah. Vickie will take care of her. She's real capable, that girl."

"She is for sure," said Leah, getting up to pour coffee. "But what happens now? Can you get along with Sam?"

Bertie sipped his coffee, recoiling from the sting the hot liquid caused on his bruised lips. "I don't know, but now that I'm back, well, I don't like to say it but we got to get Sam off the place. The way he treats Ma isn't right. And Vickie too."

Harold caught his wife's eye before speaking. "You don't think he's, you know, bothering Vickie?"

"Oh no," said Bertie. "Not that way. Least I don't think."

"Because if that was the case he could go to jail," said Harold.

"No, it's more like how he's taken over the whole works. I know he was mad about his pickup, but right after the fight he threatened to kill me. To me, that tells what's going on in his head."

Leah blew on her coffee. "Bertie, you need to be told something," she said.

"What's that?"

"Sam and your mother. Well, they're married now."

Bertie felt like the room had shifted. "What? Married?" he said. "Sam and Ma are married? They're not even…" He turned to Harold, who stared at his lap. Bertie looked back at Leah, wanting elaboration. He shook his head, searching for words. "Sam's the hired man."

Wisely, Leah let him go on.

"That couldn't of happened. Ma, she would never do that." His eyes went to the framed photo of a young Richie Lee perched on a tractor seat. This was torture. "I don't get what's going on since I left."

An air of agitation hung over the room, broken shortly by the soft lowing of a cow in the pasture.

"How come Vickie never told me? We been having lots of talks."

"It could be she never knew," said Harold. "It was only a justice of the peace thing. We weren't there, and I don't think Sam's folks were either."

"How'd you find out?" asked Bertie.

"Leah spotted it in the paper. They put who got a marriage license in the legal notices."

"God almighty," muttered Bertie.

No one spoke for a minute, allowing Bertie to absorb the shock. "So that's that," he said. "Now I don't know what to do."

Harold straightened himself on his chair and leaned forward. "Have you thought about maybe just letting it lay?"

"How's that?"

"I think what Harold means is let things cool down a while," said Leah.

Bertie looked from one to the other. They weren't listening. "I don't see how that would fix anything."

Harold folded his hands. "That's not it at all. Your mother, well, you see, she's not well, and the girl's gonna be grown up and vamoosed before you know it."

Leah shifted her position on her chair, trying to get comfortable. "That they're married changes things. The thing is, the two of us aren't sure what you'd like us to do," she said.

"But couldn't someone just talk to him?" said Bertie. "If Sam caught on that people were on to him, he might change his ways." His eyes were watering.

"I don't know if we would be the best ones to interfere," said Leah. "Don't forget the Morinvilles still live the next place over to us. Stuff like that, it's complicated." She turned to her husband for help, but none was offered.

Bertie was speechless. To his right, Harold sat like a stone. Though he knew his distant relative as someone who went out of his way to avoid disputes, he'd been imagining the man enlisting someone like Harlan Maas and a few other neighbors and beating Sam within an inch of his life, then, married or not, throwing him off the place forever.

Finally Harold spoke up. "You better bunk with us till you heal up."

"I don't mean to put you out," said Bertie, using the politeness he'd acquired from his travels.

Leah got up from her chair. "You need some rest. Go lay down in Richie Lee's room for a while. Make yourself at home."

\* \* \* \* \*

Although he didn't expect to, Bertie did manage a short nap. When he heard the TV, he came downstairs. Harold had come in from the barn to get the stock market report.

He waited for a commercial. "Say, do you suppose I could use one of your vehicles for a while? The pickup would do me."

Harold was not a man who made decisions before weighing all considerations. "How long?"

"I'd be back before supper."

"Would you mind telling me where you want to go?"

Bertie hesitated. "I'd like to run into town."

Harold brightened. "Leah would take you. She's always got errands."

Bertie sighed. Why did everything have to come so hard? "Well, there's a girl I used to know, and I just as soon keep it to myself."

"Oh," said Harold, rattled. "You go right ahead. Take the pickup. But could be she won't be so glad to see you, your face busted up like that."

"I don't even know for sure if she's around anymore," said Bertie, distressed from the pressure of his fib.

Harold pulled his gloves off. "Go where you like, but I want you to promise you'll stay away from your mother's place."

Bertie forced a smile. "Don't worry about that."

\* \* \* \* \*

From the familiar road into Rolland, all looked normal. The barley was a little green but getting close. On the long hill next to the city airport, the surface of the road was molded to washboard ridges, and Bertie geared down to first to keep from rattling his teeth. The Dunlops were working the ditch for hay, sending the sweet aroma of fresh-cut grass into the cab.

He pulled into Rolland, taking a right at Staggs and continuing past the dairy to the sheriff's office. Three county cars complete with siren and light mounts were parked in the reserved spots. Not too long ago they'd gotten by with one. He climbed the steps and entered. A woman sat behind a desk set apart by a low, curved railing. She looked up.

"Yes?"

"I'm here to see the sheriff," said Bertie. He'd expected to have to state his business and maybe flash an ID, doubting his Alaska driver's license would do, but the lady, gray-haired and about his mother's age, turned to her side and called through a doorway.

"Dale. Someone to see you."

Steel rollers clacked on their tracks as two file drawers were shut and Sheriff Aingher called out, "Come in."

A wave of discomfort passed through Bertie. He knew the sheriff, but the dealings he had with him before he left didn't go well.

"Remember me? Albert Breen? They call me Bertie?"

"You shot up a foot since I saw you," said the sheriff. "Last I heard, you were up in Alaska somewhere."

Aingher, who had been sheriff now for going on twenty years, was showing his age. In profile, he resembled his son, Dale Jr., but a series of chins drooped over his Adam's apple, and the flesh around his face made his eyes nearly invisible. He lowered his ample bottom to the corner of his desk. "What can I do for you?"

"I come to talk to you about Sam Morinville," said Bertie, not sure if he should take the chair that sat before the desk. He glanced at the open door. Aingher took the hint, walked heavily over and swung it shut.

"OK, go ahead. Does this have something to do with how you got that busted nose?"

"Kind of," said Bertie, offering what he knew was a weak smile. He went on to repeat most of what he'd told the Peaveys, altering his story slightly to emphasize Sam's harsh treatment of everybody and his own desire to one way or another have Sam banished out of the lives of the Breen family. As he spoke, he studied Aingher closely, hoping for approval of the indignation that he himself felt. But the reaction reminded him of the talk with Harold and Leah. The man just sat there on the edge of his desk bracing himself with his hands, nodding occasionally, calm as a cow after milking.

"You know they're married now, don't you?" said the sheriff after motioning to the vacant chair.

"I just found that out."

"That can change some things," said Aingher. "A man's got no right to abuse his wife, but there's the requirement of proper procedure. If Sam Morinville has actually struck your mother or neglected her basic needs like medicine, there might be a case we could act on. But would your mother be willing to bring charges and testify? And don't you think there'd be some question of credibility coming from someone who's been around not much more than a couple days in what, five years?"

Bertie didn't like the sheriff's tone. He also didn't like having to look up at the man after accepting a seat. And why all this rigmarole? In Alaska, things like this were tended to on the spot.

"But we got rights, too," said Bertie, flustered and searching for the correct words. "Sam's trying to kick me off the farm. He even threatened me, and I'll testify to that!"

The sheriff hopped off the desk and pulled open a file drawer. Mumbling to himself, he pushed it shut with too much force, rattling the light fixture on the ceiling. Bertie waited. The office carried the smell of the ink they used in the old ditto machine back in grade school. The sheriff opened another drawer.

"Here we are," he said. "You might not need to see this, but there it is in case." He held a manila folder stuffed with pink carbon copies of various official-looking forms.

"What's all that for?" said Bertie.

"These are property tax records from all the years I've had this job, but it's only the last couple you'd be interested in."

"How's that?"

"Just listen," said Aingher. With his free hand he slid a pair of glasses from his shirt pocket. Using his teeth to pull the temples back, he began reading aloud:

"Chippewa County Real Estate Tax Statement, parcel numbers two thousand such and such, jurisdiction Dark Lake township. Physical location such and such, legal description, OK, here we are: statement name, Morinville, Samuel E."

The sheriff closed the folder and repocketed his glasses. He looked at Bertie, waiting for him to speak.

"What's that mean?"

"It means that where it says Sam Morinville, a few years ago it would have said Fawn Breen, and a few years before that, Sidney Breen."

For the second time that day, Bertie was dumbfounded. "You mean it's saying Sam owns the farm?"

"No one told you that either?" said the sheriff. "I'm sorry to be the one."

"But something's not right," said Bertie. "Can I see that paper?"

Aingher handed it over. "That there's just the tax statement," he said. "To see the actual proof, you got to go down the hall to the Register of Deeds. You're welcome to do that, but I can save you the bother. It says in a whole bunch of words that Sam owns the entire property, except the household or what they call personal possessions—you know, clothes and so forth. All the rest—buildings, livestock, machinery, you name it—belongs to Sam."

"Just him alone?"

"Afraid so. Nothing from now on will mention Mrs. Morinville."

*Mrs. Morinville.* The words nearly choked Bertie. "The land too?"

"The whole kit and caboodle. And the paper that says so is called a quitclaim and that's the last thing that's got your mother's name on it."

"Ma would never have seen to that on her own. You know she gets spells where she doesn't know what's she doing. I bet Sam bamboozled her into it." Bertie looked toward the window. The sun struck the venetian blinds, producing a horizontal ripple effect that hurt his eyes.

"Oh, I wouldn't be surprised at that," said Aingher. "But from what I've seen, it's awful hard to prove."

Desperate now, Bertie sensed his voice rising. "If only my dad was alive. And how come is it that just some of the records are kept here and not all of them?"

Long accustomed to people becoming emotional in his office, the sheriff held his composure while he explained. "Like I said, these are tax records. When people don't pay their property taxes, it's the job of the county sheriff to try to collect them. Every time I have to take up a case like that, I first check to make sure the right people are being billed. I can look up who owns every square foot of property in Chippewa County."

Bertie went silent while he let this all find its place. He felt as if all the evil forces in the world were grouped against him. Then, just to fill in space, he asked if the taxes were being paid.

"They're up to date now," said the sheriff. "They were unpaid for the first year or so that Morinville took over the property."

"Took over? You mean stole," said Bertie. "Didn't Sam have to pay us something for it?"

"That's out of my area," replied Aingher. "But I don't think so. Sometimes they put in words like 'consideration,' but it doesn't mean much."

"But there's got to be a way to get it back," said Bertie. "That land's been in the Breen family since going way back."

Aingher sounded hesitant. "Like I say, that's just not my bailiwick. You'd have to talk to an attorney. But if I had to take a guess, I'd say that unless you wanted to buy him out or he voluntarily signed the title back, there wouldn't be any easy way."

"How about if Sam died?" asked Bertie.

"Well, I suppose it would go back to your mother if she was still living. Unless Sam assigned it to any of his own heirs. I imagine that's not too likely to happen."

"What about if he committed a crime and was sent to jail?"

The sheriff sighed. "That depends. If it was a serious crime and it was proved that any property owned was acquired through criminal activity, it could pretty much certainly be taken away, but it would be a while."

The sun had moved past the window. The sheriff glanced at his watch and then at the door. "Is there something else I can help you with?" he said.

Bertie knew it was time to depart. He'd been there a while, but he wasn't ready.

"Mr. Aingher," he began, purposely wanting to sound formal and serious. "You know my sister, Vickie. She's fifteen years old."

"I know of her. I know she's not Sam's child, yeah."

"Molesting a minor person, that's a serious offense, right? You know, like touching them and so on."

Aingher sat back on the corner of his desk and folded his arms. "Yes, that will put someone in prison, for good sometimes." He unfolded his arms, cupping one knee in his hands. "But before you say too much, I want to warn you. If you're going to make something up about any of the people we been talking about, don't do it."

The sheriff paused as if to gather his thoughts. "I got to say that, myself, I got no feelings to lose for Sam Morinville, but if you bring false charges knowingly, I won't be on your side. And what's more, I got to tell you that I have my doubts because if something was going on, you'd of told me about it first off."

Bertie looked around at the spindle holding odd sizes of paper and at the sheriff's hat hanging on a rack made of a diamond willow topped by a set of deer antlers. He felt out of place.

"So, is there anything more you want to talk about?" asked the sheriff, coming to his feet.

"No," said Bertie quietly. He looked at his hands, so soft and sensitive now that he wasn't toiling at hard labor.

"All right, we'll just both forget about this last part of our conversation," said the sheriff. He tugged at his pants, trying to cinch them up higher on his belly.

"You know, sometimes the law is all cockeyed, but it's still the law. And if it's worth something to you, I want to let you know that as long as I'm around, I'll keep an eye on things up there."

To Bertie, the promise sounded hollow. Just the same, he stood, took the sheriff's hand and thanked him.

He drove out of town, past Bergstrom Motors where Sam probably bought his pickup, past Larsen Feed and Grain which, his mother claimed, wouldn't give Sam credit because he was Indian, and past Milo's Bar where Sam most likely hung out when he came to town in his fancy clothes. By the time he arrived at Peaveys, having driven the Chevy a slow, thoughtful distance, he had made his decision.

*****

He lay in bed the next morning waiting for it to grow quiet downstairs, indicating Harold had gone out to do morning chores. He ate the oatmeal Leah had kept warm for him, thanked her and told her he was going out for a hike and wouldn't be back for a while.

He estimated that on foot it would take at least two hours depending on how far off the highway it was. The road in was not hard to find after Harlan Maas had pointed it out, even though it was unmarked and overgrown with poplar. Harlan had said there was another road off the one connecting to the highway, but Bertie couldn't even guess how distant that was. The trees formed a canopy over the narrow trail, and Bertie couldn't see how a truck could make it through. No doubt a better way in existed from the south. He followed a curve and a sign appeared, fancy and solid with store-bought brass letters: *PRIVATE*.

A hundred yards farther, he reached a high mesh fence topped with barbed wire. A wide steel gate stretched across the trail. A thick creosote-soaked post embedded firmly in the earth supported one side of the gate; the other side, the one with the latch, rested in a wide pool of mud that looked treacherous enough to swallow a vehicle.

For someone walking, however, the gate presented no barrier. Bertie grabbed the top bar and at once received a jolt that caused him to jerk away and cry out. Only then did he see the white insulators. The fence and gate were electrified.

He wiggled out of his jacket and draped it over the rail to use as an insulator. Concentrating so as not to allow bare skin to touch metal, he planted one foot on the other side and, in a crouch, twisted himself through, butt first. Straightening up, he noticed a weathered tag screwed into the top bar. *Prop. of Prophetstown Cemetery Assn.* If nothing else, these people had a lot of nerve.

A shallow ditch that looked hand-dug lay parallel to the gate. It wasn't adequate to stop a car, and Bertie wondered about its purpose. He took a long step to cross it but failed to notice a thin trip wire, and as his foot caught it, a bell sounded in the distance, shattering the quiet woodsy air. For an instant, he wanted to bolt. This wasn't the way he'd planned to announce his presence, but here he was. He gathered himself and waited.

Shortly, the roar of an unmuffled engine sounded and a motorcycle coasted to a stop within a cloud of blue smoke.

"You see the sign?" said the rider, shouting over the noise of the motorcycle. He was a lean, young man with a long face and ears protruding like mushrooms on a log.

"I saw," said Bertie, nodding sharply and doubting he could be heard over the raucous machine.

The man reached for the ignition and the deafening roar eased. "What do you want?"

"I'm trying to get to the Able place," said Bertie.

The man wore a green visor that exposed a sunburned scalp through his thinning hair. "You got business there?"

"Not exactly. What I want takes a little explaining."

The man didn't like this bit of hedging. "I think you better go back where you come from. I'll walk you past the fence case you can't find the way." He hopped off the motorcycle, probing for the kickstand with the toe of his boot.

At this, Bertie took a gamble. "What this has to do with is an Indian I know who's got some comeuppance due."

This amused the man, and he broke into a grin. "What'd they do, these Indians? They running off with your cows?"

"It's just the one and I'd rather not say yet," said Bertie.

The driver peered at Bertie's muddy feet. "What's your name?"

"Albert Breen. We farm up there by Dark Lake."

The man studied Bertie, his curiosity up. "Where's your rig?"

"I walked."

"From Dark Lake?"

"I been staying at Peaveys. That's their place over next to—"

"Why's that?"

Bertie realized he'd get nowhere with this character. "Look, Mister, I told you what I need. Now why can't you let me in? It won't take long."

The man wiped his mouth and turned his neck around like he was checking to see if anyone followed. "Don't go no farther till I get back," he said.

This time, the wait was longer before the man reappeared, on foot this time. He came so close before halting that Bertie could see individual hairs on the stubble of his chin. "You did say your name was Breen, right?"

"That's right."

"Lucky for you, the old man's in a good mood today," he said, apparently not liking the idea himself. "Come on then."

As the sound of a throbbing generator increased in volume, they walked a quarter mile uphill over the trail, which gradually became wider. At the top of the hill, they reached another gate, this one with a rusting cattle guard, that the man swung open.

As they proceeded, various structures took shape—a stone barn, a corral, an unpainted two-story house with a lightning rod pointing to the clouds, a windmill with a TV antenna in place of the fan and vanes, a variety of smaller buildings—all unpainted—and four trailer houses set in a circle around the large house like defense outposts.

Three dogs, gray and thick-chested, charged from behind a trailer, stopping at Bertie's feet. Visible through an upstairs window hung a Confederate flag, its red faded to pink. A fenderless Dodge pickup rested under a tree with its tires off, hood up and motor dangling by a chain from the stoutest limb.

Bertie's guide directed him to a building that must have once been a country schoolhouse, complete with a squat belfry. A boy in a dirty plaid shirt gaped wide-eyed from behind a cottonwood.

The inside of the building had been hollowed out all the way down to a dirt floor. Along one wall, three chest freezers sat on a platform side by side, their compressors humming.

Though the double-wide door and windows were open, an aroma of decay nearly overwhelmed Bertie. The light was poor, but in the center of the room a man in a baseball cap with the bill backward stood gutting a deer hanging from a hook attached to a sturdy tripod. A pile of guts, shiny and bloody-blue, lay at the side. On the floor by the door lay two more dead deer awaiting cleaning, their tongues protruding, their soft eyes half-lidded.

"Virgil?" Bertie's guide spoke above the sound of the compressor motors.

Butcher Virgil worked with his shirt off, exposing arms bloody to his broad shoulders. He glanced at Bertie and resumed his work. The knife he held in his left hand looked fearsomely large and sharp. The deer had been field-dressed, and Virgil was now removing skin and limbs, cutting the carcass into roasts and steaks. He functioned with great skill and deftness, slipping the knife deep inside the cavity and extracting the organs cleanly—the kidneys, the stomach, the intestines.

He wiped the knife blade on his pants and slid it into a sheath on his leather belt. He turned, exposing an upper torso of stringy muscles enclosed in a covering of sagging skin. "Go ahead. Talk."

Bertie swallowed, trying not to heed the stench and the pile of offal near his feet. "There's this Indian, Sam Morinville, he works for my mother." He waited, trying to judge the level of interest. "Anyhow, that's how it all got started." He paused again.

"What in particular got started?"

"Sam, I think he's bothering my sister. She's only fifteen." There. He got it out.

Virgil adjusted the bill of his cap. "In what manner?"

"What?"

"How's he bothering her?"

"You know. Sexually."

The older man lowered his jaw, exposing bare pink gums. "What's your name again?"

Bertie told him, wondering how many times he'd have to repeat it.

"Breen?"

"Yeah, like I told this other—"

"And your sister's name?"

"Victoria. Vickie, we call her."

"And that's your home by Dark Lake, the house with the weather vane. Place that needs painting."

"Well, yeah."

"And her age at her last birthday—fifteen, you say?"

"Vickie? Yes, fifteen," said Bertie, trying to tame his hopes.

With great deliberation, Virgil unsheathed his knife and held it to the light. "I'm about to enlighten you with my conclusion, Albert Breen," he said. "What I subscribe to is that you yourself are responsible for the molestation of your sister and now that she's missing her monthlies, you're jumping on the opportunity to put it on somebody else. Sam Morinville is as available as anyone."

"Oh no, that's not how it is," protested Bertie.

Virgil continued, ignoring Bertie's objection. "I don't know why you hoped for a solution by approaching us, but your responsibility is to tend to problems of your own creation."

He motioned to the man who'd escorted Bertie in. "Jeffrey. Escort Mr. Breen the hell out of here."

Still gripping the knife menacingly, he called to Bertie. "May I assume no one will be told of your visit?"

Wanting to preserve what dignity he still owned, Bertie ignored the warning. Needing no assistance, he pivoted on his heels and walked away, seeking to conceal his humiliation. Behind him, the generator hummed and the muted voices of the men took up their business. The air itself seemed undisturbed by Bertie's presence, as if reinforcing the insult that his best efforts made absolutely no difference to anyone or anything.

Just the same, he barely regretted making up the story he told Virgil Able. After all, this was a man who was no stranger to untruth. The real sin was that Bertie had likewise lied to himself. He had assumed he owned the right to create a fib about Vickie being in danger. Never mind that she was so capable of protecting herself that she marched around with a hammer tied to her belt. In the end, Bertie had foolishly counted on the Ables to put a stop to a problem that was never there in the first place.

The Ables saw what Bertie failed to recognize, and that's why they laughed him off the place. This was the price he had to pay for lying. Before he reached the main road, he realized that to keep on trying to fix things only created opportunities for more lies.

And for all his efforts, he'd accomplished nothing more than being thrown permanently off two different farms in less than forty-eight hours.

* * * * *

Two days later, Harold drove Bertie to Rugby so he could catch the train going west. As they crossed gushing Willow Creek south of Dunseith, it occurred to Bertie that there were no streams he could think of that ran through the hills of what used to be home. Everything flowed away and down. Of course, if someone wanted to follow a river, he could go just a few miles over to the Des Lacs, track it to the Souris, and then to the Assiniboine up in Canada. Or he might make his way down to the Missouri and ride it to the Mississippi and point south. It was all downstream, all going away. And like the rivers, for Bertie there was no going back.

# CONSEQUENCES

## 1 | What Girls Say

Vickie Breen, having been summoned from study hall with three others, all boys, waited on a metal chair adorned with the gold-and-purple Bulldog decal outside the principal's office. She sat for a good fifteen minutes. The door opened and out sulked Rodney Bergstrom, a kid from town who thought he was hot stuff because his dad owned the Ford garage. Only he didn't look so hot now, all white in the face from the bawling out he must have just gotten.

Behind him stood Mr. Hoffart, pointing at Vickie like she'd been chosen to come up on stage and get sawed in half.

"This is getting to be a habit, is it not?" said Mr. Hoffart after easing the door closed.

Vickie knew that such questions were not intended to be addressed. She waited mutely, her eyes fixed on the wooden floor where shallow grooves had formed beneath her feet from the endless line of delinquents who'd sat here before her.

"I'll get to the point," said the principal. "This isn't just about your repeated violations of the dress code or the opened pack of cigarettes found in your locker. It has to do with your behavior outside the school grounds." He paused, gauging whether his words were absorbed. The aroma of his cologne, *Old Spice* it was called, made Vickie's eyes water.

"You know to what I'm referring, don't you?"

Vickie speculated whether he thought she would be stupid enough to admit it if she did.

"No," she answered, trying on what she considered a convincing appearance of ignorance.

"I think you do," Mr. Hoffart said, tugging at a desk drawer that seemed to stick.

Vickie pondered whether he knew that the kids called him "Principal Who Farts." Probably. Grown-ups weren't as dumb as kids thought.

The drawer came open and he held up a block-lettered poster made with a red felt-tip pen proclaiming *GIRLS SAY YES TO BOYS WHO SAY NO*. It was decorated with a female stick figure with cone-shaped breasts batting her eyes at a long-haired boy peeking out from behind the letter *O*. Vickie regarded the poster with calculated interest. She'd drawn one of the boy's eyes larger than the other.

"You were seen tacking it up," said Mr. Hoffart. He turned the poster toward himself. "On good cardstock, too. I'm assuming it came from our art department."

He rolled the poster tightly in his hands. "It's not just what you did," he said, "but where you chose to place it—the door outside the Selective Service office." He sighed as if to let his statement sink in.

"And do you know who brought it to my attention?" He didn't wait for an answer. "Max Plummer. In case you aren't aware, he happens to be president of the school board."

The principal was a frail, sharp-featured man whose attire never fit him right. A standard crew cut that went out of style in the late fifties allowed a shiny bald spot to show through his thin hair.

"Do you believe that acts like this are clever—encouraging the breaking of the law? Let me explain something. Yes, our country allows for free expression, but in practice this is necessarily overridden by community standards. What is acceptable in Berkeley is unsatisfactory in Rolland."

Vickie ached to point out the paradox, but Hoffart, with his bony hands flying all about and his narrow face reddening, would not be willing to argue the point.

"Mr. Plummer and other board members have let it be known that actions of your kind are improper and offensive. It's my job as an administrator to see that their decisions are complied with."

He paused to let his words sink in.

"From this point on, you will refrain from manufacturing public displays such as this sign. You are furthermore ordered to cease speech or actions that demean our government or cast aspersions upon your school."

Not fully understanding, Vickie began, "But how—"

At once, Mr. Hoffart's hand shot up in a *stop* gesture. "You are a smart young lady. You will know what actions are out-of-bounds."

Forced to acknowledge that such a statement was true, Vickie also knew there was nothing in the way of penalty that would make much difference. Mr. Principal Who Farts could write letters till his hand broke off and it would make no difference to how well she slept at night. Just the same, she reasoned that out of pride she should allow herself a mild protest. "Do you mean I'm not even supposed to say my opinion like in civics class?"

Mr. Hoffart was ready for such a question. "Mr. Peterson tells me that, rather than participating, you habitually dominate discussions, allowing no one else to speak or disagree."

This example amused Vickie. In truth, most of those brainwashed students didn't know civics from Christmas tree tinsel.

Mr. Hoffart went on. "Now, I must inform you that in the event of violation of this policy, there will be consequences."

*Consequences.* The word had not been used before. The principal's tone of voice was distant, more reasoned. Rather than expressing anger like before, he had assumed an air of confidence, as if he had thought this all out previously.

He slid his ballpoint pen from his breast pocket and studied it for an endless minute as if it might display the words he'd been searching for. "What you may not know is that in extreme cases administration has the right to apply chastisements beyond the standards set out in the code of conduct."

Vickie unconsciously sat up straighter in her chair.

Mr. Hoffart lifted his chin, a gesture flaunting his power. "In legal terms, it means letting the punishment fit the crime. The potential gradations, to be effective, must be such that the student is forced to take them seriously. A common practice might be the loss of privilege. For example, a football player seen drinking or violating laws beyond school policy may lose the right to participate."

Vickie frowned, not yet connecting the illustration to herself.

"In case you're in doubt, this would apply to all extracurricular activities." The principal waited for a retort.

"Mr. Wenslas is of the belief that you are developing into quite a talented violinist," he said.

With that, Vickie grasped what was coming.

"The arrangement in this particular instance means that if you conform to established standards you'll be allowed to continue with music, which, incidentally, is the single subject in which you're demonstrating above-average grades." His eyes brightened.

*He's enjoying this,* thought Vickie. *He must hate me.* She hated him in return.

"If you violate the directive," he went on, comfortably in control now, "your name will be deleted from the list of those eligible to participate in band or orchestra functions. That includes rehearsals, concerts and competitions, as well as a probable trip to Minneapolis in the spring to perform at the Midwest regional competitions."

Vickie could not hold back a sudden sob. Nothing in life brought her joy like touching the bow to the strings of a perfectly tuned violin.

But the principal wasn't through. "I shouldn't need to remind you that the instrument you use is the property of the school district. It was purchased for your benefit at the request of Mr. Wenslas with discretionary funds, which the board monitors closely."

Vickie listened to this gibberish, which she'd heard several times before.

"Therefore," said the principal, "if your name does not appear on rosters of Mr. Wenslas's music classes, you won't have permission to use the violin."

"That's no fair," cried Vickie, thrusting herself forward in her chair. "Mr. Wenslas wants me to practice every day. He told me I was the best violinist he ever had." Stopping for breath, she could see the man wasn't budged.

Hoffart adjusted his suit coat where it had slid off his shoulder. "Victoria," he said, speaking slower. "Please appreciate the gravity of the situation. You're fortunate Mr. Plummer didn't haul you in here by the ear. He wanted you expelled on the spot."

Not only did Vickie doubt that statement but she despised Mr. Hoffart further for trying to make himself sound like a hero. "That's so mean," she said, knowing she must sound like a five year old. "Punishing me for something that doesn't have to do with school."

"Mean it might be," said Mr. Hoffart. "But bear in mind it hasn't transpired yet. Again, it won't have to. No more politicking, in particular no actions that suggest resistance or defiance toward lawful decisions made by duly elected officials at all levels of government. You're clear on that?"

Now she was crying. She nodded through her tears.

"I repeat. You will adhere strictly to the school policy, including but not restricted to dress, speech and respect. No more upside-down flags sewn on your apparel, no more jeans or slacks, no smoking, no foul language, no scuffling in classrooms or hallways, no displays of disrespect to teachers or administrators such as interrupting, creating a spectacle or otherwise interfering with decorum and proper order."

Vickie's nose was running. A box of Kleenex rested on Mr. Hoffart's desk, but Vickie didn't dare ask for it.

"You may consider this session as your first warning," said Mr. Hoffart. "There will be no second."

With that, he took a paper from his desk and made a slow, deliberate mark on the bottom with his pen. "Now, do you have any questions?"

As he waited for a response, he clicked his Paper Mate deliberately with his thumb.

"No," she said, wiping her nose with her hand.

"Well, I have a question for you," said Mr. Hoffart.

Vickie looked up.

"I know you have a brother in the armed forces. How do you think he feels about your attitude?"

Vickie swallowed, gathering herself. "May I have a Kleenex?" she asked. Mr. Hoffart handed her the box. She pulled several out, one by one, and wiped her eyes and face.

"My brother only joined the army because Sam Morinville cheated us out of our farm," she said. "He had nowhere else to go. He was forced into it just like you are forcing me to do stuff I don't like and to be a person I don't care to be."

With that, she handed the principal the box of tissues and rose from her chair.

"You haven't been dismissed yet," said the principal.

Vickie glanced at him, wanting to speak, but thought better of it and walked out, leaving the door open behind her.

## 2 | Memories of Cabbage

Bertie had never been much of a letter writer, but lately his messages became more frequent and lengthier. When he joined the army, he spoke well of the roof-over and the three squares a day. But after being sent to faraway Vietnam, he painted a more truthful picture of army life—nights without sleep, unending rain and the misery of humping through bamboo and elephant grass with a full rucksack, always wondering when you might step on a snake or have to hit the deck to avoid Charlie's potshots.

Then lately, maybe because his remaining time in the war zone was being measured in weeks, his messages took on a happier tone. One recent letter in which he spoke of specifics for a hopeful future was Vickie's favorite. Written with a ballpoint that was evidently running dry, for some words could be made out only by straining to see the groove the dry ball made in the paper, he promised that when he got home they would first find a way to get the farm back from Sam and send him away forever. They would then seek help for their mother, maybe take her to the Mayo Clinic over in Minnesota. Finally, they would begin setting money aside for Vickie to go to college to study music.

Unusual for him, he talked of how much he missed her and the life they had on the farm, reminding her of the happy moments they enjoyed even after Sam came along and Mama became sicker. He spoke of their favorite summertime foods—corn on the cob, fresh tomatoes, fried cabbage. He remembered the cool fall evenings listening to Vickie play her violin. He said that when he couldn't sleep or was out on patrol, he could hear her play "Morning Has Broken," and it made him feel at peace.

She smiled at the memory. That was an easy piece. She couldn't wait for him to hear her play now.

With that in mind, she decided not to tell Bertie about Mr. Hoffart's dire warnings that if she wanted to continue playing the violin, she would have to go along with rules that made no sense. Although she knew that Bertie would be proud of her, she did not want to have him return to find her in disgrace. She would do what they wanted, at least for a while.

She began by asking Leah Peavey if she would make some not-too-fancy school outfits on her sewing machine. In addition to spending yet more time on violin practice, Vickie started bringing books home. Although it enraged her to hear hateful remarks about dropping atom bombs on the enemy, she turned away or bit her lower lip to hush herself. And one Friday afternoon when the entire student body was herded into the gym for lyceum preceded by the singing of the national anthem, rather than slouching and gazing indifferently around, she stood straight with her hand over her heart, though she only mouthed the words.

She was surprised one day to see Rodney Bergstrom catch her eye on the way out of civics class.

"You got a second?" he said.

She was unsure of herself—this was her first time wearing the plaid jumper and blouse that Leah had stitched for her. "I guess so."

"I was thinking maybe if you want to go to the homecoming dance we could go together," he said, nervously tapping his geometry textbook against the side of his leg.

Vickie had never been on a single date and never believed a boy would admit interest in her, let alone a boy from town, one who was popular and from a rich family.

"I don't know. I guess so," she said, uneasy.

"OK then," said Rodney, smiling, the silvery braces on his teeth glinting in the artificial light. Then the bell rang and he was off to his next class while Vickie desperately tried to remember the combination to her locker.

\* \* \* \* \*

That afternoon, as usual for a Friday, Vickie got off the bus at the Peavey farm. Naturally, she told Leah about the invitation to the dance, trying to minimize her excitement. Driving Vickie home later, Leah chattered excitedly about the dress she would make for the dance, but only if she had time, since Richie Lee was due home from his basic training in ten days.

As she listened, picturing herself in formal wear, Vickie couldn't help but wonder—what did Rodney or anyone see in her that would make them want to take her anywhere? Her unstylish hair was trimmed so short it barely covered her saucer ears. Red acne marks spotted her forehead. If only she were tall like her brother and mother, but she barely topped five feet. Worse, she knew at school people thought of her as weird—this sawed-off girl from the bush who looked like a boy and sounded like one of those Communists we were fighting. She even knew what she was called behind her back—"Bitchy Vickie."

Not that anyone would mistake Rodney for Steve McQueen. But who could tell about boys? Anyway, if Vickie was to change, going on dates was certainly an inevitable part of it. As Leah prattled on, Vickie began seeing herself in a light blue taffeta dress, her hair combed out, maybe even wearing fingernail polish.

By the end of the next week, however, Rodney had made no effort to contact her since the brief meeting in the hallway. She'd sighted him a few times standing with his pals as they poked one another, laughed seemingly over nothing and created fart sounds with their mouths.

Her worries were not eased after world history class when a boy's voice sounded from behind her. "Hey, BV, wait up."

She wheeled around. Doug Voltmer and Danny Ingebretson were walking in lockstep toward her. "What did you call me?" she asked.

Ignoring the question, Danny, the taller of the two, said they had a question. "We heard you're going to homecoming with Bergie. Is it true?"

She looked from one to the other. Why would they want to know? "If that's what he told you."

"Good. Thanks, Vickie," said Danny.

"Yeah, thanks," said Doug, grinning and elbowing his companion in the ribs.

*God,* thought Vickie as the two hurried away, guffawing. *Just what is the matter with boys anyhow?*

## 3 | A Weary Farmhouse

Leah Peavey changed the sheets and finished cleaning Richie Lee's bedroom in anticipation of his return home. As she looped the cord around the handle of the vacuum, she tried to imagine what he would be like when he emerged from the train. Not that he could change much in six weeks, but a mother would see differences that extended beyond the shaved military-looking haircut and the crisp uniform with the sewed-on stripe. For one thing, he'd be slimmer. For another, he'd project an air of maturity with that detached look in his eyes that soldiers take on after a while.

Hoping Harold might have finished his business in town early so he could change the flat on the Plymouth for her before she went to town, she glanced out the window toward the east, and then west toward the Morinvilles. A strange sedan had pulled off the highway and was rolling toward their farmhouse. While various vehicles driven by nurses, social workers and the like kept coming and going ever since old man Morinville had been permanently bedridden from the accident in his grain bin, this one looked different—cleaner and cautiously driven. She grabbed the binoculars from the hook by the window and trained them on the car. Two men occupied the vehicle, the driver and a passenger, both wearing military-style hats, sitting erect and staring directly ahead. A small blue flag of some kind was mounted on the front fender. She let the binoculars fall against her stomach.

*Oh, dear god, no!*

Something had happened to Richie Lee—she knew it. The officers must be trying to deliver notification but got the wrong place.

But no, the terrifying thought eased as the car came to a stop. Both mailboxes were clearly marked with the family names, and they'd never make such a mistake in something like that.

For an unreasonable instant, Leah concluded—even hoped, she was ashamed to admit, since she rather liked what she knew of the boy—that the men were bringing news concerning Casey, the Morinville son, who was also planning to go into the service.

But she wasn't thinking straight, for that made no sense either—Casey hadn't left home yet. Following a pause during which the men looked to be in conference, one of them, the passenger, got out and knocked on the Morinville door. It was answered at once by Mrs. Morinville, who spoke briefly and seemed to point in various directions before closing the door, renewing Leah's worries.

Yet the impossibly slow sedan, rather than reversing its course over the brief distance to the Peavey place, commenced west and soon disappeared over the hill. Leah waited, frozen in place, for the sedan to turn around. But it did not. The dust on the road settled and the peace of the countryside returned.

Bursting with curiosity and dread, she hurried across the ditch and around the fence separating the properties and knocked on her neighbors' door, not so loud as to sound bossy but strong enough to be heard.

Mrs. Morinville opened it at once. From the porch, Leah could see into the living room, where a metal contraption hung over the bed where Mr. Morinville lay. The smell of disinfectant and sickness permeated the air.

"I'm sorry to bother you," said Leah. "I couldn't help but notice. What did those men want?"

"They wouldn't say exactly," said Mrs. Morinville, looking off in the direction the car had vanished. "Just how to get to the Breens."

Leah gazed toward the empty highway. "Breens? You don't think…"

"Why else would the army send someone out here?"

Each woman, a mother of a soon-to-be soldier, turned her eyes to the other, seeking reassurance and finding comfort in the fleeting exchange.

"Oh, lord," said Leah. She leaned closer to see the man's watch on Mrs. Morinville's wrist, trying to read it upside down. Two hours remained before school let out.

"I hate to ask," she said. "The car's laid up and Harold's gone with the truck. Is there any way you could take me on over to Breens?"

"Of course."

On the way, the women spoke amicably, as if under the crisis, rules imposed by old animosities were suspended. They talked about wheat crops, rain, the scarcity of chokecherries and much else except what their purpose was in bouncing along in the Morinville's ancient pickup at twenty-five miles an hour.

Then, oddly, Mrs. Morinville changed the topic. "I haven't seen Sam in over a year," she said.

Leah struggled for a moment, searching for a neutral response. "Is that so?"

"He's never even been to visit Etienne," said Mrs. Morinville. "Once in a while I see him go by on the way to town. But he never stops."

They turned in at the washboard road leading up to the Breen house, still marked by its prominent rooster weather vane. The government car, parked a respectable distance from the house, had been turned around so as to face the highway. Mrs. Morinville steered her pickup toward a hillock by the barn, wanting to avoid coming between the house and the government car.

Leah perceived Mrs. Morinville's hesitation after she shut the engine down. "Come in with me please. I'd appreciate it."

Sam Morinville apparently spotted their vehicle, for he stood waiting inside the porch door. Ignoring Leah, he acknowledged his mother with his eyes down and a brief, mumbled, "Hello."

The two officers sat on the couch in identical positions, feet flat on the floor, shoulders back, hands resting on their laps. Fawn Breen occupied the easy chair, her head lolling back and slightly to one side, knees spread obscenely, a bunched-up blanket resting on her lap.

At the sight of the visitors, the officers came to their feet in unison and turned toward the women, alert but not quite at attention. The closer officer spoke first, lowering and then raising his chin ever so slightly to introduce himself and his companion. Leah couldn't catch their names, which were buried in a gush of words that included their ranks, occupations in the army and where they were stationed.

The one doing the speaking, who Leah realized was a chaplain, looked much older than the other. "May I assume you've ascertained our purpose here today?" he asked.

"It's about Bertie?" said Leah, though the officer had directed his question toward Mrs. Morinville, perhaps because she was the older lady.

He turned to Leah. "Yes, ma'am. It concerns Specialist Albert Breen."

"What?" demanded Leah, glancing toward Mrs. Morinville for encouragement.

The officer locked eyes with her for a long second. "It is a sad duty fallen upon us to report that your loved one has been killed in action. We hope it may comfort you to know that Albert was an exemplary soldier, loved by all with whom he came in contact. Major Eisley and I offer our sincerest condolences."

Leah glanced at Fawn, whose eyes were fixed on the chaplain though she had not altered her position on the chair nor displayed any comprehension of the officer's words. "Thank you," said Leah.

Major Eisley spoke. "May I inquire if the two of you are relatives?"

"I'm distantly related," said Leah. "Mrs. Morinville is a neighbor."

"I'm related too," said Mrs. Morinville. "By marriage. Albert would be my stepgrandson."

Leah turned her head toward Mrs. Morinville. Leah, though she knew that the statement was technically true, felt jarred out of the exchange.

The major, maybe sensing an awkwardness, asserted control at once, producing a small bundle of forms that he'd concealed somewhere in his unwieldy uniform. This acted as the cue for everyone to find a seat, and he set about going over the duties and responsibilities of the army that would include but not be limited to arranging for the service, helping file claims, notifying other relatives, placing the obituary in appropriate newspapers and so on. He went on to promise that he and Chaplain Thompson would be in the area for two more days, and that they would remain in close touch for any assistance required by the family.

At this point, Leah saw fit to interrupt. "Sir," she said, looking from one to the other. "What about his sister, Vickie? Is anyone seeing to her? She's in school."

"It's being attended to, we assure you," responded the major, speaking in precise, complete sentences. "We've been in contact with the school and expect her arrival soon. But thank you for bringing it up."

As the conversation ended, Fawn pulled herself out of her chair and shuffled toward the bathroom, making no effort to hold her bathrobe in place.

As they waited for her return, Leah formed impressions that would remain with her. The officers, for instance, how they contrasted with the shabby furniture and dirty windows, so unsoiled they looked, like they'd been dry-cleaned right along with their stiff, brown uniforms. Sam had taken on a confused, restless demeanor, as if feeling he'd been brought here to say or do something, though he had no hint of what. Of all the occupants in the ancient, weary farmhouse, only Ida Florence Morinville held herself unruffled, a dignified expression of serenity and acceptance on her face as she listened to the officers. Once, briefly, she extended a hand and patted Leah on the thigh, offering both silent consolation and encouragement.

But above all, Leah came to grasp that this scene might be repeated in her own home. Many of the same people—perhaps even the same notification officers—might gather one day in her living room. She could picture Harold in his chair, speaking only a bare minimum of words, his knees crossed, hands clasped, his gray face an unreadable mask. In time, he would modify the static arrangement of molecules in his mind and arrive at some level of acceptable tolerance. But would she?

After several minutes, Fawn had not come out. Leah, seated closest to the bathroom, kept her ears tuned for the sound of flushing. The officers maintained their stoic faces. Two more minutes passed before she got up, stepped to the bathroom door and tapped on it. "Fawn?"

She opened the door just a crack and called again before pulling it wider and noticing the open window. "She's not in there," she said.

Sam, the only person familiar with Fawn's habit of disappearing, turned to his mother. "See what she does? She took off again."

Hoping Sam could deal with the officers, Ida Florence and Leah hurried outside and spotted Fawn nearly out of sight, her long steps carrying her across the stubble field heading north. Ida Florence reached her first. With Leah's help, she got her back to the house, where they tried to talk her into lying down. She would have none of it and folded her lean form into the chair, where she stayed put, her pallid, almost bloodless face emotionless.

\* \* \* \* \*

Vickie was upset for allowing herself to become distracted. She loved it when she reached what she thought of as her *drift*—the mood or state she reached when her fingers moved with their own will and the bow rested so lightly on the strings, teasing them as if tickling someone with a feather. The notes became abstract—black marks on white paper.

But this afternoon in the music room, that state eluded her. Maybe it was because she always had difficulty with a Vivaldi. She refused to accept the possibility that she was upset because Rodney had yet to follow up with plans for the dance. She would put the piece aside and practice fingered octaves. Wanting to check the tuning first, she scooted her chair toward the piano and reached for the A key. Just then, Mr. Wenslas interrupted her—something that rarely happened.

"Mr. Hoffart needs to see you," he said.

Vickie scowled and set the violin on its stand.

She reached the door just as it opened and Mr. Hoffart entered. At least she wouldn't have to go to his office.

"There's been an emergency at home," he said. "Mr. Kenny will drive you there."

"My home? What kind of emergency? Is it my mother?"

"I don't believe so, but I don't have the details. Mr. Kenny will meet you by the shop door."

She went back to pack the violin and bow and found that Mr. Wenslas had already done so. He handed it to her wordlessly. She stopped at her locker to pick up her books and sweater, wishing she'd taken the chance to speak with Rodney earlier.

Mr. Kenny waited in his big blue car with the engine running. A number of teachers owned Volkswagens or Chevrolet sedans, but even Vickie, though she was uninterested in cars, knew Mr. Kenny drove a Pontiac GTO, a model much admired by most of the boys as well as several girls, more than a few of whom also admired Mr. Kenny himself.

Being alone in the car with the teacher was difficult. She took no classes from Mr. Kenny and barely knew him. She was relieved when, a couple miles out of town, he turned on the car radio, which was tuned to one of the Winnipeg stations.

"Winnipeg," he said, as if replying to a question. "I wonder what it's like to live up there." He gazed past the hills to the north.

"It's nice, I think," said Vickie.

Emboldened by that meaningless snippet of conversation, she asked Mr. Kenny if he knew what the emergency was.

"Sorry," he said. "They only asked me if I'd drive a student home. They usually send someone who doesn't have a class, and that was me. We had to cancel biology lab because a pipe broke."

Though she should have expected he'd avoid an answer, Vickie wanted to try again, believing that Mr. Kenny must know something. "My mother gets sick often. Do you think she's gotten worse?"

Mr. Kenny slowed before passing a grain truck. "I have no way of knowing, but if something like that were the case, don't you think they'd bring her in to the hospital?"

"I suppose so. Maybe Sam had some kind of accident."

"Sam?"

"He works on the farm." Vickie immediately wished she'd let it drop with her mother. As always, she was never going to admit that Sam was married to Mama or that he was prone to accidents when he was drunk. Like when he got the combine wedged into the barn door or the time he neglected to secure the gate and it took a whole day to round up the cows.

Only when they were a mile from home did a different thought, one which she'd pushed from her mind like a tiresome song, hit her.

"I wonder if it has something to do with Bertie," she said aloud.

"Who?"

"Bertie, my brother. He's a soldier in Vietnam."

"Oh, I hope not," said Mr. Kenny.

He turned the radio off, a trifling act, but one that deepened Vickie's worry. It was like he was preparing her for the proper mood to fit the bad news that was about to come.

"You'll have to tell me where to turn," he said.

Vickie spotted the strange car first, a long black sedan with a sheen of dust on it from the gravel road. Parked farther away from the house was a beat-up pickup that looked like the one the Morinvilles owned.

Mr. Kenny must have taken some meaning from the situation, for he couldn't seem to get away fast enough, wheeling around in the driveway the second Vickie exited the car.

She looked around, seeing the cows in the pasture. Ordinarily, they'd be brought in the barn for milking by this time of day.

She entered quietly, walking through the kitchen to the living room, where six faces turned toward her. The soldiers sprang to their full height. Mama sat wrapped in a blanket and barely stirred except to whimper like a child in a light sleep, looking as bloodless and unhealthy as always. Sam seemed to want no part of the scene, lingering behind and staring out the window. Mrs. Morinville struggled to heave herself up from the armless folding chair that she occupied.

Leah approached her, arms spreading. That told her all she needed to know for the time being.

Leah later said she would never forget Vickie's first words. "How come nobody had the sense to at least make coffee?"

* * * * *

At first, she hated the soldiers. It was like they themselves killed Bertie. After all, they could have been the ones fighting, allowing Bertie to remain out of harm's way. One of them was a chaplain, a man of God supposedly. How come he was involved with an organization whose purpose was to kill God's children?

But they were friendly and not at all like the men who marched in parades with rifles on their shoulders and scowls on their faces. They gave the impression of being in no hurry to leave. Vickie couldn't have faulted them if she'd wanted to.

Not long after Vickie's arrival, Mrs. Morinville said she had to get back home to tend to her husband. Leah said she'd stay and have Harold pick her up later. Sam used the departure of his mother as an excuse to go out and start the chores. Leah took Fawn to rest, leaving Vickie with the soldiers. Studying their sympathetic faces, she realized that they were the closest people available that could tell her about what happened to her brother.

"Could I ask you some questions?" she said hesitantly, unaware and uncaring about proper procedure.

"That's part of why we are here," said the chaplain.

First, she wanted to know how long ago Bertie died.

They advised her that it had been ten days.

She counted back in her mind. That would have been a Tuesday. She tried but could not come up with exactly what she had done that day, only that she had no recollection of it being a day distinguished in any way.

"How exactly was he killed?" she asked.

They answered that he died honorably in combat.

"No, I mean did the enemies shoot him or what?"

The officer on her left, the major, not the chaplain, was quick to respond. "Albert died heroically. He didn't suffer."

"Was either one of you there?"

"No, ma'am, we weren't, no," said the major. "But we've both served in Vietnam in the past, if that's what you're curious about. And we have studied the full report on the…" He paused.

"The circumstances," offered Vickie.

"Yes, the circumstances. Thank you."

"Then what were the circumstances?"

The chaplain, wanting to help, cut in. "We've communicated directly with the commanding officer of your brother's squad. He's in his second tour now. An outstanding officer. He spoke highly of Albert's bravery."

"Then he was there when Bertie died?"

"That's correct."

"What did he say exactly, about Bertie?"

"He remarked on your brother's valor and is recommending a medal."

"Yes, but did he say how he died?"

"Only that he didn't suffer. He'd have felt nothing."

*They always say that,* thought Vickie. If you thought it over well, it seemed impossible that you could go from being strong and healthy and talking and digesting your food and breathing to being nothing as fast as a light goes out when you turn the switch.

"Did it happen in a fight with shooting back and forth?"

"It was a nighttime ambush," said the major.

Vickie thought about that, trying to picture it.

"Were they in the jungle?"

"The official report states that it occurred near a village."

"Is the village in a jungle?"

"The terrain varies," said the major, who was providing all the information now.

"What's the name of the village?"

The major reached for the briefcase between his shiny shoes. He flipped through several papers, pursed his lips and looked up. "We will get you that information as soon as we can."

"The officer. Was he close by when Bertie died?"

"Yes, that's a reasonable assumption. You understand that a battlefield is a place of chaos."

"Can I know the officer's name?" said Vickie.

Again, the major reached into his briefcase, but before he could come up with an answer, the chaplain broke in. "That would be Lieutenant Lewis."

"Lewis?"

"Gregory P. Lewis."

"Were there other soldiers that got killed?"

"Two others, yes, unfortunately. And four wounded."

Vickie measured this for a minute or two. "What kind of wounds?"

The major shifted forward on the couch, trying to get more comfortable. "You are a most curious young lady," he said.

"I want to know how my brother died," said Vickie, her eyes glued on the major.

The major glanced at the chaplain. "Of course. It was a mortar attack. You recognize what that involves?"

"Like grenades?"

"Right. Only more powerful. It was a direct hit. All the victims had multiple, grave injuries."

That detail stifled Vickie momentarily.

"How did they take him away?"

"Operating procedures call for helicopter evacuation when and where it's safe to land. There was some delay while the area was cleared."

"Where is he now?"

"Your brother is on the way home. The aircraft carrying him would have landed in Delaware this morning. From there he'll be put on a train accompanied by an honor guard."

"I want to see him."

"We very much advise against that," said the chaplain.

"Why?"

"The unfortunate reality is that disfigurement happens in battle casualties. Just the same, I assure you that remains are handled with great respect. I can tell you that most families who are granted permission to view their loved ones come to regret it in time."

Vickie chose not to pursue her request just then. She could tell by their words that she could have her way if she tried.

\* \* \* \* \*

For the remainder of the weekend, people came and went. They brought food, mostly hamburger casseroles or large still-steaming pots of macaroni and Velveeta. Sam stayed out of sight, especially when his mother and brother, Casey, visited. The officers returned but not for long. True to their word, they had looked up the name of the village near the battle: Lai San. Leah stayed all day Saturday and spent most of the time cleaning the house.

As the weekend passed, Vickie tired of car doors slamming, constant rapping at the door, timid visitors in Sunday garb saying the same thing, heads bowed slightly. Why did people in mourning always look older, wrinklier, and have watery eyes, like they themselves were all set for the grave?

\* \* \* \* \*

By Sunday night, she knew where she wanted to go and how to make up for what had happened. When the house was at last clear of visitors, she went to her room and studied the dress patterns Leah had given her to choose from. At first, she'd selected three she liked best. Now they all looked more or less the same. Modest, below the knee, offering little of interest, designed to convey an impression of innocence and sweet fakery. She wadded them into a ball. Homecoming? She didn't even know how to dance. Rodney Bergstrom, a rich kid who wore his greasy black hair swept back like Elvis and picked his nose in study hall—how small of her to think that such a person counted for anything.

She opened the violin case and lifted the instrument out carefully. She loosened the strings so that they rested just above the fingerboard. With a clean chamois she wiped the body until light reflected through the two layers of walnut varnish. Finally, she replaced it in the velvet case that always reminded her so much of a coffin. In the morning, she would take it over to Leah and ask her to see that it was returned to the school.

# SOMETHING TO LOOK FORWARD TO

### 1 | Who Didn't Like Butter?

"I can't hear you," said Drill Instructor Sgt. Peter Axelee. Fine droplets of spit flew out of his mouth, gleaming in the hot sun.

"*Yes*, Drill Sergeant!" screamed Private Peavey.

"I still can't hear you!" shouted the DI, pitching forward from the waist.

Richie Lee tried again, aware of how his puny voice was swallowed by the croaky bass of the DI. "Yes, Drill Sergeant."

"That's piss-poor. Give me twenty," said the DI.

Richie Lee dropped to all fours and completed the push-ups.

"On your feet, Cheesedick," said Axelee. Richie Lee stood, trying to roll his shoulders back.

"I gave you an order. What do you say when you hear an order?"

"Yes, Drill Sergeant," said Richie Lee.

"Louder."

"Yes, Drill Sergeant."

"Now get down and beat your face for twenty more on account of being the A-one shitbird in the unit."

"Yes, Drill Sergeant."

\* \* \* \* \*

*If I'd only known,* thought Richie Lee Peavey.

He'd talked his parents into letting him sign up for the army in return for an early release from reform school—a place that seemed like paradise now. On top of that, he'd been allowed a year of freedom to do whatever he wanted. He'd considered working for wages part of the year and then allowing himself some traveling, maybe out to California to check out the ganja and flower girls. But he ran into snags, including a citation for driving under the influence following a car accident that totaled the family's station wagon and an incident with an underage girl in which the charges were dismissed when the judge was advised that Richie Lee had pledged to join the armed services.

Now he was at Fort Sill in the third week of basic training, being introduced to the value of endless push-ups on the quad in the Oklahoma heat. To make it worse, he could tell by this early point that most of the Joes hated him. He had—or used to have—only two friends. One was Bengston, a fat, stuttering kid from Minnesota who was scared of everything—guns, spiders, thunder and lightning, girls. Why the army took him was a mystery. As with Richie Lee, the DI hated Bengston, calling him "lard-ass" and making him do push-ups until he collapsed.

Bengston only lasted twelve days. That was when combat training started and the recruits loaded their M16s with live ammo and shot at plywood cutouts shaped like enemy soldiers. After a predetermined number of rounds, each squad knelt low in a trench dug behind the row of cutouts to allow them to get the feel of bullets zinging over their heads. Bengston found this terrifying and would slide his hands under his helmet to shield his ears.

The day it happened, the squad took their turn in the trench behind the targets with Richie Lee at one end and Bengston at the other. Richie Lee lay there smelling the cordite, which made him think of the duck blind back home, and waited for the roar of a dozen M16s going off at once. The command rang out: "Ready! Aim! Fire!"

The noise and smoke ended with recruits screaming and crying, "Medic!" One guy, a lanky kid from Ohio, came running toward Richie Lee, puking his guts out.

Bengston had either gone total yahoo or misheard the commands and stood up at the worst time—the army classified it as a suicide while the young man's parents claimed otherwise. Either way, he was dead. So now Richie Lee felt more alone and isolated than ever. His only remaining friend—if he could be called that—among the thousands on base was his bunkmate, Spec-4 Marquis, a kid from some big-city shithole ghetto back east. Marquis was a quiet, sullen, untrusting guy. Richie Lee figured that rather than actually enjoying his company, Marquis only tolerated it, owing to the fact that he was black and believed that Richie Lee never really knew how it was. But they were bunkmates and they'd have to get along for at least a few more weeks.

\* \* \* \* \*

They'd barely cleaned out Bengston's locker and dug the bloody mud out of the trench when word came that Richie Lee's distant cousin Bertie was KIA in Vietnam. He'd come to attention before the lieutenant in the CO's office, who ordered him to stand at ease after he delivered the news.

"Was the deceased an immediate relative?" asked the blue-eyed, scrawny lieutenant, who must have been one of those ROTC types that the army was accepting now.

Richie Lee thought a minute. "A cousin, sort of."

"A cousin? In that case, you won't be given leave to attend services," said the lieutenant. "You will be excused from duty for the remainder of the day with a strong recommendation that you visit the base chaplain. You know where he's located, right?"

"Yes, Sir," said Richie Lee, taking by the tone of his superior's voice that he should come to attention and salute.

"Very good. On behalf of the commander in chief, I express the army's condolences. That will be all."

\* \* \* \* \*

After allowing ten wasted minutes for the chaplain to appear, Richie Lee walked back to the barracks, where he stretched out on his less than perfectly made cot and stared at the ceiling with his hands folded behind his head. It felt weird to have nothing to do. He tried to sleep, but the shouting outside, the distant roar of gunfire and the constant clatter, so unlike the stillness of the farm, kept him awake. He tried to think. Bertie got killed. He should feel sad, but he could never quite forget that Bertie had let him down after he'd managed to escape from reform school. His thoughts drifted from Bertie to his bunkmate, Marquis.

Marquis Jackson, a slow-to-speak, muscular black from Camden, New Jersey, was one of those guys who calculated how much to do to get by. He was the envy of many in the squad if for no other reason than he clearly didn't give a shit. He maintained his boots with barely enough of a shine to prove that he did something to them, and that something was better than nothing. He reacted to commands with a delayed, slurring "yah-sir" that, in the strictest sense, indicated compliance while maintaining self-respect. And standing supposedly at attention, he took on a slight slouch as precise as the pose of a ballet dancer.

He also owned a little Philco cassette player that he concealed under his mattress. When he got high he liked to listen to Coltrane or Jimi. Occasionally, he put on Dylan. The device was strictly non-reg, but nobody mentioned it because how do you punish a guy who doesn't care what happens to him?

\* \* \* \* \*

Two weeks following the news about Bertie, Richie Lee was surprised by a letter from his dad, only the second that he could recall ever receiving. He lay on the bunk slowly reading it while Marquis rested on his rack, humming to himself.

*Dear Son Richie Lee,*

*Sometimes the best mark of a man is to let out that he was wrong. What I did way back I'm not ashamed of. I was younger and that was how I felt about things. But what happened to Bertie Breen got me thinking. He went on his own steam and did what he figured was right and I don't have to tell you that going off to war is a lot tougher now than back in my time. That's why I'm proud of you for sticking with it and now I wish I hadn't tried to stand in your way. I don't believe in war but there's another matter and that's got to do with keeping a promise. You agreed to something and now you got to pay it back. That's the sign of a good man. That's about all I got to say except me and your mother are looking forward to seeing you when you're done down there in Texas.*

*Your dad*

Richie Lee couldn't help but smile. His dad was so backward he didn't even know that Fort Sill was in Oklahoma. When finished, he flopped over on the bunk and pounded his pillow a couple times.

"Marquis," he said. "Ain't you afraid of getting killed?"

"Shee-it," answered Marquis, his standard reply to half the comments addressed to him.

"Guys are getting it every day," said Richie Lee. "I know two already if you count Bengston. What scares me is things happen in threes."

Marquis made no response. Maybe he'd never heard of that fact.

"I shouldn't even be here, you know," said Richie Lee. "It was supposed to be a choice, but it really wasn't." Richie Lee knew that was mixed-up reasoning, but blame had to be given.

Marquis was smoking a joint. He offered it to Richie Lee, who declined, planning to roll his own blunt later.

"What do you think the chances are that they'll send us to 'Nam?" asked Richie Lee.

Marquis rolled toward him. "They ever give you a choice of Jersey or Vietnam, you take 'Nam."

Richie Lee thought about that, trying to picture enemies shooting at you when you drove to the store for a bottle of milk. "You know, I heard that if you score good in basic, they might keep you stateside and have you be an instructor."

Marquis broke into a coughing fit that ended with a high-pitched cackle.

"What's funny?"

"How you gon' teach sumpin' you never even learned your own self yet?"

"It's only because Axelee hates me," said Richie Lee. "He won't be there when we go for AIT."

Marquis grunted something Richie Lee couldn't catch before reaching beneath his mattress for his music player. Richie Lee waited until he loaded the tape he wanted.

"Marquis, what's it like over there? Is it what they say?"

"Shee-it."

"No, really."

"Like I tol' you, Vietnam be no worse than East Camden. Besides, I hear green's cheap."

"Sometimes I even think about going over the hill. Do you ever?"

Marquis answered with a cackle.

"What's so funny now?"

"You. You so fucked up you probably run the wrong way and end up in Havana, Cuba and think you home free."

"No. Really. You think you could skip?"

"A brother don't do that. They shoot him for sure. You maybe be OK."

Richie Lee began the story that Marquis had heard many times. "I ran away from reform school and made it a long time before I got ratted on."

"Shee-it," muttered Marquis and reached for his tape player.

Richie Lee looked closer at the letter. Feeling it in his fingers, he noticed that the onionskin paper it had been written on was thin as Kleenex but resisted tearing. It resembled premium paper, known to burn well with no aftertaste. It should be better than a blunt where the paper still contained nicotine, which wasn't good for you. He tore the letter in half and folded one of the halves over the other. Reaching for the little bag with the drawstring that he kept in his slant pocket, he shook a generous row of weed over the curved paper, licked one edge and rolled his creation into a cylinder. He pulled hard on the joint and let his head loll. He drew another hit. The paper burned too hot. He crumpled the other half of the letter into a ball and threw it across at Marquis, who lay with his box on his belly, listening intently with his eyes closed to Dylan singing "Tangled Up in Blue."

Two weeks more and basic would be over.

* * * * *

Bertie Breen's body arrived in his flag-draped, army-issued regulation casket, accompanied by a contingent of young and slim soldiers in crisp brown uniforms.

With Bertie's mother incapacitated and Sam Morinville undependable, it fell to Leah Peavey to help Vickie with funeral arrangements, so the next day, she and

Vickie drove to the small Prophetstown cemetery to choose a gravesite. Bertie's father, Sidney, who had also died before his time, was buried there, and they planned the fresh grave to be next to his.

As they emerged from their vehicle, the sun broke through the overcast and the wind died, making for a gorgeous Indian summer day. It had been dry lately, and with fall looming, the flattened grass in the graveyard had turned a lifeless russet, giving even the smallest markers an unusual prominence. Within view of the Breen plots lay the graves of Leah's father, Omar Tuttle, and Freddy Morinville, who more than a handful of folks still believed to be Omar's murder victim, less than twenty feet from each other.

Leah trailed Vickie, watching the girl gaze at first one marker, then the other, spending an intense minute staring at the marker of her purported father, Sidney Breen. Leah knew what she was thinking. The man had died too early to have been her biological father. Apparently, Vickie had not been told of her origins.

Not wanting to address questions at the moment, Leah moved on to Freddy's grave, which she'd never visited up close. It looked like a forgotten piece of ordinary prairie—a few dried-up weeds and some washed-out gravel punctured with gopher holes. It even lacked a proper stone. A small sign from the funeral home, so rusty and crusted over with dirt that you could hardly read it, remained the only trace of his life.

A late-season patch of dandelions blossomed on the slope leading to the creek. She remembered when they were kids and Freddy would rub a dandelion on her nose and tell her that if her nose turned yellow, it meant she liked butter. She smiled. Who didn't like butter?

\* \* \* \* \*

At the ceremony, Vickie gathered with the others clustered around the open hole that had been prepared to swallow Bertie in his coffin. How unlike themselves people looked in their suits and best dresses, so brushed, so stiff and clean. Richie Lee's dad kept tugging on his collar like his necktie was choking him. Leah stood silently next to Mrs. Morinville, who looked so tired and sad you'd think she was the mother of Bertie Breen. Little wonder, though, considering the burden of caring for her husband, who'd been incapable of talking or walking since almost suffocating in a grain bin accident. Their son, Casey—the exact opposite in every way of his brother Sam—was there, while Sam himself had the sense to stay away.

Vickie positioned herself behind Mama, who sat in a metal folding chair, the only mourner not standing. Leah, who seemed to be getting bossier, had insisted that Vickie wear a dress, and now Vickie had the terrible sensation that the nylon on her right leg was slipping. From time to time, Leah looked over at Mama like she was afraid she might leap up again and run off like she did the other day. After an hour's search, Vickie had found her in the hayloft, raving about the goat that was either her imaginary friend or enemy.

The things the preacher said sounded like words that you could plug in for the death of anyone. There was nothing that fit Bertie. The preacher had never met him, never knew how he could filet a Northern in half a minute or recite all the state capitals and U.S. presidents even though he never completed high school. The man could not know how smart Bertie was, how he figured out on his own that you had to put rosin on the strings of a violin to make it produce music. He'd never heard Bertie tell a joke or seen him hoe a bean row. Never knew Bertie could hit a crow on the fly with a rock if he wanted to, except he never wanted to. The red-faced minister had already left everybody standing around watching the road after losing his way trying to get to the cemetery, and now he had to be paid twelve dollars for his services.

The real tributes to Bertie would come ten years from now when people would reminisce on how diffcrent or how goofy he was. They'd say things like, "Remember that time Bertie Breen tried to ride his bike up a ramp like he saw at the fair and just about broke his neck?"

A delegation from the Legion commanded by Max Plummer, the man whose complaint about Vickie's poster got her in trouble at school, waited to perform their duty. Bertie would have laughed at how unsoldierly they were, with their bellies spilling over their belts and each wearing different-colored pants and shoes. Their time came and they fired a salute, fascinating and startling the children in attendance. To Vickie, the volley sounded flat and hollow, like from a cap gun.

An embarrassing interlude occurred as the flag covering Bertie's casket was folded properly into a triangle and presented to Mama. She wasn't prepared to receive it, and while she peered at it trying to determine what it was, the flag slipped out of her bony fingers into the dust at her feet.

While everyone tried to disregard the desecrated flag, Mr. Murray from the funeral parlor began lowering Bertie into his grave. Some sort of complicated contraption with cranks and pulleys and cables held the coffin suspended, and it was quite the chore to see that it stayed level, requiring Murray to scoot from one corner to another making adjustments. After the coffin reached bottom, family members dropped in handfuls of blue wildflowers, an act that almost, but not quite, brought a tear to Vickie's eye.

Several of the attendees glanced with discomfort at the stoic face of Fawn before turning to Vickie.

"Sorry," they said. Or, "He was a fine boy." Or, most often, "Just let us know if we can do anything." Some extended their hand. Others sought to get an arm around her for an embrace, but Vickie stiffened and they got the message.

That attended to, the mourners moved off while kids scurried around looking for empty shell casings before being herded to their cars. Before the cemetery even cleared, two workmen started shoveling dirt like they couldn't wait to get Bertie properly covered in the ground.

Vickie didn't linger. Though she never did get to see him, she knew he was gone, bombed to pieces, and this was where he'd stay. In fifty or a hundred years, somebody would come along and run a hand over an eroded tombstone and wonder for about three seconds just who Albert Breen was that he ran off and got killed way back in 1968.

## 2 | It Takes Time

Vickie stood in the potato patch thinking how things changed since the death of Bertie. The farm now seemed hollow, empty and dangerous. In that brief time, Sam Morinville had assumed an air of cheerless optimism, like a person who just learned that he didn't have cancer after all. For one thing, he acted like he thought she quit school just so she could help him. In fact, she didn't consider that she actually *quit* school. She just quit going. There was a difference. If anyone wanted to know, she would just say that she had to stay home to see to her ailing mother.

Just a month ago, when she received from Bertie a photograph of him napping on a pile of sandbags, Mama was all smiles as she taped the picture to the door of the spice cabinet. The following day she arose early and cooked a pot of oatmeal and prunes and even washed out the saucepan. Later, she washed a load of whites and hung it on the clothesline. But within a week, Sam found her by the rock pile, where she'd carried a bushel basket of canned vegetables and, jar by jar, had begun smashing them on the rocks, insisting they'd been poisoned.

Vickie pushed the fork into the dry soil and twisted it, pulling up a vine to which four small potatoes clung. From the patch, she could see the side of the house where, high in the second story window, Mama peered out into her small world.

As a kind of check to see how she was today, since she and Sam were going to town, Vickie waved energetically and called out, "Mama, come down. It's nice outside."

But Mama stayed fixed in her pitched-forward way, still as a ghost. No wonder the woman was sickly—she never got the sun and never ate unless forced to.

Day after day, she wore the same old robe that drooped on her like a rag hanging from a nail.

As she helped her mother get dressed for town, Vickie reminded herself of the need for understanding. Sick people don't stay steadily sick on an even basis. They go up and down, just like everything else in life. Still, dressing her was like dressing a doll—limbs had to be bent, feet lifted to push into shoes, all the while no expression told a thing about what was going on in her head. Maybe Mama would never get better. Maybe Vickie would never escape this life.

Hours later, Fawn Morinville, formerly Fawn Breen, stood in front of the SuperValu in Rolland staring at a sun-bleached poster promoting a horse race on the reservation that had been held weeks before. She twisted her head this way and that like a person trying to read something upside down, and when she finally got her fill of the barely legible print, she removed her jacket and spread it over a shopping cart that had been left outside. Then she took off her shoes and socks and placed them neatly in the cart. Next went her faded T-shirt, her jeans, her bra and torn panties. Vacant of eye and wearing only white anklets, she padded barefoot around to the entrance, triggering the automatic door opener that had been recently installed.

The few shoppers at that time of day carried on, ignoring the spectacle by scrutinizing the labels on the red-and-white cans of Campbell's Condensed Chicken Gumbo as if they'd never seen them before. By the time the store manager, Leo Larush, summoned Officer Lundberg from his cribbage game at the pool hall, Fawn had completed a circuit of the store and placed a single item in her car—a carton of Bridgeman's small curd cottage cheese.

"What are you doing, Missus?" asked Lundberg, trying to come up with her name as he shuffled around trying to shield her with a length of butcher paper provided by Larush.

She appeared to come to her senses briefly before seizing Larush's hand and giving it a smack that startled him. "How do you like that?" she said.

Just then, Lundberg was interrupted by Useless Johnston, who said he was needed at Milo's to break up a fight involving Sam Morinville and Jeff Able before they killed each other. Lundberg hurried out, placing Fawn in the care of Leo, who knew nothing better than to take her to the hospital.

\* \* \* \* \*

Vickie knew something was wrong when they failed to return in time for milking. Sure as could be, the Peaveys' car came bouncing into the yard, moving too fast for the potholes. At least that was a good sign. When arriving vehicles moved as slow as a funeral cortege, that meant something not so good.

Vickie went out to meet them. Leah got out first.

"What is it?" asked Vickie, ignoring the rural niceties of extending a welcome no matter how dire the situation.

Leah waited as her husband caught up. "Oh, your mother had an incident," she said.

Vickie guessed Leah must have practiced on the way up since most of her speech that she went on to deliver spilled out in two quick paragraphs, the first stating what happened in the grocery store and the second that Vickie's mother was to be taken to the sanatorium in Jamestown.

"What about Sam?" asked Vickie.

"Oh, he wasn't even there," said Leah, making a sour face. "He got in some ruckus at Milo's and they locked him up. He'll be out tomorrow. Harold will do the chores till then."

Vickie was left to contemplate this while Harold headed for the barn and Leah cleared the dirty dishes from the table, though that was none of her business.

*****

"We were talking on the way out," said Leah, her hands in the suds. "We think you should come and live with us until we know more about your mother."

"You mean it might be a long time?"

"Oh, you know Doc Thwarp, you can't get much definite out of him. He thinks the pills aren't working anymore so we just need to be realistic."

"But I don't want to be in the way when Richie Lee comes home. It's soon, isn't it? What if Mama isn't back?"

Leah looked around for a towel. "We have plenty of room. I think you need to prepare yourself. You remember Mrs. Jolliffe from the dime store? This was a few years ago. She had a nervous breakdown and she was down in Jamestown for over a year before they let her out."

"A year?"

"Vickie, you know it wouldn't work for just you and Sam. Richie Lee will only be home a while before he goes off to advanced training. Casey Morinville can help Sam on the farm at least until he goes away to college."

*College.* That distant goal of so many young people or their parents. Could there be any other word that she heard so often and knew so little about? Casey was a polite and smart boy, but as a Morinville, he hardly fit the idea of someone connected to college.

"We think that's the best thing for a while," said Leah.

It bothered Vickie that Leah always said "we" when it was really just her making all the decisions. Not that she wasn't probably right. If only Sam would just… disappear.

"What exactly did he do that he's locked up for? Sam, I mean," said Vickie. "Are you sure they'll let him out right away?"

Leah must have read Vickie's mind. "If you're hoping to live all by yourself on the farm you need to forget the notion right now," said Leah. "And you have to agree to a few things. You need to go back to school."

"I don't want to go back to school," said Vickie immediately.

"But everybody needs education. You're aware of that."

"I already know more than everybody in that school," said Vickie. She didn't really believe it but liked the way it sounded.

Leah was taken aback and offered a kind of twisted smile. "Well. That may be, but don't you see? If you're back in school you can start playing your violin again."

Nobody would get it, thought Vickie. How could they know that the violin was one of the *reasons* she quit going to school? "It's just a plaything, a hobby."

Leah knew better. "You don't believe that. You're still upset about Bertie. It takes time. You're not alone. We loved him too, you know."

Vickie was further angered by the claim. After all, Leah's own son might be going to war. If something happened to him, did she think that time alone would fix it?

\* \* \* \* \*

Richie Lee came home expecting his folks to be excited. For maybe the first time in his life, he finished something he started. Never mind that he barely made it, and that just before the final dismissal he was told in front of his platoon by one of the sergeants that he was a disgrace to the service and if he didn't shape up, he was bound for one of two places: the brig or a body bag.

But his parents had their minds on other things.

His mom was tied up with worries about aunt Fawn, who'd been committed to the insane asylum, which ended up with Vickie coming to live with them for a while. His dad was complaining again about the combine with its underpowered engine that overheated and set the chaff on fire, resulting in belts needing replacing. The kid that he'd hired from town to drive truck ran into the auger, shutting down operations for half a day. At this rate, his dad went on, he'd never get to all the things that needed fixing before the cold set in.

With this in mind, Richie Lee saw no choice but to dig out his barn clothes and get to work. His dad had not exaggerated the tasks awaiting attention. The supports below the cattle guard to the small pasture had been washed out, creating a convenient path for the cows to pass through at their whim. The roof on the milk house leaked. The old low spot by the mailbox could use a load of gravel, and just about every wooden building on the place was at least a year overdue for painting.

Richie Lee was curious about Vickie. He'd heard that she had become a hell-raiser, a nuisance in school, which didn't surprise him considering what it must have been like with her mother laid up most of the time and having Sam Morinville for company. The strange thing he found out about her—and Richie Lee could barely believe it—was that she'd turned into a hippie even before Bertie got killed. If that was true, she must be awful lonely living in North Dakota.

He spotted her on her knees, pulling the last of the carrots from the vegetable garden. She had changed in the last couple years, grown up, but still showed a little of her baby fat. She looked sad, all right—you could see it in her face—but also on guard, catching your eyes like she was figuring you might try to pull something. She was pretty in a bush country way, solid and boyish, no fancy-pants bullshit to her and not at all like those skags at the cathouse off base where Richie Lee went once with some of the guys near the end of basic. And she didn't look like a hippie—her outfit was clean and her hair barely reached below her ears, let alone down to her butt like those girls hanging around the bus station in Oklahoma City.

Interesting how she was supposed to be a troublemaker. Richie Lee could teach her a few things about trouble.

After a clumsy greeting during which she offered her hand, dirty fingernails and all, he told her he was sorry about Bertie.

She turned away. "Yeah," she said, hesitating like she meant to say more, but that was all.

Richie Lee let it go. She must be tired of hearing it. Besides, if she really was one of those rebels, she must want little to do with the likes of him.

The first couple days, the two didn't see much of each other. It rained the third day, shutting down outside work. After dinner, Richie Lee's mother suggested a game of whist. "Adults against the kids," as she put it. Vickie had her nose in a *Life* magazine and didn't look up. Something was going on with her and Mom. She mostly stayed in her room when Mom was around. And here he thought they got along good, at least according to his mother's letters. Vickie finally agreed to the game but didn't look happy about it, and as they played, Dad grumbled and looked at the rain streaking down the living room windows.

\* \* \* \* \*

The teachers' conference had given Vickie the whole week off, and when the weather cleared, Dad resumed his fieldwork, placing Vickie and Richie Lee in charge of the repairs needed around the farmyard.

Like with Mom and Dad, Vickie had little to say to Richie Lee. Sometimes he thought she was avoiding him. But he did notice right off that Vickie was a willing worker, not at all like hippies were supposed to be. She was hard to decipher.

Once, after he finished painting one side of the toolshed, he stood admiring his work when she came along and patted him on the shoulder. The touch was so light it felt like an accident, but it sent a jolt through him like a brush with an electric fence. He wondered—was that supposed to be a compliment or what?

Another time, he had to ask her to hold a board in place over the barn door while he got a nail in. While she stood on an overturned tub, he managed to drive the nail nearly all the way in before it bent. "That'll keep it for now," he said.

Vickie pushed her weight against the board. "No, you better put another one in."

"Nah, it's good enough for government work," he said, smiling, using the familiar saying he'd acquired at base.

"It's just gonna come off in no time. You need to make sure," said Vickie, refusing to let go.

Richie Lee drove another nail in, this one all the way.

Vickie hopped off the tub and turned to him.

"What happens after you finish your advanced training?"

Richie Lee was surprised. He'd seen nothing to suggest that she knew the first thing about the military. "AIT? You get ten days leave and then you're deployed."

"What's that mean?"

"You get sent to a place that needs men with your kind of training."

"Men?"

"Yes," said Richie Lee, watching her face for a hidden meaning.

"Like to Vietnam?"

"Maybe. I hope not. It all depends."

"Then you don't know."

"Not yet. They send you a letter."

"When?"

"After AIT. Like I said, during that leave you get your orders, and after it's over, away you go."

Vickie had nothing more to say, leading Richie Lee to conclude that she was just talking to fill up spaces with words that were no more important than the exact number of nails you put in a board to hold it in place.

\* \* \* \* \*

Some days, Vickie gathered her hair in a tight ponytail, sometimes in a short braid like Mr. Wong, who owned a restaurant off base, and other times, nothing at all, giving him the notion that hair was not a great concern to her. She tended to go about in the same outfit—an old, faded man's shirt under bib overalls complete with hammer loops on each leg, and on her feet buckle overshoes with bits of manure and straw clinging to the sides. Once, in a hurry, Richie Lee walked out of the barn and came upon her squatting to pee. The suspenders hung to the side and the fabric bunched at her thighs, baring a horizontal stripe of white flesh. Rattled, Richie Lee turned away but not before catching a glimpse of her face. She showed no trace of embarrassment, just the same distant gaze that men assumed when relieving themselves into a ditch, expressing no thoughts at all, or at least not any that had to do with the task at hand.

As the days passed, they shared more time, mostly on projects that required two people. They talked about lots of things with two exceptions. Vickie would neither open a conversation nor carry on one that had to do with Sam or her mother. The other subject she avoided was what Richie Lee was facing.

Richie Lee assumed that besides her one question about AIT, she wasn't much interested in army life. Then that very day, she surprised him. She'd just come out of the barn carrying a pitchfork over her shoulder, fitting the image townspeople had of a farmer, and said to him, "So, what was it really like learning to be a soldier?"

Richie Lee was stirring a fresh can of paint for the door of the machine shop, liking the way the swirls of brown blended smoothly into beige. "I don't know. It's the way you learn everything else. Practice it lots. Get to know how to go about things the right way."

"Like how to kill your enemy with a knife?"

Richie Lee looked up. Was she making a connection to his going after Sam Morinville with a knife when he was a kid—the incident that landed him in reform school?

"Well, it's all part of combat training, using a bayonet and hand-to-hand techniques," he said, trying to read her intent.

"How do they train you? With dummies to stab?"

"They got plenty of dummies for sure," said Richie Lee, trying desperately to lighten the mood.

Vickie was not amused. "Think you could do that—*kill someone?*" Her eyes looked capable of burning holes in his face, so intently did she gaze at him.

"I don't know," said Richie Lee truthfully. "I hope I never have to find out."

On Saturday afternoon after chores, his dad offered Richie Lee the use of the car if he wanted to go into town, seeing as how he'd been working long hours.

"I'm sort of tired," said Richie Lee, not wanting to admit the real reason that he'd rather stay home. Why couldn't Dad suggest that both he and Vickie go into Rolland for a movie? Had his parents failed to notice how they hung out even when not working?

Not that it should affect matters. Richie Lee would be gone in a few days.

Following the usual Saturday night supper of meat loaf, mashed potatoes and creamed corn, Richie Lee and his dad took to the living room, his dad in the easy chair, Richie Lee on the couch. From years of experience, he knew that his dad would turn on *Gunsmoke*, which they'd get to watch till it was over while his mother waited impatiently, switching to Lawrence Welk at the first chance. But tonight the TV stayed silent. Richie Lee was sorry he'd decided not to go to town after all.

"So, you got my letter then?" his father began.

"Yeah, I did," said Richie Lee after a pause, during which he struggled to formulate a suitable answer.

"So, what did you think?"

"It was fine."

"You took in what I meant then?"

Richie Lee glanced at the grandfather clock in the corner. His mind felt like the pendulum, swinging first one way, then the other. "Mostly," he said, knowing that response was inadequate. As he expected, his dad wouldn't let it go.

"Which part didn't you get?"

This mortified Richie Lee, for he couldn't recall one thing about the letter other than the paper it was written on. He hated that this had the marks of a close personal discussion. That wasn't the way of the family.

He took a stab, concluding that whatever he said would be better than proving his dislike of obvious familiarity. "I think I got it all. I want to serve my country and do my part."

"That's good," said his dad, to Richie Lee's astonishment. "You know then that you have my backing. Don't let what I done way back affect you."

To Richie Lee's relief, the women came in from the kitchen.

"What? No *Gunsmoke?*" said his mother, clicking the television on.

Midway through Lawrence Welk, Richie Lee's dad's chin dropped to his chest. Soon after that, his mother lowered her knitting to her lap and her head lolled to the side.

With no one making the effort to change the channel, *Laugh-In* started, a program that Richie Lee never liked. He looked at Vickie, noticing her sour expression.

"Want to go for a walk or something?" he said.

Vickie's eyes went from one dozing parent to the other and then to the TV screen. "Might as well," she said.

They proceeded outside but only got as far as the porch step, where Richie Lee sat and rubbed the top of one shoe with the sole of the other. "My feet are sore," he said. "Must be from all that marching."

Richie Lee thought he deserved at least a chuckle of sympathy. The girl seemed to have no feelings or sense of humor.

"You and your dad were having a talk. What was it about?" she asked.

Richie Lee explained the letter and the background, trying to minimize any connection between his dad's long-ago actions and his own.

"Wait a minute. It was OK for him to do what was right, but not for you to? Even when there's an illegal war involved?"

He'd touched a nerve. "Well, it's more complicated than that." He should have steered the conversation to something else. That's what they advised in basic. His remark to his dad came to him. "It just seems right to serve my country."

The way Vickie swerved around told him that was the wrong thing to say. "Whose country? Who are you serving? The people who get rich making guns? Johnson and Nixon? You think they care about you? Why don't you consider serving me or your mama?"

Naturally, Richie Lee had heard these things constantly, even on the base from guys who you'd think would want to fight. He needed to change the subject.

"Know what?" he said.

"What?" she answered sharply.

"Chicken's butt," he replied, elbowing her.

She couldn't help but smile at the worn-out expression that ceased being funny some time in third grade. But quickly the moment of humor expired. "You don't think much of me, do you?" she said.

"That's not so. I like you fine."

"That's not what I mean."

"No, really, I like getting to know you. You're nice," said Richie Lee, growing uneasy.

"You never listen to what I have to say."

"I do too!" said Richie Lee, a little too emphatically.

The remark seemed to muzzle Vickie, further disturbing Richie Lee.

"You're different from what I thought," he added, near panic now. "Do you know how I feel?"

"Of course," said Vickie, a note of disgust in her voice.

He should never have opened his stupid mouth. Moreover, his foot was itching terrible and he knew he'd look silly interrupting things to scratch it. "It sounds like you don't feel the same way. Sorry. Anyway, I know we're related so nothing can come of it."

"Oh, shut up," said Vickie, sounding genuinely angry. "Don't you see the real problem? Do you think I want to have an attitude of love for someone who is all happy to march off and get killed for no good reason? Why would I want to go through that again?"

Stunned, Richie Lee had no reply, though he did see in her words, or so he thought, a suggestion that maybe she did or would come to like him. "I don't know what I can do about that situation," he said.

Again he had misspoken. "Jesus H. *Christ*!" said Vickie, springing to her feet. "People like you are the problem. Don't they teach soldiers to be brave?"

"Sort of," said Richie Lee weakly, reluctant by this point to say anything at all.

"Well, then *be* brave. Be new and different. Picking the right thing takes bravery too." She turned to go inside, then reeled around again. "If you do care about me, you'll figure out what I mean in time. Think about it. Good night."

Richie Lee gave his foot a good scratching as he waited a few minutes until things looked peaceful inside the house. For the first time that he could remember, he had something decent to look forward to.

# LAWS OF THE HILLS

On the Saturday following Richie Lee's departure for AIT, Vickie disappeared, alarming the Peaveys before reappearing in late afternoon. Leah refrained from quizzing her, but after supper as they sat over dessert, Harold, in his detached innocence, asked her what she'd been up to all day.

Vickie reached for the cake pan to mop up a swipe of the yellow frosting with her finger.

"Taking the lay of the land," she answered with an enigmatic smile, marking, in Leah's opinion, the first time a fifteen-year-old girl had found need for that particular turn of phrase.

\* \* \* \* \*

On Tuesday, Vickie poured herself an extra bowl of Cheerios before going out early to wait for the school bus, but when the bus returned in the afternoon, Vickie wasn't on it. Leah waited half an hour before calling Mr. Hoffart at school, who checked with the secretary, Mrs. Juergens, and learned that Vickie had been absent the entire day.

"She's not ill?" asked Hoffart.

"Not at all," said Leah. "In fact, she's perking up since going back."

"I noticed that yesterday," said Hoffart. "Perhaps she's prepared to take up the violin again."

Hoffart then contacted the bus driver, Hank Legassee, who stated that Vickie definitely had not been at the stop for a ride that morning. He claimed he even waited a couple extra minutes.

To Leah, the logical place to look would be the Breen farm, even though Vickie wouldn't remain there long with Sam around. Just the same, she suggested that Harold drive over and check.

Restless, Leah hesitated only a minute before dialing her neighbors, the Morinvilles. As she waited through the three interminable cycles of four longs and two shorts that was the Morinvilles' specific ring on the party line, she experienced the familiar flush of shame she suffered over any involvement with that family. All these years and the only time she bothered to contact them was when something went wrong.

At last an answer came, but the connection was so bad that Leah could hardly identify the voice on the other end. Nor apparently could whoever answered understand her. After a minute of confusion, she spoke very deliberately, but not so loud as to sound angry. "This—is—Leah—Peavey. I—will—come—to—your—place."

She'd barely had time to zip her jacket and get out the door when she spotted Mrs. Morinville making her way around the barbed wire fence marking the property line.

After the obligatory exchanged greetings, Leah explained. *Had Mrs. Morinville seen Vickie?*

Mrs. Morinville had not. But she offered to help if need be.

Harold returned to find his wife and Mrs. Morinville making their way through the high grass bordering the back of the barn and fields beyond. He reported having found no sign of the girl. And, he added, Sam was not around. His pickup was gone and the place looked untended.

Harold joined the women in searching around both farmyards as well as the outbuildings. At Leah's request, Harold even wiggled into his leaky old hip boots and waded out into the slough for a good distance, but that fear was abandoned when he found that it was only six inches deep at the middle.

"If only Casey wasn't staying in town all night," said Mrs. Morinville, recounting stories of how her son had located the Maas boy, who'd failed to return from a deer hunting trip, after a search party was about to give up. By then it was long past suppertime, and Mrs. Morinville, having left Etienne by himself for as long as she dared, apologized and said goodbye while Harold responded to the ceaseless bellering of the cows and set up for milking.

Leah put a pot of water on to boil. Without a notion of what she wanted to cook, she hiked out to the barn to check with Harold on how long before he got the chores done. While there, she acted on a hunch to check the haymow just in case. She took the good flashlight and clambered up the wobbly ladder, startling a barn cat, which in turn startled her. The hay, stacked in Harold's perfect rectangles, still smelled sweet, but the dusty silence told her that, aside from the cat and the usual resident mice, nothing living would be found there.

She circled the house again, directing the beam toward the bushes, toward the pile of gravel covering the hole where the outhouse used to be, then toward Morinvilles, where light shined in the kitchen and upstairs windows. Back inside, she turned off the burner under what water hadn't boiled away, dumped it in the sink and put the pot on its shelf.

The darkness outside helped create an eerie sensation of danger. Leah's dad had related stories of the days when bears and bobcats lived in the hills. Maybe Vickie had gone to see her brother's grave and somehow fallen in the creek and drowned. Many were the dangers of the outside world.

At Harold's urging, she placed a long-distance call to the hospital in Jamestown. After some delay, she was advised that Mrs. Breen had had no visitors. When Harold announced he was going to bed, Leah asked him to go out and turn on the lights in the barn and to leave the yard light on. She herself was going to wait up. If nothing happened overnight, they could phone the sheriff's office in the morning to report her missing.

Well aware of Vickie's habits, Leah tried to suppress her worries. After all, she was just as likely to come riding up on a bicycle or parachute from a helicopter as she was to get eaten by a bear. Then, standing out in the porch with her arms folded, staring into the blackness, the obvious answer came to her.

*Richie Lee!*

Her son and Vickie had spent several days together before he completed his army training. She'd given it little thought, but now her woman's intuition told her something else. *The girl had run off to be with Richie Lee!*

On impulse, she headed back inside the house to go wake Harold. But then what? They came to know long ago the difficulty involved in getting even an emergency message to a soldier in training. They should have contacted the sheriff immediately. He would know how to get over military barriers. Overcoming the urge to do otherwise, she allowed Harold to sleep, resuming her vigil in the rocking chair, gazing at the window, checking the clock, listening through the overwhelming silence of the house and the immense outdoors.

A light tap, barely audible, sounded from the kitchen door. At last! She leaped from the rocker and nearly toppled to the floor. Her foot had fallen asleep. She reminded herself to stifle her anger and let Vickie have her say first. She limped over and pulled the door open, puzzled why she would come to the kitchen door and not the front.

"I saw your lights on," said Ida Florence Morinville, her hands grasping a shawl pulled over her head like a scarf. "I thought I should keep you company. If you want."

Dazed but covering her disappointment, Leah stepped aside. But of course, the back door. In her early childhood, people from the reservation came by in horse-drawn wagons with their pails of chokecherries for sale and timidly walked all the way around the house as if they were servants.

At the kitchen table with their chipped mugs of coffee, conversation was sparse at first. Mrs. Morinville looked uneasy and self-conscious, just as Leah herself had been during the brief times she'd been inside the Morinville home. Then too, Mrs. Morinville had seated herself uncomfortably with one buttock almost over the side of her chair. Leah wished she would adjust herself before she slipped to the floor in a heap like a pillow sliding off the bed.

"You're sure I'm not bothering you," said Mrs. Morinville for the third time.

"It isn't a bother," insisted Leah as she tried to think of something to offer with the coffee. She hadn't had time to bake in weeks, and the pantry held only those fig bars that Harold loved and she detested. No doubt they were stale and dry, but with luck Mrs. Morinville would decline. She peeled away the wax paper in which Harold had clumsily wrapped the half-open package and placed a half dozen bars on a dessert platter.

Mrs. Morinville's face lit up. "Are those fig bars?" she said, reaching. She slid a corner of one into her mouth and bit down. She withdrew the bar and studied it before pushing it back in and trying again. When she still failed to bite through, she used her fingers to wedge the treat between her side teeth, where she was able to snap it in two like a peppermint stick.

Leah had bad memories of the one time she attempted to pay a social call on her neighbor by baking her a peach cobbler. So nervous was she that she burned the bottom of the dish, then carted it over anyway, where it was attacked by flies as soon as she took the cover off.

But this time there was no disaster. The bar, dipped in coffee, softened in Mrs. Morinville's mouth, and she chewed with evident pleasure, though she did decline Leah's offer of another.

The women drank a second and then a third coffee, all the while completely ignoring the issue which led to their meeting. Eventually, Mrs. Morinville was obliged to use the toilet. When she returned, she'd undone the rubber band that held her hair in place, giving the impression that she planned to stay for a while.

"I bet she's at some friend's place," she said. "Rebecca pulled that stunt a bunch of times."

"I don't think so," replied Leah. "Something did occur to me though." She went on to recount Richie Lee's leave, and how he and Vickie got along so well. "I wonder if she ran off to try and visit him."

"How far could she get on her own? I think she'll turn up around here." Mrs. Morinville leaned forward in her chair. "If it makes you feel any better, I tried something like that myself when I was a girl."

"You did?"

"Yes, with a boy, a white kid. He had a car. We didn't get a long way. Or at least I didn't." Mrs. Morinville's heavy-lidded eyes half closed, as if the memory were one she could not face. "I was sixteen."

Leah was eager to hear more, but she had to mind her manners. Mrs. Morinville's coffee cup was empty. She offered more from the percolator. Mrs. Morinville declined. "No, thank you, I'm getting the shakes."

Concerned that her neighbor was about to abandon her, Leah blurted out an offer. "How about some wine to balance it out?" She made the offer half-jokingly, having no idea if Mrs. Morinville ever allowed herself such luxuries.

Mrs. Morinville brightened. "You got wine?"

"It's pretty old," said Leah. "I got it from Aunt Dolores years ago. Does it go bad?"

This brought a smile. "When Sam was still at home we never had it around long enough to tell. But I'll try some."

Leah rooted through a kitchen drawer until she found a corkscrew on Richie Lee's old Boy Scout knife. Together, the women managed to get the cork out while several shreds drifted to the bottom like pennies dropped into a fountain.

Leah thought she should get the good glasses out of the sideboard, but she'd have to drag the stool over and Mrs. Morinville's chair blocked the way. She found two jelly jars in the pantry and filled each to the brim.

To her, the pale pink liquid smelled like flowers. She held her glass up, watching the flecks of cork tumble, then swallowed a good third.

"Whoa," said her guest. "You don't drink much around here, do you?"

Leah, blinking, admitted that Harold only took a beer now and then, and she herself, having married before she reached legal age, had never gotten the hang of enjoying alcohol. In fact, she had never tasted wine, not even in church.

"You need to go easy. Slow down. How do you like it?"

"It's got its own taste. Kind of like fruit juice that's been in the fridge too long. A little sugar wouldn't hurt."

Mrs. Morinville's eyes twinkled, and she smiled.

After a few minutes, when the broken handle on the sideboard began doubling in her vision, Leah understood why the wine should not be too hastily consumed. She waited, gauging the level of Mrs. Morinville's glass before she drank more of her own.

The wine made her reluctant to speak—the very opposite of what she thought alcohol was supposed to do, and Mrs. Morinville also allowed herself to be overtaken by muteness.

"Ida Florence?" she said and brought a hand to her mouth to suppress a giggle.

The other woman looked up.

"It's hard to say your name. It makes me feel grown-up. My mother always made me call you Mrs. Morinville."

"She was a proper woman, your mother."

"Ida Florence," said Leah, trying out the words.

"It's a long time that Lucille's been gone," said Mrs. Morinville. She lifted her glass. "I better finish this and get back home."

"Oh, you don't have to!" Leah spat the words out so suddenly that Ida Florence looked at her in alarm.

"I mean you don't have to rush off," said Leah, using an expression that was a favorite of her mother's. "Why don't we sit in the living room where it's more comfortable?"

With an immense sigh of relief, Ida Florence eased herself into Harold's easy chair while Leah dragged out one of the old kitchen chairs and set the wine bottle on the mahogany end table between them.

As Leah monitored the pace of wine consumption, she studied Ida Florence, who appeared to be sinking lower into her chair and discarding any degree of discomfort. She tried to imagine what the woman was like as a girl.

"What happened that time you just mentioned, with that boy?" Leah asked, reassured by her neighbor's easy consent to stay. "Did you get in trouble?"

"Trouble?" Ida Florence reached behind her and pulled her hair away from the chair. "Considering I was already in trouble, it couldn't get much worse."

"Oh, I didn't mean to pry," said Leah, rattled.

"No, it's OK. Those things happened then too. Anyway, the guy, I knew he wasn't too happy about how his luck had turned. So there I was, not even a fifty-cent piece in my purse, no home that would have me back and running to nowhere with a person who'd be plenty happy if I changed my mind or fell off a dock and drowned."

Leah couldn't help but relate this to Vickie. Could that be what was going on? No, it hadn't been long enough to know. But then again. She pushed the thought from her head. It must be the wine.

"What did you do?"

"Huh? Oh. I got hold of Etienne and after a while we got married."

Leah smiled. "I know what it's like to marry too young."

Ida Florence nodded. "Except we didn't have nothing. First we lived in the old shack where I grew up. It was vacant by then. But we couldn't even afford coal, so we had to live with his folks." She pursed her lips and burped silently. "I'll have some more of this good wine if you don't mind."

The bottle looked small in Ida Florence's big hand. Leah watched as she poured, such delicate movements.

"That was you that put flowers on Freddy's grave, wasn't it?" asked Mrs. Morinville. She set the wine bottle down.

"Just a few dandelions and clover. It looked so bare. I felt sorry for Freddy."

"I know," said Ida Florence. "He had it hard, Freddy did. You ought to still bear in mind how it was. How Etienne never took to him. He picked on the poor boy, griping about having to buy him shoes and a decent outfit for school."

"Yeah," said Leah, though she didn't really remember.

"Oh, yes. That was when Etienne changed. He got meaner. That's where Sam gets it, you know. And he never liked seeing you kids being friends."

"I don't think Daddy did either," said Leah.

"Everyone could tell that," said Ida Florence, her tone one of hostile resignation. "Those two, they hated each other. And then when Etienne heard you were carrying a baby, he about lost his mind. But that wasn't all."

Something about her neighbor's account didn't feel right to Leah, but she let her go on.

"You see, on top of raising a kid that wasn't his, the boy was half-white. And it didn't help that the other part was Sioux."

"But he knew that, right?"

Perhaps because she was enjoying a rare chance to boast, Ida Florence attempted to explain. "The Sioux and Chippewa, they don't get along in history. The Chippewa, they're farmers, they're more peaceful, and they take what the whites give them.

"Now you take the Sioux, they were what you call 'nomadic.' Where the buffalo went, they followed. When the whites tried to stop them, they fought back. You heard of Sitting Bull?"

Ida Florence gave no chance for Leah to answer. "He was Sioux. He beat Custer. Crazy Horse too."

Then, maybe believing she'd said too much, Ida Florence went suddenly silent but for one more brief comment.

"Me, I'm Sioux."

Like nearly every schoolchild, Leah knew the outlines of that segment of history, but she listened with fascination just the same. "And so Freddy had to suffer because of his blood. That's terrible."

"Well, yes, for that and the mistake he made."

"Mistake?"

"We can call it that. The mistake both of you made."

Leah looked away, unable to meet Ida Florence's eyes.

"I used to wonder what it would've been like to have you for my daughter-in-law," said Ida Florence. She raised her glass dreamily. "Richie Lee would be my first grandchild."

Leah was flabbergasted. Mrs. Morinville still believed that Freddy was Richie Lee's father? Of course, there were rumors, but she thought they'd gone away when she and Harold were married so quickly after Richie Lee was born.

"It was nice of you to think that," said Leah. A meaningless remark, but she knew she had to say something, as Ida Florence kept looking at her in expectation. How she could not know the truth about the pregnancy baffled Leah. Even Richie Lee's grade school classmates had once taunted him about his dad and grandpa being the same person.

Now was the time to correct the long-held impression. Just the same, there was something sweet about what Ida Florence said. To think she considered Richie Lee her grandchild. How it must have hurt to watch him from across the short yards of dirt bridging the homes and think that she would never come to know him.

"Who knows what might have come to pass eventually?" said Leah, as much to herself as to the older woman. "We were just kids. You know how it is when you got in mind a person that you thought you liked and then you see them grown up and they aren't like you thought at all?"

Ida Florence threw her shoulders back with a whoop. "Lord, if that isn't so. Lots of times when I was disgusted with Etienne, I would wonder how come I never stuck with my boyfriend. But the truth is Eddie was a miserable son of a bitch."

Light began to show over the hills to the east. In not too long the rooster would be crowing and Harold would get up. Both women were exhausted and a little drunk. Leah felt sick to her stomach but wanted the night to go on. "From what I've seen, you made the right choice then."

At that, Ida Florence stared at her so long and intently that she felt she'd been reprimanded. Finally, the still air broke as Ida Florence spoke softly. "I'll tell you something."

But before she could continue she felt a sneeze coming. She jerked from her pocket a man's red handkerchief, turned away and blew her nose loudly.

"I will tell you something about Etienne Morinville," she said, resuming. "He took me in, but that was the last good thing he ever done. It wasn't just Freddy. He was about as mean to me, and it got worse after Freddy died when you'd think he'd at least feel sorry for me." She paused as if to measure Leah's reaction.

"The first time he hit me wasn't even a week after we got married. I still think he was trying to kill the baby. What did I know? I let it go on for a couple years.

But not long after Sam was born, I got fed up one day and I whacked him across the face with the mop handle. You ever notice that crooked nose? That was my doing." She paused and hacked loudly into her hand. "Sorry," she said as she leaned back, breathing heavily.

Leah stood, intending to fetch a glass of water, but found she dared not walk. She let herself fall back in her chair, praying that, for once in his life, Harold would oversleep.

With a groan, Ida Florence sat up and looked around. "Wait a minute," she said. "Just wait." She reached for the wine bottle and held it to her lips. "So long as we're talking like this, there's something else." She wiped her mouth and held the bottle before her as if to check its contents. "There's more," she said.

Leah at first thought her remark referred to the wine. She squeezed her eyes shut to make the dizziness go away.

"Freddy," said Ida Florence. "Nobody knows this, but probably somebody guessed." She hesitated, maybe trying to find the right words. "Most people naturally agreed that it was your dad Omar that killed Freddy. Maybe you thought so too."

She looked at Leah as if for confirmation, but Leah couldn't have spoken a word at that moment to save her life.

Ida Florence reached again for the hankie before continuing. "It wasn't your dad. It was my husband. Etienne was responsible. He shot my Freddy."

Leah felt like every ounce of air was being sucked from her lungs. Her insides hurt. Her heart pounded. How Ida Florence delivered her words, in the plain, unexcited tone of a newscaster, made it worse. She may as well have been instructing her on how to can beets.

"No," she said, at first denying so firmly what she wanted to believe. "Etienne, did he tell you that?"

Ida Florence shook her head. "When I found the gun in the slough the year it dried up, I figured it out. He loved that old shotgun. He'd have never lost it that way. I didn't let on that I knew, and I never told nobody else. But every time I thought I should tell what I knew, I go back to how I felt when he drove all that way to bring me home."

Trembling, Leah responded, "I can't look down on you for that." Immediately, she knew it was a lie. She wanted very much to blame Mrs. Morinville for what amounted to shielding Etienne. And she wanted to march over with the butcher knife and plunge it into the heart of the evil man, never mind if he was helpless. But such rage wouldn't come. Nor did she feel the lifting of any burden. Mostly, she wanted to cry, and she couldn't even do that.

"You could fit in a thimble all the words we spoke in the years after that," said Ida Florence. "I know he's all sick now, but that's no punishment. I'm the one that got punished. Freddy was my son."

Overwhelmed with disbelief and emotion, Leah again struggled to her feet. She wanted to go outside but knew that was beyond her capability. She barely reached the kitchen sink, where she hooked her elbows into the basin, sensing her knees would not support her. In three loud, overpowering heaves, she retched the contents of her stomach into the sink. Lesser spasms followed as she tried to turn the faucet on. She felt the weathered brown hand reassuringly move her own hand out of the way as clear, cold water swirled through the basin, carrying away the vomit.

Ida Florence helped a grateful Leah to the sofa. Though past being able to speak, she comprehended what Ida Florence whispered in her ear, her husky voice strong.

"From now on, everything is our secret," she said.

\* \* \* \* \*

Leah awoke on the sofa with her hands crossed over her chest like a dead person. A cover lay twisted over her knees. From the kitchen came the faint clack of metal on metal, the sound of a cupboard being opened gently, the smell of burned bread crumbs in the toaster. Harold was trying not to make noise but not quite succeeding. Leah sat up and brushed her hair from her eyes.

Harold stood in the doorway, holding a mug of coffee to warm his hands. "Looks like somebody had a party."

Leah managed to lift her head to offer a vacant smile. Her husband waited for elaboration. None was offered. Leah knew that was the end of it, ignoring the fact that nothing like this had happened in their entire marriage.

"So no sign of the girl?" said Harold, going to the window.

Leah rested her elbows on her knees, letting her hands dangle. *The girl.* That state of affairs seemed a million miles away. She never wanted to taste wine again. She looked toward the floor where she'd last seen the bottle. It was gone, thank goodness.

"We'll need to drive into town if we want to make a report," said Harold. "The lines are down."

"The lines are down?" said Leah, unable to summon energy to rephrase the question in her own words.

"You never heard that wind come through? We can get going soon as I finish chores."

*Chores.* In a way, that's all there was to life. The door closed. Leah pictured her husband pausing on the step while he studied the sky, then the buildings, and finally the field to the north before making his way patiently to the barn on a path he'd followed a thousand times.

In that moment, she felt a deep love for him.

Summoning her willpower, she fetched herself to her feet to begin her own chores for the day while Harold finished in the barn. Although her hands could almost achieve the task by themselves, she had to concentrate: shoo the hen off the nest, reach in and pick up the warm egg, place it in the wicker basket. Go on to the next.

She was nearly paralyzed by her thoughts. *Etienne Morinville, a man who murdered his own son and had never been made to face justice.* In a short while, she'd be face-to-face with the person who could make this right. All Leah had to do was say the words.

\* \* \* \* \*

It was still early when they pulled in at the sheriff's office. On the front lawn, Johnny Landry hoisted the flag.

Inside, Delilah Poitra, who Leah remembered from their school days as Delilah Olson, advised them that the sheriff had been out on a case most of the night but left instructions that if the Peaveys came to the office, they should go on around to the residence.

"How did he know we might come?" asked Leah.

"You'll have to get that from him," she said, well-practiced. "You know where it is, right?"

They left the car where it was and followed the sidewalk around the courthouse past the jail to the sheriff's quarters. Marlys Aingher greeted them at the door and invited them in like they were old friends. As they passed through the kitchen, Leah noted the spicy aroma of a fresh-baked cake. An oversize coffee maker bubbled determinedly on the counter. "Take a seat and I'll let him know you're here," said Marlys.

This hospitality worried Leah. It felt too arranged, like they were being groomed to receive bad news. She shot an enquiring glance at her husband. He'd taken on the manner he assumed when away from the comfort of his cows and machinery—erect posture, hands on the arms of the chair, facial expression hollow.

She looked around the room. The apartment had been built long ago, around the same time as the old courthouse. A one-person elevator had been installed on the stairs, no doubt to accommodate the Aingher son's disability from wounds in Vietnam. A fireplace was boarded over and concealed by two panels on which yellow flowers had been drawn. On the mantle rested various photos, most of them of Marlys herself. She'd pridefully kept her trim figure, Leah would give her that, even if her shoulders were a little too broad for a woman. Decades ago, she'd been engaged to Harold. Now it was impossible to think of them as a couple.

The sheriff had been sleeping. His sparse hair sprouted up in the back like Junior in Dick Tracy and his pants bore the wrinkles of having been tossed in a corner. Leah tried to imagine his reaction if she disclosed what Mrs. Morinville had told her the night before. The man looked unworthy of the news.

Aingher shook hands with both of them and took a seat next to Harold.

"I was expecting you folks," he said, yawning and scratching his head.

"Then you know where Vickie's at," said Leah. "Did she try to see Richie Lee?"

"No, she didn't go anyplace far away, but I can tell you she's getting along fine for now."

"Then you've got her in jail here in town, right?"

"No, she's not even in town."

"But where is she?"

At that moment, Marlys entered carrying a plastic tray. With her stomach still roiling from the night before, Leah couldn't bear to think of food. She accepted a coffee and set it beside her. Marlys retreated to the kitchen.

"I'm sorry, I can't tell you," said Aingher, breaking his coffee cake in half, ignoring the fork. "And she's not in any kinda fix. She's in a place that she went to by her own choice."

The sheriff crammed half of the cake into his mouth. "Sorry," he repeated, his mouth full.

Energized now by the sheriff's attitude, Leah fumed. As always, this man wanted to make use of every ounce of his authority.

Harold broke in finally. "It would help if you let us know a little more. We don't know if we're coming or going here."

"I wish I could be more open with you folks," said Aingher. "But there's an agreement I made and for everybody's good, I'm bound to stick to it. Victoria is safe, and she's where she wants to be for the time being. How long she stays depends on her as much as anything."

But Aingher's talk of an agreement did nothing to appease Leah. She looked at her husband, but he'd said his piece. She gathered herself. "I for one don't like one thing about this." She did her best to lock eyes with the sheriff. "We're responsible for her. We're blood relatives and we have the right to know what you did with her. There are laws about everything. I thought you swore to uphold them."

Sheriff Aingher remained unperturbed. He waited Leah out, nodding slightly at the end of each sentence. When she at last finished, he coughed quietly into his hand.

"Leah, what you say is absolutely so," he said. "It's all on record, and it's true too that there are books full of all sorts of problems of right and wrong. But if you looked a little closer, you might see that most matters are not so off base as you think. You were born and raised in the bush, and I imagine you know better than anybody that sometimes the laws in the books count for less than the laws of the hills."

\* \* \* \* \*

It took each of the empty and silent miles home past the sagging granary at Disruds, the turnoff to the golf course and the blind crossing where the school cook Mrs. Sutton was killed by a train before Leah's thoughts came to rest. Sheriff Aingher had looked so smug as he sat there with his shirt half-buttoned, talking with warm cake stuffed in his mouth, enjoying the power. That alone was enough to make Leah even more determined to learn where Vickie was. She reviewed the conversation with the sheriff. He said the girl wasn't in town, but that she was safe.

Laws of the hills be damned. As soon as they arrived home, she was on the phone to Mrs. Morinville.

"You know," she began. "This is a long shot, but I don't know what to do. I know that Casey gets around easy and stays out of trouble. And I remember you telling me about him making a map of all the farms around here and Rolland. If you don't mind, I'd like to ask him for a favor."

Two days later, Leah Peavey found out what she wanted to know.

# NO GOOD REASON

Virgil Able firmly believed that Rolland rated high on the list of targets the Russians planned to bomb first. This was thanks to the factory that made jewel bearings for guided missiles—one of only two such places in the world. When the family built its bomb shelter after the Cuba nuclear scare, Virgil ordered the boys to construct the walls facing town the thickest even though Rolland sat more than twenty miles away. To Vickie, that represented one more reason to avoid the town and its narrow-minded citizens, and now that she'd quit school for good, she saw little need to ever go there since her new family—she had to remind herself that it was also her old family—grew, hunted or cobbled together all that they required to survive.

After living here for only a little over a month, she knew how to field dress a deer, set a rabbit trap, seine for perch and attend to a variety of indoor tasks like dying wool and making candles. Moreover, she contributed skills of her own that she'd absorbed from the mother who raised her, such as preparing willow bark for a tea that cured Virgil's headaches.

The homeplace, as the Ables called their property, consisted of a large four-square house with dormer windows and multiple lightning rods, along with an assortment of small trailer houses, sheds, stables and half-built structures. Water on two sides and a stockade on the third protected the grounds. Two routes led in—one barely a road that no one used if in a hurry and the main one itself difficult to follow because of various gates and barriers. Vickie shared a room in the big house with two of the girls, both younger. Everyone had their own horse and was responsible for caring for it, even little Maida, who was only five. Virgil selected a bay named Dandy for Vickie, an animal that reminded her of Bertie's old horse.

Except for the prayer meeting every night after supper that felt like it went on longer than a chemistry lab at school, everything about the place suited Vickie. As long as you put in your time in the garden or stable, you were free to do what you liked. You could talk dirty, but saying swear words involving God or Jesus would get you in bad. You could smoke if you wanted, but nobody did. Instead they all chewed, even the smaller girls. Vickie didn't like the taste, so she gave up tobacco entirely. And you didn't have to wear a dress or fancy shoes that hurt your feet. In fact, the boys went barefoot.

Although she was content living on the homeplace, Vickie missed being connected more closely with the outside world. Seldom was the TV or even a radio turned on, nor was a newspaper available other than outdated *Grand Forks Herald*s that were used to start fires. One morning, she stood by as Virgil sharpened his knives outside the butcher shop. The grindstone was rigged with pedals like a bicycle, and as he pumped, he held a blade so close to the stone that Vickie was afraid sparks would fly into his eyes. When he paused to run his thickly calloused thumb across the knife's edge to check the sharpness, he caught Vickie's eye, a gesture that told her it was all right to interrupt his work.

"Do you think it's right when a country makes people go fight in a war for no good reason?" she asked.

She knew that was out of the blue, but this was important because what Virgil thought would guide the view of everybody else. But, instead of answering, he returned to his task, probably to think it over. After a minute, he checked the sharpness again and wiped the knife on his trousers.

"What I think is that what you do is you cultivate ignorance in matters beyond your sphere of influence," he said.

It took Vickie a minute to untwist the words and still they made little sense. Virgil occasionally used big words or spoke in riddles, but this was a new one. "But if you want to get along in the world, you should know what the government is up to, shouldn't you?"

"Why?" replied Virgil.

"Well, if people don't show they worry, who knows what will happen? The government could take over everything if nobody stops it."

"Unquestionably, and when that happens the only people who endure will be those who know how to make do for themselves. Like us."

\* \* \* \* \*

When Sheriff Aingher drove into the muddy yard the day after she arrived, Vickie ran into the woods, afraid he'd come to take her back to Peaveys. But it turned out that his visit was nothing extraordinary. To the contrary, he was welcomed—and, far from hauling her away, he sat down to chat with her on the back porch like he was an old family friend, which in a way he was.

The sheriff, a man who used to frighten her because he only came to deliver bad news, explained that he wanted to assure himself that she'd come to the place all on her own and in fact had no wish to go elsewhere.

"You know that if you want to stay you have to follow the directions of the family, just like anywhere else," he warned. "But first there's a rule that comes from me." His voice grew stern. "You don't ever go along when someone goes out for errands. You got nothing to do with that."

As Vickie would learn, "going for errands" meant that Virgil and one of the older boys left after sunset and were back before dawn with some item or commodity considered vital. One night it was a post-hole digger, another time a bushel of flaxseed. Vickie knew that this meant the item would be stolen, but for the sheriff to come right out and say it like that shocked her.

Another requirement, one that surprised her only a little, was that if she intended to avoid returning to school in Rolland, she must keep up with lessons that old Sally Able would provide.

There were other expectations that she knew about, such as never talking to outsiders about the Ables or what may be going on at the homeplace.

"You got any questions for me while I'm still here?" asked Aingher.

She did in fact have a couple. "Can I see Richie Lee Peavey when he comes home?"

The sheriff expected that. "Maybe. So long as you go over to the Peavey farm. Richie Lee wouldn't be welcome here. And you better make sure you are welcome there."

Vickie appreciated that. "I know," she said. "I shouldn't have left like I did. But don't you see? If I'd told them, they'd have tried to stop me—especially if I said I wanted to go live with the Ables."

She waited for the sheriff to acknowledge her argument, but he looked unconvinced. What's a person supposed to do, she thought. If you are honest, you're prevented from going after something you want. No wonder kids turn into rebels.

They'd been sitting side by side on the step, but Sheriff Aingher came to his feet, towering over her. "There's something you're missing here," he began. "We're flying by the seat of our pants. You're not an adult. Everybody's trying to do the best they can."

"I know," she said.

"Good. Now I have to go. Is there anything else you need to know?"

Chastened as she was, Vickie was afraid to mention the one remaining thing important to her, but this might be her best chance.

"Can you fix it so I can stop at the house?"

"You mean your house, the Breen place? What do you want there?"

"I haven't been to the farm since that night they sent Mama away. There's stuff I want—my jacket, things that belong to Mama, pictures of Bertie, you know. I might never live there again."

"It would have to be when Sam's not there. Even if you think he's off somewhere, I don't want you going near the place on your own."

This didn't satisfy Vickie. "Well, when could I go? It would be like Sam to throw away what he thinks isn't worth something."

"I can't say," said the sheriff, anxious to leave. "How about you talk it over with Virgil. See what he thinks."

As Aingher hurried to his car, Virgil emerged from the slaughterhouse with a large venison roast wrapped in bloody newspaper from the freezer. The sheriff thanked him, shook his hand and placed the roast in his car trunk before pulling away.

\* \* \* \* \*

When Harlan Maas drove by the Breen farm, he took in again the sight of the cows milling around the barn. Usually by this hour of the morning they'd be grazing in the pasture. This was unusual—especially since Sam's pickup sat in its usual place in the weed-overgrown yard. He pulled in and waited in his cab for a minute, gazing around. Something wasn't right. Two white chickens emerged from under the porch, clucking and pecking in their jerky way. He stepped down and called, "Anybody here?" The chickens looked up at him before returning to their important tasks of the day.

He banged hard on the door of the house, but no one answered. He searched through the barn, thinking maybe Sam encountered an accident and couldn't move. This happened to farmers operating by themselves. Just last winter, Fred Garrison's hired man had tripped and fallen through the hatch between the haymow and the manger, catching his parka on a nail. He kicked and twisted as best he could, being crippled up with rheumatism, but couldn't free himself and eventually either choked to death or froze.

The calves were hungry and bellering. Seeing a human, they demanded to be fed. Harlan followed the fence line bordering the pasture while calling Sam's name. Back near the house, he located the old well, but it was coated in ice and boarded up tight. In the yard there were traces of tire tracks that didn't match the new tubeless Firestones on Sam's pickup, and two or three sets of footprints made by boots, but all of that didn't mean much. With the Breen house prominently visible from the road, travelers often drove in to seek directions or to turn around.

He tried the front entrance and found it unlocked, which was typical of farmhouses in the area. The cookstove was cold to the touch. White bacon grease flecked with black particles had congealed in a frying pan and twin slices of bread waited in the toaster. He looked inside the bathroom and downstairs bedroom, noting the mess, which was to be expected of a man who now lived by himself and wasn't too much on staying clean in the first place.

Before going upstairs, he prepared himself. Sam Morinville was still a young man, but his size and the way he tended to his health made him as likely as the next person to have a heart attack. The covers were in a heap and the dirty pillow had been tossed to the floor, but the room was otherwise empty.

He let the calves out, left the barn door leading to the pasture open and drove on into town to notify the sheriff.

To Harlan, Sheriff Aingher wasn't all that interested, coming out with only a few questions: how long had it been since he'd seen Sam, did anything seem to be missing and, to Harlan's annoyance, was he sure the pickup was there? The sheriff allowed that he might have to run up and take a look in a couple hours, but more than likely Sam was on a bender or shacked up somewhere. He reminded Harlan to let him know if he saw something different.

By the time Aingher got around to heading north, Harlan was through in town and ended up following the sheriff all the way up. Curious and wanting to be helpful, he turned in at the Breen farm and eased in behind the sheriff's dusty cruiser. He stood by, keeping out of the way, while Aingher more or less repeated Harlan's search.

After standing on his tiptoes to peer into Sam's pickup, the sheriff walked to the road to check the mailbox, where he withdrew the assortment of circulars and magazines.

"Got any ideas?" asked Harlan.

"Sure don't," answered Aingher, sorting through the mail. "Things look normal."

"You seen them tire tracks then?" said Harlan, pointing.

Aingher studied the mail in his hands as he spoke. "Could have been just about anybody, such as Howie Mitchell with the mail. I'll have Stan call him."

"Awful strange that he'd disappear like that," said Harlan.

"It does happen," said Aingher. "Since I been sheriff, I've had three I can think of that just vanished into thin air."

A loud mooing sounded from the barn. Both men turned in that direction.

"I guess we'll need to get someone to look after the livestock," said Aingher.

"I can do it for a couple days," said Harlan. "Them cows are already leaking. Be lucky if they don't get mastitis. Long as I'm here, I might as well get 'em milked."

As Harlan herded the cows into the barn, he realized he'd left his cigarettes in his truck. Emerging from the side door of the barn, he saw Aingher staring at the tire tracks. With what looked like a deliberate gesture, the sheriff dragged the side of his foot along the tire tracks and kicked dirt over the footprints. *What was that about?* wondered Harlan.

He felt the sheriff's eyes on him as he reached for his Chesterfields on the seat of the pickup. Aingher continued to stare at him.

"I guess there's lots of folks around that never thought much of Sam Morinville," said Harlan, shaking a cigarette from the pack. Before lighting it, he held the pack toward the sheriff, who unexpectedly accepted the offer. Harlan struck a match and lit both of their smokes.

The sheriff inhaled deeply. "You're sure right about that, Harlan."

Aingher levered his long body into his car. As it pulled away, Harlan dropped his cigarette and ground it into the loose dirt. No one had to tell him that whatever this was, it was none of his business.

# JUST A LITTLE WAR

## 1 | The Half of It

Home again following completion of his AIT, Richie Lee Peavey lay awake the first two nights deliberating what was to become of him. Waiting for his orders felt like doing detention in reform school. What if, as he feared, the army ordered him to report to San Francisco for embarkation to Vietnam? After all, they trained him as an infantryman, and despite what you heard, few other places in the world needed armed soldiers.

All they talked about on the news now was Vietnam. A *conflict*, they called it. While his parents stared at Walter Cronkite with his dark moustache and bushy eyebrows, Richie Lee stared at his parents. Being told how many American boys died that day froze his dad in his chair with his hands resting on his belly like a Buddha statue, while his mom set her sewing down and studied the TV like a complication she couldn't solve.

On top of all that, he was going batshit trying to reason out what was with Vickie. She'd quit writing after only one letter. So there. After not hearing from her for two weeks, he quit too.

But where was she? Not here at the farm, that was for sure, and not at her own place. He thought his parents or at least his mom would explain it right off, but no. The talk of the countryside, he soon gathered, centered not on Vickie but on the disappearance of Sam Morinville. Nobody gave a hoot about Vickie, so finally, on an afternoon when his dad went to town, Richie Lee asked his mother.

She was chopping carrots with the butcher knife. "Vickie?" she said. "I thought she would've told you. She moved in with the Ables."

"What?" Richie Lee thought he hadn't heard right.

His mom didn't answer. Every few seconds, if she didn't hold the knife square to the cutting board, an orange piece of carrot rolled off the counter to the floor.

"That bunch that's always raising a ruckus?"

His mother put the knife in the sink and turned toward him, folding her arms as if daring him to challenge her forthcoming answer. "She hightailed it out just like that. Not even a goodbye or a go to hell! We haven't set eyes on her since except one time that your father saw her riding a horse up by Prophetstown."

"Jeepers," said Richie Lee, taken aback by his mother's quick fury. "And she's living with the Ables."

"That's right."

"What come over her? I don't get it."

"Don't look at me," said his mother, stooping to gather the slices of carrot from the floor.

"I always thought she was sort of funny or strange even. Do you suppose she got some mental thing from her mother?"

"I can't say. Is that the truck I hear? Your dad must be back. I got to get busy."

In his awkward way, Richie Lee's dad told him that he'd get by without his help in the field.

"You just take it easy and enjoy yourself," he said. "You earned it."

Hearing this worried Richie Lee more than ever. His dad was treating him like a prisoner before his last meal. Did he think he was doomed?

He pulled the map out of the kitchen drawer and located Hallock, Minnesota, his friend Bengston's hometown. He thought about driving over there to look up Bengston's mom and dad. He could tell them what all took place, how their son had come to want to get himself killed. But no, his folks would know most of it, and Richie Lee wasn't the kind of person who did that sort of thing.

Nothing acted to speed or slow the flow of time, and nothing could take his mind off the worry at hand. All he could do was wait.

For the next couple days, he put on jeans and a T-shirt and drove into town, hoping to contact a few old friends. But he'd lost touch with people his age. While they'd been playing football or saving for a broken-down car, he was burning his days in detention down at what they now called the North Dakota State Training School. Many had gone on to college or into the service themselves, and the few yet in the area had grown older and bigger in appearance but smaller in outlook.

What would college be like? Lots of guys that went to college got deferments. But they were lucky. Or smart. Anyway, it was too late for him.

\* \* \* \* \*

Leah Peavey told herself once again that the time had come to prepare for parting with her only child. She once dreamed of how she would use the year after he was released from reform school to make up for her failures as a mother. She might reacquaint him with church where he could meet a nice girl. She would cultivate in him a desire for learning. She would demonstrate her love. She might even try to help him understand the truth behind his parentage.

Then, of course, he came home toughened, no longer a little boy. He was sullen, distant. He bickered with his father, slept late, came home smelling of beer. Above all, she questioned her own decision to encourage him to go into the army in return for an early release from school.

She knew Harold would reassure her, tell her she was only doing what she thought right. But that wasn't what Leah wanted. She wanted punishment. She wanted him to grab her by the shoulders and scream in her face, "I warned you. Now look!"

That would never happen. Harold would return to his chores, to watching Jackie Gleason and to picking his nose in his easy chair when he thought his wife wasn't looking. It was up to her if Richie Lee was ever to change. Or up to him to change himself.

Hauling a basket of sheets and towels to put away, she was surprised to find her son stretched out on his bed with a book open. It had been so quiet she thought he was outside. He barely looked up as she entered the room.

"What's that you're reading?" she asked.

"A physics book. I found it in the attic," he said, holding the book up so she could see the title.

"That all you got to read?"

He looked up. "It's a funny thing. Just since thinking about what could happen, lots of stuff I never cared about seems interesting now. Like this schoolbook. I can't make much sense of what it's about, but last night I spotted an airplane way up there in the sky and it made me curious how it stayed up so high against gravity. And then I got to wondering about the different kinds of plants by the slough and how that Bell person made a contraption that sends our voice a thousand miles away. It's like I got to know everything."

His eyes took on a sorrowful appearance. "I'm almost nineteen years old and all I can do is shoot an M16—and I don't do that so good."

Despite the bleak mood in the little room, Leah had to smile. "When I was nineteen, I was an old married woman, and I don't know if I did such a good job at that."

Richie Lee lifted his hand tentatively, giving Leah the sensation that he was about to touch her. "Don't say that. I think back now and wonder how you managed."

"You don't know the half of it," said Leah, averting her eyes so he wouldn't see her emerging tears. She pulled a hankie from the basket and blew her nose. "I know what we should do," she said, brightening suddenly. "Let's go to town."

"To Rolland? What for?" asked Richie Lee, frowning.

"Just to do whatever, like a date. Know what else? Let's see if Ida Florence and Casey can come with us. We'll make it a party. I see Rebecca's car over there. She should be able to stay with old Etienne for a while."

"Wait a minute," said Richie Lee. "The Morinvilles?"

"Of course."

"I thought—"

Leah cut him off. "Things change."

"I would like to see Casey, all right," said Richie Lee, interpreting the tone of his mother's words as her having no interest in elaborating on the things that change. "Last I heard, he was going to UND."

"He was, yes, but now there's a hitch whether the army will pay for his schooling. Have him tell you about it. Anyway, get cleaned up. I'll call Ida Florence."

In the bathroom, Richie Lee puzzled over how that all came about. It was good news, but in a way, it felt like he was more distant than ever from the life he used to know.

He heard his mother call twice before he finally felt OK to go. With his freshly scrubbed skin gleaming, he knew he looked like a youngster set for his first day of school instead of the combat-ready soldier he would become. A white Band-Aid covered a razor cut on his cheek.

They rode in a single car with Richie Lee driving and the mothers in the back. As the women chatted easily, the boys found it difficult to find a comfortable topic. Richie Lee couldn't put the contrast out of his mind. Casey had grown into a good-looking young man, outgoing and popular at school. In contrast, Richie Lee was an overweight, ostracized failure. If things went right for him, Casey would be going to college and eventually becoming an army officer, while Richie Lee was a lowly PFC. Just the thought of it made Richie Lee sit up straighter in his seat and pull his gut in.

After words about crops and weather fell flat, Casey opened a subject they couldn't avoid. "So, I guess you're expecting your orders," he said, concern in his voice.

"Any day now," said Richie Lee, trying to sound casual.

"I sympathize with you," said Casey. "Not knowing what's in store."

"Vietnam's where they're sending everybody," said Richie Lee.

"How do you feel about that?" asked Casey.

Before Richie Lee could answer, he became aware that the women had gone silent, apparently to hear what the boys were talking about. This halted his thoughts as if a switch had been tripped. At last, something came to him. "I put in for Disneyland, but they said the waiting list was too long to bother."

Everyone chuckled, breaking the ice.

They stopped first at the drugstore, where Leah bought three rolls of expensive color film for the Brownie. She wanted to take snapshots of the little group out on the sidewalk, but Ida Florence objected to being included. Leah contented herself finally with a shot of the boys, who, with the ice broken, grinned broadly. Standing by was Useless Johnston, visible in the background, gawking at what must have looked to him to be an event of note.

They moved on next to Pam and Joyce and Deb's Café for a meal—all four ordering the special, meat loaf with mashed potatoes and gravy, after being huffily told by Joyce that they'd come too early for anything else. They joked about this, the smoky-smelling café being well-known for its limited offerings.

When Joyce advised that she was fresh out of pie, they drove to the Dairy Queen, where they found the line so long they were forced to skip dessert, Leah vowing to pick up a pint of ice cream to share with Harold. Next, Casey and his mother backtracked to the drugstore to confer with the pharmacist Monte on what they could use for Etienne's bedsores. This gave Leah the opportunity to drag Richie Lee to the Merc to try on clothes, including shoes, discovering that his shoe size had increased from eight and a half to ten in barely a year.

"Cripes, Ma," he complained. "The army makes sure I got plenty to wear."

"They're for when you come back," she said.

As he stood before the mirror shrugging his way into a blue suit coat, Richie Lee studied his mother's face behind him as she scrutinized the fit. He'd never noticed. They had the same rounded chin, distrustful eyes and large upper teeth. Gazing at her, he was overtaken with a fierce impulse to throw his arms about her.

The group reunited two doors down the street at the Ben Franklin store, where Leah wanted to pick up writing paper. Spotting the Halloween outfits on display, Casey whispered something in Richie Lee's ear. They grinned as Richie Lee tried on a Nixon mask and Casey found one of Hubert Humphrey.

They then feigned a fistfight complete with grunts and cries of pain before collapsing to the floor on their backs with their arms askew. While the mothers stood by, both embarrassed and amused, other customers hurried over to watch, laughing good-naturedly.

On the way home, with Casey and his mother trading places, they relived the cheerful hours, during which no one spoke a word about Richie Lee's imminent departure. Watching the Morinvilles disappear into their home left Richie Lee with an unexpected sorrow that he might never see them again.

In contrast, Richie Lee's mother was still smiling as they entered the house, where his dad waited for his supper. That's when they discovered that their strawberry ice cream had melted into the hot ham sandwich and fries they'd brought for Harold so Leah wouldn't have to cook. The pitiful look on his dad's face when he saw the pink mess brought Richie Lee out of his regretful mood.

* * * * *

The orders came by registered mail. Howard Mitchell, the rural carrier, left a notice in the mailbox requiring Richie Lee to drive into the post office in Rolland to sign the yellow-and-green forms that would prove that his orders were in his hands. His dad offered to keep him company, but Richie Lee said he might just as well go alone.

Mr. Mears, the clerk at the post office, was the father of Terry Mears, a kid that Richie Lee knew from grade school. Ordinarily, Richie Lee might inquire what had become of Terry, but right now he could only think about the orders. Mr. Mears retrieved the bulky envelope, checked the forms and pushed the envelope across the counter like it was no more important than a seed catalog from Northrup. For him, it was business as usual—sort of like the drill sergeant at basic, part of the rotten system that forced unlucky people like Richie Lee into bad situations that they didn't deserve.

By pure determination, Richie Lee made himself walk to the pickup without opening the envelope. He slid behind the steering wheel and tore the flap, destroying the envelope in his nervousness. He pulled a smaller envelope out. He read the label. *Voucher, one person one-way rail transportation from Rugby, North Dakota, to San Francisco, California. Present at station. Further information enclosed. Read carefully.*

*Jesus.* They were sending him to Vietnam.

Inside were listed all the dates, times and places he was required to be, how to get there, to whom to report, what to bring.

*Jesus, god.* Vietnam!

All the way home, he felt like he was driving through sludge. The pickup kept slowing like a tired horse, and Richie Lee had to make an effort to keep the accelerator depressed. As the vehicle drifted to the middle of the road, cars passed, their horns blaring. He ignored them. How strange that people, animals and trees swaying in the breeze could go about their lives as if all was well.

He pulled into the yard. His dad emerged from the barn in his slow way, double-checking to see that the sliding door was snug on its railing. He had taken to wearing suspenders now when he did chores. With his earflaps down in the warm weather, he looked like the dumbest country hick alive.

Richie Lee gathered his papers and headed for the house, leaving his father gaping at him. At the steps, he remembered that his mother had wanted him to stop at SuperValu and pick up a can of Crisco.

Crisco.

He tried to slip inside quietly, but the sticky door caught and made a sound like a string breaking on a guitar. His mother turned, her blue apron in one hand, the end of a strap dangling on the floor. Her forehead formed wrinkles. He wished she would speak. She was trying to read him. He handed her the letter. The raucous, insincere voice of a man delivering a commercial for Alka-Seltzer on TV blared from the living room.

She frowned at the contents as she read, then turned the envelope over and scanned the back as if it might offer better news.

"Oh."

The single word became submerged in the storm of a breath. In a single motion, his mother flung her broad arms around him.

Not even when she first saw him in the hospital after the incident with Sam Morinville had she done that. Richie Lee bit down on his lower lip to keep from sobbing, pulling away only when he heard his dad's footsteps on the porch.

And then, just like that, the farm and its residents rearranged themselves and an air of normality returned. Leah set the peeled potatoes on the burner. After finding his reading glasses, Harold sat at the table to study Richie Lee's orders, then turned on the kitchen radio to catch the closing livestock report. Richie Lee himself read through an article in *Popular Mechanics* on how to build your own sailboat. Out on the road, Casey Morinville passed briefly into view, finishing his afternoon run. The phone rang, and Leah stretched the cord into the pantry and spoke for less than a minute.

Supper was simple. Fried hamburger with pan gravy, boiled spuds and string beans.

Conversation was equally modest.

*I see Ericksons finally got their pole barn up.*

*I heard they're gonna gravel all the way to Gordon Lake.*

*Old man Bergstrom had a stroke and they shipped him to Fargo. How come not Minot? They probably got better equipment for that in Fargo.*

Only once did anyone stray from the safe exchanges that prevailed in every family seeking to preserve the compulsory illusion that all was well.

"I just wish they could send you someplace safe," said Leah, shattering a spell of quietness that had gone on too long.

Richie Lee smiled. "I hear Disneyland don't need no soldiers."

Leah laughed hardest despite having heard the joke once already. Even stoic old Harold allowed himself an audible chuckle.

The day ended.

## 2 | No Hard Feelings

With three days remaining, Richie Lee took the twelve-gauge out to the blind on the west side of the lake hoping to get a shot at a goose, but mostly seeking quiet time alone, as his folks were getting on his nerves. High overhead, a flight passed, the determined honking the only sound in the autumn air. As Richie Lee surveyed them, they descended on a course that would bring them in directly overhead. But suddenly they beat their wings frantically and, in an explosion of feathers and noise, gained altitude and made for the far side of the water and out of shotgun range. Smart birds they were.

Startled by a crashing through the reeds to his left, Richie Lee turned the gun in that direction. At first, he thought it was a deer, but it was moving too leisurely. Then he heard the chuff of a horse. The reeds parted, revealing Vickie Breen leading a rusty-brown mare.

"Whoa, don't shoot me," she said, raising her hands in pretend horror.

"I'm not shootin' nobody, least of all the geese you scared off," said Richie Lee.

Vickie led the horse to the water's edge so she could drink. The girl looked sunburned and muscular, wearing pants and a checkered blouse that displayed feminine curves formerly concealed by baggy jeans and a man's long-sleeved shirt.

"Having any luck?"

"Not yet, and I for sure won't with that horse standing there in plain sight."

"Never mind Dandy," said Vickie. "You won't get a shot anyway. You're set up in the wind. Geese won't come in where there's rough water. And where's your decoys?"

"Too much bother. I'm just fooling around," said Richie Lee, trying to hide his annoyance. "Where'd you learn about goose hunting?"

"From Virgil and the boys."

"The Ables? They teach you how to rustle cattle too?"

Vickie patted the ground, checking for dampness before sitting. "All right, I know you're mad at me," she said. "I'm sorry I quit writing—I couldn't help it. But you got to hear me out. Did you keep in mind what we talked about?"

"We talked about how good it felt to get to know each other."

"Forget that for a minute. Tell me, did your orders come?"

Richie Lee looked away. "Yeah."

"And is it Vietnam?"

"Uh-huh."

"No surprise, right?"

"Right."

"Listen, Richie Lee. I know how you can get to Canada."

Richie Lee turned his head and gazed across the water to the north as if peering into the country itself. "So do I. You go to the border, tell the customs guys where you're going and when you'll be back, and they wave you across."

Vickie didn't crack a smile. "Right, and when you don't return, they send somebody after you. I've talked to people who can get you across and nobody will ever know."

"Is that so. Who would that be? Your Able friends?"

"Nope. If I told you, you wouldn't believe it."

Richie Lee was more irritated than curious. Like this silly little teenager had such connections. "Why don't you tell me and see if I do?"

Vickie folded her arms. "Act stupid all you want," she said. "Just bear in mind that in a week you'll be in a jungle full of snakes and tigers and enemies trying to shoot you in the face."

"You're the one acting," said Richie Lee. "You pretend like you know so much. Quit making up things. You never been out of Chippewa County. You could get yourself in real trouble if the wrong people heard some of the things you say."

"Think so? Are you claiming I'd get criticized for talking about napalm and bombs dropped on children?"

"That's what they call propaganda, and you know it. They can fake pictures too."

"This comes direct from Bertie. He told me about what it's really like in his letters. He told me other things too."

"Like what?"

"He said he wanted me to talk to you."

"Yeah?"

"He said I should do whatever I needed to keep you from going over there."

Richie Lee shook his head. "You know, Vickie, I don't think it's right to put words in Bertie's mouth."

"I still got the letters." Vickie looked up, her eyes boring into his like headlights. "You wouldn't be the first American soldier to go up to Canada. Did you know that?" She waited for a reply.

"Of course. They don't keep news from us if that's what you're worried about."

"You can't tell me you haven't thought about it."

"Every guy I knew in basic thought about it. Like they say, the one thing you can't take away from a soldier is his right to wish and bitch. That's different from actually doing it. I wouldn't even know how to get started."

"I just told you there's help."

Richie Lee stared at her. There was no denying her determination. "So how do they help—drop you on the other side of the border and shake your hand?"

"There's an organization that takes you in once you get across."

"Is that right? They're gonna feed me and pay my rent too?"

Vickie reached into the vest pocket of her jacket. "Here." She held out a wad of money wrapped in a sturdy green rubber band.

"What's this?" Richie Lee jerked his hands back as if the bundle was on fire.

"It's $1,000, Canadian money. See the picture of the Queen?"

"Where'd you get it?"

"It's insurance money from Bertie. He made it so it went to me because he was afraid if he put Ma's name, Sam would get it."

Richie Lee eyed the thick wad of warm, slightly sweaty paper that Vickie pressed against his chest. "That don't mean Bertie intended for me to have it."

"Consider it as part of keeping you from going over there."

"Well, I still can't take it," said Richie Lee. "Supposing they never do find Sam Morinville. That's money that ought to go to fixing up your place."

"This isn't all of it by a long ways," said Vickie.

Very carefully, Richie Lee broke the shotgun, pocketed the shells, then reseated himself, by now thinking what he could do with $1,000. "OK, just say I was fool enough to try something like that. There's lots of other considerations."

"Like what?" Vickie responded, going to her knees to rearrange her position before resettling herself on the dry grass.

"First, if I get caught, it's desertion. They warn you in basic. You can get shot."

"They're not going to shoot you and you know it."

Richie Lee did know it. According to Bengston, no one had been shot for deserting since World War II when some poor fellow got executed to make an example. Bengston even knew the guy's name: Eddie Slovak.

"I never been on my own yet in my own country. How can I get by in a place that's foreign?"

Vickie took a breath. "You remember going up to Manitoba for picnics when we were kids. They spoke English, same as you and me. You'll be seen to just like in the army only better. The first thing they do is join you up with other Americans, and then you'll get a choice of where you want to go. It might be like in a lumber mill or on a farm someplace where you won't get noticed."

"I don't want to work in no lumber mill in Canada for the rest of my life."

"Everybody knows the war won't last long. It's just a little war." Vickie thrust her chin out, challenging him to come up with a counterpoint.

He took the bait. "Not so little for Bertie." At once, he saw the hurt in her eyes. So she did have soft spots.

But she recovered immediately. "When it's over, the government will be so glad that they'll let you and all the others come back, no hard feelings."

"Just say. If I was to go along, you'd need to let me know who the person in charge of getting me over is."

"What difference would it make?"

"I'd just like to know if it's somebody I can trust. You see, whatever I try never turns out. I got put in reform school when all I did was keep Sam from picking on me. Then I tried to run away, but that got me nowhere. Next thing, I got wrangled into joining the service and look what happens."

"I can't give you the name, but I will say that if this person can't be trusted, then nobody can."

"Well, that means you're saying that I first have to trust you."

Immediately, Richie Lee knew he'd gone too far. Vickie sprang to her feet like a rocket. Her face reddened as she jammed her fists into her sides. "You know what, Richie Lee Peavey? Sometimes you could make me throw up. You want to hear about things that don't turn out? How about having your brother dead and your mother in the insane asylum? What about living with a bunch of people everybody hates?"

Ashamed, Richie Lee focused his gaze on the horse, so calm, so uncaring what these foolish humans were in such a fuss about.

Vickie wasn't through. "Bertie probably knew he'd never come back. The best thing he could do was keep someone else from winding up the same way. This doesn't all have to do with you. He wanted to know somebody would be here for me to depend on when he wasn't, and that somebody is you. Don't you see?"

"And what good would I do you if I'm in Canada?"

"I just *said*. It's only for a little while." Now she sounded more like a girl her age. The tears started. "I don't want you getting killed."

"I'm not planning on it," said Richie Lee.

"Then don't take the chance." Vickie brushed Dandy's mane with her hand to calm her before mounting. "Please consider what I say. To honor Bertie's memory."

\* \* \* \* \*

The money felt like ten pounds of iron in his pocket. Richie Lee knew that in accepting it, Vickie would think he agreed to her crazy plan. Taking it, in a way, put the decision in her hands.

With his departure a day and a half off, he was as jittery as a sparrow on a fence. He leapt from one task to another, failing to finish the first while unsure what came next. He misplaced a photo of his parents and spent fifteen minutes crawling around searching only to find it in his shirt pocket. He left the refrigerator door open, walked outside barefoot, and poured two tall glasses of apple juice and touched neither. After ignoring the juice, he filled a glass with water and drank it in one long swallow, thinking how good it tasted compared to the water at the bases that smelled like a swimming pool.

The telephone jangled and he nearly jumped out of his skin. Since it was never for him, he let his mother answer. He waited for the innocent rhythms of her voice before resuming his thoughts.

"Richie Lee?" she called. "It's Vickie." She rolled her eyes in distaste as she handed him the phone.

"It's all set," announced Vickie with such exuberance Richie Lee was sure his mother heard.

"Yes," he said brightly, unaware that he had aped the girl in volume.

"They want you to do just like I told you," said Vickie.

"OK," replied Richie Lee automatically, willing his mother to leave him alone.

"You sound funny," said Vickie. "Are you all right?"

"Sure."

"OK," said Vickie. "I won't be there, so this is my goodbye."

Richie Lee knew this was his last chance. He held the phone, which smelled of his mother's hand lotion. She'd gone upstairs. With his free hand, he picked up the glass paperweight that her long-dead Aunt Dolores had gotten at the Chicago World's Fair. He shook it and a cascade of swirling snow descended over a miniature pond surrounded by buildings. It brought a memory of being wrapped head to toe in a huge coat and pulled in a sled over the frozen slough by his dad, his breath frosty, his nose dripping.

"OK," he said.

"Take into account, Richie Lee, this is for the good of everybody, not just us. I'm so proud of you." Vickie's voice was buoyant, cheerfully confident, like a TV quiz host.

"I know," he said, and with an ominous click, the line went silent.

He replaced the receiver and set the paperweight back on its doily. With that, he let himself think of Canada. The country was part of England, maybe like a colony, he thought. He remembered getting home from visits to Boissevain just across the border, his jacket stuffed with fireworks, which were illegal in North Dakota. It was true that Canadians talked with a funny accent, but it was the same language. Their cars looked like ours, as did the houses they lived in. Their police were called Mounties; he still had a plastic model of one of them lying facedown in his old toy box.

Vickie had spoken like an adult, using words he knew were not her own. For that, he guessed she'd been coached, which he took to be a good thing. Because of her convincing manner, he found himself sold on the crazy scheme, and he felt his spirits lighten. In the time it took for those thoughts to pass through his mind, he came to believe that all would yet be well.

# IN ALL THE DAYS IN THIS HOUSE

Ida Florence knew from the beginning that it was a mistake to try to keep him at home after the accident, but she wouldn't have it any other way. Living in a hospital was no good—people coming in and out every couple hours, strangers giving you a bath and holding you over the toilet, cold tile floors and solid walls that shimmered like a bell.

Not that there was much choice—the money would run out before the next frost.

Yet caring for him at home took its toll. She wasn't aware of the last time she slept more than four hours straight. Casey, who was to begin college come fall and was still recovering from his own injuries in the accident, had his hands more than full trying to run the farm by himself. So when her daughter, Rebecca, offered to move back with her own son, Charlie, Ida Florence accepted the offer eagerly.

As it turned out, Rebecca was not being that generous. She'd lost the latest of her string of jobs in town and had no place else to go. Until lately, she mostly made use of free babysitting for Charlie while she went out and partied five nights a week. Charlie himself was now school-age and demonstrating the rowdiness of a fresh generation. On top of that, she was pregnant again, this time refusing to say or maybe ignorant of the identity of the father. Now, while Ida Florence ran around trying to catch her breath, Rebecca, heavy in her pregnancy, sat in her father's old easy chair with her feet spread, complaining about the heat and how life had treated her while smoking one cigarette after another with the things costing sixty cents a pack.

Ida Florence had judged poorly too about how much money they'd save keeping Etienne at home. The materials required to care for an invalid were endless— the hospital bed and medicines, special food because Etienne couldn't chew, the wheelchair, the diapers, the special bedding, the surgical dressings and the blood pressure cuff. Even the night-light cost four dollars. The visits from the county nurse were free, but other things required, like the toilet chair and the harness for bathing, were not.

Just when Ida Florence began thinking they might squeeze by if the crop was good and nothing else went bad, something did. The notice from the university arrived, reminding Casey that the deposit on his dorm room for the fall semester was overdue. Both Ida Florence and Casey had believed that his college would be paid for by the ROTC, but it turned out that financial assistance wouldn't begin until successful completion of his first two years.

They had already sold off a quarter section of land to Harold Peavey, an action that would have surely caused Etienne to have a stroke if he hadn't been previously rendered senseless and brain-damaged. But that money had mostly gone to cover the old hospital bills. To further reduce the amount of land under tillage would be a foolish mortgage of the future at a time when anybody could see that, to survive, farms must grow larger. All she could do now was cross her fingers and hope nothing else came along—sickness, hail, fire.

Many a calamity could appear, but nothing would alter Ida Florence's determination on one matter. Casey was going to college, and nothing on earth would stand in the way.

\* \* \* \* \*

That morning, Rebecca was driving Charlie into town for his pre-school physical while Casey planned to use the drizzly day to repair fence along the field north of the slough. Casey resembled his father in at least one way—he would throw himself into a job without a break until dinner, no matter how wet or hungry. That allowed Ida Florence the time alone with her husband that she would need.

Ever since they set up Etienne's bed in the living room where she could see him from the kitchen, Ida Florence had developed the habit of calling to him as if he were sitting in his chair with his chin on his chest, catching the briefest of naps while waiting to be summoned to the table.

"Wash up. It's just about ready," she'd say. Or, "Go call the kids before the spuds get cold."

Even before Etienne got hurt, there was little to say from ordinary day to ordinary day, but Ida Florence liked to hear the sound of her own voice, as well as any reply, even if it had been little more than a grunt that had to be interpreted by tone. Lately she would have been happy to hear even the barest meaningless murmur, anything aside from the slow, labored, rattling breathing and occasional involuntary cough. He hadn't spoken a word since the accident, though once Rebecca claimed she heard him ask for water. But that was Rebecca.

She pulled the blanket down to expose his face and upper chest. They'd quit shaving him long ago. Though he'd never had much of a beard, his face had become patchy like an untended garden. With no exposure to weather, his skin had softened, and the deeply embedded dirt of many years had worked its way to the surface and vanished.

Of all the physical changes—the withered limbs, the overgrown, yellowish fingernails, the constant drool—what bothered Ida Florence most were his eyes. When open, they resembled the plastic eyes in one of Rebecca's old dolls—unchanging and vacant as Little Orphan Annie's. Then sometimes a sudden light from outside caused his eyes to roll slightly, as if the doll had been jostled, spooking her.

On the other hand, the stench of soiled bedding never bothered her anymore. She could make a joke out of it. Her life had turned to shit.

In a way, she knew this would be both easier and harder than she had anticipated. She would use a pillow so as not to leave marks—one of those newer ones that felt squishy like a sponge instead of the old lumpy kind with their prickly feathers. She leaned over him, gripping the pillow near the middle with both hands while her memory brought her back to when Etienne rescued her from a hopeless predicament and bestowed on her a new life—one with promises that would be forever unfulfilled.

She had learned from her father Howahkan, descendant of the great Lame Wolf, that all things in life come down to two things: money or blood. She wished she could tell Etienne that after all their early years of poverty and struggle, this had to do with both.

She debated fleetingly whether she should give him a kiss on the forehead, then with the strong hands that served her well, clamped the pillow down to banish such a thought. Even with the arthritis in her fingers, her grip was robust as ever. Holding the pillow in place over her husband's mouth and nose, she applied increasing pressure with her forearms and elbows, praying that it would be over soon, reasoning that he had so little life left in him.

His head rolled feebly toward one side and a shoulder twisted over against the pillow. She applied more pressure, using her weight to counter the resistance. One leg came up, tenting the blankets, then settled. Ida Florence let go of the pillow for a moment to get a better grip and Etienne reacted with a cavernous inhalation that she thought beyond his powers. She replaced the pillow, using her strong hands to assure it covered his face more tightly. She held it for longer than she knew necessary before standing back and allowing it to slide to the floor. She touched a finger to his bare throat, limp and wrinkled with age, feeling for the throb of a pulse. She smoothed his hair and with the corner of the sheet wiped the saliva from his chin.

She stood back. "I'm Sioux," she said.

In all the days in this house, it had never felt so quiet.

"I'm Sioux," she repeated.

# A KIND OF COURAGE

As Richie Lee lay fully clothed atop his bed, he imagined what it would be like if he accidentally fell asleep.

He would hear the voice of his father, tentative, unsure, heard a million times before and drifting up the stairs like a whiff of unwelcome air: "Better get up. We're gonna be late for the train." His dad, a man who never in his life had missed an appointment, would certainly not miss this one. After all, hadn't he said he was proud of his son?

He turned on his side, his hands beneath his cheek. He heard his dad cry out in his sleep, his mother moan as if in response. All was silent, and at last it was time.

He knew the house so well that he avoided the board that always screeched like its nails were being pulled out. At the bottom, he remembered his billfold. Vickie had told him he should take nothing so that when his parents discovered him missing, they would think he only went for a walk, but he wasn't going anywhere without his license and his little bit of U.S. folding money. He tiptoed back up, thinking of when he and others would sneak past the monitor's bedroom at reform school to have a cigarette outside in the cold.

In a way, it seemed like ever since then not a thing had happened.

Careful to hold the screen door so it wouldn't slam, he stepped into the familiar farmyard odor of cow dung, swamp and dust from the road. Colder air moving in from the north made every star stand out against the black sky. Like so much else, he'd never paid attention to the sky. On this clear night, it was deep, measureless, engulfing. It was easy to believe in a heaven on such a night.

Walking unhurried, the better to hear any vehicle approaching, he made his way a mile and a half to the T marking the turn to Gordon Lake. There, in the tall grass below the *CAUTION* sign, he found the bag just where Vickie assured him it would be.

She hadn't said exactly when the car would come for him, only that he should be at the pickup place no later than midnight. To kill time, he opened the bag, a well-used canvas duffel with a sticky zipper. Vickie said she would pack it herself, and she'd done a good job. The jeans were well-worn and maybe a little long for him, but the brown sweater was a good fit. She could have done better on the food, which consisted mostly of a box of Oreo cookies, a half jar of peanut butter and a can of RC Cola. But these must be intended only for an emergency, which must mean that good meals would be available wherever he was going. More alarming was the presence of a compass—a nice Boy Scout model in a leather case. Adding to such a concern was a still-folded map of Manitoba. There were gloves, too, and a stocking cap and a blanket. He changed into the clothes and pulled on the cap.

This killing time in the dark brought to mind his hiding out in the woods near the Breen farm when he ran away from reform school. The first night by himself, before he sorted out the natural from the dangerous, he found every little sound alarming. When all was silent, he could hear an amazing distance. A car approaching sounded close but took forever to arrive.

And how immense and exciting the sky was when he was alone. At first glimpse, the stars displayed no pattern, as if they were thrown in the air randomly like a cluster of sparks. But when he watched for a while, he made out not just the Big Dipper that anyone could recognize, but other formations that resembled animals or people. After gazing at a cloudy area, he realized he was looking at the Milky Way. When he discerned that one of the sparks had changed position, he apprehended that he'd been observing a planet. As for the stars, it saddened him to think that those visible on Earth no longer existed. Only their light, which took millions of years to reach Earth, was evidence that they once burned bright and hot. But at least they left that. A person like himself who had never done much of anything in his time might leave nothing at all.

When at last he heard a car, he backed into the stand of birch to wait. Vickie had explained that the vehicle taking him away would drive at a slow speed past the corner, then turn around and come within twenty or thirty yards of him before it stopped. He was not to let himself be seen until then.

He caught sight of the lights, just a faint, steady yellowish glow that intensified into a blinding brilliance. The accompanying sound became a growl and then a roar. Richie Lee stood perfectly still in the trees as the vehicle whizzed past, leaving behind a veil of dust that settled bit by bit. In a while, the air cleared again and the stars revealed themselves brighter than ever.

He gazed back toward the east. If it were light, he'd be able to make out the top of a silo at the farm. He pictured the barn, the chicken coop, the house, painted every four years with the same shade of white bought from Stagg Hardware in town. That house, with its smoky furnace and heavy storm windows, was the only place he'd ever lived where he wasn't told when he could eat and when he had to get up. Funny how only the good sticks in your mind. He remembered with warmth and longing the two or three times his dad took him fishing. But in fact, Richie Lee never liked fishing—the sharp hook catching on his pants, the line always tangling, the waiting for something to bite.

Another car neared, neither slow nor fast, rolling at a steady speed as if floating above the ground. It drew abreast of him, not braking—if anything, accelerating. Richie Lee strained to see the driver, but in the dim light could only make out a man's profile—although it bore a familiarity that he could not place.

He watched as it went on for a quarter mile or so until the brake lights flashed. The car made a U-turn and moved toward him, its headlights on full bright. As it slowed to a stop near his hiding place, he picked up the duffel bag at his feet and patted himself down to make sure he hadn't dropped anything. In that instant, the driver's door opened and the dome light illuminated the face of Sheriff Dale Aingher.

Richie Lee paused, stupefied. *Vickie had set a trap and he'd fallen into it.* He waited, afraid to show himself.

The sheriff pushed the door open wider, freeing the sounds of Buck Owens singing on KFYR. Stepping out, Aingher spread his legs, unzipped and urinated into the dirt while leisurely scanning the woods.

Despite his consternation, this amused Richie Lee. There must be a regulation against law officers peeing on a private road. The whole spectacle served to make him feel bolder. Maybe this was how lawmen hoped to capture smugglers and AWOL soldiers trying to cross the border—by sitting in a warm car listening to cowboy music. While Richie Lee crouched in the bushes, frightened and indecisive, the sheriff behaved like he had all the time in the world, getting back in his car and rapping his knuckles on the dashboard as he sang along to the song "I've Got a Tiger By the Tail."

Then Richie Lee figured it out. How stupid could he be? The sheriff was not only interested in Richie Lee—he wanted mostly to catch the person responsible for the whole business of illegally escorting people across the border.

He debated. Should he sneak away back farther into the woods? Whoever was supposed to take him across the border should be here by now. Or maybe the sheriff didn't intend to stop him—or possibly he didn't even know it was him.

Just as he made up his mind to move deeper into the brush, the headlights on Aingher's car faded out, as did the interior light. The sounds from the radio and the engine ceased. The only sign of life in the car was the red tip of a lit cigarette bobbing in the air. The door opened, and the sheriff stepped out and ground his cigarette deliberately with his boot, creating an audible crunch in the gravel.

"Richie Lee Peavey?" he called.

The boy didn't move.

"Richie Lee?" he repeated, louder this time. "Come on out. I don't have all night."

Richie Lee stood, unsure whether to leave the duffel bag. What use would he have for it now? But he picked it up and walked slowly into the open, raising his feet high over the brush.

"How are you?" asked the sheriff, extending a hand. Richie Lee had not expected this but out of habit accepted the handshake.

Aingher held a back door of the car open, and Richie Lee climbed in.

"Better leave that up here with me," said Aingher, reaching for the bag.

After the sheriff wiggled in behind the wheel, he reached for a notebook and wrote something in it. "Goddamn it," he said suddenly. "Lead broke." He reached into the glove compartment, pulled out another pencil and resumed writing. After wedging his notebook over the visor, he turned on his two-way radio, listened to the meaningless static for a moment and turned it off.

His business apparently completed, he carefully adjusted his rearview mirror so he could see Richie Lee's face. "You're all right there for now," he said. "But if a car comes along, sit still. Don't try to duck or anything. Then about a mile before the border you'll have to get in the trunk with your bag. They won't be busy this time of night, so if Carlson is on duty, he'll want to jabber for a while. You just stay put."

"Carlson?" said Richie Lee.

"You know. The customs agent. The guy with the wooden leg."

Aingher looked at his watch. He'd made no effort to start the car. Richie Lee sat as still as a post, confused but afraid to ask a question for fear of setting events in motion. Finally, he couldn't restrain himself. "We're not going to town?" he said.

The sheriff half turned in his seat. "To town? What for?"

At this, Richie Lee began to make sense of it. "Then it's you? You're the one driving me to Canada?"

"Well, yeah. What did you think I was doing up here in the middle of the night? Hunting gophers?"

"I just never thought it out," said Richie Lee, at a loss.

The sheriff lowered his window and cocked his head, contemplating the sky. "Pretty night."

Evidently, he was still in no hurry to depart. That was reassuring. Looking at the thick neck and upright posture of Aingher, Richie Lee's memory went back to a long drive when he was very small. He'd fallen asleep in the back seat and awakened frightened and confused before catching sight of his father, hands on the wheel, in control, protective.

"You know, Son, when I found out who it was they wanted me to take, I almost backed out," said the sheriff. "Me and your dad, we go back a long way. You know, don't you, that that's going to be the worst part for me. To look your folks in the eye and pretend like I don't know what became of you."

One more lie to his long-suffering parents, thought Richie Lee. This after all the times he'd let them down.

"Now, you were told what to do when we get across to the drop-off place, weren't you?" said Aingher.

"She said just to wait and keep out of sight, like I did here," answered Richie Lee. At once, he realized he shouldn't have said "she." But the sheriff displayed no reaction.

"Yes. There'll be someone meeting you if it goes right."

"What happens if it don't go right?" asked Richie Lee.

Aingher let go a lung-draining breath and twisted around so Richie Lee could see his face. "You mean you spent all that time down in Mandan and never picked up that much? What you do when you're in a fix is you keep your mouth shut. You're only the second one I know of to cross here. We're so out of the way that the Canucks won't catch on. You're not technically AWOL for a few days yet. Most that would happen would be you'd get a talking-to and a warning before they'd bring you back over to this side."

Richie Lee took little comfort in the sheriff's explanation. "What about if *you* wind up getting found out?"

"When was the last time you heard of a law officer being charged with anything around here?" said Aingher. "Besides, I'm about to retire."

A vehicle with a single headlight came over the hill. Aingher looked at it, squinting. "That's Harlan Maas headin' home," he said. "He usually pulls over by a turnaround for a while to sleep it off. Must be in a hurry tonight."

They waited until the pickup rolled out of sight. "I got to ask," said Richie Lee. "How come you're involved in all this? Is it because of what happened to Dale?"

Aingher took a while to answer. "I asked myself the same thing. I knew when he went what could happen. Sometimes we gauge that we just have to do something and we don't know why."

"After I caused so much trouble for you, I wouldn't hold it against you if you wanted nothing to do with me," said Richie Lee.

"You did your share and then some, all right," said Aingher.

They'd been sitting beside the road for half an hour, and Richie Lee felt a growing restlessness. It was torture sitting here trying to talk to the sheriff and act like they were friends when he was about to commit a crime.

Aingher must have sensed it. "Might as well take it easy," he said, stretching his arms before resting both hands around the back of his neck. "I was thinking about what you said about causing a ruckus here and there. You know you just made it worse by running away."

He spoke into the windshield. Richie Lee leaned forward to hear him, even though by catching a few words, he knew what he was being told.

"But you did your time, sort of, and now you're—oops, hold it," said the sheriff, his voice low and steady. "Don't move."

Richie Lee froze, terrified.

"OK, look over there to the left, just under the tallest oak."

Richie Lee saw nothing at first, but as he watched, three deer materialized in the dimness, a doe and two fawns, staring straight on at the car with its two invaders.

"Ain't this wonderful country to live in?" said the sheriff. He opened his door and clapped his hands sharply. The deer disappeared into the brush, their white tails twitching. "See how close they came? I love it up here in the bush."

Growing up in the area, Richie Lee had seen hundreds of deer, but the sheriff's reaction made these three seem special. He wished he'd been the one to spot them first.

The sheriff took up where the conversation was interrupted. "Anyway, after paying for what you did, how do you look on what you're doing now?"

"What do you mean?"

"What exactly is the action you're taking to clear up the problem you have now?"

Richie Lee took a minute to sort out the question. "You mean the problem that the army wants to send me somewhere I got no wish to go? Well, I'm doing what I need to, to keep that from happening."

"In other words…" said Aingher.

"I'm running away, if that's what you want me to say."

"You're sure about that?" The sheriff's eyes went to the rearview, where he held his gaze.

"I thought you were here to help me," said Richie Lee.

"I am."

Baffled and uneasy, Richie Lee sat mute, hoping the subject would change.

"Your folks ever tell you I was there the night you were born?" said Aingher.

"You were?"

"I sat with your dad and we talked over old times while we waited for you. Your mother had a tough time there for a while."

Richie Lee had no idea exactly what brought that up but let it go. At the moment, the memory of his mother and Mrs. Morinville laughing so hard when he and Casey put on their show in the dime store was the one he preferred.

"How come you were there?" he asked.

"I just was. But the funny thing was that before that, we never got along too good, Harold and me."

That sparked Richie Lee's curiosity. "Really? My dad never said. Why was that?"

The sheriff waited as another car passed, this one heading in the direction of town. "Call it a difference of opinion. We even had a fistfight."

"You and my dad?" Richie Lee leaned forward.

"Oh, he got the worst of it, but only because I had people helping me, three against one. Still, I never saw a man take a beating like he did that night, and he never even said a word. He just took it, like maybe he decided he was at fault after all, so he just accepted what was happening. That showed me a kind of courage, which was part of what the disagreement was about in the first place."

Aingher peered over in the direction of the trees.

"I'm not like my dad at all," said Richie Lee.

"Maybe you aren't and maybe you are," said the sheriff. "But when it comes to figuring out what's best, we all got to make our own decision no matter who we are." He raised his window and started the car.

As they began to move, Richie Lee pulled his knees together and rocked forward.

"You OK back there?" asked the sheriff.

Richie Lee swallowed. He pictured himself bolting from the car and running full-speed across the stubble field, tripping but not falling. His dad would be up in an hour, having to rise earlier than usual to do chores before taking him to the train.

"When I was in basic, my dad wrote me a letter that said he was proud of me," said Richie Lee.

Aingher either chose not to answer or Richie Lee didn't hear him.

"But before that, after they brought in the army recruiter, he drove all the way to Mandan through a blizzard to try and talk me out of joining."

Again, the sheriff made no response.

"I guess he couldn't make up his mind or else he was saying two things at once," said Richie Lee.

Aingher braked carefully but didn't move his head. He let the car coast to a stop at a pull-off before speaking. "I'll tell you one thing," he began. "Your dad's not only the gutsiest man I ever knew, he's one of the smartest, and he was saying a lot more than you think." He glanced at his watch. "Yup, it's about time," he said, and put the car back in gear.

"Can you wait a minute?" said Richie Lee.

"Take your time," said the sheriff.

"I'm not ready," said Richie Lee.

"I expect that's so."

"I got to explain something."

"You don't have to say a word."

"I'm sorry."

"It's all right, Richie Lee. It's OK. Do you want me to drop you by your place?"

"I guess I'll walk," said Richie Lee.

Aingher extended a hand. "Good luck to you, Son."

The black car pulled away at a measured pace, the engine not straining. It glided over the hill and disappeared except for the arc of its lights that soon faded. Richie Lee realized that in his eagerness he'd left the canvas bag behind. It felt good to be rid of it.

From where he stood, he judged it to be about a three-mile walk home, but that would bring him back too early. He wanted to arrive just as the sun was clearing the horizon to the east. By that time, his dad would have finished milking and his mother would be up fixing breakfast. If he approached from the south, he'd see them through the window sitting across from each other at the table, their silhouettes formed from the light over the sink.

He knew that if he followed the road, someone was sure to come along even this time of night, so he set off through the woods. He'd always had difficulty with directions, as he learned quickly in boot camp, a failing that had earned him a ton of extra push-ups—so he calculated that if he went west the proper distance and then north, he should run directly into the farm.

It was rough going at first. The brush was thick in this area and he had to keep making his way around potholes, which tended to push him farther away from the road that would serve as a rough guide.

Still, he appreciated the calm that came only in the predawn day. The night air descended around him as if to take him in. He looked to the northeast where shimmering lights danced like ghosts. To the right hung the Big Dipper, which helped mark north. The familiar mossy aroma from the potholes made him think of the north pasture and how much he would miss home.

With his shoes wet and the darkness making progress more difficult than expected, he wished he had someone like Casey Morinville leading him. He felt sorry for Casey, having his dad die not long after his brother Sam up and disappeared. No matter now that Richie Lee kept bad memories of Sam going way back. Like everyone, he wondered what became of him. He'd considered asking the sheriff, but that didn't seem right. Sam might be dead at the bottom of Devils Lake or hiding out in Coeur d'Alene, Idaho. Wherever he was, he was beyond harming Richie Lee.

His thoughts turned to others—Vickie's mother, who the doctors said might never get out of the mental hospital, Vickie herself, Casey himself, Ma and Dad.

Sure, Ma would be upset, but just for a while. Maybe before too long she would share his absolute belief—that he would come through this just fine. He knew that in his heart.

It wouldn't be long till Vickie got over being mad at him for not doing what she wanted. Probably about the time he was enjoying his first R & R, she'd be off somewhere carrying a sign about how the government ought to clamp down on people who eat lime Jell-O.

He tried to imagine what his folks would say when he reached the house. Not much, he supposed. His dad hardly ever spoke about anything outside the farm. Most likely, he'd be fretting about missing the train. His mother would look him up and down and say, "Where'd you get those pants? They don't fit you, you know."

What would he himself say? That he'd be good and obey orders, that this would make a man of him for sure, that he wanted to apologize for causing so much worry over the years? Or maybe he'd just say, "I guess I'll have another couple of them sausages."

So deep into remembrance had he fallen that he failed to notice a cloud cover had moved in, and with it, a chill. He stopped to rest on a fallen log so rotted through that it gave in like an easy chair when he sat. He looked around, realizing he'd drifted out of sight of the road. He listened hard. Off to his right, something, a frog maybe, jumped into water. He stood. The seat of his pants was damp from the log. He looked up. The sky was like a dark blanket thrown over a window. Nothing marked a possible direction he might follow. Now he wished he had the duffel bag with the compass Vickie had packed.

But then, as he fought his growing alarm, the clouds shifted and a patch of sky appeared. He stared toward the heavens. The handle of the Big Dipper showed itself, hazy at first, then bright and clear. From there, he could make out the Little

Dipper and, at the tip of its handle, Polaris, the North Star, superior to any magnetic compass for it marked true north, the way home.

As the sky opened further, it seemed that during the time he'd believed himself lost, billions more stars had appeared, maybe one for every person who ever lived, each leaving light as a sign that it once existed, and as a reminder that he too carried the good light of life.

That he too would leave something behind.

# AUTHOR'S NOTE

When I decided in mid-life that I wanted to become a writer the standard advice then as now holds that one should write about things most familiar. But when I searched for the right words to shed light on Alaska where I had lived for several years, or to talk about pharmacy which provided me with an income, I got nowhere.

Up to now in my late-blooming literary career I've been primarily a short story writer. Eventually I noticed that most of the stories for which readers expressed admiration were reminiscent of the society as well as the times that prevailed during my youth in the Turtle Mountain region of North Dakota. I also realized that my short stories had a chronological continuity to them. It made sense to string them together making, in effect, a long story. Thus, this novel is as much a child of adoption as one of birth.

As I wrote about the interactions of the three principal families in *True North* and how they battled through the challenges of their lives, I encountered an unexpected realization. What I thought was a permanent antipathy toward the area that formed my attitudes, personality, and sensibilities faded to be replaced by a growing affection. I discovered that the more I was compelled to think about the area, the more it became a place where nothing happens to one where everything happens. I realize now that this is a phenomenon well-known to writers. Put under a microscope, a subject will reveal a nature previously unknown or well concealed.

The Turtle Mountains, yes, mountains, though they rise less than a thousand feet above the surrounding prairie, encompass an area of lakes, woodlands, lush greenery, wild animals, and hidden places. Winters remain harsh and many of the flaws listed above still exist though to a lesser degree. But it is loved both by those who went away, those who stayed, and all in search of deep truths about themselves. It is home in the way a house when viewed from afar is only a house, but once inside becomes a home. Even if we cannot access those elements that made us who we are, our minds and imaginations will bring us back again and again.

# ACKNOWLEDGMENTS

*In gratitude*

Jen Corrigan, Art Staniforth, Hank Nuwer, Jon Dunlop, Peggy Schell, Glenda Stormes-Bice, Erin Todey, Paula Curran, Keith Shimp, Marijo Grimes, Timothy Fay, and the staff of the Ames Public Library. Special thanks go to my wonderful editor Jamie Rich, and to my great and dear writing friend Paul Hedeen who has been my accurate and ceaseless guide from beginning to end.

*And to the memory of Marianne Malinowski*

# ABOUT THE AUTHOR

Born and raised in the small town of Rolla, North Dakota, Gary Eller was a late starter to writing. After earning a degree in pharmacy from North Dakota State University, he worked in Idaho, Nevada, and for several years in Kodiak, Alaska. He began writing seriously after studying at the University of Iowa Writers' Workshop where he completed an M.F.A. in Creative Writing.

Eller's previous collection of short fiction, *Thin Ice and Other Risks*, was well-received and described as "reminiscent of Raymond Carver's best work." In addition to many short stories, he has published nonfiction articles on such varied topics as commercial fishing in Alaska, rare museum collections, and post-divorce life. He's also conducted interviews and published several articles on the craft or writing. His focus in the nonfiction genre, however, has been on baseball, one of his many loves.

His writing awards include the River City Award in Fiction, the Fowler Prize, and a Minnesota Voices Award, among others. He is a former Pushcart Prize nominee and recipient of a Creative Writing Fellowship from the National Endowment for the Arts.

Eller has taught fiction and nonfiction at Iowa State University and lectured widely on aspects of creative writing.

Before returning as a writer to what he regards as the redemptive qualities of the Midwest, Eller was rescued twice in reality (once by helicopter from sub-Arctic Alaska wilderness, and once from bear country on Kodiak Island) and countless times metaphorically.

He lives and writes in Ames, Iowa, while spending part of each summer in his family's cabin on scenic Lake Upsilon in the Turtle Mountains of North Dakota, the area where most of *True North* is set.

Lightning Source UK Ltd.
Milton Keynes UK
UKHW011021031221
394932UK00005B/134/J